Two by Two

ALSO BY NICHOLAS SPARKS

The Notebook
Message in a Bottle
A Walk to Remember
The Rescue
A Bend in the Road
Nights in Rodanthe
The Guardian
The Wedding
Three Weeks with My Brother (with Micah Sparks)
True Believer
At First Sight
Dear John
The Choice
The Lucky One
The Last Song
Safe Haven
The Best of Me
The Longest Ride
See Me

NICHOLAS SPARKS

Two by Two

sphere

SPHERE

First published in the USA in 2016 by Grand Central Publishing
First Published in Great Britain in 2016 by Sphere

1 3 5 7 9 10 8 6 4 2

Copyright © Willow Holdings, Inc. 2016

The moral right of the author has been asserted.

*All characters and events in this publication, other than those
clearly in the public domain, are fictitious and any resemblance
to real persons, living or dead, is purely coincidental.*

A CIP catalogue record for this book
is available from the British Library.

Hardback ISBN 978-0-7515-5002-3
Trade Paperback ISBN 978-0-7515-5003-0

Printed and bound in Great Britain by
Clays Ltd, St Ives plc

Papers used by Sphere are from well-managed forests
and other responsible sources.

To you, my loyal reader:
Thank you for the last twenty years

CHAPTER 1

And Baby Makes Three

W_{ow!}" I can remember saying as soon as Vivian stepped out of the bathroom and showed me the positive result of the pregnancy test. "That's great!"

In truth, my feelings were closer to . . . Really? Already?

It was more shock than anything, with a bit of terror mixed in. We'd been married for a little more than a year and she'd already told me that she intended to stay home for the first few years when we decided to have a baby. I'd always agreed when she'd said it—I wanted the same thing— but in that moment, I also understood that our life as a couple with two incomes would soon be coming to an end. Moreover, I wasn't sure whether I was even ready to become a father, but what could I do? It wasn't as though she'd tricked me, nor had she concealed the fact that she wanted to have a baby, and she'd let me know when she stopped taking the pill. I wanted children as well, of course, but she'd stopped the pill only three weeks earlier. I can remember thinking that I probably had a few months at least before her body readjusted to its normal, baby-making state. For all I knew, it could be hard for her to become pregnant, which meant it might even be a year or two.

But not my Vivian. Her body had adjusted right away. My Vivian was fertile.

I slipped my arms around her, studying her to see if she was already glowing. But it was too soon for that, right? What exactly is glowing, any-way? Is it just another way of saying someone looks hot and sweaty? How were our lives going to change? And by how much?

Questions tumbled around and around, and as I held my wife, I, Russell Green, had answers to none of them.

Months later, the big *IT* happened, though I admit much of the day remains a blur.

In retrospect, I probably should have written it all down while it was still fresh in my mind. A day like the big *IT* should be remembered in vivid detail—not the fuzzy snapshots I tend to recall. The only reason I remember as much as I do is because of Vivian. Every detail seemed etched into her consciousness, but then she was the one in labor, and pain has a way of sometimes sharpening the mind. Or so they say.

What I do know is this: Sometimes, in recalling events of that day, she and I are of slightly differing opinions. For instance, I considered my actions completely understandable under the circumstances, whereas Vivian would declare alternately that I was selfish, or simply a complete idiot. When she told the story to friends—and she has done so many times—people inevitably laughed, or shook their heads and offered her pitying glances.

In all fairness, I don't think I was either selfish or a complete idiot; after all, it was our first child, and neither of us knew exactly what to expect when she went into labor. Does anyone really feel prepared for what's coming? Labor, I was told, is unpredictable; during her pregnancy, Vivian reminded me more than once that the process from initial contractions to actual birth could take more than a day—especially for the first child—and labors of twelve hours or more were not uncommon. Like most young fathers-to-be, I considered my wife the expert and took her at her word. After all, she was the one who'd read all the books.

It should also be noted that I wasn't entirely deficient on the morning in question. I had taken my responsibilities seriously. Both her overnight bag and the baby's bag were packed, and the contents of both had been checked and double-checked. The camera and video camera were charged and ready, and the baby's room was fully stocked with everything our child would need for at least a month. I knew

2

the quickest route to the hospital and had planned alternate routes, if there happened to be an accident on the highway. I had also known the baby would be coming soon; in the days leading up to the actual birth, there'd been numerous false alarms, but even I knew the count-down had officially started.

In other words, I wasn't entirely surprised when my wife shook me awake at half past four on October 16, 2009, announcing that the contractions were about five minutes apart and that it was time to go to the hospital. I didn't doubt her; she knew the difference between Braxton Hicks and the *real thing*, and though I'd been preparing for this moment, my first thoughts weren't about throwing on my clothes and loading up the car; in fact, they weren't about my wife and soon-to-be-born child at all. Rather, my thoughts went something like this: *Today's the big IT, and people are going to be taking a lot of photographs. Other people will be staring at these photographs forever, and— considering it's for posterity—I should probably hop in the shower before we go, since my hair looks as though I'd spent the night in a wind tunnel.*

It's not that I'm vain; I simply thought I had *plenty of time*, so I told Vivian I'd be ready to go in a few minutes. As a general rule, I shower quickly—no more than ten minutes on a normal day, includ-ing shaving—but right after I'd applied the shaving cream, I thought I heard my wife cry out from the living room. I listened again, hear-ing nothing, but sped up nonetheless. By the time I was rinsing off, I heard her shouting, though strangely it seemed as though she was shouting *about* me, not *at* me. I wrapped a towel around my waist and stepped into the darkened hallway, still dripping. As God is my wit-ness, I was in the shower for less than six minutes.

Vivian cried out again and it took me a second to process that Viv-ian was on all fours and shouting into her cell phone that I was IN THE DAMN SHOWER! and demanding WHAT IN THE HELL CAN THAT IDIOT BE THINKING?!?!?!? *Idiot*, by the way, was the nicest term she used to describe me in that same conversation; her language was actually quite a bit more colorful. What I didn't know was that the contractions that had been five minutes apart were now only two minutes apart, and that she also was in back labor. Back labor is excruciating, and Vivian suddenly let out a scream so powerful

3

that it became its own living entity, one that may still be hovering above our neighborhood in Charlotte, North Carolina, an otherwise peaceful place.

Rest assured, I moved into even higher gear after that, slapping on clothes without completely toweling off, and loading the car. I supported Vivian as we walked to the car and didn't comment on the fact that she was digging her fingernails into my forearm. In a flash, I was behind the wheel and once on the road, I called the obstetrician, who promised to meet us at the hospital.

The contractions were still a couple of minutes apart when we arrived, but Vivian's continuing anguish meant that she was taken straight to labor and delivery. I held her hand and tried to guide her through her breathing—during which she again offered various colorful sentiments about me and where I could *stick the damn breathing!*—until the anesthesiologist arrived for the epidural. Early in the pregnancy, Vivian had debated whether or not to get one before reluctantly deciding in favor, and now it appeared to be a blessing. As soon as the medication kicked in, her agony vanished and Vivian smiled for the first time since she'd shaken me awake that morning. Her obstetrician—in his sixties, with neat gray hair and a friendly face—wandered into the room every twenty to thirty minutes to see how dilated she was, and in between those visits I called both sets of parents, as well as my sister.

It was time. Nurses were summoned and they readied the equipment with calm professionalism. Then, all at once, the doctor told my wife to push.

Vivian pushed through three contractions; on the third, the doctor suddenly began rotating his wrists and hands like a magician pulling a rabbit from his hat and the next thing I knew, I was a father.

Just like that.

The doctor examined our baby, and though she was slightly anemic, she had ten fingers, ten toes, a healthy heart and a set of obviously functioning lungs. I asked about the anemia—the doctor said it was nothing to worry about—and after he squirted a bunch of goop in our baby's eyes, she was cleaned and swaddled and placed in my wife's arms.

Just as I'd predicted, photos were taken all day long but strangely, when people saw them later, no one seemed to care about my appearance at all.

It's been said that babies are born looking like either Winston Churchill or Mahatma Gandhi, but because the anemia lent a grayish pallor to my daughter's skin, my first thought was that she resembled Yoda, without the ears of course. A *beautiful* Yoda, mind you, a *breathtaking* Yoda, a Yoda so *miraculous* that when she gripped my finger, my heart nearly burst. My parents happened to arrive a few minutes later, and in my nervousness and excitement, I met them in the hallway and blurted out the first words that came to mind.

"We have a gray baby!"

My mother looked at me as though I'd gone insane while my father dug his finger into his ear as if wondering if the waxy buildup had clouded his ability to hear effectively. Ignoring my comment, they entered the room and saw Vivian cradling our daughter in her arms, her expression serene. My eyes followed theirs and I thought to myself that London had to be the single most precious little girl in the history of the world. While I'm sure all new fathers think the same thing about their own children, the simple fact is that there can only be one child who is actually the *most precious in the history of the world*, and part of me marveled that others in the hospital weren't stopping by our room to marvel at my daughter.

My mom stepped toward the bed, craning her neck to peer even closer.

"Did you decide on a name?" she asked.

"London," my wife answered, her attention completely devoted to our child. "We've decided to name her London."

My parents eventually left, then returned again that afternoon. In between, Vivian's parents visited as well. They'd flown in from Alexandria, Virginia, where Vivian had been raised, and while Vivian was thrilled, I immediately felt the tension in the room begin to rise.

I'd always sensed that they believed their daughter had *settled* when deciding to marry me, and who knows? Nor did they seem to like my parents, and the feeling was mutual. While the four of them were always cordial, it was nonetheless obvious that they preferred to avoid each other's company.

My older sister, Marge, also came by with Liz, bearing gifts. Marge and Liz had been together longer than Vivian and I had—at the time, more than five years—and not only did I think Liz was a terrific partner for my sister, but I knew that Marge was the greatest older sibling a guy could have. With both my parents working—Dad was a plumber and Mom worked as a receptionist at a dentist's office until her retirement a few years back—Marge had not only served as a substitute parent at times, but as a sibling confidante who helped me wade through the angst of adolescence. Neither of them liked Vivian's parents either, by the way, a feeling that had coalesced at my wedding, when Vivian's parents refused to let Marge and Liz sit together at the main table. Granted, Marge had been in the wedding party and Liz had not—and Marge had opted to wear a tuxedo, not a dress—but it was the kind of slight that neither of them had been able to forgive, since other heterosexual couples had been allowed the privilege. Frankly, I don't blame Marge or Liz for being upset about it, because I was bothered, too. She and Liz get along better than most of the married couples I know.

While our visitors came and went, I stayed in the room with my wife for the rest of the day, alternately sitting in the rocking chair near the window or on the bed beside her, both of us repeatedly whispering in amazement that *we had a daughter*. I would stare at my wife and daughter, knowing with certainty that I belonged with these two and that the three of us would forever be connected. The feeling was overwhelming—like everything else that day—and I found myself speculating what London would look like as a teenager, or what she would dream about, or what she would do with her life. Whenever London cried, Vivian would automatically move her to her breast, and I would witness yet another miracle.

How does London know how to do that? I wondered to myself. *How on earth does she know?*

6

There is another memory from that day, however, that is all mine.

It occurred on that first night in the hospital, long after our final visitors had left. Vivian was asleep and I was dozing in the rocking chair when I heard my daughter begin to fuss. Before that day, I'd never actually held a newborn, and scooping her into my arms, I pulled her close to my body. I thought I'd have to wake Vivian, but surprising me, London settled down. I inched back to the rocking chair and for the next twenty minutes, all I could do was marvel at the feelings she stirred within me. That I adored her, I already knew, but already, the thought of life without her struck me as inconceivable. I remember whispering to her that as her father, I would always be there for her, and as if knowing exactly what I was saying, she pooped and squirmed and then began to cry. In the end, I handed her back to Vivian.

CHAPTER 2

In the Beginning

I told them today," Vivian announced.

We were in the bedroom, Vivian had slipped into her pajamas and crawled into bed, the two of us finally alone. It was mid-December, and London had been asleep for less than an hour; at eight weeks, she was still only sleeping three to four hours at a stretch. Vivian hadn't complained, but she was endlessly tired. Beautiful, but tired.

"Told who what?" I asked.

"Rob," she answered, meaning her boss at the media company where she worked. "I officially let him know that after my maternity leave was up, I wouldn't be coming back."

"Oh," I said, feeling the same pang of terror I'd felt when I'd seen the positive pregnancy result. Vivian earned nearly as much as I did and without her income, I wasn't sure we could afford our lifestyle.

"He said the door was always open if I changed my mind," she added. "But I told him that London wasn't going to be raised by strangers. Otherwise, why have a child in the first place?"

"You don't have to convince me," I said, doing my best to hide my feelings. "I'm on your side." Well, part of me was, anyway. "But you know that means we can't go out to dinner as much and we'll have to cut back on discretionary spending, right?"

"I know."

"And you're okay with not shopping as much?"

"You say it like I waste money. I never do that."

The credit card bills sometimes seemed to indicate otherwise—as did her closet, which bulged with clothes and shoes and bags—but I could hear the annoyance in her tone, and the last thing I wanted to do was argue with her. Instead, I rolled toward her, pulling her close, something else on my mind. I nuzzled and kissed her neck.

"Now?" she asked.

"It's been a long time."

"And my poor baby feels like he's about to blow up, doesn't he?"

"Frankly, I don't want to risk it."

She laughed and as I began to unbutton her pajama top, a noise sounded on the baby monitor. In that instant, we both froze.

Nothing.

Still nothing.

And just when I thought the coast was clear and I let out a breath I didn't even know I'd been holding, the noise from the baby monitor began in full force. With a sigh, I rolled onto my back and Vivian slipped from the bed. By the time London finally calmed—which took a good half hour—Vivian wasn't in the mood for a second attempt.

In the morning, Vivian and I had more luck. So much luck, in fact, that I cheerfully volunteered to take care of London when she woke so that Vivian could go back to sleep. London, however, must have been just as tired as Vivian; it wasn't until I'd finished my second cup of coffee that I heard various noises but no cries, emanating from the baby monitor.

In her room, the mobile above the crib was rotating, and London was wiggly and full of energy, her legs shooting like pistons. I couldn't help but smile and she suddenly smiled as well.

It wasn't gas; it wasn't a reflexive tic. I'd seen those, and I almost didn't believe my eyes. This was a real smile, as true as the sunrise, and when she emitted an unexpected giggle, the already brilliant start to my day was suddenly made a thousand times better.

I'm not a wise man.

I'm not unintelligent, mind you. But wisdom means more than being intelligent, because it encompasses understanding, empathy, experience, inner peace, and intuition, and in retrospect, I obviously lack many of those traits.

Here's what else I've learned: Age doesn't guarantee wisdom, any more than age guarantees intelligence. I know that's not a popular notion—don't we frequently regard our elders as wise partially because they're gray and wrinkled?—but lately I've come to believe that some people are born with the capacity to become wise while others aren't, and in some people, wisdom seems to be evident even at a young age.

My sister Marge, for instance. She's wise, and she's only five years older than I am. Frankly, she's been wise as long as I've known her. Liz, too. She's younger than Marge and yet her comments are both thoughtful and empathetic. In the aftermath of a conversation with her, I often find myself contemplating the things she'd said. My mom and dad are also wise and I've been thinking about it a lot these days because it's become clear to me that even though wisdom runs in the family, it bypassed me entirely.

If I were wise, after all, I would have listened to Marge back in the summer of 2007, when she drove me out to the cemetery where our grandparents were buried and asked me whether I was absolutely sure that I wanted to marry Vivian.

If I were wise, I would have listened to my father when he asked me whether I was sure I should strike out on my own and start my own advertising company when I was thirty-five years old.

If I were wise, I would have listened to my mom when she told me to spend as much time with London as I could, since kids grow up so fast, and you can never get those years back.

But like I said, I'm not a wise man, and because of that, my life pretty much went into a tailspin. Even now, I wonder if I'll ever recover.

Where does one begin when trying to make sense of a story that makes little sense at all? At the beginning? And where is the beginning?

Who knows?

So let's start with this. When I was child, I grew up believing that I'd feel like an adult by the time I was eighteen, and I was right. At eighteen, I was already making plans. My family had lived paycheck to paycheck, and I had no intention of doing the same. I had dreams of starting my own business, of being my own boss, even if I wasn't sure what I was actually going to do. Figuring that college would help steer me in the proper direction, I went to NC State but the longer I was there, the younger I seemed to feel. By the time I collected my degree I couldn't shake the notion that I was pretty much the same guy I'd been in high school.

Nor had college helped me decide on the kind of business I'd start. I had little in the way of real-world experience and even less capital, so deferring my dream, I took a job in advertising for a man named Jesse Peters. I wore suits to the office and worked a ton of hours and yet, more often than not, I still felt *younger* than my actual age might indicate. On weekends, I frequented the same bars I did in college, and I often imagined that I could start over as a freshman, fitting right in with whatever fraternity I happened to join. Over the next eight years there would be even more changes; I'd get married and purchase a house and start driving a hybrid but even then, I didn't necessarily always feel like the adult version of me. Peters, after all, had essentially taken the place of my parents—like my parents, he could tell me what to do *or else*—which made it seem as though I was still *pretending*. Sometimes, when sitting at my desk, I'd try to convince myself: *Okay, it's official. I'm now a grown-up.*

That realization came, of course, after London was born and Vivian quit her job. I wasn't quite thirty years old and the pressure I felt to provide for my family over the next few years required sacrifice on a scale that even I hadn't expected, and if that isn't being a grown-up, I don't know what is. After finishing at the agency—on days when I actually made it home at a reasonable hour—I'd walk through the door and hear London call out, "Daddy!" and always wish that I could spend more time with her. She'd come running and I'd scoop her up, and she'd wrap her arms around my neck, and I'd remind myself that all the sacrifices had been worth it, if only because of our wonderful little girl.

In the hectic rush of life, it was easy to convince myself that the important things—my wife and daughter, my job, my family—were going okay, even if I couldn't be my own boss. In rare moments, when I imagined a future, I would find myself picturing a life that wasn't all that different than the one I was currently leading, and that was okay, too. On the surface, things seemed to be running rather smoothly, but I should have taken that as a warning sign. Trust me when I say that I had *absolutely no idea* that within a couple of years, I'd wake in the mornings feeling like one of those immigrants on Ellis Island who'd arrived in America with nothing but the clothes on their back, not speaking the language, and wondering, *What am I going to do now?*

When, exactly, did it all begin to go wrong? If you ask Marge, the answer is obvious: "It started going downhill when you met Vivian," she's told me more than once. Of course, being Marge, she would automatically correct herself. "I take that back," she would add. "It started way before that, when you were still in grade school and hung that poster on your wall, the one with the girl in the skimpy bikini with the big bahoonas. I always liked that poster, by the way, but it warped your thinking." Then, after further consideration, she would shake her head, speculating, "Now that I think about it, you were always kind of screwed up, and coming from the person who's always been regarded as the family screwup, that's saying something. Maybe your real problem is that you've always been too damn nice for your own good."

And that's the thing. When you start trying to figure out what went wrong—or, more specifically, where *you* went wrong—it's a bit like peeling an onion. There's always another layer, another mistake in the past or a painful memory that stands out, which then leads one back even further in time, and then even further, in search of the *ultimate truth*. I've reached the point where I've stopped trying to figure it out: The only thing that really matters now is learning enough to avoid making the same mistakes again.

To understand why that is, it's important to understand me. Which isn't easy, by the way. I've been me for more than a third of a century, and half the time, I still don't understand myself. So let me start with this: As I've grown older, I've come to believe that there are two types of men in the world. The marrying type, and the bachelor type. The marrying type is the kind of guy who pretty much sizes up every girl he dates, assessing whether or not she could be *The One*. It's the reason that women in their thirties and forties often say things like *All the good men are taken.* By that, women mean guys who are ready, willing, and able to commit to being part of a couple.

I've always been the marrying type. To me, being part of a couple feels *right*. For whatever reason, I've always been more comfortable in the presence of women than men, even in friendship, and spending time with one woman *who also happened to be madly in love with me* struck me as the best of all possible worlds.

And it can be, I suppose. But that's where things get a bit trickier because not all marrying types are the same. There are subgroups within the marrying types, guys who may also consider themselves to be *romantic*, for instance. Sounds nice, right? The kind of guy that most women insist they want? It probably is, and I must admit that I'm a card-carrying member of this particular subgroup. In rare instances, however, this particular subtype is also wired to be a *people pleaser* and when taken together, these three things made me believe that with just a bit more effort—if only I tried a little harder—then my wife would always adore me in the same way I adored her.

But what was it that made me that way? Was it simply my nature? Was I influenced by family dynamics? Or did I simply watch too many romantic movies at an impressionable age? Or all of the above?

I have no idea, but I state without hesitation that the *watching too many romantic movies* thing was entirely Marge's fault. She loved the classics like *An Affair to Remember* and *Casablanca*, but *Ghost* and *Dirty Dancing* were up there too, and we must have watched *Pretty Woman* at least twenty times. That movie was her all-time favorite. What I didn't know, of course, was that Marge and I enjoyed watching it because we both had massive crushes on Julia Roberts at the time, but that's beside the point. The film will probably live on forever because it *works*. The characters played by Richard Gere and Julia Roberts had...*chemistry*. They talked. They learned to trust each other, despite the odds. They fell in love. And how can one possibly forget the scene when Richard Gere is waiting for Julia—he's planning to take her to the opera—and she emerges wearing a gown that utterly transforms her? The audience sees Richard's awestruck expression, and he eventually opens a velvet box, which holds the diamond necklace Julia will also be wearing that evening. As Julia reaches for it, Richard snaps the lid closed, and Julia's sudden joyful surprise...

It was all there, really, in just those few scenes. The romance, I mean—trust, anticipation, and joy combined with opera, dressing up, and jewelry all led to *love*. In my preteenage brain, it just clicked: a how-to manual of sorts to impress a girl. All I really had to do was remember that girls had to *like* the guy first and that *romantic gestures* would then lead to *love*. In the end, another romantic in the real world was created.

When I was in sixth grade, a new girl joined the class. Melissa Anderson had moved from Minnesota, and with blond hair and blue eyes, she shared the look of her Swedish ancestors. When I saw her on the first day of school, I'm pretty sure I went slack-jawed and I wasn't the only one. Every guy was whispering about her and there was little doubt in my mind that she was far and away the prettiest girl who'd ever set foot in Mrs. Hartman's class at Arthur E. Edmonds elementary school.

But the difference between me and the other guys at school was that I knew exactly what to do while they did not. I would woo her and though I wasn't Richard Gere with private jets and diamond necklaces, I did have a bicycle and I'd learned how to macramé bracelets, complete with wooden beads. Those, however, would come later. First—just like Richard and Julia—we had to get to *like* each other. I began to find reasons to sit at the same table with her at lunch. While she talked, I listened and asked questions, and weeks later, when she finally told me that she thought I was nice, I knew it was time to take the next step. I wrote her a poem—about her life in Minnesota and how pretty she was—and I slipped it to her on the school bus one afternoon, along with a flower. I took my seat, knowing exactly what would happen: She'd understand I was different, and with that would come an even greater epiphany, one that would lead her to reach for my hand and ask me to walk her home as soon as we got off the bus.

Except it didn't work out that way. Instead of reading the poem, she gabbed with her friend April the whole way home, and the following day, she sat next to Tommy Harmon at lunch and didn't talk to me at all. Nor did she speak to me the following day, or the day after that.

14

When Marge found me sulking in my bedroom later, she told me that I was trying too hard and that I should just be myself.

"I am being myself."

"Then you might want to change," Marge retorted, "because you're coming across as desperate."

Problem was, I didn't think twice. Did Richard Gere think twice? He clearly knew more than my sister, and again, here's where wisdom and I were obviously traveling in opposite directions along the highway. Because *Pretty Woman* was a movie and I was living in the real world, but the pattern I established with Melissa Anderson continued, with variations, until it eventually became a habit I couldn't break. I became the king of romantic gestures—flowers, notes, cards, and the like—and in college, I was even the "secret admirer" to a girl I happened to fancy. I opened doors and paid for dates, and I listened whenever a girl wanted to talk, even if it was about how much she still loved her ex-boyfriend. Most girls sincerely liked me. I mean that. To them, I was a *friend*, the kind of guy who'd get invited to hang out with a group of girlfriends whenever they went out, but I seldom succeeded in landing the girl I'd set my sights on. I can't tell you how many times I've heard, *"You're the nicest guy I know, and I'm sure you'll meet someone special. I have two or three friends I could probably set you up with . . ."*

It wasn't easy being the guy who was *perfect for someone else*. It often left me brokenhearted, and I couldn't understand why women told me that they wanted certain traits—romance and kindness, interest and the ability to listen—and then didn't appreciate it when it was actually offered to them.

I wasn't altogether unlucky in love, of course. In high school, I had a girlfriend named Angela during my sophomore year; in college, Victoria and I were together most of my junior year. And during the summer after graduation from college, when I was twenty-two, I met a woman named Emily.

Emily still lives in the area, and over the years, I've seen her out and about. She was the first woman I ever loved, and since *romance* and *nostalgia* are often intertwined, I still think about her. Emily was a bit of a Bohemian; she favored long flowered skirts and sandals, wore little makeup, and had majored in fine arts with an emphasis on painting. She was also beautiful, with chestnut hair and hazel eyes that were flecked with gold, but beyond her physical appearance, there was more. She was quick to laugh, kind to everyone she met, and intelligent, a woman who most thought was perfect for me. My parents adored her, Marge loved her, and when we were together, we were comfortable even when silent. Our relationship was easy and relaxed; more than lovers, we were friends. Not only could we talk about anything, she delighted in the notes I'd place under her pillow or the flowers I'd have delivered to her workplace for no reason whatsoever. Emily loved me as much as she loved romantic gestures, and after dating her for a couple of years, I made plans to propose, even putting a deposit down on an engagement ring.

And then, I screwed it up. Don't ask me why. I could blame the booze that night—I'd been drinking with friends at a bar—but for whatever reason, I struck up a conversation with a woman named Carly. She was beautiful and she knew how to flirt and she'd recently broken up with a long-term boyfriend. One drink led to another, which led to more flirting, and we eventually ended up in bed together. In the morning, Carly made it clear that what had happened was simply a fling, with no strings attached, and though she kissed me goodbye, she didn't bother giving me her phone number.

There are a couple of very simple Guy Rules in this sort of situation, and Rule Number One goes like this: *Never ever tell*. And if your sweetheart ever suspects anything and asks directly, go immediately to Rule Number Two: *Deny, deny, deny*.

All guys know these rules, but the thing was, I also felt guilty. Horribly guilty. Even after a month, I couldn't put the experience behind me, nor could I seem to forgive myself. Keeping it secret seemed inconceivable; I couldn't imagine building a future with Emily knowing it was constructed at least in part on a lie. I talked to Marge about it, and Marge was, as always, helpful in that sisterly way of hers.

"Keep your stupid trap shut, you dimwit. You did a crappy thing and you should feel guilty. But if you're never going to do it again, then don't hurt Emily's feelings, too. Something like this will crush her."

I knew Marge was right, and yet...

I wanted Emily's forgiveness, because I wasn't sure I could forgive myself without it, and so in the end, I went to Emily and said the words that even now, I wish I could take back.

"There's something I have to tell you," I began, and proceeded to spill everything.

If forgiveness was the goal, it didn't work. If trying to build a long-term relationship on a foundation of truth was another goal, that didn't work either. Through angry tears, she stormed off, saying that she needed some time to think.

I left her alone for a week, waiting for her to call while moping around my apartment, but the phone never rang. The following week, I left two messages—and apologized again both times—but she still wouldn't call. It wasn't until the following week that we finally had lunch, but it was strained, and when she left the restaurant, she told me not to walk her to her car. The writing was on the wall and a week after that, she left a message saying it was over for good. It crushed me for weeks.

The passage of time has lessened my guilt—time always does—and I try to console myself with the idea that at least for Emily, my indiscretion was a blessing in disguise. I heard from a friend of a friend a few years after our breakup that she'd married an Australian guy and whenever I caught a glimpse of her, it appeared as though life was treating her well. I'd tell myself that I was happy for her. Emily, more than anyone, deserved a wonderful life, and Marge felt exactly the same way. Even after I'd married Vivian, my sister would sometimes turn to me and say, "That Emily sure was something. You really messed that up, didn't you?"

I was born in Charlotte, North Carolina, and aside from a single year in another city, I've lived there all my life. Even now, it strikes me as almost impossible that Vivian and I met in the place where we did, or even that we ever met at all. After all, she, like me, was from the South; like mine, her job required long hours, and she seldom went out. What are the odds, then, that I'd meet Vivian at a cocktail party in Manhattan?

At the time, I was working at the agency's satellite office in

Midtown, which probably sounds like a bigger deal than it really was. Jesse Peters was of the opinion that pretty much anyone who showed promise in the Charlotte office had to serve at least a little time up north, if only because a number of our clients are banks, and every bank has a major presence in New York City. You've probably seen some of the commercials I've worked on; I like to think of them as thoughtful and serious, projecting the soul of integrity. The first of those commercials, by the way, was conceived while I was living in a small studio on West Seventy-Seventh between Columbus and Amsterdam and trying to figure out whether my ATM accurately reflected my checking account, which showed a balance with just enough funds to purchase a meal deal at a nearby fast-food place.

In May 2006, a CEO of the one of the banks who *loved my vision* was hosting a charity event to benefit MoMA. The CEO was seriously into art—something I knew nothing about—and even though it was an exclusive, black-tie event, I hadn't wanted to attend. But his bank was a client and Peters was my *do-what-I-tell-you-or-else* boss, so what could I do?

I remember almost nothing about the first half hour, other than that I clearly didn't belong. Well over half the people in attendance were old enough to be my grandparents, and practically everyone was in a different stratosphere when it came to our respective levels of wealth. At one point, I found myself listening as two gray-haired gentlemen debated the merits of the G IV when compared to the Falcon 2000. It took me a while to figure out that they were comparing their private jets.

When I turned away from the conversation, I saw her boss on the other side of the room. I recognized him from late-night television, and Vivian would later tell me that he considered himself an art collector. She'd wrinkled her nose when she said it, implying that he had money but no taste, which didn't surprise me. Despite famous guests, his show's trademark humor was best described as lowbrow.

She was standing behind him, hidden from my line of sight, but when he stepped forward to greet someone, I saw her. With dark hair, flawless skin, and cheekbones that supermodels dream about, I was sure she was the most beautiful woman I'd ever seen.

At first I thought she was his date, but the longer I watched, the more confident I was that they weren't *together*, that she instead worked for him in some capacity. Nor was she wearing a ring, another good sign . . . but really, what chance did I have?

Yet the romantic within me was undeterred, and when she went to the bar to get a cocktail, I sidled up to the bar as well. Up close, she was even more gorgeous.

"It's you," I said.

"Excuse me?"

"The one the Disney artists think about when they draw the eyes of their princesses."

Not great, I'll admit. Ham-handed, maybe even cheesy, and in the awkward pause that ensued, I knew I'd blown it. But here's the thing: She laughed.

"Now there's a pickup line I've never heard before."

"It wouldn't work on just anyone," I said. "I'm Russell Green."

She seemed amused. "I'm Vivian Hamilton," she said, and I almost gasped.

Her name was *Vivian*.

Just like Julia Roberts's character in *Pretty Woman*.

How does one actually know when another is *right* for you? What kind of signals does that entail? To meet a person and think, *This is the one with whom I want to spend the rest of my life.* For example, how could Emily seem right, and Vivian seem right, when they were as different as night and day? When the relationships were as different as night and day?

I don't know, but when I think about Vivian, it's still easy to remember the heady thrill of our first few evenings together. Where Emily and I were warm and comfortable, Vivian and I burned hot, almost from the very beginning, as if our attraction were fated. Every interaction, every conversation seemed to amplify my growing belief that we were exactly what each was looking for in the other.

As the marrying type, I began to fantasize about the paths our life together would take, our passionate connection burning forever.

Within a couple of months, I was certain I wanted Vivian to be my wife, even if I didn't say as much. Vivian took longer to feel the same way about me, but by the time we'd been seeing each other six months, Vivian and I were a *serious item*, testing the waters about how each felt about God, money, politics, families, neighborhoods, kids, and our core values. More often than not, we were in agreement, and taking a cue from yet another romantic movie, I proposed on the viewing deck of the Empire State Building on Valentine's Day, a week before I had to move back to Charlotte.

I *thought* I knew what I was getting when I dropped to one knee. But thinking back, Vivian *knew* with certainty—not only that I was the kind of man she wanted, but *needed*—and on November 17, 2007, we took our vows in front of friends and family.

What happened next? you may wonder.

Like every married couple, we had our ups and downs, our challenges and opportunities, successes and failures. When all the dust had settled, I came to believe that marriage, at least in theory, is wonderful.

In practice, though, I think a more accurate word is *complicated*.

Marriage, after all, is never quite what one imagines it will be. Part of me—the romantic part—no doubt imagined the entire venture as an extended commercial for Hallmark cards with roses and candles and everything in soft focus, a dimension in which love and trust could surmount any challenge. The more practical side of me knew that remaining a couple over the long term took effort on both sides. It requires commitment and compromise, communication and cooperation, especially as life tends to throw curveballs, often when we least expect them. Ideally, the curveball slides past the couple with little damage; at other times, facing those pitches together makes the couple more committed to each other.

But sometimes, the curveballs end up smacking us in the chest and close to the heart, leaving bruises that never seem to heal.

CHAPTER 3

And Then What?

*B*eing the sole provider for the family wasn't easy. By end of the week, I was often exhausted, but one particular Friday evening stands out. London would turn a year old the following day, and I'd spent the day slaving over a series of sales videos for Spannerman Properties—one of the largest real-estate developers in the Southeast—as part of a major advertising push. The agency was earning a small fortune for their efforts and the executives at Spannerman were particularly demanding. There were deadlines for every stage of the project; deadlines made even more difficult by Spannerman himself, a man with a net worth of two billion dollars. He had to approve every decision, and I had the sense that he wanted to make my life as miserable as possible. That he disliked me, I had no doubt. He was the kind of guy who liked to surround himself with beautiful women—most of the executives were attractive females—and it went without saying that Spannerman and Jesse Peters got along famously. I, on the other hand, despised both the man and his company. He had a reputation for cutting corners and paying off politicians, especially when it came to environmental regulations, and there'd been numerous op-eds in the newspaper blasting both him and the company. Which was part of the reason they'd hired our firm in the first place—their image needed serious rebranding.

For most of the year, I'd worked punishing hours on the Spanner-man account, and it was far and away the most miserable year of my life. I dreaded heading into work, but because Peters and Spannerman were buddies, I kept my feelings to myself. Eventually, the account was handed off to another executive at the agency—Spannerman decided that he wanted a female executive, which surprised no one—and I breathed a sigh of relief. Had I been forced to continue with Spannerman, I probably would have ended up quitting.

Jesse Peters believed in bonuses as a way to keep employees motivated, and despite the never-ending stress associated with the Spannerman account, I was nonetheless able to maximize every bonus. I had to. I've never been comfortable unless I was able to put money into savings and our investment account, but the bonuses also helped to keep the balances on our credit cards at zero. Instead of shrinking over the past year, our monthly expenses had grown larger, despite Vivian's promise to cut back on "running errands," which was how she'd begun to refer to shopping. Vivian seemed incapable of entering Target or Walmart without spending at least a couple of hundred dollars, even if she'd gone to pick up laundry detergent. I couldn't understand it—I speculated that it filled a sort of unknown emptiness inside her—and when particularly exhausted, I sometimes felt resentful and used. Yet, when I tried to discuss the matter with her, it often led to an argument. Even when tempers didn't flare, however, little seemed to change. She would always assure me that she only bought what we needed, or that I was lucky because she'd taken advantage of a sale.

But on that Friday night those concerns seemed distant, and when I entered the living room, I saw London in the playpen, and she offered me the kind of smile that never ceased to move me. Vivian, as beautiful as ever, was on the couch flipping through a house and garden magazine. I kissed London and then Vivian, enveloped in the scent of baby powder and perfume.

We had dinner, talk running to what each of us had done that day, and then began the process of getting London ready for bed. Vivian went first, bathing her and dressing London in her pajamas; I read to her and tucked her in bed, knowing she'd fall asleep within a few minutes.

Downstairs, I poured myself a glass of wine, and noticed that the bottle was getting close to empty, which meant that Vivian was probably on her second glass. Glass one was a maybe when it came to fooling around; glass two made it likely, and as tired as I was, I felt my mood lift.

Vivian was still thumbing through the magazine when I sat beside her. In time, Vivian angled the magazine toward me.

"What do you think of this kitchen?" she asked.

The kitchen displayed in the photograph had cream cabinets topped with brown granite countertops, the color palette matched by the detailing on the cabinets. An island stood amidst gleaming state-of-the-art appliances, a suburban fantasy.

"It's gorgeous," I admitted.

"It is, isn't it? Everything about the kitchen speaks to class. And I just love the lighting. The chandelier is breathtaking."

I hadn't even noticed the lighting and leaned closer. "Wow. That is something."

"The article said that remodeling a kitchen almost always adds value to a house. If we ever decide to sell."

"Why would we sell? I love it here."

"I'm not talking about selling it now. But we're not going to live here forever."

Oddly, the thought that we wouldn't live here forever had never crossed my mind. My parents, after all, still lived in the same house where I'd grown up, but that's not what Vivian really wanted to talk about.

"You're probably right about it adding value," I said, "but I'm not sure we can afford to remodel our kitchen right now."

"We have money in savings, don't we?"

"Yes, but that's our rainy-day fund. For emergencies."

"Okay," she said. I could the disappointment in her tone. "I was just wondering."

I watched as she carefully folded the corner of the page down, so she could find the photo later, and I felt like a failure. I hated to disappoint her.

Life as a stay-at-home mother was good for Vivian.

Despite having a child, Vivian could still pass for a woman ten years younger, and even after London was born, she was occasionally carded when ordering a cocktail. Time had little effect on her, yet it was other qualities that made her particularly unusual. Vivian had always struck me as mature and confident, self-assured in her thoughts and opinions, and unlike me, she's always had the courage to speak her mind. If she wanted something, she'd let me know; if something was bothering her, she never held her feelings in reserve, even if I might be upset by what she said. The strength to be who you are without fear of rejection from others was something I respected, if only because it was something I aspired to myself.

She was strong, too. Vivian didn't whine or complain in the face of adversity; if anything, she became almost stoic. In all the years I've known her, I've seen her cry only once, and that was when Harvey, her cat, passed away. At the time, she was pregnant with London and Harvey had been with her since she was a sophomore in college; even with her hormones in overdrive, it was less like sobbing than a couple of tears leaking onto her cheeks.

People can read whatever they want into the fact that she wasn't prone to weeping, but the fact was, there hasn't been much for Vivian *to* cry about. To that point, we'd been spared any major tragedies and if there was anything at all that might have been a cause for disappointment, it was that Vivian hadn't been able to become pregnant a second time. We'd begun trying when London was eighteen months old, but month after month passed without success, and though I was willing to see a specialist, Vivian seemed content to let nature take its course.

Even without another child, though, I usually felt lucky to be married to Vivian, partly because of our daughter. Some women are better suited to motherhood than others, and Vivian had been a natural. She was conscientious and loving, a natural nurse unfazed by diarrhea or vomit, and a model of patience. Vivian read London hundreds of books and could play on the floor for hours; the two of them went to parks and the library, and the sight of Vivian pushing London in a jogger-stroller was a common one in our neighborhood. There were other activities and scheduled playdates with neighborhood kids, preschool classes, and the usual doctors' and dentists' appointments, which meant that the two of them were always on the go. And yet when I think back on those first years of London's life, the image of Vivian that most comes to mind is the expression of absolute joy on her face, whether holding London or watching our daughter gradually discover the world. Once when London was about eight months old and sitting in the high chair, she happened to sneeze. For whatever reason, London found that highly amusing and began to laugh; I offered a fake sneeze, and London's laughter became uncontrollable. While I found the experience delightful, for Vivian, it was *more*. The love she felt for our daughter eclipsed everything else, even the love she felt for me.

The all-consuming nature of motherhood—or Vivian's view of it, anyway—not only allowed me to concentrate on my career, but it also meant I seldom had to take care of London on my own, so I never really learned how challenging it could be. Because Vivian made it look easy, I thought it was easy for her, but over time, Vivian became moodier and more irritable. Basic household chores also took a backseat, and I often came home to a living room littered from wall to wall with toys and a kitchen sink filled with dirty dishes. Laundry piled up, carpets weren't vacuumed, and because I've always disliked a messy house, I eventually decided to bring someone in twice a week to clean. During London's toddler years, I added a babysitter three afternoons a week to give Vivian a break during the day and I began watching London on Saturday mornings, so Vivian could have some Me Time. My hope was that she would have more energy for us as a couple again. To my mind, it seemed that my wife had begun to define herself as Vivian and a mother and that the three of us together were a family, but that being a wife and part of a couple had gradually become an inconvenience to her.

Yet most of the time, our relationship didn't bother me. I figured we were like most married couples with young children. In the evenings, we generally talked about the *stuff of life*: conversations about children or work or family, or what to eat or where to go on the weekend, or when to bring the car in for an inspection. And it wasn't as though I always felt like an afterthought; Vivian and I began to set aside Friday nights as date nights. Even people at work knew about our date night, and unless there was an absolute emergency, I would leave the office at a reasonable hour, put some music on in the car on the way home, and be smiling as soon as I walked in the door. London and I would spend time together while Vivian dressed up, and after London went to sleep, it almost felt as though Vivian and I were dating again.

Vivian also humored me when work was particularly stressful.

When I was thirty-three, I'd considered trading in my *respectable* car—the hybrid—for a Mustang GT, even if the trade-in wouldn't have caused much of a dent in the purchase price. At the time it didn't matter; when I took it on a test drive with the enthusiastic salesman, I heard the throaty roar of the engine and knew it was a car that would elicit envious glances as I drove down the highway. The salesman played right along and when I told Vivian about it later, she didn't tease me about being too young for the middle-age crazies, or worry aloud that I clearly wanted something different than the life I was leading. Instead, she let me indulge the fantasy for a while, and when I finally came to my senses, I bought something similar to what I already had: another hybrid with four doors, extra storage in the trunk and an excellent safety ranking in *Consumer Reports*. And I've never regretted it.

Well, maybe I regretted it a *little*, but that's beside the point.

And through it all, I *loved* Vivian, and never once did I waver from the conviction that I wanted to spend my life with her. In my desire to show it, I thought long and hard about what to buy her for Christmases, anniversaries, birthdays, as well as Valentine's and Mother's Day. I had flowers delivered to her unexpectedly, tucked notes under her pillow before heading off to work, and would sometimes surprise her with breakfast in bed. Early on, she appreciated those gestures; in time, they seemed to lose a bit of luster because she'd come to expect them. So I'd rack my brain, trying to think of another way to please her, something that would let her know how much she still meant to me.

And in the end, among other things, Vivian received the kitchen she'd wanted, just like the one in the magazine.

Vivian had always planned to go back to work once London started school, something part-time, which would still allow her to spend her afternoons and evenings at home. Vivian insisted that she had no desire to be one of those moms who became permanent volunteers in the classroom, or decorated the cafeteria at the holidays. Nor did she want to spend her days in an otherwise empty house; in addition to being a great mother, Vivian is also brilliant. She'd graduated from Georgetown University summa cum laude, and prior to becoming a mom and housewife, she'd served as a successful publicist not only for the talk show host in New York, but at the media company where she'd worked until London came along.

As for me, I'd not only maximized every bonus since starting at the agency, I'd received promotions as well, and by 2014, I was heading up some of the agency's major accounts. Vivian and I had been married for seven years, London had recently turned five, and I was thirty-four years old. We'd not only remodeled the kitchen of our home, but we also had plans to remodel the master bathroom as well. The stock market had been kind to our investments—especially Apple, our largest holding—and aside from the mortgage we had no debts. I adored my wife and child, my parents lived nearby and my sister and Liz were my best friends in the world. From the outside, my life seemed charmed, and I would say as much to anyone who asked.

And yet deep down, part of me would also have known that I was lying.

As well as things had been going at work, no one who reported to Jesse Peters ever felt comfortable or secure in their job. Peters had started the agency twenty years earlier and with offices in Charlotte, Atlanta, Tampa, Nashville, and New York, it was far and away the most prominent agency headquartered in the Southeast. Peters, with blue eyes and hair that had gone silver in his twenties, was legendary for being both shrewd and ruthless; his modus operandi had been to run other agencies out of business either by poaching clients or undercutting fees; when those strategies didn't work, he'd simply buy out his competitors. His successes further inflated his already massive ego to megalomaniacal proportions, and his management style fully reflected his personality. He was certain that his opinions were always correct, and he played favorites among the employees, frequently pitting one executive against the other, effectively keeping everyone on edge. He fostered a climate in which most employees attempted to claim more credit on successes than they deserved, while hinting that any failures or mistakes were the other guy's fault. It was a brutal form of social Darwinism, in which only a select few had any chance for long-term survival.

Fortunately, for more than a decade I'd been relatively spared the savage rounds of office politics that had caused more than one nervous breakdown among the executive staff; early on because I was too subordinate to care about, and later on because I brought in clients who appreciated my work and paid the firm accordingly. Over time, I suppose I convinced myself that because I made Peters a lot of money, he considered me too valuable to torment. After all, Peters wasn't nearly as hard on me as he'd been on others in the agency. While he'd chat with me in the hallway, other executives—some with more experience than I—would often emerge from Peters's office appearing shell-shocked. When I'd see them, I couldn't help but breathe a sigh of relief—and maybe even feel a little smug—that such a thing had never happened to me.

But assumptions are only as accurate as the person who makes them, and I was wrong about virtually everything. My first major promotion had somewhat coincided with my marriage to Vivian; my second promotion had occurred two weeks after Vivian had come to the office to drop off my car after it had been in the shop, one of those drop-ins that could go catastrophically wrong but in this case had caused the boss to join us in my office before eventually taking us to lunch. The third promotion came less than a week after Peters and Vivian spent three hours talking at a client's dinner party. Only in retrospect did it become clear that Peters was less interested in my work performance than he was in Vivian, and it was that simple truth that had kept him from zeroing in on me all along. Vivian, I should note, bore a striking resemblance to both of Peters's former wives, and Peters, I suspected, wanted nothing more than to keep her happy… or if possible, marry wife number three, even if it cost me my own marriage.

I'm not kidding. Nor am I exaggerating. Whenever Peters spoke to me, he never failed to ask me how Vivian was doing, or comment on what a beautiful woman she was, or ask how *we* were doing. At client dinners—three or four times a year—Peters always found a way to sit beside my wife, and every Christmas party included the sight of them, heads together in a corner. I probably could have ignored all of this, if not for Vivian's response to his obvious attraction. Though she didn't do anything to encourage Peters, she didn't do anything to *discourage* his attention either. As terrible as he was as a boss, Peters could be quite charming around women, especially beautiful ones like Vivian. He would listen and laugh and offer just the right compliment at exactly the right time, and because he was also as rich as Midas, it struck me as possible—even likely—that Vivian was flattered by his interest. His attraction toward her was, for her, par for the course. Guys had been vying for her attention ever since she'd been in elementary school and she'd come to *expect* it; what she didn't like, however, was the fact that it sometimes made me jealous.

In December 2014—the month before the most fateful year of my life—we were getting ready for the agency's annual office Christmas party. When I expressed my concerns about the situation, she heaved an aggravated sigh.

"Get over it," she said and I turned away, wondering why it was my wife seemed so dismissive of my feelings.

To rewind a bit on Vivian and me:

As rewarding as motherhood had been for Vivian, marriage to me seemed to have dimmed in its appeal. I can remember thinking that Vivian had changed in the years we'd been married, but lately, I've come to believe that Vivian didn't change so much as simply evolve, becoming more of the person she'd always been—a person who gradually felt to me like a stranger.

The shift was so subtle as to barely be noticeable. In the first year of London's life, I accepted Vivian's occasional moodiness and irritation as something normal and expected, a phase that would pass. I can't say I enjoyed it, but I grew used to it, even when it seemed to border on contempt. But the phase never seemed to end. Over the next few years, Vivian seemed to grow more angry, more disappointed, and more dismissive of my concerns. She frequently grew angry over even minor things, hurling insults I could never imagine even whispering aloud. Her aggression was swift and pointed, usually aimed at getting me to apologize and back down. As someone who disliked conflict, I eventually reached the point where I nearly always retreated as soon as she raised her voice, no matter what grievances I might have held.

The aftermath of her anger was often worse than the attack itself. Forgiveness seemed unobtainable, and instead of continuing to discuss things or simply putting them behind her, Vivian would withdraw. She would say little or nothing to me at all, sometimes for days, answering questions with one or two words. Instead, she would focus her attention on London, and retreat to the bedroom as soon as our daughter was tucked in, leaving me alone in the family room. On those days she radiated contempt, leaving me to wonder whether my wife still loved me at all.

And yet there was an unpredictability to all of these things, rules suddenly changing and then changing again. Vivian would be in her anger forthright, then passive-aggressive, whichever seemed to fit her mood. Her expectations of me became increasingly fuzzy and half the time, I wasn't sure what to do or not to do, rehashing events in the wake of a blowout, trying to figure out what I might have done to upset her. Nor would she tell me; instead, she'd deny that anything was wrong or accuse me of overreacting. I often felt as if I were walking through a minefield, with both my emotional state and the marriage on the line...and then suddenly, for reasons that were equally mysterious to me, our relationship would revert to something approaching *normal*. She'd ask about my day or whether there was anything special I wanted for dinner; and after London went to bed, we would make love—the ultimate signal that I'd been forgiven. Afterward, I'd breathe a sigh of relief, hopeful that things were finally returning to the way they used to be.

Vivian would deny my version of these events, or at least my interpretation of them. *Angrily.* Or she'd cast her actions and behaviors as responses to things I'd done. She would say that I had an unrealistic view of marriage, and that I'd somehow expected the honeymoon to last forever, which just wasn't possible. She claimed that I brought work stress home, and that I was the one who was moody, not her;

that I resented the fact that she'd been able to stay at home and that I often took my resentment out on her.

Whatever version of events was objectively true, in my heart what I wanted more than anything was for Vivian to be happy. Or, more specifically, *happy with me*. I still loved Vivian, after all, and I missed how she used to smile and laugh when we were together; I missed our rambling conversations and the way we used to hold hands. I missed the Vivian who'd made me believe that I was a man worthy of her love.

Yet, with the exception of our Friday evening date nights, our relationship continued its gradual evolution into something I didn't always recognize, or even want. Vivian's contempt began to *hurt* me. I spent most of those years being disappointed in myself for constantly letting her down, and vowing to try even harder to please her.

Now, fast-forward back to the night of the Christmas party again.

"Get over it," she'd said to me, and the words continued to play in my mind, even as I dressed. They were sharp, dismissive of my concern and devoid of empathy, but even so, what I remember most about that evening was that Vivian looked even more stunning than usual. She was wearing a black cocktail dress, pumps, and the diamond pendant necklace I'd given her on her last birthday. Her hair fell loose over her shoulders, and when she emerged from the bathroom, all I could do was stare.

"You look beautiful," I said.

"Thank you," she said, clutching her handbag.

In the car, things were still tense between us. We stumbled through some small talk, and when she discerned I wasn't going to bring up Peters again, her mood began to thaw. By the time we arrived at the party, it was almost as though she and I had come to an unspoken agreement to pretend that my comment and her response had never been uttered at all.

Yet, she'd heard me. As annoyed as she'd been, Vivian stayed by my side virtually the entire evening. Peters chatted with us on three separate occasions and twice asked Vivian if she wanted to get something to drink—it was clear he wanted her to join him at the bar—and on both occasions, she shook her head, telling him that she'd already ordered from one of the waiters. She was polite and friendly as she said it, and I found myself wondering whether I'd been making too much of the whole Peters situation after all. He could flirt with her all he wanted, but at the end of the night she would head home with me, and that was all that really mattered, right?

The party itself was largely forgettable—it was no better or worse or even all that different from any other office Christmas party—but after we got home and let our teenage babysitter go, Vivian asked me to pour her a glass of wine and check in on London. By the time I finally made it to the bedroom, there were candles lit and she was wearing lingerie...and...

That was the thing about Vivian; trying to guess what she was going to do next was often pointless; even after seven years, she could still amaze me, sometimes in blissfully tender ways.

Big mistake.

That's pretty much the way I think about that evening now, at least when it came to my career at the agency.

Jesse Peters, it turns out, wasn't pleased that Vivian had avoided him, and by the following week, a distinct cooling breeze began flowing from his office toward mine. It was subtle at first; when I saw him in the hallway on the Monday following the party, he walked past with a curt nod, and during a creative meeting a few days later, he asked everyone questions but me. Those types of minor snubs continued, but because I was buried in yet another complex campaign—for a bank that wanted a campaign centered on integrity but that also felt *new*—I thought nothing of it. After that came the holidays and because the office was *always* a bit crazed at the beginning of a new year, it wasn't until the end of January when I registered the fact that Jesse Peters had barely spoken to me for at least six weeks. At that point, I began swinging by his office, but his assistant would inform me that he was on a call or otherwise busy. What finally made me understand the depth of his peevishness with me came in mid-February, when he finally made time to see me. Actually, through his secretary, and then mine, he *requested* to see me, which essentially meant I had no choice. The firm had lost a major client, an automotive dealer with eight locations throughout Charlotte, and it had been my account. After I walked him through the reasons I thought the client had chosen another firm, he fixed me with an unblinking stare. More ominously, he neither mentioned Vivian nor asked about her. At the conclusion of our meeting, I walked out the door feeling much like the executives I used to feel superior to, the ones I'd seen teetering on the edge of a nervous breakdown. I had the sinking feeling that my days at the Peters Group were suddenly numbered.

Even harder to bear was the fact that it wasn't because of anything I did or didn't do for the auto dealer—a man in his late sixties—that made him leave. I've seen the print ads and commercials from the agency that took over the account and I still believe that our ideas were more creative and more effective. But clients can be fickle. A downturn in the economy, change in management, or simply the desire to cut expenses in the short run can lead to changes that affect our industry, but sometimes, it has nothing to do with business at all. In this case, the client was going through a divorce and needed money to pay for the settlement; cutting advertising for the next six months would save him more than six figures, and he needed to hoard every penny, since his wife had hired a notoriously cutthroat lawyer. With court costs rising and a nasty settlement in the making, the guy was trimming every expense he could, and Peters knew it.

A month later, when another client pulled the plug—a chain of urgent care clinics—Peters's displeasure with me was even more evident. It wasn't a major client—frankly, it barely classified as even a *medium* client—and the fact that I'd signed three new clients since the beginning of the year seemed to matter to him not at all. Instead, after again summoning me, he ventured aloud that *"you might be losing your touch"* and that *"clients may have stopped trusting your judgment."* As a final exclamation point to the meeting, he called Todd Henley into the office and announced that from that point on, we'd be *"working together."* Henley was an up-and-comer—he'd been at the agency five years—and though he was somewhat creative, his real skill was navigating the political waters of the agency. I'd known he was gunning for my job—he wasn't the only one, but he was the most sycophantic of the bunch. When he suddenly began spending more time in Peters's office—no doubt claiming more credit than he deserved for any ad campaign we were working on—and leaving with a self-satisfied smirk I knew I had to start making plans.

My experience, position, and current salary didn't leave many options. Because Peters dominated the advertising industry in the Charlotte area, I had to cast a wider net. In Atlanta, Peters was number two in the market and growing, gobbling up smaller agencies and landing new clients. The current market leader had gone through two recent transitions in leadership and was now in a hiring freeze. After that, I contacted firms in Washington, D.C., Richmond, and Baltimore, thinking that being closer to Vivian's parents would make the move from Charlotte more palatable to Vivian. Again, however, I couldn't land so much as an interview.

There were other possibilities, of course, depending on how far away from Charlotte I'd be willing to move, and I contacted seven or eight firms throughout the Southeast and Midwest. And yet with every call, I also grew more certain that I didn't want to leave. My parents were here, Marge and Liz were here; Charlotte was home for me. And with that, the idea of *starting my own business*—a boutique advertising agency—began to rise from the ashes like the mythical phoenix. Which, I realized, also happened to be a perfect name...

The Phoenix Agency. Where your business will rise to levels of unprecedented success.

All at once, I could see the slogan on business cards; I could imagine chatting with clients, and when visiting my parents, I casually mentioned the idea to my father. He told me straight out that it wasn't a good idea; Vivian wasn't thrilled about it either. I'd been keeping her informed about my job search and when I mentioned my idea for the Phoenix Agency, she'd suggested I try looking into New York and Chicago, two places I considered nonstarters. But still, I couldn't shake off my dream, and the advantages began to tumble through my mind.

As a solo operator, I'd have little in the way of overhead.

I was on a first-name basis with CEOs and other executives throughout Charlotte.

I was excellent at my job.

I'd be a boutique firm, catering to only a few clients.

I could charge the client less and earn more.

Meanwhile, at the office, I began running numbers and making projections. I called clients, asking if they were satisfied with the service and pricing they were getting from the Peters Group, and their answers bolstered my certainty that I couldn't fail. Meanwhile, Henley was verbally slipping me into concrete loafers and tossing me overboard every time he walked into Peters's office, and Peters actually began to scowl at me.

That was when I knew Peters would fire me, which meant I had no choice but to strike out on my own.

All I had left to do was officially tell Vivian.

What could be better than celebrating my future success on date night?

Granted, I could have chosen another night, but I wanted to share my excitement with her. I wanted her support. I wanted to share my plans and have her reach across the table to take my hands while saying *I can't tell you how long I've been waiting for you to do something like this. There's no doubt in my mind you'll be a success. I've always believed in you.*

About a year later, when I confessed to Marge my hopes for that night, she'd actually laughed aloud. "So let me get this straight," she'd said to me. "You basically ripped away her sense of security and told her you were about to turn your lives upside down . . . and you honestly believed she'd think it was a good idea? You had a child, for God's sake. And a mortgage. And other bills. Are you out of your mind?"

"But . . ."

"There are no buts," she said. "You know that Vivian and I don't always agree, but on that night, she was right."

Maybe Marge had a point, but hindsight is twenty-twenty. On the night in question after we'd put London to bed, I grilled steaks—about the only thing I could actually cook well—while Vivian prepared a salad, steamed some broccoli, and sautéed green beans with shaved almonds. Vivian, I should add, *never* ate what might be considered *unhealthy* carbs—bread, ice cream, pasta, sugar, or anything that included white flour—all of which I considered to be rather tasty and indulged in during my lunches, which probably explained my love handles.

Dinner, however, was tense from the beginning. My intention to keep things light and easy seemed only to put her more on edge, as if she were preparing herself for whatever might be coming next. Vivian had always been able to read me like Moses read the Commandments, and her growing unease made me try even harder to keep things breezy, which only made her sit even straighter in her chair.

I waited until we were nearly finished with the meal. She'd eaten two or three ounces of her steak and I'd refilled her glass of wine when I started to tell her about Henley and Peters and my suspicion about being fired. She merely nodded, so I gathered my courage and launched into my plans, walking through my projections while under-scoring every reason for the decision. As I spoke, she may as well have been carved from marble. She sat as still as I'd ever seen her, not even glancing at her glass of wine. Nor did she ask any questions until after I'd finished. Silence filled the room, echoing against the walls.

"Are you sure that's a good idea?" she finally offered.

It wasn't the ringing endorsement that I'd wanted, but she didn't storm off either, which I took as a good sign. Silly me.

"Actually," I admitted, "it scares the hell out of me, but if I don't do it now, I don't know if I ever will."

"Aren't you kind of young to start your own agency?"

"I'm thirty-five. Peters was only thirty when he started his agency."

She pressed her lips together and I could almost see the words forming in her mind—*but you aren't Peters*. Thankfully, she didn't say that. Instead, she drew her brows together, though not a single wrin-kle showed. The woman really was a marvel when it came to aging. "Do you even know how to start your own agency?"

"It's like starting any other business, and people start businesses all the time. Essentially, it comes down to filing the appropriate paperwork with the government, hiring a good lawyer and accountant and setting up the office."

"How long would that take?"

"A month, maybe? And once I'm in an office, I'll start signing clients."

"If they decide to hire you."

"I can get the clients," I said. "I'm not worried about that. Peters is expensive, and I've worked with some of these clients for years. I'm sure they'll jump ship if given the chance."

"But you still won't be earning anything for a while."

"We'll just have to cut back a bit on a few things. Like the cleaning lady, for instance."

"You want me to clean the house?"

"I can help," I assured her.

"Obviously," she said. "Where are you getting the money for all this?"

"I was planning to use some of the money from our investments."

"Our investments?" she repeated.

"We've got more than enough to live on for a year."

"A year?" she asked, echoing me a second time.

"And that's with no income at all," I said. "Which isn't going to happen."

She nodded. "No income."

"I know it seems scary right now, but in the end, it's all going to be worth it. And your life isn't going to change."

"You mean aside from expecting me to be your maid, you mean."

"That's not what I said..."

She cut me off before I could finish. "Peters isn't just going to sit back and applaud your courage," she pointed out. "If he thinks you're trying to poach his clients, he'll do whatever it takes to run you out of business."

"He can try," I said. "But in the end, money talks."

"He's got more of it."

"I'm talking about the clients' money."

"And I'm talking about money for our *family*," she said, a hard edge coming into her voice. "What about us? What about me? Do you expect me to simply go along with this? We have a child, for God's sake."

"And I'm supposed to just give up my dreams?"

"Don't play the martyr. I hate when you do that."

"I'm not playing the martyr. I'm trying to have a discussion..."

"No you're not!" she said, her voice rising. "You've telling me what *you* want to do, even if it might not be good for our family!"

I exhaled slowly, concentrating on keeping my voice steady. "I've already told you that I'm sure Peters is going to fire me and there's no other jobs around here."

"Have you tried to talk to him?"

"Of course I've tried to talk to him."

"So you say."

"You don't believe me?"

"Only partly."

"What part?"

She slammed her napkin onto her plate and rose from the table. "The part where you're going to do what you want to do, even if it's detrimental to us and our child."

"Are you saying that I don't care about our family?"

But by then, she'd left the room.

That night, I slept in the guest room. And while remaining somewhat cordial while answering questions with one- or two-word answers, Vivian didn't otherwise speak to me for the next three days.

As good as Marge was at keeping me alive during my youth and offering pearls of wisdom when it came to my flaws, there was a part of her that resented having to babysit me once her teenage years kicked in. She began spending an inordinate amount of time on the phone, and as a result, I watched a lot of television. I can't speak for other kids, but I learned much of what I know about commercials and advertising simply by osmosis. I didn't learn it in college, nor did I learn it from my older, more experienced cohorts at the agency, since half of them were spending their creative energy trying to sabotage the careers of the other half, courtesy of Peters. Not knowing what else to do when I was thrown headfirst into the job, I'd listen as clients described what they wanted to achieve, tap into my well of memories, and come up with new spins on old commercials.

It wasn't quite that simple, of course. Advertising encompasses a lot more than simply television commercials. Over the years, I'd generated catchy slogans for print ads, or billboards; I'd scripted radio commercials and infomercials; I'd helped to redesign websites and created viable social media campaigns; I'd been part of a team that prioritized Internet searches and banner ads targeted to specific zip codes, income, and educational levels, and for one particular client, I conceived and executed the use of advertising on paneled trucks. While virtually all of that work was completed in-house at Peters by various teams, as a solo operator, I'd be responsible for whatever the client needed, and while I was strong in some areas, I was weaker in others, particularly when it came to tech. Fortunately, I'd been in the business long enough to know local vendors who provided the services I'd need, and one by one, I made contact with them.

I hadn't been lying to Vivian when I told her I wasn't worried about landing clients, but unfortunately, I made a mistake, one that was filled with irony. I forgot to plan an advertising campaign for my own business. I should have spent more money putting together a high-quality website and creating promotional materials that reflected the firm I intended to have, not the one I was building from the ground up. I should have put together some quality direct mailings that would inspire clients to reach out to me.

Instead, however, I spent the month of May making sure that the infrastructure was in place to accommodate my success. Using vacation days, I hired a lawyer and accountant, and had the appropriate paperwork filed. I leased an office with a shared receptionist. I purchased office equipment, signed leases for other equipment, and stocked my office with the supplies I knew I'd need. I read books on starting a business, and all of them stressed the importance of being adequately capitalized, and in mid-May, I submitted my two-week notice. If there was any dimming of my excitement, it had to do with the fact that I'd underestimated my start-up costs, while the regular bills still kept coming. The year of no income I'd mentioned to Vivian had shrunk to nine months.

But no matter. June first rolled around, and it was time to officially launch the Phoenix Agency. I sent letters to clients I'd worked with in the past, explaining the services I could offer while promising significant savings, and I let them know that I hoped to hear from them. I started making calls, lining up appointments, and after that, I leaned back in my chair, waiting for the phone to ring.

CHAPTER 4

———— ✕ ————

The Summer of My Discontent

L*ately, I've come to believe that having a child jumbles our sense of time, stirring together past and present as if in an electric mixer. Whenever I looked at London, the past was often propelled to the front of my thoughts as memories took hold.*

"Why are you smiling, Daddy?" London would ask me.

"Because I'm thinking about you," I'd answer, and in my mind's eye, I would see her as an infant asleep in my arms, or her revelatory first smile, or even the first time she rolled over. She was a little more than five months old and I'd put her down for a nap on her tummy while Vivian went to a yoga class. When London woke, I did a double take while I realized she was lying on her back and smiling up at me.

Other times, I would remember her as a toddler and the cautious way she crawled or held the table as ballast while she was learning how to stand; I remember holding her hands as we paraded up and down the hall-way before she could walk on her own.

There is much, however, that I missed, especially when it came to firsts. I missed her first word, for instance, and was out of town when London lost her first baby tooth. I missed the first time she ate baby food from a jar, and yet, it didn't much change my excitement when I eventually witnessed those things. For me, after all, it was still a first.

Sadly, though, there is much that I don't remember. Not everything can be reduced to a single event. When exactly did she move from toddling to walking? Or how did she move from that first word to speaking in short sentences? Those periods of incremental and inevitable improvement now seem to blur together and it sometimes feels as though I turned my back for an instant, only to discover a new version of London had taken the place of the old one.

Nor am I sure when her room and toys and games changed. I can visualize the nursery in amazing detail, right down to the wallpaper border that featured images of baby ducks. But when were the blocks and stuffed animals in the shape of caterpillars put back into a box that now sits in the corner? When did the first Barbie make her appearance, and how did London begin to imagine Barbie's fantasy life, one that included the color of clothing Barbie must wear when she's in the kitchen? When did London begin to change from being a daughter named London, to London, my daughter?

I occasionally find myself aching for the infant and toddler I'd once known and loved. She's been replaced now with a little girl who had opinions about her hair, asked her mom to paint her nails, and would soon be spending most of her day at school, under the care of a teacher I had yet to meet. These days, I find myself wishing I could turn back the clock so I could more fully experience London's first five years: I'd work fewer hours, spend more time playing on the floor with her, and share her wonder as she focused on the flight path of butterflies. I wanted London to know how much joy she added to my life and to tell her that I did the best I could. I wanted her to understand that even though her mother was always with her, I loved her as much as any father could possibly love a daughter.

Why then, I sometimes wonder, do I feel as if that's not enough?

The phone didn't ring.

Not in the first week, nor the second, nor even the third. While I'd met with more than a dozen different potential clients and all had expressed initial interest, my office phone remained mute. Even worse, as the month neared its end, none of them would make additional time to speak with me when I reached out to them, and their secretaries eventually reached the point where they asked me to stop calling.

Peters.

His fingerprints were all over this, and I thought again about Vivian's warning to me. "If he thinks you're trying to poach his clients, he'll do whatever it takes to run you out of business."

By the beginning of July, I was both depressed and worried, a situation made worse by the most recent credit card bill. Vivian had obviously taken my words to heart about her life not changing; she'd been *running errands* like crazy, and since I'd let the cleaning lady go, the house had become a regular disaster. After work, I'd have to spend an hour picking up around the house, doing laundry, vacuuming, and cleaning the kitchen. I had the sense that Vivian seemed to view my taking over of the domestic duties—and the credit card bill—as some kind of worthwhile penance.

Our conversations since I'd started my business had been superficial. I said little about work; she casually mentioned once that she'd begun putting out feelers about finding some part-time work. We talked about our families and made small talk about friends and neighbors. Mostly, though, we talked about London, always a safe topic. We both sensed that the slightest offense or misspoken word might lead to an argument.

The Fourth of July fell on a Saturday, and I wanted nothing more than to spend the day decompressing. I wanted to tune out concerns about money or bills or clients who ignored my calls; I wanted to stop the little voice in my head that had begun to wonder whether I should get a second job or start looking for jobs in other cities again. What I wanted was to escape adulthood for a day and then cap the holiday weekend off with a romantic evening with Vivian, because it would make me feel like she still believed in me, even if her faith was getting wobbly.

But holiday or not, Saturday morning was Vivian's *Me Time*, and soon after waking, she was out the door to yoga class, after which she would go to the gym. I gave London some cereal and the two of us went to the park; in the afternoon, the three of us attended a neighborhood block party. There were games for the kids, and Vivian hung with other mothers while I sipped on a couple of beers with the fathers. I didn't know them well; like me, until recently, they'd tended to work long hours, and my thoughts continually wandered to my looming financial fiasco, even as they spoke.

Later, while the fireworks blossomed in the sky above the BB&T Ballpark, I continued to feel the tension in my neck and shoulders.

On Sunday, I felt no better.

Again, I hoped for a day to unwind, but after breakfast, Vivian told me she had some *errands to run* and would be gone most of the day. The tone she used—both casual and defiant—made clear that she would be out of the house for most of the day, and was more than ready for an argument if I wanted one.

I didn't. Instead, with my stomach in knots, I watched her hop in the SUV, wondering not only how I was going to hold myself together, but how I was going to keep London entertained for an entire day. In that moment, however, I remembered a slogan I'd conceived in the first year of my advertising career.

When you're in trouble and need someone in your corner . . .

I'd written it into a commercial for a personal injury attorney and even though the guy was disciplined by the bar and eventually lost his license to practice, the ad had caused a flood of other local attorneys to advertise with our firm. I was responsible for most of them; the go-to guy when it came to any form of legal advertising and it made Peters a ton of money. A couple of years later, an article appeared in *The Charlotte Observer* and noted that the Peters Group was considered to be *the ambulance chasers of the advertising world*, and a few banking and real-estate executives began to balk at the association. Peters reluctantly pulled the plug on those same clients, even though it pained him, and years later, he would sometimes complain that he'd been extorted by those same banks he had no trouble exploiting, at least when it came to the fees he charged them.

Still, I *was in trouble and I needed someone in my corner . . .* and I made the spur-of-the-moment decision to visit my parents.

If they're not in your corner, you're in real trouble.

It's hard for me to imagine my mom without an apron. She seemed convinced that aprons were as essential as a bra and panties when it came to women's wear, at least when she was at home. Growing up, she'd be wearing one when Marge and I came down to breakfast;

she put one on immediately after walking in the door after work, and she'd continue wearing one long after dinner had been concluded and the kitchen had been cleaned. When I'd ask her why, she'd say that she liked the pockets, or that it kept her warm, or that she might have a cup of decaffeinated coffee later and didn't want to spill it on her clothes.

Personally, I think it was just a quirk, but it made buying her Christmas and birthday gifts easy, and over the years, her collection had grown. She had aprons in every color, every length and style; she had seasonal aprons, aprons with slogans, aprons that Marge and I had made her when we were kids, aprons with the name "Gladys" stenciled onto the fabric, and a couple of them even had lace, though she considered those too racy to wear. I knew for a fact that there were seven boxes of neatly folded aprons in the attic, and two entire cabinets in the kitchen were dedicated to her collection. It had always been something of a mystery to Marge and me how our mom went about selecting her Apron of the Day, or even how she could find the one she wanted amidst all the others.

Little about her apron-wearing habit had changed after she'd stopped working. My mom had worked not because she loved her job but because our family needed the money, and once she stepped away, she joined a gardening club, volunteered at the senior center, and was an active member of the Red Hat Society. Like Vivian and London, it seemed as though she had something planned every day of the week, things that made her happy, and it was my distinct impression that the aprons she'd been selecting over the last few years reflected a more cheerful disposition. Plain aprons had been banished to the bottom of the drawer; at the top were aprons patterned with flowers and birds, and the occasional slogan such as *Retired: Young at Heart but Older in Other Places.*

When I arrived with London in tow, my mom was wearing a red and blue checkered apron—without pockets, I couldn't help but notice— and her face lit up at the sight of my daughter. Over the years, she'd begun to resemble less the mother I'd known and more the kind of grandmother that Norman Rockwell might have created for the cover of *The Saturday Evening Post*. She was gray-haired, pink-cheeked, and soft in all the right places, and it went without saying that London was equally thrilled to see her.

Even better, both Liz and Marge were at the house. After a quick hug and kiss from all of them, their attention shifted completely to my daughter, and I pretty much became invisible. Liz scooped her up almost as soon as London burst through the front door and all at once London was talking a mile a minute. Marge and Liz hung on her every word, and as soon as I heard the word *cupcakes*, I knew that London would be occupied for at least the next couple of hours. London loved to bake, which was odd since it was something that Vivian didn't particularly enjoy, what with all the white flour and sugar.

"How was your Fourth?" I asked my mom. "Did you and Dad see the fireworks?"

"We stayed in," she said. "Crowds and traffic are just too much these days. How about you?"

"The usual. Neighborhood block party, and then we went to the ballpark."

"So did we," Liz said. "You should have called us. We could have made plans to meet."

"I didn't think about it. Sorry."

"Did you like the show, London?" Marge asked.

"They were super pretty. But some of them were really loud."

"Yes, they were."

"Can we go start the cupcakes now?"

"Sure, sweetie."

Strangely, my mom didn't follow the three of them. Instead, she hovered near me, waiting until they were in the kitchen before finally smoothing the front of her apron. It was what she always did when she was nervous.

"You okay, Mom?"

"You need to talk to him. He needs to go to the doctor."

"Why? What's up?"

"I'm worried he might have the cancer."

My mom never said simply "cancer." It was always *the* cancer. And the idea of *the cancer* terrified her. It had taken the lives of her parents

46

as well her two older siblings. Since then, *the cancer* had become a regular topic of conversation with my mom, a bogeyman waiting to strike when it was least expected.

"Why would you think he has cancer?"

"Because the cancer makes it hard to breathe. That's the same thing that happened to my brother. First, the cancer takes your breath, and then it takes the rest of you."

"Your brother smoked two packs of cigarettes a day."

"But your dad doesn't. And the other day, he had trouble catching his breath."

For the first time, I noticed the natural pinkness in her cheeks had faded.

"Why didn't you tell me? What happened?"

"I'm telling you now," she said. She drew a long breath. "On Thursday, after work, he was on the back porch. I was cooking dinner, and even though it was blazing hot outside, your father got it in his head to move the planter with the Japanese maple in it from one end of porch to the other, so it wouldn't get so much sun."

"By himself?" There wasn't a chance I could shift the thing an inch. It must have weighed a few hundred pounds. Maybe more.

"Of course," she answered, as if I was dumb to even ask. "And after he'd moved it, it took him a few minutes to catch his breath. He had to sit down and everything."

"It's no wonder. Anyone would breathe hard after that."

"Not your father."

She had a point, I admitted. "How was he afterward?"

"I just told you."

"How long did it take him to get back to normal?"

"I don't know. A couple of minutes maybe."

"Did he have to lie down on the couch or anything like that?"

"No. He acted like nothing was wrong with him at all. Got himself a beer in fact and put on the ball game."

"Well, if he seemed fine..."

"He needs to go to the doctor."

"You know he doesn't like doctors."

"That's why *you* need to tell him. He won't listen to me anymore. He's as stubborn as a drain clogged with gizzards and bacon grease, and he hasn't been to the doctor in years."

"He probably won't listen to me either. Did you tell Marge to ask him?"

"She told me that it was your turn."

Thanks, Marge. "I'll talk to him, okay?"

She nodded but by her distracted expression, I knew she was still thinking about *the cancer.*

"Where's Vivian? Isn't she coming?"

"It's just London and me this afternoon. Viv's running some errands."

"Oh," my mom said. She knew what *running errands* meant. "Your dad should still be in the garage."

Thankfully, the garage offered shade, lowering the temperature to something barely tolerable for a man like me, who was used to an air-conditioned office. My dad, on the other hand, probably didn't even notice, or if he did, wouldn't complain. The garage was his sanctuary, and as I entered, I marveled at how organized and cluttered it was at exactly the same time. Tools hung along the wall, boxes of wires and assorted gizmos I couldn't name, and a homemade workbench with drawers full of every kind of nail, screw, and bolt in existence. Engine parts, extension cords, garden equipment; it all had a place in my dad's world. I've always believed that my dad would have been most comfortable in the 1950s, or even as a pioneer.

My dad was a large man, with broad shoulders, muscular arms, and a mermaid tattoo on his forearm, a remnant from his stint in the navy. During my childhood, he'd loomed like a giant. Though he was a plumber who'd worked for the same company for almost thirty years, it seemed like he could repair anything. Leaking windows or roofs, lawnmower engines, televisions, heat pumps; it didn't matter to him; he had an innate knowledge of exactly the part he'd need to get whatever was broken working perfectly again. He knew everything there was to know about cars—as long as they were built before everything was computerized—and spent his weekend afternoons tinkering on the 1974 Ford Mustang he had restored twenty years ago and still drove to work. In addition to the workbench, he'd built numerous things around the house: the back deck, the storage shed, a vanity for my mother, and the cabinets in our kitchen. He wore jeans and work boots no matter what the weather, and had a colorful style of profanity that emphasized verbs, not adjectives. It went without saying that he cared little for pop culture and had never seen a single minute of anything that could be considered reality TV. He expected dinner on the table promptly at six, after which he'd put on a ball game in the family room. On the weekends, he worked in the garden or in the garage in addition to taking care of the lawn. He wasn't a hugger, either. My dad shook hands, even with me, and I was always conscious of the calluses and strength in his grip.

When I found him, he was half under the Mustang, with only his bottom half showing. Talking to my dad in the garage was often like talking to a poorly stored mannequin.

"Hey, Dad."

"Who's there?"

In his midsixties, my dad had begun to lose his hearing.

"It's me, Russ."

"Russ? What the hell are you doing here?"

"I thought I'd bring London over to say hi. She's inside with Mom and Marge and Liz."

"Cute kid," he said. From my dad, that was about as gushy a compliment as he'd ever offer, even though he adored her. Truth was, he loved nothing better than to have London sit in his lap while he was watching a ball game.

"Mom says you couldn't catch your breath the other day. She thinks you should see a doctor."

"Your mom worries too much."

"When was the last time you saw a doctor?"

"I don't know. A year ago, maybe? He said I was fit as a fiddle."

"Mom says it was longer than that."

"Maybe it was..."

I watched his hand pick through a series of wrenches by his hip and then vanish under the car. It was my cue to ease up, or at the very least change the subject. "What's up with the car?"

"Small oil leak. Just trying to figure out why. I think the filter might be faulty."

"You would know." I, on the other hand, wouldn't have been able to find the oil filter. We were different, my dad and me.

"How's business?" he asked.

"Slow," I admitted.

"I figured it might be. Tough thing, starting your own business."

"Do you have any advice?"

"Nope. I'm still not even sure what it is that you do."

"We've talked about this a hundred times. I come up with advertising campaigns, script commercials, and design print and digital ads."

He finally rolled out from beneath the car, his hands and fingernails grease-stained.

"Are you the one who does those car commercials? The ones where the guy is always yelling and screaming about the latest great deal?"

"No." I'd answered this question before, too.

"I hate those commercials. They're too loud. I use the mute button."

It was one of the reasons I tried to talk dealership owners out of raising their voices—most viewers hit the mute button.

"I know. You've told me."

He slowly began to rise. Watching my dad get up was like watching a mountain forced upward by the collision of tectonic plates.

"You said London was here?"

"She's inside."

"Vivian, too, I guess."

"No. She had some things to do today."

He continued to wipe his hands. "She doing women stuff?"

I smiled. For my dad—an old-fashioned sexist at heart—*women stuff* described pretty much everything my mom did these days, from cooking and cleaning to clipping coupons and grocery shopping.

"Yes. Women stuff."

He nodded, thinking that made perfect sense, and I cleared my throat. "Did I tell you that Vivian's thinking of going back to work?"

"Hmm."

50

"It's not because we need the money. She's been talking about this for a while, you know. With London starting school, I mean."

"Hmm."

"I think it will be good for her. Something easy, something part-time. She'd be bored otherwise."

"Hmm."

I hesitated. "What do you think?"

"About what?"

"Vivian thinking of going back to work. My new agency."

He scratched at his ear, buying time. "Did you ever think that maybe you shouldn't have quit your job in the first place?"

My dad, as much of a man's man that he was, wasn't a risk taker. For him, having a steady job and receiving a regular paycheck more than outweighed any potential reward of running his own business. Seven years ago, the former owner of the plumbing business had offered to let my dad buy it; my dad had passed on the offer, and the business was purchased by another, younger employee with entrepreneurial dreams.

To be frank, I hadn't expected him to offer me much in the way of career advice. That, too, was outside my dad's comfort zone, but I didn't hold it against him. He and I had led different lives; where I'd gone to college, he'd graduated from high school and spent time on a destroyer in Vietnam. He'd married at nineteen and was a father by twenty-two; his parents had died in a car accident a year after that. He worked with his hands while I worked with my mind, and while his view of the world—black and white, good and bad—may have seemed simplistic to some, it also provided a road map for how a real man was supposed to lead his life. Get married. Love your wife and treat her with respect. Have children, and teach them the value of hard work. Do your job. Don't complain. Remember that family—unlike most of those people you might meet in life—will always be around. Fix what can be fixed or get rid of it. Be a good neighbor. Love your grandchildren. Do the right thing.

Good rules. Actually, they were *great* rules and for the most part, they'd stayed intact throughout his life. One, however, had fallen by the wayside, and was no longer on his list. My dad had been raised Southern Baptist, and Marge and I had gone to services on both Wednesday evenings and Sundays throughout our youth. We'd gone to vacation Bible school every summer, and my parents never questioned whether or not to go to church. Like the other rules, it wasn't abandoned until soon after Marge told my parents that she was gay.

I can only imagine how nervous Marge must have been. We'd been raised in a church that believed homosexuality was a sin, and my parents marched to the beat of that very same drummer; maybe even more so, because they were from a different generation. My dad ended up meeting with the pastor, a real fire-and-brimstone kind of guy. The pastor told my dad that Marge was choosing a life of sin if she surrendered to her nature, and that they should bring her in to pray, in the hope of finding God's grace.

My dad was a lot of things—hard at times, gruff, profane—but he also loved his kids. He believed in his kids, and when Marge told him that she hadn't chosen a lifestyle—that she'd been born that way—he nodded once, told her that he loved her, and from that day onward, our family stopped attending services.

There are a lot of people in the world, I think, who could learn a lot from my dad.

"You look like crap," Marge said to me. We'd retreated to the back porch with a couple of cupcakes while Mom, Liz, and London continued to bake another batch. My dad was in the family room, enjoying the cupcakes while watching the Atlanta Braves, no doubt waiting for London to join him. She always called him Papa, which I thought was sort of cute.

"You always know just what to say to make a guy feel great."

"I'm being honest. You're pasty."

"I'm tired."

"Oh," she said. "My mistake. It's not like I know you, and can tell when you're lying. You're stressed."

"A little."

"New business not going well?"

I shifted in my seat. "I guess I thought it would be a little easier to get clients. Or at least one client."

"They'll come. You just need to give it time." When I didn't respond, she went on. "How's Vivian handling it?"

"We don't really talk about it much."

"Why not? She's your wife."

"I don't want her to worry. I figure I'll talk to her when there's something good to tell her."

"See? That's where you're wrong. Vivian should be the one person you can talk to about anything."

"I guess."

"You guess? You two really need to work on your communication skills. See a counselor or whatever."

"Maybe we should schedule an appointment with Liz. Being that she's a therapist, I mean."

"You couldn't afford her. You're not making any money."

"That makes me feel a lot better."

"Would you rather I blow smoke up the old back door?"

"As delightful as that sounds, I'll pass."

She laughed. "The point is, I've seen it happen over and over."

"Seen what happen?"

"The same mistakes people make when starting a business," she said, taking another bite. "Too much optimism on the revenue front and not enough pessimism when it comes to either business or household expenses. In your case, credit cards."

"How would you know that?"

"Hello? Vivian and her *errands*? The bill arriving in the middle of the month? This isn't the first time we've had this conversation."

"The balance was a little high," I finally admitted.

"Then take some advice from your sister with the CPA. Cancel it. Or at least put a limit on it."

"I can't.

"Why not?"

"Because I told her that her life wasn't going to change."

"Why on earth would you say something like that?"

"Because there's no reason she should have to suffer."

"You know how crazy that sounds, right? Shopping less is not equivalent to suffering. And besides, you're supposed to be partners, both of you on the same team, especially when things get tough."

"We are on the same team. And I love her."

"I know you love her. If anything, you love her too much."

"There's no such thing."

"Yeah, well...I'm just saying that she's not always the easiest person to be married to."

"That's because she's a woman."

"Do I have to remind you whom you're talking to?"

I hesitated. "Do you think I made a mistake? By going out on my own?"

"Don't start second-guessing yourself now. Unless you were willing to move halfway across the country, you didn't have a choice. And besides, I have the feeling that it's all going to work out for the better."

It was exactly what I needed to hear. And yet as she said it, I couldn't help wishing that Vivian had said it, not my sister.

"I take it the cooking classes are still going well?" I said to Liz half an hour later. For Christmas last year, I'd bought her a couple of classes at a place called the Chef's Dream, but she'd enjoyed it so much, she had continued on her own. By then, I was on my second cupcake. "These are great."

"Those are more your mom's doing. We don't really do a lot of baking. Right now, we're learning French cuisine."

"Like snails and frog legs?"

"Among other things."

"And you eat it?"

"They're better than the cupcakes, believe it or not."

"Have you talked Marge into going yet?"

"No, but that's okay. And I enjoy having a bit of alone time. Besides, it's only one night a week. It's not that big of a deal."

"Speaking of Marge, she thinks I'm a doormat."

"She's just worried about you," Liz said. With long brown hair, oval eyes the color of coffee, and an easygoing demeanor, she was more the *class secretary* type than *head cheerleader* type, but I'd always thought that made her even more attractive. "She knows you're under a lot of pressure and she worries about you. How's Vivian these days?"

"She's okay, but she's feeling the pressure, too. I just want her to be happy with me."

"Hmmm."

"That's it?"

"What else am I supposed to say?"

"I don't know. Challenge me? Give me advice?"

"Why would I do that?"

"Because, among other things, you're trained as a counselor."

"You're not my patient. But even then, I'm not sure I could help."

"Why not?"

"Because counseling isn't about changing someone else. It's about trying to change yourself."

On our way to the car, I held London's hand.

"Don't tell Mommy I had two cupcakes, okay?"

"Why?

"Because it's not good for me and I don't want her to be sad."

"Okay," she said. "I won't. I promise."

"Thanks, sweetie."

London and I returned at six to an empty house with a batch of vanilla cupcakes.

When I texted Vivian, asking where she was, she replied *Still have a couple of things to do—will be home in a little while*. It felt annoyingly cryptic, but before I could text again, London was tugging on my sleeve and leading me toward the pink three-story Barbie Dreamhouse she'd stationed in the corner of the living room.

London *adored* Barbie, was *over the moon* for Barbie. She had seven of them, two pink Barbie convertibles, and a plastic tub filled with more outfits than a fully stocked department store. That every doll had the same name seemed not to matter to London at all; what fascinated me even more was that every time Barbie moved from one room in the pink three-story Dreamhouse to another or changed activities, London believed that a wardrobe change was imperative. This occurred roughly every thirty-five seconds, and it went without saying was that the only thing that London enjoyed more than changing Barbie's wardrobe was having Dad do it for her.

For the next hour and a half, I spent four full days changing Barbie's outfits, one right after the other.

If that doesn't make sense, I have to admit that it didn't make much sense to me either. It probably has something to do with the theory of relativity—time being relative and all that—but London didn't seem to care whether I was bored or not as long as I kept the outfits a-changing. Nor did she seem to care whether I understood her reasoning as to the particular outfit she wanted. Somewhere around the three-day mark on that late afternoon, I remember reaching for a green pair of pants when London shook her head.

"No, Daddy! I told you that she needs to wear *yellow* pants when she's in the kitchen."

"Why?"

"Because she's in the *kitchen*."

Oh.

Eventually, I heard Vivian's SUV pull into the drive. Unlike my Prius, it got horrible gas mileage, but it was large, safe, and Vivian had insisted she'd never drive a minivan, even though it was far more economical.

"Your mom is home, sweetheart," I offered, expelling a sigh of relief as London raced for the door. As soon as she opened it, I heard her call out "Mommy!" I straightened up the play area before following her. By the time I reached the front steps, Vivian was already holding London, the rear hatch open, and I did a quick double take. Her hair, I saw, was noticeably shorter, now shoulder length and closer in style to what it had been when I'd first met her.

She smiled up at me, squinting in the waning summer sunlight. "Hey hon!" she called out. "Would you mind grabbing some of the bags?"

I descended the steps, listening as London chattered away, telling Vivian about her day. When I was close, Vivian lowered London to the ground. By her expression, I knew she was waiting for a reaction.

"Wow," I said, offering her a quick kiss. "This brings back memories."

"You like?" she asked.

"You look beautiful. But how you did you pull this off on Sunday? Where on earth would even be open?"

"There's a salon downtown that offers Sunday appointments. I've heard great things about one of the hairdressers there and I decided to give her a try."

Why she hadn't mentioned it that morning, I had no idea. She'd also, I noticed, gotten a manicure, and hadn't mentioned that either.

"I love it, too, Mommy," London said, breaking into my thoughts.

"Thanks, sweetie," she said.

"I made cupcakes at Nana's today."

"You did, huh?"

"And they're so good, Daddy had two of them."

"Really?"

My daughter nodded, obviously forgetting all about her promise to me. "And Papa had four!"

"They must be delicious." Vivian smiled. She reached into the car, pulling out a couple of the lighter bags. "Would you mind being a helper with the groceries?"

"Okay," London said, reaching for them. While London made her way toward the steps, I noted in Vivian a hint of mischievousness, her good mood evident.

"Two cupcakes, huh?"

"What can I say?" I shrugged. "They were tasty."

She began reaching for more bags, handing four to me. "It sounds like the two of you had a good time today."

"It was fun," I agreed.

"How are your parents?"

"They're all right. Mom's worried about Dad having the cancer again. She said he had trouble catching his breath the other day."

"That doesn't sound good."

"There's more to the story, but I'm pretty sure it's nothing to worry about. He seemed fine to me. Mom's right, though. He does need to get a checkup."

"Let me know when you round up the team of wild horses you'll need to drag him in there. I want to get a photo." She winked before glancing at the front door, her way of flirting. "Would you mind bringing in the rest of it?" she asked. "I want to visit with London."

"Of course," I said.

She kissed me again and I felt the flicker of her tongue against my lips. Definitely flirting. "There are some more bags in the backseat, too."

"No worries."

I began reaching for the bags of groceries as she walked away. Absently glancing toward the backseat, I expected to see more of the same.

But it wasn't groceries. Instead, the backseat was stacked with bags from various high-end department stores and I felt my stomach lurch. No wonder my wife was in such a good mood.

Trying my best to ignore the sensation in my gut, it took me three trips to unload the SUV. I set the department store bags on the dining room table and I was just about finished putting away the groceries when Vivian wandered into the kitchen. Opening the cupboard, she pulled out a couple of glasses and retrieved a bottle from the wine refrigerator below the cabinet.

"I assume you need a glass even more than I do," she said while pouring. "London told me you played Barbies with her."

"She played. I was in charge of wardrobes."

"I feel your pain. I was there yesterday." She handed me a glass and took a sip from her own. "How are Marge and Liz?"

Though the shift in tone was subtle, I nonetheless detected a lack of interest in her question. Vivian's feelings for Marge mirrored Marge's for Vivian, which was one of the reasons why Vivian tended to get along better with Liz. That being said, although Vivian and Liz were civil and polite to one another, they weren't exactly close either.

"They're fine. London really enjoys spending time with them."

"I know she does."

I nodded toward the dining room table. "I see you went shopping."

"London needed some summer dresses."

My daughter, like my wife, would leave the house dressed as though she'd strolled out of a catalog. "I thought you already bought her summer clothes."

She sighed. "Please don't."

"Don't what?"

"Fuss at me about shopping again. I'm so tired of hearing it."

"I haven't fussed at you."

"Are you kidding?" she asked, a hint of frustration surfacing. "That's all you ever do, even when I take advantage of a sale. And besides, I also had to buy a couple of new suits for my interviews this week."

For a second I wasn't sure I'd heard her right. "You have interviews this week?"

"Why do you think I've been running around like crazy all day?" She shook her head, seemingly amazed I hadn't figured it out. "And that reminds me—you'll be able to watch London, right? On Tuesday afternoon and Wednesday morning? For maybe three hours each day or so? I'm supposed to interview with a slew of different executives at the company."

"Um...yeah, I guess," I said, still trying to wrap my head around the word "interviews." "When did this happen?"

"I found out today."

"On a *Sunday*? On a *holiday weekend*?"

"Believe me, I was as surprised as you are. They weren't even in the office on Friday. I was on my way to my hair appointment when they let me know."

"Why didn't you call me?"

"Because after that, I was rushing from here to there and I could barely believe it myself. Isn't it incredible? I think we should celebrate tonight, but first how about I show you what I bought?"

Without waiting for an answer, she led the way to the dining room and pulled out both suits—one gray and one black—draping them over the chairs. "What do you think?"

"They're very stylish," I said. I tried to avoid the sight of the price tags but I couldn't help it. My stomach did another flip-flop, then flopped again. Dollar signs danced in my head.

"The fabric is fabulous and I love the cut," she said. "And I got these, as well, to go with them." Reaching for another bag, she pulled out four blouses, setting them first against one suit, then the other. "The blouses match both suits—I was trying to save as much money as I could."

I wasn't sure what to say to that. Instead: "I'm still a little confused as to how the interviews came about. Last I heard, you were just putting out feelers."

"I got lucky," she said.

"What does that mean?"

"I called Rob a couple of weeks back and told him I was thinking about getting back into the PR game and he promised he'd let me know if he heard of anything. After that, I called my old boss from New York. Remember him?"

I nodded, wondering why she even needed to ask. We saw the guy practically every night before turning off the television.

"Anyway, he said he'd see what he could do. I didn't expect much, but I guess he talked to his manager, and his manager ended up calling me back. And, it just so happens that he knew a guy who knew a guy, and I guess my name got passed along to the right people because last Monday, I was talking to one of the vice presidents about a job and she asked me to put in a résumé and three letters of recommendation."

"You've been working on this since Monday? And never mentioned it?"

"I didn't think it would amount to anything."

"It sounds to me like you had to have some idea this might be coming."

"Oh, please. Like I could have predicted any of this." She began laying the blouses over one of the chairs. "And anyway, I had to scramble for a third recommendation. I wanted someone locally prominent, but I wasn't sure he'd agree. But sure enough, he came through and I got my paperwork in by Wednesday."

"And you said the job is in PR?"

"I'd be working directly for the CEO, not so much the company. I guess he does a lot of press conferences and interviews. A lot of his developments are on the coast, and environmentalists are always up in arms. Plus, he's got a super PAC now, and he's getting more involved in politics and wants to make sure he's always on message."

"Who's the CEO?"

She paused, running her fingers along one of the suits. "Before I tell you, just keep in mind that I haven't even been offered the job yet.

60

And I don't know whether I'd take it, even if they do offer me a position. I don't have all the details yet."

"Why won't you tell me?"

"Because I don't want you to get upset."

"Why would I be upset?"

She began slipping the bags back over the suits. "Because you know him. Actually, you've worked on some of the advertising campaigns for his company."

I connected the dots almost immediately. "It's not Walter Spannerman, is it?"

She seemed almost sheepish. "Actually, it is."

I remembered how miserable he'd made me; I also remembered his penchant for hiring beautiful women, so the fact that he was interested in Vivian didn't shock me in the slightest. "You know he's awful, right? And so is his company."

"That's why he wants an in-house PR person."

"And you'd be okay working with a guy like that?"

"I don't know. I haven't met him yet. I just hope I can impress him."

With the way you look, I'm sure he'll be impressed, I thought. "How many hours a week are they thinking?"

"Well, that's the thing," she answered. "It's a full-time position. And there's probably going to be some travel, too."

"Overnight?"

"That's what travel usually means, doesn't it?"

"What about London?"

"I don't know anything yet, okay? Let's cross that bridge when we get there. *If* we get there. For now, can we just plan to celebrate? Can you do that for me?"

"Of course," I said, but even as I said the words, I thought about Spannerman and his relationship with Peters and found myself wondering who exactly Vivian had called for that final recommendation.

But she wouldn't have done something like that, would she?

CHAPTER 5

Changes

When London was four, a small bicycle with training wheels appeared under the Christmas tree. I'd been adamant about getting her a bicycle; some of my favorite childhood memories were of pedaling hard on my Schwinn, chasing my freedom on humid summer days. Granted, most of those memories occurred between the ages of eight and thirteen, but my thinking as the holidays approached was that London would learn to ride for a year or two before the training wheels finally came off, and in a few years, she would ride as well as I had.

Vivian, however, wasn't thrilled with the idea. Though she'd owned a bicycle, she didn't have the same joyful associations that I did. I remembered asking her if she'd bought the bicycle in the weeks leading up to Christmas and each time she put me off, telling me that she hadn't had time. In the end, I'd dragged her to the store and bought it myself, spending hours assembling it like one of Santa's elves after Vivian had gone to bed.

I couldn't wait for London to give it a try, and as soon as she spotted it under the tree, she ran over and I helped her climb on. As I began to push her through the living room Vivian intervened, suggesting that we open some of her other gifts. As always, my first thought was that she received too many things: clothes and toys, finger-painting kits, a mannequin (to dress up), and a beaded jewelry–making kit. Then there were countless Barbie-related items; it took me an hour to dispose of the wrapping paper and ribbons strewn throughout the room. Vivian, meanwhile, spent that time with London and her toys and clothes, and it wasn't until almost noon that I was finally able to get London outside.

Vivian had followed us, but it struck me that she seemed to view it more as a duty than a new and exciting adventure for London. She stood on the front steps with her arms crossed while I helped London onto the seat. Watching her breaths come out in little puffs, I walked hunched over beside her, holding the handlebars. I encouraged London to pedal as we rolled up and down the street, and after fifteen minutes, she told me she was done. Her cheeks were pink and I assured her she'd done a great job. I'm not sure why, but I assumed that we'd ride two or three more times before the day was done.

Instead, she spent the rest of Christmas Day playing with her Barbies or trying on her clothes while Vivian beamed; later, she finger painted and assembled a pair of beaded bracelets. I wasn't dissuaded, however; I had the week off, and I made it a point to bring her out to ride at least once a day. Over the next few days, as she grew more coordinated and less wobbly, I would release the handlebars for periods of increasing duration. London giggled when I pretended she was going so fast that I couldn't keep up. We stayed out longer each time, and when she finally announced that she was finished, I would hold her hand as we walked toward the front door. She would jabber on excitedly to Vivian, and I was certain that London had caught the same bicycle-riding bug that I had and would insist on riding every day while I was at work.

But that didn't happen. Instead, when I came home from work—by then it would be dark and London would often be in her pajamas—and asked London if she rode, she always said that she hadn't. Each time, Vivian had a reason for not bringing her out—it was raining, or they had errands to run, or London might be getting a cold, or even that London didn't want to. Still, after work when I'd park in the garage, I'd see the little bicycle that made my daughter laugh, collecting dust in the corner. And every single time, I felt a faint ache in my heart. I must not know my daughter as well as I thought I did, or perhaps London and I simply liked different things. And though I'm not proud to admit it, I sometimes found myself wondering whether Vivian didn't want London to ride her bike simply because it was something I wanted London to do.

In retrospect, I think I believed that quitting my job would be the most significant event of 2015 for my wife and me. I ended up being wrong, of course; striking out on my own was simply the first domino in a long line of dominoes that would begin to topple, with even larger dominoes to come later.

The following week was domino number two.

Because Vivian wanted to prep for her interviews on Monday, I came home from the office at noon. I cleaned the house and did the laundry while trying to keep London entertained, which wasn't as easy as it sounded. On Tuesday afternoon, while Vivian interviewed, I brought London to a late lunch at Chuck E. Cheese, a place Vivian would never set foot in. After eating, she played some of the games in the arcade, hoping to win enough tickets to trade them for a pink teddy bear. We didn't come close, and by my calculations, I could have simply purchased three of them for what I'd spent in game tokens.

On Wednesday, I opted for our usual Saturday morning routine of breakfast and the park, but it was impossible for me to ignore my growing anxiety concerning work. I kept imagining that potential clients were trying to reach me, or worse, standing outside an office that was obviously closed, but whenever I called the receptionist, I was informed there were no messages.

With my initial list of potential clients amounting to nothing, I started cold-calling businesses. Starting Wednesday afternoon and all day Thursday, I made more than a couple of hundred calls. I consistently heard the words *not interested*, but kept at it and eventually managed to line up five meetings the following week. The businesses weren't the kind of clients that the Peters Group normally targeted— a family-owned restaurant, a sandwich shop, two chiropractors, and a day spa—and the fees would likely be low, but it was better than nothing.

At home, Vivian said little about her various interviews. She didn't want to jinx them, she explained, but she seemed confident, and when I told her about my meetings the following week, her mind was clearly elsewhere. Looking back, I should have taken it as a sign.

On Friday morning, I'd just walked in the kitchen when I heard Vivian's cell phone begin to ring. London was already at the table, eating a bowl of cereal. Vivian checked the incoming number and wandered to the back patio before answering. Thinking it was her mother—her mother was the only person I knew who would call that early—I poured myself a cup of coffee.

"Hi, sweetie," I said to London.

"Hi, Daddy. Is zero a number?"

"Yes," I answered. "Why?"

"Well, you know I'm five, right? And before that, I was four?"

"Yes."

"What was I before I was one?"

"Before you were one, we would talk about your age in months. Like, you're three months old, or six months old. And before you were a month old, your age was measured in weeks. Or even days."

"And then I was zero right?"

"I guess you were. Why all the questions?"

"Because I'll be six in October. But really, I'll be seven."

"You'll be six, honey."

She held up her hands and began counting, holding up a finger or thumb with every number she pronounced. "Zero. One. Two. Three. Four. Five. Six."

By then, she was holding up five fingers on one hand and two on the other. Seven in total.

"That's not how it works," I said.

"But you said I was zero, and that zero was a number. There's seven numbers. That means, I'll be seven, not six."

It was too much to process before I'd finished my first cup of coffee. "When did you think of this?"

Instead of answering, she shrugged and I thought again how much she resembled her mother. At that moment, Vivian stepped back into the kitchen, her face slightly flushed.

"You okay?" I asked.

At first, I wasn't sure she'd heard me. "Yeah," she finally offered. "I'm fine."

"Everything okay with your mom?"

"I guess so. I haven't talked to her in about a week. Why would you ask about Mom?"

"Wasn't that who you were talking to?"

"No," she said.

"Who was on the phone?" I finally asked.

"Rachel Johnson."

"Who?"

"She's one of the vice presidents at Spannerman. I interviewed with her on Wednesday."

She added nothing else. I waited. Still nothing.

"And she was calling because?" I persisted.

"They're offering me the job," she said. "They want me to start Monday. Orientation."

I wasn't sure whether congratulations were in order, but I said it anyway and even in that moment, I still had no inkling whatsoever that my entire world was about to be turned upside down.

Work that day didn't feel...*normal*, and that was saying something, since nothing about work had seemed normal since I'd gone out on my own. I began to put together PowerPoint presentations for the meetings I'd scheduled. They would offer a general overview of various ad campaigns I'd worked on, discussed the dollar value of advertising for the client's specific business, and preview the kind of work I could do for them. If the potential clients showed interest, I'd follow that up with a more specific proposal at a second meeting.

Even though I made significant headway, my thoughts would occasionally wander back to what I learned that morning.

My wife would be going to work on Monday, for Spannerman.

Good God.

Spannerman.

Still, it was date night and I was looking forward to spending the evening with Vivian. When I walked in the door, however, I felt as though I'd stepped into the wrong house. The living room, dining room, and kitchen were a mess, and London was parked in front of the television, something I'd never seen at that time of night. Vivian was nowhere to be seen, nor did she answer when I called for her. I walked from one room to the next, finally locating her in the den. She was seated in front of the computer researching all things Spannerman, and for the first time in our married life, she seemed almost frazzled. She was wearing jeans and a T-shirt and her hair looked as though she'd been twisting strands of it for most of the day. Beside her was a thick binder—she had printed and highlighted a thick sheaf of pages—and when she turned toward me, I could see that romance was not only off the table, but hadn't even crossed her mind all day.

I hid my disappointment and after some small talk, I suggested we order Chinese food. We ate as a family, but Vivian remained distracted, and as soon as she finished eating, she went back to the den. While she clicked and printed, I cleaned the house and helped London get ready for bed. I filled the bathtub—London had reached the age where she could wash herself—brushed her hair and lay beside her in bed reading an assortment of books. In another first, Vivian simply kissed our daughter goodnight without reading a story, and when I found her back in the den, she told me that she still had another few hours to go. I watched television for a while and went to bed alone; when I woke the following morning, I found myself staring at Vivian and wondering how late she'd finally turned in.

She was back to her normal self soon after waking, but then again, it was Saturday morning. She was out the door right on schedule for her *Me Time*, and for the fifth time in seven days, I found myself playing Mr. Mom, if only part-time. On her way out the door, Vivian asked if I could take care of London for the day; she told me that she hadn't quite finished the research from the night before and also had some things she needed to grab for work.

"No problem," I said, and as a result, London and I found ourselves back at my parents' place. Marge and Liz had gone to Asheville for the weekend, so London had my mom all to herself most of the day. Nonetheless, my mom found time to sidle up to me and mentioned that since I'd failed in my task of getting my dad to the doctor, Marge would be bringing him on Monday.

"It's good to know that one of our kids really cares about their father," my mom remarked.

Thanks, Mom.

My father, as usual, was in the garage. When I walked in, he poked his head around the hood of the car.

"You're here," he said to me.

"I thought I'd swing by with London."

"No Vivian again?"

"She has some things to do for work. She got a job and starts on Monday."

"Oh," he said.

"That's it?"

He took a handkerchief from his back pocket and wiped his hands. "It's probably a good thing," he finally said. "Someone in your family should be earning some money."

Thanks, Dad.

After visiting with him for a bit—and with London happily baking with Nana—I sat on the couch in the living room, absently watching golf. I'm not a golfer and I don't generally watch golf, but I found myself staring at logos on golf bags and shirts while trying to calculate how much money had gone to the advertising agencies who'd come up with that idea.

The whole thing depressed me.

Meanwhile, I texted Vivian twice and left a voicemail without getting a response; the house phone also went unanswered. Figuring she was out and about, I stopped at the grocery store on the way back from my parents', something fairly rare for me. I usually only went to the store when we were out of something or when I was in the mood for something specific for dinner; I was the kind of shopper who used a handheld basket as opposed to a cart, like I was in a race to see how fast I could get out of there. For London, I grabbed a box of macaroni and cheese, slices of turkey breast and pears, which was only somewhat healthy, but also happened to be her favorite. For Vivian and me, I selected a New York strip and sashimi-grade tuna fillet that I could put on the grill, along with the makings for a salad, corn on the cob, and a bottle of Chardonnay.

While I hoped to make up for our lost date night, I also simply wanted to spend time with Vivian. I wanted to listen to her and hold her and discuss our future. I knew there were going to be changes in our lives, even challenges, and I wanted to promise that we'd get through them together as a couple. If Vivian felt more fulfilled and accomplished at work, she just might bring that better mood home with her; if we shared parenting more equally, we might begin to see each other in ways more conducive to a closer relationship. In the evenings, we'd visit about our days, revel in our successes and support each other in our struggles, and the extra money would make things easier as well. In other words, things would only get better for Vivian and me, and tonight was the first step in the process.

Why, then, did I feel so unsettled?

Maybe it was because Vivian never called or texted me back, nor was she home when London and I returned.

What had been odd gradually grew concerning, but I didn't text or call, because I knew that I wouldn't be able to hide my annoyance, which would no doubt put an end to the evening before it started. Instead, I marinated the steak and placed it in the fridge before starting to dice the cucumbers and tomatoes for the salad. London, meanwhile, pulled the husks from the corncobs. Thrilled to help make dinner for *Date Night*, she diligently picked away at the silken threads then would hold the corn up for me to examine before setting it aside and starting on the next. I prepared the macaroni and cheese, peeled and sliced a pear, added turkey to her plate and sat with London while she ate. With still no word from Vivian, I put on a movie for London and sat with her until I finally heard the SUV pull into the drive.

London was already out the front door as soon as my wife stepped out of the SUV and I watched Vivian scoop her up and give her a kiss. She kissed me as well and asked if I could bring the bags inside. Figuring it was groceries, I opened the back hatch after Vivian and London had vanished inside and saw a *mountain* of bags from Neiman Marcus and half a dozen shoe boxes with Italian names.

No wonder she hadn't called or answered. Vivian had been *busy*.

Like the week before, it took multiple trips to unload all the items she'd purchased and by the time I finished, Vivian was sitting beside London on the couch, London leaning into her.

Vivian smiled at me before mouthing that she wanted a few more minutes with London. I nodded, reminding myself again not to show the slightest hint of irritation. In the kitchen, I poured two glasses of wine and brought one of them to Vivian before returning to the back porch where I fired up the grill. Knowing it would take a few minutes to heat up, I went back inside and sipped at the wine while taking stock of the dining room table where I'd heaped her things. In time, Vivian kissed London on her head then slid away. She beckoned me to meet her near the goodies. She leaned in for a quick kiss as I approached.

"London said she had a fun day with you."

"I'm glad," I said. "I'm guessing you had a pretty full day, too."

"I did. After I finished with my research, I raced from one store to the next. By the end, all I really wanted to do was come home and relax."

"Are you hungry? I picked you up some fresh tuna and I've already got the grill going."

"Really? Tonight?"

"Why not?"

"Because I've already eaten." Vivian must have seen my expression and her tone acquired an edge of defensiveness. "I didn't know you were planning to make dinner tonight. All I knew was that I hadn't eaten breakfast or lunch, and I was so hungry that my hands began to shake. I ended up stopping at a café on the way out of the mall. You should have let me know and I would have just grabbed a snack."

"I called and texted, but you never responded."

"My phone was in my purse and I didn't hear it. I didn't see your texts or that you'd called until I was almost home."

"You could have called me."

"I just told you that I was rushing around all day."

"To the point you couldn't even check your phone?"

"Don't make it sound like I was trying to ruin your night on purpose," she said with a sigh. "You can still grill the steak. I'm sure London is hungry."

"She already ate," I said, thinking that what I really wanted was for my wife to have missed talking to me as much as I'd missed talking to her.

"Oh," she said. "Do you want to see what I bought?"

"Yeah, okay," I said.

"Would you mind getting me another half a glass of wine first? I want to organize my things before I show you."

I nodded, wandering back to the kitchen in a daze, still trying to sort through what had just happened. She had to assume we'd have dinner, so why had she stopped to eat? And why hadn't she checked her phone? How was it that my wife could feel no need to check in on her family? I refilled her glass, returning to the dining room wanting to ask more questions, but by then, Vivian had various outfits either spread on the table or draped over the back of the chairs.

"Thanks, hon," she said, reaching for the glass. She kissed me again and set her glass aside without taking a sip. "I bought a navy blue suit, too. It's gorgeous, but it was a little big in the hips, so I'm having it altered," she began, then proceeded to present one outfit after another. As she did, I caught sight of one of the receipts from the bags and felt my heart skip a beat. The total, on that one receipt, was more than half the mortgage.

"Are you okay?" she asked when she was finished. "You seem like you're upset."

"I'm just wondering why you didn't call me."

"I already told you. I was busy."

"I know, but..."

"But what?" she asked, her eyes flashing. "It's not like you called and texted every minute when you were at work either."

"You were shopping."

"For *work*," she said, the anger in her voice now plain. "Do you think I wanted to stay up half the night and then race around all afternoon? But you didn't give me much of a choice, did you? I have to *work* because *you* quit *your* job. And don't pretend I didn't see you inspecting those receipts, so before you get on *that* high horse again, maybe you should remind yourself that your little adventure has cost a lot more than I spent today, so maybe you should look in the mirror."

"Vivian..."

"You need to stop acting like I'm the bad guy. You're not exactly perfect."

"I never said I was."

"Then stop finding fault with everything I do."

"I'm not..."

By then, however, she'd already left the dining room.

71

For the next half hour, we avoided each other. Or rather, she avoided me. She'd always been better at it than I was. I know because I kept peeking at her, hoping to detect a thaw in her mood, and found myself wondering why we couldn't seem to discuss anything that bothered me without it turning into an argument.

I grilled the tuna and the steak, hoping she'd at least taste the food, and set the table on the back porch. After bringing the food over, I called for Vivian, only to see her emerge with London in tow.

I put small portions on both their plates and though both Vivian and London took a few bites, my wife's silent treatment continued. If there was one positive from the meal, it was that London didn't seem to notice, since she and her mom chatted as though I wasn't there at all.

By the time we finished dinner, I was as annoyed with Vivian as she was with me. I went to the den and fired up my computer, thinking I'd continue working on my presentations, but it turned out to be a pointless exercise, since I continued to replay all that had happened.

I couldn't escape a gnawing sense of failure. Somehow, I'd blown it again, even though I wasn't sure exactly what it was I'd done so wrong. By then, Vivian had already begun the process of getting London ready for bed and I heard her as she descended the steps.

"She's ready for a story," she said. "Not a long one, though. She's already yawning."

"All right," I said, and in her expression, I thought I saw the same kind of remorse that I was feeling about the evening. "Hey," I said, reaching for her hand. "I'm sorry about the way tonight turned out."

She shrugged. "It's been a stressful week for both of us."

I read to London and kissed her goodnight; when I found Vivian in the family room, she was already in her pajamas, a magazine open in her lap, and the television turned to some reality show.

"Hey," she said, as soon as I sat beside her, seemingly more interested in the magazine than me. "I had to change out of my clothes into something comfy. I'm wiped out. I'm not sure how much longer I'm going to last before turning in."

I understood what she hadn't specifically verbalized: The idea that the two of us might make love later was out of the question.

"I'm tired, too."

"I can't believe she'll be starting school next month. It doesn't seem possible."

"I still don't know why they start so early," I said, picking up the thread of the conversation. "Didn't we always start school after Labor Day when we were in school? I mean, why August twenty-fifth?"

"I have no idea. Something about the mandatory number of school days, I think."

I reached for the remote control. "Would you mind if I found something else to watch?"

Her eyes suddenly flashed toward the TV. "I was watching that. I just wanted something brainless to help me unwind."

I put the remote control down. For a while, neither of us said anything. Finally: "What do you want to do tomorrow?"

"I'm not sure yet. I know I have to pick up the suit that's getting tailored, but that's about it. Why? What are you thinking?"

"Whatever you'd like to do. You've been so busy this week, we haven't been able to spend much time together."

"I know. It's been absolutely crazy."

Though I might have been imagining it, she didn't sound as bothered by the recent schedule as I was. "And about dinner tonight..."

She shook her head. "Let's not talk about it, Russ. I just want to relax."

"I was trying to tell you that I was getting concerned when I didn't hear from you..."

She lowered the magazine.

"Really?"

"What?"

"You want to do this right now? I told you that I'm tired. I told you I didn't want to talk about it."

"Why are you getting upset again?"

"Because I know what you're trying to do."

"What am I trying to do?"

"You're trying to get me to apologize, but I didn't do anything wrong. Do you want me to say that I'm sorry for getting a good job? Or to apologize for trying to dress like a professional? Or for getting a bite to eat because I was shaking? Did you ever stop to think that maybe you should apologize for trying to pick a fight in the first place?"

"I wasn't trying to pick a fight."

"That's exactly what you were trying to do," she said, staring at me like I was crazy. "You got upset as soon I told you that I'd already eaten, and you wanted to make sure I knew it. So I tried to be sweet. I invited you to the dining room to show you what I got. I kissed you. And right after that, you started in on me, just like you always do."

I knew there was some truth in what she said. "Okay, you're right," I said, trying to keep my voice steady. "I'll admit that I was disappointed that you'd eaten before you got home—"

"Ya think?" she said, cutting me off. "And that's the thing with you. Believe it or not, you're not the only one with feelings around here. Did you ever stop to think about the pressure I've been under lately? So what do you do? Make things hard as soon as I walk in the door and even now, you can't let it go." She stood from the couch and kept talking as she started to leave the room. "I just wanted to watch my show and read my magazine and sit with you without fighting. That's it. Was that too much to ask?"

"Where are you going?"

"I'm going to lie in bed for a while, because I want to relax. You're welcome to join me, but if you'd rather start arguing again, then please don't bother."

Then she was gone. I turned off the television, sitting in silence for the next hour, trying to figure out what had happened to my wife and me.

Or, more specifically, how I could make things better between us.

I woke up late on Sunday to an empty bed.

I tossed on a pair of jeans before trying to tame the oddly shaped waves of hair that greeted me in the mirror every morning. It was a disappointing predicament, made worse by the fact that Vivian usually woke looking already groomed.

Since Vivian had been asleep by the time I crawled into bed, I wasn't sure what to expect but as I approached the kitchen, I could hear my wife and daughter laughing.

"Good morning," I said.

"Daddy!" London called out.

Vivian turned and winked, smiling at me as though the night before had never happened at all. "Perfect timing," she offered. "I just finished making breakfast."

"It smells fantastic."

"Come here, handsome," she said.

I approached, assuming she was trying to gauge my mood, and when I was close, she kissed me. "I'm sorry about last night. You okay?"

"Yeah, I'm okay. And I'm sorry, too."

"How about I make you a plate of food? I made the bacon extra crispy for you."

"That would be great."

"Coffee's ready, too. The creamer should be right there."

"Thanks," I said. I poured a cup and brought it to the dining room table, taking a seat next to London. I kissed the top of her head as she reached for her milk.

"How're you doing, sweetie? Did you have any good dreams?"

"I can't remember," she said. She took a gulp of milk, which left the trace of a milk mustache.

Vivian brought two plates to the table, with scrambled eggs, bacon, and toast, placing them in front of us. "Do you want some juice? There's some fresh-squeezed orange juice."

"Sounds great. Thanks."

Vivian brought those over as well, along with her own plate. Unlike ours, her plate had a small portion of scrambled egg whites and fruit.

I took a bite of bacon. "What time did you get up?"

"An hour ago, maybe? You must have been exhausted. I don't think you even heard me get out of bed."

"I guess I must have been," I said.

"I will say that if you hadn't gotten up, I was about to send London back there to jump on you."

I turned toward London, my mouth agape. "You wouldn't have done that, would you? If I was still sleeping?"

75

"Of course I would have," London said, giggling. "Guess what? Mommy is taking me to the mall to pick up her clothes, and then we're going to the pet store."

"What's at the pet store?"

"Mommy said I could get a hamster. I'm going to name her Mrs. Sprinkles."

"I didn't know you wanted a hamster."

"I've wanted a hamster for a long time, Daddy."

"How come you never told me, sweetie?"

"Because mom said you wouldn't want one."

"Well, I don't know," I said. "It's a lot of work taking care of hamsters."

"I know," she said. "But they're so cute."

"They are cute," I admitted, and for the remainder of breakfast, I listened while London tried to convince me she was old enough to take care of a hamster.

I was sipping my second cup of coffee in the kitchen while Vivian began loading the dishwasher; in the living room, London was playing with her Barbies.

"She's old enough to have a hamster, you know," Vivian commented. "Even if you'll have to clean the cage."

"Me?"

"Of course," she said. "You're the dad."

"And in your mind, helping my daughter clean a hamster cage is part of the job description, right?"

"Think of it as a good way to bond with her."

"Cleaning hamster poop?"

"Oh, hush," she said, nudging me. "It'll be good for her. She'll learn responsibility. And besides, it's a lot easier than getting her a puppy. She's also in love with the neighbor's Yorkie, you know, so consider yourself lucky. Did you see the newsletter from the country club?"

"Can't say that I did."

"They've got some good programs for kids, including tennis. It's three days a week at nine in the morning for four weeks, so it wouldn't interfere with any of her other activities. Monday, Tuesday, and Thursday."

From where I was standing, I could see my daughter and noted again how much she resembled her mother. "I don't know if she'd like it," I answered. "And about London. I've been meaning to ask—what are you thinking when it comes to her?"

"What do you mean?"

"Day care," I said. "You're starting work tomorrow. Who's going to watch her?"

"I know, I know." A tinge of stress colored her response as she rinsed and loaded another plate into the dishwasher. "I meant to research some day cares last week, but I just didn't have the time. It's been all I can do to keep my head above water and I still feel like I'm not prepared for tomorrow. The last thing I want is for Walter to think I'm an idiot while we're at lunch."

"Lunch with Walter?"

"My new boss? Walter Spannerman?"

"I know who he is. I just didn't know you'd be having lunch with him tomorrow."

"I didn't either until this morning. I woke up to an email with my orientation schedule. They have me on the run all day tomorrow—human resources, the legal department, lunch, meetings with various vice presidents. I have to be there at seven thirty in the morning."

"Early," I said. I waited, wondering if she'd return to the subject of who would be watching London. She rinsed some utensils and loaded them in the dishwasher, remaining quiet. I cleared my throat. "And you said you haven't been able to find a day care center for London?"

"Not yet. I called some friends and they said the day cares they use are good, but I still want to see for myself, you know? Do a walk-through, meet the staff, discuss the kinds of programs they can offer. I want to make sure it's the right place for her."

"If you have the names, I can call and make an appointment for us."

"Well, that's the thing. I have no idea what kind of hours to expect this week."

"I'm sure I'd be able to set up an evening appointment."

"It's probably better if I do it, don't you think? I'd hate to have to cancel."

"So...what's the plan for tomorrow then? For London?"

"I wouldn't be comfortable with just dropping her off in some strange place. Would you? I want what's best for her."

"I'm sure that if you pick one of the places that your friends use, she'd be fine."

"She's already nervous enough about me going back to work and she was pretty upset this morning. That's why we had a family breakfast, and I suggested getting a hamster. I don't want her to feel like we're abandoning her this week."

"What exactly are you saying?"

Vivian closed the dishwasher door. "I was hoping that you would watch her this week. That way, London will have time to adjust."

"I can't. I have client meetings every day this week."

"I know I'm asking a lot and I hate to do this to you. But I don't know what else to do. I was thinking that you could either bring her to your office or maybe even work from home. When you have your meetings, you can drop her at your mom's. It would only be a week or two."

A week? Or *two*?

The words continued to reverberate in my mind, even as I answered. "I don't know. I'd have to call my mom and ask if she's okay with that."

"Would you? I'm already nervous enough about my new job, and I don't want to have to worry about London, too. Like I told you, she was really upset this morning."

I scrutinized London; she hadn't seemed upset at breakfast, and didn't appear upset now, but then Vivian knew her better than I did. "Yeah, okay. I'll call her."

Vivian smiled before moving close and slipping her arms around my neck.

"Trying to surprise me with dinner last night was very sweet. And I was thinking that I might just be in the mood for a glass of wine after London goes to bed." She kissed my neck, her breath hot on my skin. "Do you think you might be up for something like that?"

Despite myself, I suddenly wondered whether the entire morning— her appearance, her cheerful mood, breakfast—had simply been part of a plan to get what she wanted, but when she kissed my neck a second time, I forgave her.

Vivian and London were out until midafternoon. While they were gone, I finished the presentation for the chiropractor, the first of the meetings. In the meantime, I'd also tidied up the house and then called my mom. I told her about my client meetings the following week, and asked her if I could drop London off on Monday.

"Of course you can," she said.

I was hanging up the phone just as Vivian and London pulled in the drive, and I could hear London calling for me even before I made it out the door.

"Daddy, Daddy! Come here, quick!"

I trotted down the steps, watching as she held up a small clear plastic cage. From a distance, my first thought was that I was seeing double because there appeared to be two hamsters, one black and white, and the second, brown. London was grinning from ear to ear as I approached.

"I got two of them, Daddy! Mrs. Sprinkles *and* Mr. Sprinkles."

"Two?"

"She couldn't pick," Vivian said, "so I figured, why not? We had to get the cage anyway."

"And I got to hold Mr. Sprinkles the whole way home!" London added.

"You did, huh?"

"He's so sweet. He just sat there in my hands the whole time. I'm going to go hold Mrs. Sprinkles next."

"That's great," I said. "I like their cage."

"Oh, this is just their carrying cage. Their real cage is in the back. Mommy said you can help me put it together. It's huge!"

"She did, huh?" I said, and I was struck with visions of past Christmas Eves, when I'd spent hours assembling various…things—painter's desk, Barbie's Dreamhouse, the bicycle. Suffice it to say, I found it much more difficult than my father probably would have. Vivian must have known exactly what I was thinking because I felt her slip her arm around me.

79

"Don't worry," she said. "It won't be that hard. And I'll be your cheerleader."

Later that night, after we'd made love, I was lying on my side, tracing the small of Vivian's back with my finger. Her eyes were closed, her body relaxed, beautiful.

"You still haven't told me much about what your job actually entails."

"There's not much to tell. It's the same kind of work that I used to do." She sounded sleepy, the words coming out almost in a mumble.

"Do you know how much you might be traveling?"

"Not yet," she answered. "I guess I'll find out."

"That might get tricky with London."

"London will be okay. You'll be here."

For whatever reason, I'd expected her to say more: how much she'd miss London, or that she was hoping to find a way to travel less. Instead, she drew long steady breaths.

"Do you know your salary yet?"

"Why?"

"I'm trying to figure out our budget."

"No," she said. "I don't know yet."

"How can you not know?"

"There's the base salary, bonuses, and different kinds of incentives. Profit sharing. I sort of tuned out when they started to explain it to me."

"Do you even have a ballpark estimate?"

She flopped a hand onto my arm. "Do we really have to do this now? You know I hate talking about money."

"No, of course not."

"I love you."

"I love you, too."

"Thanks for watching London this week."

Or two weeks, I immediately thought, but I kept the words to myself. "You're welcome."

I couldn't fall asleep, and after staring at the ceiling for an hour, I slipped from the bed and padded toward the kitchen. I poured a small glass of milk and finished it in a single swallow, thinking that since I was up, I might as well check in on London. I entered her room and could hear the hamster wheel squeaking and whirring, a hamster party in the middle of the night.

Thankfully, London seemed not to notice. She was sound asleep, her breaths deep and steady. I kissed her on the cheek before pulling up the covers. She shifted slightly and as I stared down at her, I felt a tug at my heart, a mixture of pride and love and concern and fear, a mixture that mystified me in its intensity.

Afterward, I sat outside on the porch. The night was warm and the sound of chirping crickets filled the air; I vaguely remembered something from my childhood when my dad had told me that the frequency of chirps roughly correlated with the temperature, and I wondered whether it was true, or just something that fathers say to their sons on late summer evenings.

Pondering that question seemed to free other thoughts, and I suddenly understood why sleep seemed so elusive.

It had to do with Vivian and the fact that she hadn't told me her salary. I didn't believe her when she said she'd tuned out when it was being explained to her, and that bothered me as well.

In all the years we'd been married, I'd always shared with Vivian exactly what I'd earned. To me, sharing such information was a prerequisite of marriage; the last thing any couple should harbor was financial secrecy. Secrecy could be corrosive, and ultimately stemmed from a desire to control. Or maybe, I was being too hard on her. Maybe it was simply she hadn't wanted to hurt my feelings because she'd be earning an income while my own business was floundering.

I couldn't figure it out. Meanwhile, I'd been handed the responsibility for our daughter, and all at once, the real reason for my insomnia seemed all too obvious.

Our roles in the marriage had suddenly been reversed.

CHAPTER 6

Mr. Mom

When I was young, my parents would load the camper and bring Marge and me to the Outer Banks every summer. Early on, we stayed near Rodanthe; later we stayed farther north, near the area where the Wright brothers made aviation history. But as we grew older, Ocracoke became our spot.

Ocracoke isn't much more than a village, but compared to Rodanthe, it was a metropolis, with shops that served ice cream and pizza by the slice. Marge and I spent hours roaming the beaches and the shops, collecting seashells and lounging in the sun. In the evenings, my mom would make dinner, usually burgers or hot dogs. Afterward, we'd capture fireflies in mason jars before finally falling asleep in a tent while our parents slept in the camper, stars filling the nighttime sky.

Good times. Some of the best in my life. Of course, my dad recalls them differently.

"I hated those family trips," he confessed to me when I was in college. "You and Marge would fight like cats and dogs on the whole drive down. You'd get sunburned on the first day and you'd whine like a baby the rest of the week. Marge would spend most of the week sulking because she wasn't with her friends, and if that wasn't bad enough, as soon as your skin began to peel, you'd throw the remains at Marge to make her scream. You two were a total pain in the ass."

"Then why did you bring us every year?"

"Because your mother made me. I would have rather gone on vacation."

"We were on vacation."

"No," he said, "we were on a family trip, not a vacation."

"What's the difference?"

"You'll figure it out."

For the first three years of London's life, trips out of town required D-Day–like preparations, diapers and bottles and strollers; snacks and baby shampoo, entire bags packed with toys to amuse her. While out of town, we visited places that we thought she would enjoy—the aquarium, McDonald's playgrounds, the beach—running ourselves ragged, with little time to ourselves and even less time to relax.

Two weeks before London's fourth birthday, however, Peters sent me to Miami for a conference, and I decided to use a few vacation days after it ended. I made arrangements for my parents to take care London for four days, and while Vivian had initially been hesitant to leave our daughter, it didn't take long for both of us to understand how much we'd simply missed being . . . free. We read magazines and books by the pool, sipped piña coladas, and took naps in the afternoon. We got dressed up for dinner, lingered over glasses of wine, and made love every single day, sometimes more than once. One night we went to a nightclub and danced until well after midnight, sleeping in the next day. By the time we returned to Charlotte, I finally understood what my dad had meant.

Kids, he meant, changed everything.

It would have been more appropriate, I suppose, if it had been Friday the thirteenth, instead of Monday the thirteenth since everything about Vivian's first day of work seemed *off* somehow.

For starters, Vivian hopped in the shower first, which threw off a morning schedule that had been years in the making. Unsure what to do, I made the bed and went to the kitchen to start a pot of coffee. While it brewed, I decided to make Vivian a breakfast including egg whites, along with berries and slices of cantaloupe. I made the same for myself, thinking it wouldn't hurt to drop a few pounds. My pants, I'd noticed, were beginning to nip at my waist.

While I was cooking, London joined me in the kitchen and I poured her a bowl of cereal. Her hair was puffed up and messy, and even I could see that she was tired.

"Did you sleep okay?" I asked.

"Mr. and Mrs. Sprinkles kept waking me up. They kept getting on the wheel and it squeaks."

"That's not good. I'll see if I can make it stop squeaking, okay?"

She nodded as I poured my first cup of coffee. It wasn't until I was on my third cup that Vivian finally made it to the kitchen. I did a double take.

"Whoa." I smiled.

"You like?"

"You look fantastic," I said, meaning it. "I made you breakfast."

"I don't know how much I can eat. I'm so nervous, I'm not hungry."

I reheated the egg whites in the microwave while Vivian sat with London, listening as London told her about the noisy wheel.

"I told her I'd see if I can make it quieter," I said, bringing the plates to the table.

Vivian began to nibble at her food while I sat. "You'll need to use the detangling spray on London's hair this morning before you brush it. It's next to the sink, in the green bottle."

"No problem," I said, vaguely remembering that I'd seen Vivian do it before. I scooped a forkful of eggs.

She turned her attention to London. "And your dad is going to sign you up for tennis camp today. You're going to love it."

I hesitated, my fork hovering just above the plate. "Wait..." I said. "What?"

"Tennis camp? We talked about this yesterday. Don't you remember?"

"I remember that you mentioned it. I don't remember any decision though."

"The sign-up for camp is today, and they're pretty sure it's going to fill up fast, so you should try to be there around eight thirty. They'll start taking names at nine. Her art class is at eleven."

"I need to go over my presentation."

"It's not going to take long to sign her up, and you can go over it while she's doing art. There's a coffee shop a couple of doors down in the same complex. She'll be fine if you don't stay—I usually just drop her off and leave for the gym. What time's your meeting?"

"Two."

"See? That's perfect. Her class ends at twelve thirty, so you can drop her at your mom's afterward. You know where the studio is, right? In that strip center just down from the mall with the TGI Fridays?"

I knew the strip mall she was talking about, but my mind was more focused on my rapidly expanding to-do list.

"Can't we just call the club and sign her up?"

"No," Vivian said. "They need a copy of the insurance card, and there's a waiver that has to be signed."

My mind continued to whirl. "Does she have to go to her art class today?"

Vivian turned toward London. "Do you want to go to art class today, sweetheart?"

London nodded. "My friend Bodhi is there," she said, pronouncing it *Bodie*. "He spells it B-O-D-H-I and he's really nice. I told him that I'd bring Mr. and Mrs. Sprinkles in today so he could see them."

"Oh, that reminds me. You'll need to grab more shavings, too, from the pet store," Vivian added. "And don't forget about dance class later this afternoon. It's at five, and the studio is in the same shopping center as Harris Teeter." Vivian stood from the table and kissed London before giving her a squeeze. "Mommy will be home after work, okay? Make sure you put your dirty clothes in the hamper."

"Okay, Mommy. Love you."

"Love you, too."

I walked Vivian to the door and opened it for her before offering a quick kiss.

"You'll knock 'em dead," I said.

"I hope so." She touched her hair carefully. Reaching into her purse, she handed me a folded piece of paper. "I wrote London's schedule down to make it easier for you."

I scanned the list. Art classes on Mondays and Fridays at eleven, piano lessons Tuesdays and Thursdays at nine thirty. Dance class on Monday, Wednesday, and Friday at five. And starting next week, tennis camp, on Mondays, Tuesdays, and Thursdays at eight.

"Wow," I volunteered. "That's quite the schedule. Don't you think it's too much?"

"She'll be fine," Vivian said.

For whatever reason, I expected a longer goodbye, maybe a bit more chitchat about her being nervous or whatever, but instead she turned and walked briskly toward her car.

She never glanced back.

Don't ask me how, but somehow, I pulled it all off. Shower, shave, and throw on my work duds; check. Detangler spray before brushing London's hair and get her dressed for the day; check. Clean the kitchen, and start the dishwasher; check. Sign London up for tennis camp and bring her to art class along with Mr. and Mrs. Sprinkles; check and check. Go over the presentation, drop London off at my mom's, and make it to the meeting with the chiropractor with a couple of minutes to spare; check, check, and check.

The chiropractor's office was a rinky-dink storefront in a run-down industrial area, not the kind of place anyone might feel comfortable seeing a health practitioner. A single once-over revealed that my potential client was in desperate need of my services.

Unfortunately, the client felt otherwise. He was interested in neither the PowerPoint presentation I'd prepared nor anything I had to say, especially when compared to the interest he showed in the sandwich he was eating. He was irked that it didn't have any mustard. I know this because he told me three times, and when I asked if he had any questions at the end of my presentation, he asked me if I had any packets of mustard in my car that I could spare.

I wasn't in the best of moods when I picked up London from my mom's, and after swinging by the pet store, we headed home. I hopped back onto the computer and worked until it was time for dance, but finding London's outfits took some time since neither of us had any idea where Vivian put them. We were a few minutes late leaving the house and London grew fretful as the clock continued to tick.

"Ms. Hamshaw gets really, really mad if you break her rules."

"Don't worry. I'll just tell her it's my fault."

"It won't matter."

It turns out London was right. Just inside the entrance was a seating area occupied by five unspeaking women; directly ahead was the dance floor, the two areas separated by a low wall with a swinging door. To the right were cases filled with trophies; the walls were decorated with banners proclaiming various students and teams as winners of national competitions.

"Go on in," I urged.

"I can't walk onto the floor until I'm told I can proceed."

"What does that mean?"

"Stop talking, Daddy. Parents are supposed to be quiet when Ms. Hamshaw is talking. I'll get in even more trouble."

Ms. Hamshaw—a stern woman with iron-colored hair pulled into a tight bun—barked directions at a class comprised of five- and six-years-olds. In time, she strode toward us.

"I'm sorry about being late," I began. "London's mom started work today and I couldn't find her dance outfit."

"I see," Hamshaw interrupted, staring up at me. She said nothing else, simply telegraphed her disapproval before finally putting a hand on London's back. "You may proceed onto the floor."

London shuffled through the door and into the studio, her eyes downcast.

Hamshaw watched her *proceed* before turning her attention on me again. "Please don't let it happen again. Late arrivals disrupt the class, and it's already hard enough to keep my students focused."

Stepping outside, I called my receptionist only to learn there were no messages, then spent the rest of the hour watching London and the other girls as they did their best to please Ms. Hamshaw, who seemed pretty much unpleasable. More than once, I saw London gnawing on her fingernails.

When class was over, London trailed a few steps behind as we made our way to the car, her shoulders curled inward. She said nothing at all until we pulled out of the parking lot.

"Daddy?"

"Yes, sweetheart?"

"Can I have Lucky Charms when we get home?"

"That's not dinner. That's breakfast. And you know your mom doesn't like you having sugary cereals."

"Bodhi's mom lets him have Lucky Charms as a snack sometimes. And I'm hungry. Please, Daddy?"

Please, Daddy spoken in that most plaintive of voices. As a father, how could I say no?

I hit the grocery store and grabbed the box of cereal, arriving home three minutes later than I otherwise would have.

I poured her a bowl, shot Vivian a text asking when she'd be home, and squeezed in some more work, feeling as though I'd been whip-sawed since the moment I crawled out of bed. I must have lost track of time; when Vivian finally pulled in the drive, I noticed it was coming up on eight o'clock.

Eight?

London beat me to the door and I watched as Vivian scooped her up and kissed her before putting her back down.

"Sorry I'm late. There was an emergency at work."

"I thought you were doing orientation."

"I did. Pretty much all day. And then at four o'clock, we found out that a journalist from the Raleigh *News & Observer* is planning an alleged 'exposé' of one of Walter's developments. All at once, we were in crisis mode. Including me."

"Why you? It's your first day?"

"That's why they hired me," she said. "And I have a lot of experience in crisis management. My boss in New York was always in trouble with the press. So anyway, we had to meet and come up with a plan and I had to touch base with Spannerman's outside publicists. It was one thing after another. I hope you saved me some dinner. I'm starved. I don't care what you made."

Oops.

She must have seen the expression on my face because her shoulders dropped slightly. "You didn't make dinner?"

"No. I got caught up with my work..."

"So London hasn't eaten?"

"Dad let me have Lucky Charms," my daughter volunteered with a smile.

"Lucky Charms?"

"It was just a snack," I said, hearing the defensiveness in my tone.

88

But by then, Vivian was barely listening. "How about we see what we can scrounge up for dinner, okay? Something healthy."

"Okay, Mommy."

"How did dance class go?"

"We were late," London answered, "and the teacher was really, really mad at Daddy." Vivian's face was tight, her displeasure as evident as Hamshaw's had been.

"Other than the emergency, how was your first day at work?" I asked her later, when we were lying in bed. I could tell she was still aggravated with me.

"It was fine. Just meetings and getting acclimatized to the place."

"And your lunch with Spannerman?"

"I think it went well," she said. She didn't add anything else.

"Do you feel like you can work for him?"

"I don't think I'll have any problems with him at all. Most of the executives have been there for years."

Only if they're females, I thought. "Let me know if he ever hits on you, okay?"

She sighed. "It's just a job, Russ."

I rose at dawn and crammed in a couple of hours of work on the computer before Vivian woke; in the kitchen, her conversation with me felt less personal than purpose driven. She handed me a grocery list and reminded me that London had a piano lesson; she also asked me to find out whether the piano teacher would be willing to work with London on Tuesday and Thursday afternoons or evenings, once school began. On her way out the door, she turned to face me.

"Could you please try to be more conscientious today when it comes to London? Get her to her activities on time and make sure she eats right? It's not like I'm asking you to do anything I haven't been doing for years."

Her comment stung, but before I could respond, she was closing the door behind her.

London came padding down the steps a few minutes later and asked if she could have Lucky Charms for breakfast.

"Of course you can," I said. Still replaying Vivian's words, there was something definitely passive-aggressive in my ready agreement. "Do you want some chocolate milk, too?"

"Yes!"

"I thought you might," I said, wondering what Vivian would think about *that*.

London ate and then played with her Barbies; I detangled her hair, made sure she was dressed for the day, and brought her to her piano lesson. I remembered to ask the teacher about changing her lesson schedule, and afterward, I raced to my parents' house.

"Oh," my mom said as soon as I stepped in the door of my boyhood home, "you're back." When she gave London a kiss, I noticed my mom wasn't wearing an apron. Instead, she was wearing a purple dress.

"Of course I'm here," I said. "But I can only stay a few minutes because I don't want to be late."

She patted London on the back. "London, sweetheart? Would you like to try one of the cookies we made yesterday? They're in the cookie jar by the toaster."

"I know where they are," London said. My daughter practically skipped to the kitchen, as if the sugary cereal hadn't been enough.

"I really appreciate you helping me out with London," I said.

"Well, see, that's the thing."

"What's the thing?"

"I have a lunch today with the Red Hat Society." She pointed to her hat, which sat on the table next door; it was the color of clown lipstick and adorned with feathers that I guessed had been plucked from peacocks.

"But I told you that I had meetings all week."

"I remember. But you only asked if I could watch London on Monday."

"I just assumed you knew that's what I meant. And London loves spending time with you."

She put a hand on my arm. "Now, Russ…You *know* how much I love her, too, but I can't watch London every day until she starts school," she said. "Like you, I have things to do."

"It's just temporary," I protested. "By next week, I'm hoping you won't have to."

"Tomorrow, I won't be here. My gardening club is hosting a tulip and daffodil workshop, and they have some exotic bulbs we can buy. I'm hoping to surprise your father next spring. You know he's never had great luck with tulips. And I volunteer on Thursdays and Fridays."

"Oh," I said, my head suddenly spinning. I heard my mom let out a sigh.

"As for today, though, and since London is already here…what time will you be finished with your meeting?"

"A quarter to twelve, maybe?"

"My lunch is at noon, so why don't you plan on coming to the restaurant to pick her up. London can sit with me and my friends until you get there."

"That would great," I said, feeling a surge of relief. "Where is it?"

She mentioned a place that I happened to know, though I'd never been there before.

"What time is your meeting again?"

The meeting. Oh crap.

"I've got to go, Mom. I can't tell you how much I appreciate this."

"Seriously?" Marge asked. "You're upset with Mom because she happens to have her own life?"

I was zipping along the highway, talking through my Bluetooth. "Weren't you listening? I have meetings all week. What am I going to do?"

"Hello? Day care? Hire a babysitter for a couple of hours? Ask one of the neighbors? Set up a playdate, and then ditch the kid?"

"I haven't had a spare minute to explore anything like that."

"You have time to talk to me right now."

Because I'm hoping you'll watch London tomorrow for a couple of hours tomorrow.

"Vivian and I talked about it. London's already having a hard enough time with Vivian going off to work."

"Is she?"

Aside from an apparent dislike of dance class, not that I've noticed. But . . .

"Anyway, I called because I was hoping that—"

"Don't even go there," Marge warned, cutting me off.

"Go where?"

"You're going to ask me if I can watch London tomorrow, since Mom closed that door. Or Thursday or Friday. Or all three."

Like I said, Marge is wise. "I don't know what you're talking about."

I could practically hear my sister rolling her eyes. "Don't play dumb and don't bother denying it, either. Why else would you be calling? Do you know how many times in the past five years you've called me at work?"

"Not offhand," I admitted.

"Zero."

"That's not true."

"You're right. I'm lying to you. You call me every day. We chat and giggle like middle-school girls for hours while I'm doodling. Hold on for a second."

I heard my sister cough, the sound deep and harsh. "You okay?" I asked.

"I think I picked up a virus."

"In the summer?"

"I had to bring Dad to the doctor yesterday and the waiting room was filled with sickness and disease. It's a wonder I didn't leave on a stretcher."

"How's Dad?"

"It'll take a few days for the labs to come in, but the stress test and EKG showed his heart was fine. Lungs, too. The doctor seemed pretty amazed, despite how surly Dad was."

"Sounds like him," I agreed. My mind circled back to London again. "What am I supposed to do with London if I can't find anyone to watch her?"

"You're smart. You'll figure it out."

"You're such a supportive and helpful sister."

"I try."

The meeting with the owners of the sandwich shop went about as well as the one with the chiropractor the day before. Not because they weren't interested. The owners, a married couple from Greece, knew that advertising would help their business; the problem was that they were barely earning enough to keep the doors open and still cover their expenses. They told me to come back in a few months, when they had a better handle on things, and offered me a sandwich as I was getting ready to leave.

"It's delicious," the husband said. "All our sandwiches are served in fresh pita bread that we make here."

"It's my grandmother's recipe," the wife added.

I had to admit that the bread smelled heaven-sent, and I could see the great care the husband took when making the sandwich. The wife asked if I wanted some chips and something to drink—why not?—and they handed me my lunch, both of them wearing smiles.

After that, they presented me with the bill.

I made it to the lunch gathering of the Red Hat Society at a quarter past twelve. Despite the inconvenience I'd no doubt caused my mom, I had the sense that my mom was proud to show off her granddaughter, who was something of a novelty in that group.

"Daddy!" London called out as soon as she saw me. She scooted off her chair and ran toward me. "They said I could come back to one of their lunches any time!"

My mom got up from the table and gave me a hug, away from the group.

"Thanks for watching her, Mom."

"My pleasure," she said. "She was a hit."

"I could tell."

"But tomorrow and the rest of the week..."

"I know," I said. "Tulips. Volunteering."

On our way out, I reached for London's hand. It was small in mine, warm and comforting.

"Daddy?" she said.

"Yes."

"I'm hungry."

"Let's go home and get you a peanut butter and jelly sandwich."

"We can't," London said.

"Why not?"

"We don't have any bread."

We went to the grocery store, where—for the first time—I grabbed a *cart*.

For the next hour, I slowly worked my way through Vivian's list, backtracking to a previously visited aisle more than once. I have no idea what I would have done had London not been there to help me, since she had a knowledge of the brands that went well beyond her five years. I had no idea where to find spaghetti squash, nor could I tell whether an avocado was ripe by squeezing it, but somehow with her and a few store employees' help I was able to cross everything off the list. While I was there, I saw mothers with children of all ages, most appearing as overwhelmed as I felt and I felt a fleeting kinship with them. I wondered how many of them, like me, would rather have been in an office instead of the meats section of the store, where it took me nearly five minutes to find the organic free-range chicken breasts that Vivian had specified.

Back home, after making a sandwich for London and unpacking the groceries, I spent the rest of the afternoon alternately working and cleaning while making sure London was okay, feeling the whole time like I was swimming against a never-ending current. Vivian arrived home at half past six and spent time with London for a few minutes before meeting me in the kitchen, where I'd started putting together a salad.

"How's the chicken Marsala coming?"

"Chicken Marsala?"

"With spaghetti squash on the side?"

"Uh…"

She laughed. "I'm kidding. I'll get it going. It won't take long."

"How was work today?"

"Busy," she said. "I spent most of the day learning about the journalist I mentioned yesterday and trying to figure out the angle he wants to take for the article. And, of course, how to contain the story once it's out and generate some positive coverage instead."

"Do you have a guess as to the kind of story it might be?"

"I suspect it's just the usual garbage, similar to what's been written before. The journalist is an environmentalist nut and he's been talking to people who claim that one of the oceanfront condo developments took a lot of shortcuts and was not only illegal, but has caused severe beach erosion on another part of the beach during the last tropical storm. Basically, it's all about blaming the rich people whenever Mother Nature strikes."

"You know Spannerman's not an eco-friendly guy, right?"

By then, Vivian was pouring herself a glass of wine. "Walter's not like that anymore. He's changed a lot since you knew him."

I doubt it, I thought. "It sounds like you've got a good handle on it," I offered instead.

"I'm just glad the article isn't coming out this week. Walter's got a big fund-raiser scheduled this weekend in Atlanta. For his PAC."

"He has a PAC now?"

"I mentioned it to you before," she said. She placed a frying pan on the stove, added the chicken and began riffling through the spice cabinet. "He started it a couple of years ago and has been funding it himself. Now he's decided to reach out to others for support. And that's what I'm going to be overseeing for the next three days. He hired an event company to run the program and while they've done a good job, he wants it to be perfect. That's where I come in. He knows I was in entertainment, and he wants me to see if I can find a musical act. Someone big."

"For this weekend? That doesn't give you a lot of time."

"I know. And I told him exactly that. I put a call in to my old boss and he gave me the names of some people to call, so we'll see. On the plus side, Walter is willing to pay whatever it costs, but it means I'll probably be working late all week. And I'll have to go to Atlanta."

"You're kidding," I said. "It's only your second day at work."

"Don't be like that," she said as she began browning the chicken. "It's not like he gave me much of a choice in the matter. Pretty much every major developer from Texas to Virginia is coming, and all the executives have to go. And it's not all weekend—I fly out Saturday morning and come back Sunday."

I didn't like it but what could I do? "All right," I said. "It sounds like you're already becoming indispensable."

"I'm trying." She smiled. "How was London today? Did she do okay at piano?"

"She did great, but I'm not sure she likes dance all that much. She was quiet after class yesterday."

"The teacher was upset because you were late. So London was upset, too."

"The instructor seems a little intense."

"She is. And that's why her dance teams win so many competitions." She nodded toward London. "While I get dinner going, will you get London into the bath?"

"Now?"

"That way, you can read to her after we eat, and get her down for the night. She's tired and like I told you, I've got a ton of work on tap."

"Sure," I said, realizing that once again, I'd likely be going to bed alone.

CHAPTER 7

Two by Two

W hen London was three and half, the three of us went on a picnic near Lake Norman. It was something we only did once. Vivian packed a delicious lunch and on our way to Lake Norman, and because the day was breezy, we stopped at a hobby store on the way to buy a kite. I'd picked the kind of kite that had been popular when I was a kid; simple and inexpensive, nothing like the kind of kites that avid enthusiasts would dream of flying.

It ended up being the perfect kite for a child. I was able to launch it myself and once it rose high, it seemed as if it was practically stuck to the sky. It didn't matter what I did; I could stand in place or walk around and when I handed London the kite reel and secured it to her wrist, it didn't matter what she did either. She could pick flowers or run around chasing butterflies; a nice couple had a small cocker spaniel, and she was able to sit on the ground and let the puppy crawl over her while the kite stayed fixed in the air. When we finally got around to having lunch, I looped the string around a nearby bench, and the kite simply hovered above us.

Vivian was in a buoyant mood, and we stayed at the park for most of the afternoon. On the way home, I can remember thinking to myself that times like this were what life was really all about, and that no matter what, I'd never let my family down.

But here and now, I was doing exactly that. Or at least, right now, it felt that way. It felt to me as though I was letting everyone down, including myself.

It was Wednesday, day three for Vivian at work, and I was on my own with London.

All day.

As I stood with London outside chiropractor number two's office, I felt almost as though I were shipping my daughter off to a foreign country. The thought that she'd sit in the waiting room with strangers made me uneasy; the newspapers and evening broadcasts had led modern parents to believe that the bogeyman was always lurking, ready to pounce.

I wondered if my parents ever worried about Marge and me like that, but that thought lasted only a split second. Of course they didn't. My dad used to have me sit on the bench outside an old tavern he occasionally frequented while he had a beer with friends. And that bench was on a corner of a busy street, near a bus stop.

"You understand that this is an important meeting for Daddy, right?"

"I know," London said.

"And I want you to sit quietly."

"And don't get up and wander around and don't talk to strangers. You already told me."

Vivian and I must have been doing something right because London did exactly as she was told. The receptionist remarked on what a well-behaved young lady she'd been during the meeting, which soothed my anxiety about what I'd done.

Unfortunately, the client wasn't interested in my services. I was *O-for-three* at that point. At the restaurant the following day, I upped that to *O-for-four*.

Forcing myself to remain optimistic, I had my best presentation to date on Friday afternoon. The owner of the spa—a blond, quick-talking woman in her fifties—was enthusiastic and though my sense was that they were already doing well, she knew who I was and was even familiar with some of my other campaigns. As I spoke with her, I felt relaxed and confident, and when I finished, I had the sense that I couldn't have done any better. But despite all that, the stars weren't aligning for me.

Not only did I fail to set up any meetings for the following week, I'd gone *O-for-five*.

Still, it was date night.

When there's nothing to celebrate, celebrate anyway, right?

That wasn't quite true, though. While I hadn't had any work success, Vivian certainly seemed to be lighting things on fire at her new job. She'd even been able to line up a musical act, a band from the eighties with a name I recognized. How she'd pulled that off, I had not the slightest idea. I'd also spent more one-on-one time with London, and that was definitely a great development.

Except...that it didn't feel all that great. With the constant running around from one thing to the next, it almost felt as though I was *working for* London instead of *enjoying time with* London.

Was I alone in feeling that way? Did other parents feel like that?

I have no idea, but date night was date night, and while London was in dance class, I swung by the store and picked up salmon, steak, and a nice bottle of Chardonnay. Vivian's SUV was in the driveway when I got home, and London jumped out of the car, calling for her mom. I followed with the plastic bag holding the goodies for dinner, only to see London zipping back down the steps. Vivian was nowhere in sight, but I heard her calling out from the bedroom.

London raced that way and I heard Vivian say, "There you are, sweetheart! How was your day?" I followed the sounds and spotted Vivian and London near the bed, upon which lay an open suitcase, already packed, along with two more empty department store bags.

Errands.

"Getting ready for tomorrow, I see."

"Actually, I have to leave tonight."

"You're leaving?" London burst out before I could.

I watched as Vivian put her hand on London's shoulder. "I don't want to, but I have to. I'm sorry, sweetheart."

"But I don't want you to go," London said.

"I know, sweetie. But when I get home on Sunday, I'll make it up to you. We'll do something fun, just you and me."

"Like what?" London asked.

"It's up to you."

"Maybe…" I watched as London's mind sorted through the problem. "We can go to the blueberry farm? The one you took me to before? And pick blueberries and pet the animals?"

"That's a great idea!" Vivian said. "Let's do it."

"And we also need to clean the hamster cage."

"Your daddy will do that for you when I'm gone. But for now, let's get you something to eat, okay? I think we have some leftover chicken and rice I can heat up. Can you wait for Mommy in the kitchen while I talk to Daddy for a minute?"

"Okay," London answered.

"So," I said, after London had left us alone, "you're off tonight."

"I have to head out in half an hour. Walter wants me and a couple of the other executives to do a walk-through with the manager of the Ritz-Carlton, to make sure it's getting set up the way Walter expects."

"The Ritz-Carlton?" I nodded. "Is that where you're staying?"

She nodded. "I know you're probably upset. Just so you know, I wasn't thrilled with knowing I'd be gone two nights either. I'm just trying to make the best of it."

"That's all you can do," I said, forcing a smile.

"Let me go spend a little time with London, okay? I think she's upset."

"Yeah," I said, "okay."

She stared at me. "You're angry with me."

"No, it's not that. I just wish you didn't have to go. I mean, I get it, but I was looking forward to spending some time with you tonight."

"I know," she said, "me, too." She leaned in for a quick kiss. "We'll make up for it next Friday, okay?"

"Okay."

"Can you zip my bag for me? I don't want to wreck my nails. I just got them done." She held up her hands for me. "Is the color okay?"

"It's great," I assured her. I secured the suitcase and pulled it from the bed. "You said you have a walk-through tonight at the hotel?"

"The whole thing has turned into a really big deal."

"Atlanta's four hours away."

"I'm not driving. I'm flying."

"What time's your flight?"

"Six thirty."

"Shouldn't you already be on your way to the airport? Or at the airport right now?"

"We're flying on Walter's private jet."

Walter. I was beginning to hate the sound of his name, almost as much as I hated the word *errands.*

"Wow," I said. "You're moving up in the world."

"It's not my jet," she said, smiling, "it's his."

"I knew you could pull it off all by your lonesome," Marge said. "You should be proud."

"I'm not proud. I'm exhausted."

We were at my parents' place by eleven on Saturday, and the day was already sweltering. Marge and Liz sat across from me on the back porch while I recounted the week I just spent in all its hectic detail. London was helping my mom make sandwiches; Dad was, as usual, in the garage.

"So? You told me yourself you finally felt like you were hitting your stride on that last presentation."

"A lot of good it did. And I've got nothing lined up for next week."

"On the bright side," Marge said, "that should make it a lot easier to get London to all her activities, *and* you'll have more time to cook and clean."

When I glared at her, Marge laughed. "Oh, lighten up. With Vivian starting work, you knew it was going to be a crazy week anyway. And you know that whole *it's always darkest before the dawn thing*? I have the feeling that dawn is right around the corner."

"I don't know," I said. "I was thinking as I drove over here this morning that I should have been a plumber like Dad. Plumbers always have work."

"True," Marge said, "but then again, there's a lot of crap involved with it."

Despite my mood, I laughed under my breath. "That's funny."

"What can I say? I bring joy and mirth to everyone around me. Even whiny little brothers."

"I haven't been whining."

"Yes you have. You've been whining since you sat down."

"Liz?"

She absently picked at the armrest before answering. "Maybe a little."

After lunch, and with the day only getting hotter, I decided to bring London to the movies, one of those animated ones. Marge and Liz came with us and seemed to enjoy it as much as London did. As for me, I wanted to enjoy it, but my thoughts kept drifting to the previous week, which made me wonder what on earth might be coming next.

After the movie, I didn't want to go home. Marge and Liz seemed content to hang out at my parents' place as well, and Mom ended up making tuna casserole, something London regarded as a treat, what with all the white flour in the pasta. She had a larger than normal portion and began to doze in the car on our way back home; I figured I'd get her in the bath, read a few stories, and spend the rest of the night zoning out in front of the television.

But it was not to be. As soon as she got in the house, she trotted to see the hamsters and I heard her voice calling to me from upstairs.

"Daddy! Come quick! I think something is wrong with Mrs. Sprinkles!"

I went to her room and peered into the cage, staring at a hamster that seemed to be making an attempt to push through the glass. Her room smelled like a barn. "She seems fine to me," I said.

"That's Mr. Sprinkles. Mrs. Sprinkles isn't moving."

I squinted. "I think she's sleeping, honey."

"But what if she's sick?"

I had no idea what to do in that case and opening the lid, I scooped Mrs. Sprinkles into my hand. She was warm, always a good sign, and I could feel her begin to move.

"Is she okay?"

"She seems fine to me," I said. "Do you want to hold her?"

102

She nodded and cupped her hands; I put the hamster in them. I watched as she brought the little critter closer to her face.

"I think I'll just hold her for a little while to make sure."

"All right," I said, kissing the top of her head. "But not too long, all right? It's already almost bedtime."

I kissed her on top of the head and headed toward the door.

"Daddy?" she asked.

"Yes?"

"You need to clean their cage."

"I'll do it tomorrow, okay? I'm kind of tired."

"Mommy said you'd clean it."

"I will. I just said I'd clean it tomorrow."

"But what if it's making Mrs. Sprinkles sick? I want you to clean it now." Not only was she not listening, her pitch was beginning to rise, and I wasn't in the mood to deal with it.

"I'll be back in a little while to get you ready for bed. Put your dirty clothes in the hamper, okay?"

For the next half hour, I flipped through the channels, finding nothing whatsoever to watch. More than a hundred channels and zippo, but then again, I was cranky on top of being tired. Tomorrow, I'd be scooping poop from a hamster cage, my client list was hovering at zero, and unless there was some sort of miracle, it would remain that way another week. Meanwhile, my wife was flying on private jets and staying at the Ritz-Carlton.

In time, I rose from my spot on the couch and went back to London's room. By then, her hamsters were back in the cage and she was playing with her Barbies.

"Hey sweetheart," I said. "Are you about ready for your bath?"

She answered without turning toward me. "I don't want to take a bath tonight."

"But you got all sweaty with Nana today."

"No."

I blinked. "What's wrong, sweetheart?"

"I'm mad at you."

"Why are you mad at me?"

"Because you don't care about Mr. and Mrs. Sprinkles."

"Of course I care about them." In the cage, both of them were moving about, no different than any other night. "And you know you need a bath."

"I want Mommy to do it."

"I know you do. But Mommy's not here."

"Then I'm not going to take a bath."

"Will you look at me?"

"No."

She sounded almost like Vivian as she said it and I was at a loss. London continued to send Barbie rampaging around the Barbie townhouse; the doll seemed on the verge of kicking over the furniture.

"How about I get the water going, okay? Then we can talk about it. I'll put extra bubbles in there."

As promised, I added extra bubbles to the water and when it was ready, I turned off the faucet. London hadn't moved; Barbie was still raging through the playhouse with Ken by her side.

"*I can't make breakfast,*" I heard her make Barbie say to Ken, "*because I have to go to work.*"

"*But daddies are supposed to work,*" Ken said.

"*Maybe you should have thought about that before you quit.*"

I felt my stomach tighten, certain that London was mimicking Vivian and me.

"Your bath is ready," I said.

"I *told* you I'm not taking a bath!"

"Just come on..."

"NO!!!" she screamed. "I'm not taking a bath and you can't make me! You made Mommy get a job!"

"I didn't make Mommy get a job..."

"YES YOU DID!" she shouted, and when she turned, I saw tears streaming down her cheeks. "She told me that she had to get a job because you're not working!"

Another father probably would have been less defensive, but I was exhausted and her words stung, if only because I felt bad enough about myself already.

"I am working!" I said, my voice rising. "And taking care of you and cleaning the house!"

"I want Mommy!" she cried, and for the first time, I realized that Vivian hadn't called today. Nor could I call her; the event was probably in full swing right about now.

I took a deep breath. "She'll be here tomorrow and the two of you are going to the blueberry farm, remember? You want to be all clean for her, don't you?"

"NO!" she shouted. "I hate you!"

The next thing I knew, I was marching across the room and seized London by the arm. She began to struggle and scream and I dragged her to the bathroom, like a bad-parent video on YouTube.

"Either you get yourself undressed and into the bath, or I'll undress you. I'm not kidding."

"GO AWAY!" she screamed and after putting her pajamas on the countertop, I closed the door. For the next few minutes, I heard her alternately crying and talking to herself while I waited outside the door.

"Get in the bath, London," I warned through the door. "If you don't, I'll make you clean the hamster cage all by yourself."

I heard her scream again; a minute later, though, I heard her climbing into the tub. I continued to wait. After a little while, I heard her playing with her tub toys without the anger I'd heard earlier. Finally, the door opened; London was in her pajamas, her hair wet.

"Can we dry my hair tonight instead of leaving it wet?"

I gritted my teeth. "Of course we can, sweetheart."

"I miss Mommy."

I squatted down and took her in my arms, breathing in the sweet-clean scent of her soap and shampoo. "I know you do," I said, and held her close, wondering how a father as messed up as I could have managed to help make something so wonderful, even as my little girl began to cry.

I read her the story of Noah and the ark as we lay in the bed together. Her favorite part, the part I had to read a second time, was when the ark was finished and the animals started to arrive.

"Two by two," I read aloud, "they came in pairs, from all over the world. Lions and horses and dogs and elephants, zebras and giraffes..."

"And hamsters," London added.

"And hamsters," I agreed, "and two by two, they boarded the ark. How will they all fit, the people wondered. But God had a plan for that, too. They made their way onto the ark and there was plenty of room, and all the animals were happy. And two by two, they stayed in the ark while the rain began to fall."

As I was finishing the story, London was fading. I turned out the light and kissed her cheek.

"I love you, London," I whispered.

"Love you, too, Daddy," she mumbled, and I crept quietly from the room.

Two by two, I thought to myself as I made my way down the stairs. London and me, father and daughter, both of us doing the best we could.

Even then, I felt like I was failing her, failing at everything.

CHAPTER 8

New Experiences

*L*ast February, when things were going from bad to worse for me at the agency, London got the flu, and it wasn't pretty. She threw up pretty much nonstop for two days, and we had to bring her to the hospital to stop the vomiting and administer fluids.

I was scared. Vivian was too, though on the surface, she exuded a lot more confidence with the doctors than I did. When she spoke to them, she was calm and cool while asking appropriate questions.

London didn't have to stay overnight, and when we brought her home, Vivian sat with her until midnight. Because she'd been awake pretty much the entire night the evening before, I took over. Like Vivian, I sat in the rocking chair and held my daughter. She was still feverish and I can remember how small and frail she felt, wrapped in a thin blanket and sweating and shivering at the same time. She woke every twenty minutes. Sometime around six, I finally put her in bed and went downstairs for coffee. An hour later, when I was pouring yet another cup, London padded into the kitchen and took a seat at the table beside Vivian. London moved lethargically and her face was pale.

"Hi, sweetheart. How are you feeling?"

"I'm hungry," London responded.

"That's a good sign," Vivian said. She put her hand on London's forehead, held it, then smiled. "I think your fever's gone."

"I feel a little better."

"Russ? Would you put some Cheerios in a bowl? Without milk?"

"Sure," I said.

"Let's try cereal without the milk, okay? I don't want your tummy to get upset."

I brought the Cheerios to the table along with my coffee and took a seat beside them.

"You were really sick," I said. "Your mom and I have been really worried about you."

"And we're going to take it easy today, okay?"

London nodded as she munched. I was glad to see her eating.

"Thanks for holding me when I was sick, Mommy."

"Of course, sweet girl. I always hold you when you're sick."

"I know," London said.

I took a sip of coffee, waiting for Vivian to say that I'd helped out as well.

But she didn't.

Kids are resilient. I know this because my mom and dad have used that expression for as long as I can remember, especially when describing their own parenting philosophy to Marge and me. *Why, why, why did you do such things to us?* we would ask. *Ah, no worries. Kids are resilient.*

In all fairness, there was some truth to their words. When London came downstairs on Sunday morning, she seemed to have forgotten completely about her tantrum from the night before. She was in a chatty mood and was even happier when I let her have Lucky Charms while I went upstairs to clean her hamster cage. I filled half a plastic bag with soiled shavings—it was disgusting—and tossed it into the garbage can. In the far corner, I saw London's bicycle and, though it was already getting hot outside, I knew what she and I could do this morning.

"Hey," I said to London when I got back inside. "Do you want to do something fun this morning?

"What?" she asked.

"Why don't we go bike riding again? Maybe without the training wheels."

"I'll fall," she said.

"I promise that you won't fall. I'll be right beside you and I'll hold on to the seat."

"I haven't ridden a bike in a long time."

And never without training wheels, I thought. "That's okay. If you don't like it or you get scared, we can stop."

"I'm not scared," she said. "But Mommy won't like it if I'm all sweaty."

"If you get sweaty, you'll just wash up. No big deal. Do you want to give it a try?"

She thought about it. "Maybe for a little while," she hedged. "When's Mommy coming home?"

As if my wife heard our daughter from miles away, my cell phone rang. Vivian's name popped up on the screen. "Well, let's find out. It's your mom," I said, reaching for it. "She must have been thinking about you." I connected the call and hit the speaker. "Hey, babe. How are you? How did it go? I've got you on speaker and London is here."

"Hey, baby girl!" Vivian said. "How are you! I'm so sorry I didn't call you yesterday. I've been running around like crazy since I've been here. How are you? How was yesterday?"

"It was so much fun," London answered. "I went to Nana's and then Daddy and me and Auntie Marge and Auntie Liz went to see a movie, and it was really funny..."

While Vivian chatted with London, I refilled my coffee and motioned that I was going back to the bedroom to change. I tossed on some shorts and a T-shirt and the pair of shoes I used to wear to the gym. Back in the kitchen, London was telling her mom about the hamsters and Vivian finally asked for me.

I picked up the phone, taking it off speaker.

"Hey there," I said.

"She's in a good mood. Sounds like you two have been having a lot of fun. I'm jealous."

I hesitated, thinking about last night. "It's been okay. How did last night go on your end?"

"Amazingly, it went off without a hitch. Walter was thrilled. The video presentations were great and so was the music. People went crazy for it."

"I'm glad it worked out."

"It did. We raised a lot of money. Turns out Walter isn't the only one who's frustrated with the current administration and Congress when it comes to development. The regulations are getting ridiculous. Developers are really getting squeezed, and it's almost impossible to turn a profit anymore."

As evidenced by Walter's private jet, I thought. "What time will you be home?"

"I'm hoping around one. But we may be having lunch with a developer from Mississippi. If that happens, it'll probably be closer to three."

"Hold on for a second," I said. I moved from the kitchen to the living room. "What about the blueberry farm?"

"I don't know if we'll be able to make it."

"But you promised London you'd go."

"I didn't promise."

"I was right there, Viv. I heard you. And I backed you up last night."

"What does that mean?"

I recounted what had happened the night before.

"Well, that's just great," she said. "You shouldn't have reminded her."

"You're saying this is my fault?"

"She's going to be even more upset."

"Because you said you'd take her."

"Just stop, Russ, okay? I was on the go for almost twenty hours straight and I've had almost no sleep. Just talk to her, okay? *Explain* it to her."

"What do you want me to tell her?"

"Please don't use that tone with me. I'm not the one who set up the lunch. I'm at Walter's mercy here, and there's a lot of money at stake."

"Spannerman already *has* a lot of money. He's a billionaire."

I heard her let out a long exhale. "Like I told you," she said, her voice taut. "I still might make it. If the lunch doesn't work out, I'll be home by one. I should know more in an hour or two."

"All right," I said, thinking about London. "Let me know."

I decided not to tell London anything until I knew more and she followed me outside, watching as I got things ready. Because the bike was covered in dust, I brought out the hose and rinsed it, then toweled it dry. I pumped the tires and made sure there were no major leaks. After that, I had to hunt for a wrench—why do tools always seem to vanish?—and removed the training wheels. Because London had grown, I raised the seat and handlebars, and when it was finally ready, London followed me out to the street and hopped on.

"Do you remember what to do?" I said, adjusting her helmet.

"I'm supposed to pedal," she said. "But you're not going to let go, right?"

"I won't let go until you're ready."

"What if I'm not ready?"

"Then I won't let go."

London began to pedal and wobbled to the left and right as I held the seat, jogging while bent at the waist. Soon I was breathing hard and sweat began to drip. Then pour. We went back and forth countless times and just when it felt like I was going to have to tell her that I needed a break, her balance began to improve, at least on the straightaways. Little by little, I was able to lessen my grip on the seat. After that, I was able to use only my fingers, just enough to be able to grab her if she tilted.

And then, I was able to let go.

Not long at first—only a few seconds—and the next time was about the same. Then, when I thought she was ready, I said the magic words.

"I'm going to let go for a second," I gasped.

"No, Daddy!"

"You can do it! Just try! I'll be right here to catch you!" I let go of the seat and sped up, jogging beside the bike for no more than a second or two. London saw me, her face a picture of wonder, and then I resumed my original position and took hold of her seat again.

"I was riding, Daddy!" she shouted. "Without your help!"

I held the seat as we turned around at the end of the cul-de-sac, and when she was balanced, I let go again, that time for five or six seconds. Then a span of ten seconds. Then she cruised the entire straightaway.

"I'm riding, Daddy! I'm riding a bike!" she squealed, and though I was sweating hard and out of breath and felt like I was dying, I was somehow able to shout back, "I know, sweetheart! You're riding a bike!"

By the time London was ready to quit, my entire body hurt and my shirt was soaked through. I rolled the bike into the garage and followed London inside; the blast of air-conditioning was the very proof of God's existence.

"Daddy needs a break," I said, still trying to catch my breath.

"Okay, Daddy," she said. I went to the bathroom and hopped in a shower with the water somewhere between cool and cold. I stayed beneath the spray until I finally felt halfway human, then dressed again and went to the kitchen.

There was a text from Vivian.

Lunch was canceled. I'm heading to the airport now. Tell London I'll be home soon.

I found London in the living room, playing with her Barbies.

"Your mom's on her way home," I said. "She should be here in a little while."

"Okay," London said, sounding strangely unmoved.

I put together a salad and grilled the salmon for Vivian while I made sandwiches for London and me. By the time Vivian walked in the door, the table was set and the food was on the table.

After a round of hugs and kisses for London, she came to the kitchen and kissed me as well.

"Wow," she remarked. "That's a pretty fancy meal for lunch."

"I had the food here, so I figured why not? How was the flight?"

"Amazing. It's so nice not having to deal with parking or security or shoving suitcases into the overhead bins. Private jets are definitely the way to travel."

"I'll keep that in mind when I begin making millions."

"What did you and London do this morning?"

"I got the bike out of the garage."

"Yeah?" she asked. "How was she?"

"She was getting pretty good by the end."

"Better you than me," she said. "It's hot out there today."

"It wasn't so bad this morning," I lied.

"Did you remember to put sunscreen on her?"

"No," I said. "I forgot."

"You have to try to remember these things. You know how much the sun can damage her skin."

"I'll remember that next time."

She kissed me again and as we had lunch, she told me about her weekend and talked to London about her activities the previous week. Afterward Vivian and London went to the car while I tidied up the kitchen.

For the first time since Tuesday, London wasn't with me. I would have worked but there wasn't anything to do, and while I thought I would enjoy my quiet afternoon, I found myself puttering around the house and thinking about London, surprised by how much I missed her.

Vivian and London got back home around five, carrying department store bags. There wasn't a smudge of dirt on my daughter's hands or face.

"Did you go to the farm?" I asked.

"No," Vivian answered, setting the bags on the table. "It was way too hot out there this afternoon. We ended up going to the mall. London needed some school clothes."

Of course she did.

Before we could speak more about it, Vivian breezed past me to the kitchen. I followed and tried to engage in conversation, but it was clear that Vivian was edgy and in no mood to mumble more than one-word answers. In the end, she made pasta and sautéed vegetables for London and me, along with a salad for herself, and dinner was eaten quickly. It wasn't until we were loading the dishes into the dishwasher that I finally asked her what was wrong.

"You didn't tell me that you took the training wheels off her bike

113

today. And that by riding her bike, you meant actually riding her bike."

"Sorry about that," I said. "I thought you understood."

"How was I supposed to know what you meant? You weren't very clear."

"Are you upset?"

"Yes, I'm upset. Why wouldn't I be upset?"

"I'm not sure why you would be."

"Because I wasn't there. Did it ever cross your mind that I might have liked to have seen London riding her bike for the first time?"

"She's still just a beginner. She can't do the turns yet without tipping over."

"So? The issue is that you went ahead and taught her to ride a bike without me. Why didn't you wait until I got home?"

"I didn't think about it."

She grabbed a dish towel and began drying her hands. "That's exactly your problem, Russ. You do this every time. Our whole life has always been about what you wanted."

"That's not true," I protested. "And how was I supposed to know you'd even want to watch? You didn't want the bike in the first place."

"Of course I wanted London to have a bike! Why would you think that? I'm the one who bought it for her for Christmas."

I stared at her, thinking, *I had to drag you to the store.* Did she really not remember it that way? Or was I going crazy?

As I pondered the question, she turned to leave. "Where are you going?" I asked.

"London needs a bath," she said. "You don't mind if I spend a little time with my daughter, do you?"

She left the kitchen, her words ricocheting in my mind.

My daughter?

After London went to bed, Vivian and I sat on the couch, the television tuned to the Food Network. Vivian was sipping a glass of wine. I thought again about bringing up the day care issue, but I wasn't sure whether or not she still angry about the bike riding incident. Her eyes flicked toward me with a quick smile, then back to her magazine. Better than being ignored, I supposed.

"Hey Viv?" I asked.

"Hmm?"

"I'm sorry you missed watching London's first bike ride. I really didn't think it was that big of a deal."

She seemed to consider my words and I watched her shoulders drop slightly.

"It's all right. I just wish I had been there to see it. I hate that I wasn't."

"I understand that. I've missed a lot of firsts over the years, too."

"But you're not her mom. It's different for mothers."

"I guess so," I said, not completely sure about that. But there was no need to point that out.

"Maybe tomorrow night, you can show me," she said, her voice soft, and I saw the Vivian that I'd fallen for so many years ago. It was uncanny, how my wife never seemed to age.

"I'm glad your event went off without a hitch. I'll bet you already have your boss eating out of the palm of your hand."

"Walter doesn't eat out of anyone's hand."

"How's next week shaping up?"

"I'll find out more tomorrow. I might have another overnight on Wednesday."

"Another fund-raiser?"

"No. This time it's a trip to D.C. And I know London's going to be upset again. It makes me feel like an awful mother."

"You're not awful. And London knows you love her."

"But it's her last summer before kindergarten, and she probably feels like I've abandoned her. She needs stability and right now, she's not getting it."

"I'm doing my best."

"I know you are. She told me that she likes spending time with you, but that it's weird."

"She said it's *weird* for her?"

"You know what she means. She's just used to me, that's all. It's been a big change for her. You know that."

"I still don't like the word *weird*."

"She's a child. She doesn't have a huge vocabulary. No big deal. You ready to hit the bedroom? We can put on the TV and relax."

"Are you making a pass at me?"

"Maybe."

"Is that a yes or a no?"

"How about I finish my glass of wine first."

I smiled, and later, when our bodies were intertwined, I found myself thinking that as hard as the previous week had been, it ended in an absolutely perfect way.

CHAPTER 9

The Past Is Never Quite Past

A few years ago, when feeling nostalgic, I reflected on some of the most meaningful days of my life. I recalled my high school and college graduations, the day I proposed and my wedding day, and of course, the day that London was born. And yet, none of those moments had been surprises, because I'd known they were coming.

I also recalled the memorable firsts of my own life, just as I recalled those firsts with London. My first kiss, the first time I slept with a woman, my first beer, and the first time my dad let me slide behind the wheel of a car. I remembered my first real paycheck and the near reverential feeling I had as I walked through the first home I'd purchased.

And yet, there were other priceless memories, memories that were neither first nor expected, but perfect in their spontaneous joy. Once, when I was a kid, my dad shook me awake in the middle of the night and brought me outside to watch a meteor shower. He'd laid a towel on the grass and as we stared up at the sky, watching trails of white racing across the sky, I sensed in the excited way he would point them out the love he felt for me, but so often had trouble expressing. I remembered the time that Marge and I stayed up all night laughing and giggling as we devoured an entire bag of chocolate chip cookies, the first night I really understood that she and I would always have each other. I thought back to the evening when my mom, after two glasses of wine, spoke about her own childhood in a way that allowed me to see her as the child she once was, someone I could have imagined as a friend.

Those moments have stayed with me forever, partly because of their

simplicity, but also because they were revelatory. Nor were they ever quite
repeated, and I can't shake the thought that if I ever tried to replicate them,
the original memories would slip through my fingers like sand, lessening
the hold I have on them now.

On Monday morning Vivian was out the door at half past seven, carrying with her a duffel bag. "I want to squeeze in a workout if I can,"
she said. "I feel like I'm getting softer by the minute."

London and I followed a few minutes later, dressed in shorts and
T-shirts. We were heading to the club for my daughter's first tennis lesson, and when I saw men dressed in ties on the road beside me, I felt
like I'd been kicked out of the only club where I'd ever wanted to be a
member. Without work, I felt like I'd lost a major part of my identity,
and if I didn't turn it around, I was going to lose myself entirely.

Time for more cold calls.

As soon as I parked the car, London spotted some girls from the
neighborhood and skipped toward them onto the court. I made my
way to the bleachers with a pad of paper and typed the words *plas-*
tic surgeons into the search engine of my phone. Like attorneys, they
were an area that Peters avoided—he considered them prima don-
nas and cheapskates—but my thinking was that doctors had money
and the intelligence to understand how advertising could benefit
their practice. There were a number of them in the Charlotte area
divided among various offices—a good sign—and I began experi-
menting with a few opening lines, hoping to find just the right com-
bination of words to keep the office manager—or the doctor, if I got
that lucky—on the phone long enough to get interested enough to set
an appointment.

"Can you believe how damn hot it is already?" I heard beside me, in
a sharp New Jersey accent. "I swear to God I'm going to melt."

When I turned, I saw a man maybe a few years older than me, built
like a block, with dark hair and bronzed skin. Above his suit, he wore
aviator sunglasses with mirrored lenses.

"Are you talking to me?"

"Of course I'm talking to you. Aside from you and me, it's like an estrogen convention out here. We're the only two guys within a hundred yards of this place. I'm Joey the Bulldog Taglieri, by the way." He scooted closer and held out his hand.

"Russell Green," I said, shaking it. "Bulldog?"

"University of Georgia mascot, my alma mater, and I've got a big neck. The nickname stuck. Nice to meet you, Russ. And if I have a heart attack or stroke out here, do me a favor and call 911. Adrian should have warned me that there wouldn't be a lick of shade out here."

"Adrian?"

"My ex. Number three, by the way. She dropped this responsibility in my lap yesterday 'cause she knew it was important to me and God knows, she's not in the favor-granting business these days. She knows I'm supposed to be in court at nine thirty, but does she care? Ask me if she cares? She doesn't care. It's not like she *had* to see her mother. Who cares if her mother's in the hospital? She's in the hospital every other week because she's a *hypochondriac*. It's not like the doctors ever find anything wrong with her. That woman's probably going to live to be a hundred." He gestured at my pad of paper. "You preparing your opening remarks?"

"Opening remarks?"

"What you say to the jury? You're a lawyer, aren't you? I think I've seen you at the courthouse."

"No," I said. "Wrong guy. I'm not a lawyer. I'm in advertising."

"Yeah? What firm?"

"The Phoenix Agency," I said. "It's my own firm."

"No kidding? The guys I use are a bunch of idiots if you ask me."

My ears perked up. "What firm are you using?"

He mentioned the name and I recognized it as a national firm that specialized in attorney commercials, which meant that for the most part, commercials were pretty much cookie-cutter, with the same images and only slight variations to the script. Before I could dwell on it, he changed the subject.

"How long have you been a member of the country club?"

"Four years or so?"

"Do you like it? I just joined."

"Considering I don't golf, I do. The food's good and the pool is a summer hangout. You can meet a lot of interesting people here."

"I'm with you on the golf thing. Tried it for a year, threw out my back, and ended up giving the clubs to my brother. I joined for the tennis. I know I don't look like it, but I'm not half bad. College scholarship, dreams of going pro, but my serve only had so much speed 'cause of my height. That's the way it goes, I guess. So now, I figured I'd get my daughter started young so that when she's a teenager, we'd have something to do together when she starts to hate me. She's the one out there with the turquoise top, by the way. Dark hair, long legs. Which one is yours?"

I pointed out London, who was standing on the back line with several other girls. "Over there," I said. "Second from the left."

"She's going to be a tall one, too. That's good."

"We'll see whether she even likes it. It's her first day picking up a racket. You said you're an attorney?"

"Yeah. Personal injury, the occasional class-action suit. I know what you're probably thinking about lawyers like me, and I really don't care. No one likes personal injury attorneys until they really need one, and then all of a sudden, I'm their best friend and their savior. And not just because I almost always get my clients the money they deserve. But because I listen. Half of this business is about listening. I learned that when I was in family law, before wife number one ran off with the neighbor and I figured out that I needed to earn a lot more money. Family law wasn't cutting it. Word of advice? Always get a prenup."

"Good to know."

He motioned toward my pad. "Plastic surgeons, huh?"

"I was thinking of expanding into that area."

"Yeah? I've made a fortune off a few of them. They may as well have been using hacksaws on a few of my clients. You want my advice with those guys? As someone who's dealt with them in the past?"

"Go ahead."

"They have God complexes but are terrible at business, so play to their egos and then promise them you can make them rich. Trust me. That'll get their attention."

120

"I'll keep that in mind."

He waved at the court. "I'm not sold on the tennis pro out there just yet. What do you think?"

"I don't know enough to even venture a guess."

"You can tell he's played, but I don't get the sense he's coached little kids before. They're a whole different ball of wax. Attention spans like gnats. The key is to keep things moving along or the kids will get restless."

"Makes sense. Maybe you should coach."

He laughed. "Now that would be something, huh? Nah, not for me. Never coach your own kid. That's one of my rules. She'd probably end up hating me even more than she already will. So what's your interest in this? Do you play?"

"No," I said. "This was my wife's idea."

"And yet, here you are."

"Here I am," I agreed, and Joey turned his attention back to what was happening on the court. I continued to jot opening lines but knew I'd have to do a lot more research before I was ready for a presentation. Every now and then, Joey would make a comment about foot positions or the proper arc to take when hitting the ball, and we'd drift back into small talk for a couple more minutes.

When the session ended, Joey shook my hand a second time.

"Are you going to be out here tomorrow?" When I nodded, he went on. "Me, too. See you then."

I left the bleachers and met London as she was exiting the court. Her face was red from the heat.

"Did you have a good time?" I asked her.

"Mom really thinks I should play. She told me this morning."

"I know she does. I was asking what you thought about it."

"It was hot. Who was that you were talking to?"

"Joey."

"Is he your friend?"

"We just met. Why?"

"Because you were acting like you were friends."

"He's a nice guy," I said, and as I we walked toward the car, I

121

reflected on what he'd said about his advertising firm being a bunch of idiots.

And, of course, that I'd see him again tomorrow.

I got London a snack, knowing she needed to cool off before art class. At the same time, my thoughts drifted to the advertising I'd done for attorneys, prior to Peters pulling the plug. I remember filming commercials in wood-shelved offices filled with law books, and recommending targeted spends on cable channels between the hours of nine and noon, when injured people might be watching.

These days, with most of the commercials nationwide put together by a single national firm, there was an opportunity for a niche in the market, if I wanted to go that route. I suspected I could get better deals at the cable companies since I had long working relationships with the key players, something the national firm didn't have. In the long run, it might not be good for my firm—I might have to go the Peters route and eventually give them up—but that day was a long way off, and I didn't want to think about it. Instead, I kept my focus on the fact that Taglieri might—just might—be open to a possible switch.

It took London less time than I thought to be back to normal, and she talked about Bodhi for most of the drive. As soon as she walked through the door of the studio, she turned and I lowered myself. She wrapped her arms around my neck and squeezed.

"I love you, Daddy."

"Love you, too," I said.

When I stood, I watched as she rushed toward a young blond boy and when they were close, they hugged each other, too.

Cute.

Then, all at once, I frowned. On second thought, I wasn't sure what to think about my little girl already hugging boys. I had no idea what was normal in such situations.

After a quick wave to the art teacher, I left for the coffee shop with my computer, figuring I'd start looking into the latest trends in legal advertising as well as any regulations that may have changed since my last advertising campaign.

I ordered a coffee, found a seat, and opened my computer. I pulled up some preliminary information and was reviewing it when I heard a voice coming from off to the side.

"Russ?"

It was impossible not to recognize her. Her chestnut hair brushed her shoulders, and was styled in a way that accented her naturally high cheekbones, while her hazel eyes were as striking as they'd always been.

"Emily?" I asked.

She started toward the table, holding a cup of coffee. "I thought that was you in the studio," she said. "How are you? Long time no see."

"I'm doing well," I said, rising from the table. Surprising me, she leaned in for a quick hug, which triggered a flood of happy memories. "What are you doing here? Why were you in the studio?"

"My son's in the class," she said. "Takes after his mom, I guess." Her smile held genuine warmth. "You look great."

"Thanks. You, too. How are you doing?" Up close, I noticed that her eyes were flecked with gold, and I wondered whether I'd never noticed before.

"I'm doing okay."

"Just okay?"

"Yeah, you know. Life."

I understood exactly what she meant and though she'd tried to hide it, I thought I heard in her tone a flicker of sadness. The next word came out almost automatically, even as I realized that spending time with a person you once loved and slept with can get complicated if one isn't careful. "Would you like to join me?"

"You sure? You look busy."

"I'm just doing some research. No big deal."

"Then I'd love to," she said. "But I can only stay a few minutes. I've got some things I want to ship to my mom and depending on the line, it can take forever."

When we were seated, I looked at her, amazed that it had been almost eleven years since our breakup. Like Vivian, she hadn't seemed to have aged at all, but I pushed the thought away, steering myself back to safer ground. "How old is your son?"

"Five," she answered. "He'll be starting kindergarten in the fall."

"My daughter, too," I said. "Where will he be going?"

When she mentioned the name of the school, I raised an eyebrow. "What a coincidence. That's where London's going, too."

"It's supposed to be great."

And expensive, I thought. "That's what I hear, too," I said. "How are your mom and dad doing?" I asked. "I haven't talked to them in years."

"They're doing well. My dad is finally retiring next year."

"From AT&T?"

"Yup—he was a lifer. He told me he wants to get an RV and travel the country. Of course, Mom wants nothing to do with that, so she's going to continue to work at the church until my dad's whimsy passes."

"St. Michael's?"

"Of course. Both my parents worked at the same place their entire lives. That just doesn't happen anymore. How about you? Are you still working for the Peters Group?"

I raised an eyebrow. "I'm impressed you remembered. But no, I left there a few months ago and went out on my own."

"How's it going?"

"It's going," I hedged.

"That's exciting. I remember you telling me you wanted to be an entrepreneur."

"I was young and naïve back then. Now, I'm old but still naïve."

She laughed. "How's Vivian?"

"She's doing well. She just started working again. I didn't realize you knew her."

"I don't. I saw her at the studio a few times earlier this summer, but she never stayed for the class. She was always dressed in workout clothes."

"Sounds like her. How's . . . your husband?"

"You mean David?" She tilted her head.

"Sure," I said. "David."

"We're divorced. As of last January."

"I'm sorry to hear that."

"I'm sorry, too."

"How long were you married?"

"Seven years."

"May I ask what happened?"

"I don't know," she said. "It's hard to explain. To say we drifted apart sounds clichéd...Lately, when people ask, I just tell them that the marriage worked until it didn't, but that isn't the answer most people want to hear. It's like they want to be able to gossip about it later, or boil it down to a single incident." As she spoke, she rubbed her thumb against her index finger. "How long have you and Vivian been together?"

"We're coming up on nine years now."

"There you go," she said. "Good for you."

"Thanks."

"So Vivian started working again?"

I nodded. "She's working for a big developer here in town. Public relations. How about you? Are you working?"

"I guess you can call it that. I still paint."

"Really?"

"My ex was good about that. Encouraging me, I mean. And it's been going well. I mean, I'll never be a Rothko or Pollock, but I'm represented by one of the galleries downtown and I sell ten or twelve pieces a year."

"That's fantastic," I said, meaning it. "You always had such talent. I remember watching you paint and wondering how you knew what to do with the colors and the..." I trailed off, trying to recall the right word.

"Composition?"

"Yes. Are you still doing modern?"

She nodded. "Sort of. I work in abstract realism."

"You know I have no idea what that means, right?"

"Basically, I start with realistic scenes as a base, but mostly I follow the brush...adding vibrant colors or geometric shapes, or random splatters and swirls and drips until I feel that it's done. Of course, a painting is never really done; I have pieces I've been tinkering with for years because they're just not right. The problem is, I'm not always sure how to make them right."

"Sounds very artsy." I grinned.

She laughed, the sound exactly what I remembered.

"As long as it would look good hanging on most people's walls and makes a person think, I'm pleased with the result."

"Oh, just that?"

"That's what the gallery owner likes to say when he's trying to sell one of my pieces, so yes."

"I'd love to see your work."

"You can stop by the gallery any time," she said. She gave me the name and I committed it to memory. "How's Marge doing? I always wanted a big sister like her."

"She's doing well—still with Liz, of course."

"The same Liz I met when we were dating?"

"Yeah. They've been together ever since. Almost eleven years now."

"Wow," she said. "Good for them. What's Liz like?"

"Kind, and thoughtful and supportive. I have no idea what she sees in Marge."

There was a glimmer of reproach in Emily's expression. "Be nice."

"You know I'm kidding. They're a great couple. I'm not sure I've ever seen them argue. They just sort of go with the flow."

"That's a good thing. And your parents? Are they still working?"

"Mom retired, but Dad's still at it full time."

"Still working on his car?"

"Every weekend."

"And your mom?"

"She's now a member of the Red Hat Society, and she wants to plant tulips." When Emily furrowed her brow, I told her about the week before.

"You know you can't be mad at her for that. She already fulfilled her parenting duties."

"That's what Marge said. Marge wouldn't help me either."

"And yet, you got everything done anyway."

"Marge said that, too."

She let out a long breath. "It's amazing where life has taken us, huh? Since we knew each other? Of course, we were just kids back then."

"We weren't kids."

She smiled. "Are you kidding? Maybe, technically, we were old

126

enough to vote, but I can definitely remember some youthful exuberance on your part. Like the time you decided to see whether you could eat that monstrous steak, so you could get your picture on the wall of the restaurant. How big was that steak again?"

The memory came back in a rush. We'd been out at the lake with a group of friends, and I spotted the restaurant sign just off the highway, advertising that in addition to my photo on the wall, there would be no charge for the meal. "Seventy-five ounces."

"You didn't even make it halfway."

"I was hungry when I started…"

"You were also drunk."

"Maybe a little."

"Good times." She laughed. She lingered before me before finally gesturing toward my computer. "But unfortunately, I should probably get going. You need to work, and I've really got to get that stuff shipped off today."

I became aware of the fact that I didn't want her to go, even if it was probably a good idea. "You're probably right."

She stood from the table. "It was nice seeing you again, Russ."

"You, too," I said. "It's been fun catching up."

"I'll see you later."

"Later?"

"When the class ends?"

"Of course," I said. "I knew that."

As she used her shoulder to push open the door, I couldn't help but notice that she glanced back at me and smiled before finally vanishing from sight.

I spent the next hour in the coffee shop researching on the Internet and was able to find two commercials for the law offices of Joey Taglieri, one of which was no longer airing. They were professional, informative, and, I had to admit, nearly the same as the kind of legal commercials I used to film. I also watched commercials from almost a dozen other law firms in town, concluding that, if anything, Taglieri's commercials were no better or worse than any of the others.

Why, then, had Joey Taglieri thought of them as idiots?

If the commercials weren't that bad, however, I still didn't think Taglieri was getting his money's worth when it came to the overall campaign. His website was distinctly out of date and lacked pizzazz, and a phone call to a buddy let me know there was nothing going on in the way of Internet advertising. Another couple of calls let me know that he didn't advertise in print or on billboards either. I wondered if he'd be open to those ideas while doing my best not to get too excited.

A call to my office helped—there was zippo, nada, zilch in the way of messages—and after leaving the coffee shop, I collected London from art class. She proudly pointed out a bowl she'd made, and I waved at Emily on my way out the door. She smiled and raised a hand—she was talking to the teacher at the time—and after bringing London home, I was unsure how best to spend the next few hours until dance class. It was too hot to bring London outside, and her day was already so full, I suspected that she might simply want to relax and play for a while.

In the end, I decided to make Vivian dinner. I perused a few cookbooks, recognizing that many of the recipes were beyond my culinary capabilities. There was, however, a recipe for Chilean sea bass, and a quick search of the cupboards indicated I had most of the ingredients. Perfect. I brought London to dance and while the class was no doubt disappointing the grim Ms. Hamshaw, I swung by the grocery store and picked up the rest. Dinner was well under way by the time Vivian walked through the door.

With rice pilaf and green bean almondine going on the stove, I couldn't step away.

"I'm in the kitchen," I called out, and soon afterward I heard Vivian's footsteps behind me.

"Wow," she noted, walking toward me. "It smells great in here. What are you making?"

When I told her, she leaned over the pots on the stove. "What's the occasion?"

"No occasion. Just thought I'd try something new. And after dinner, I figured that I'd get the bike out so you could watch London ride."

She opened the cupboard and pulled a glass from it, then the wine from the fridge. "Let's do it tomorrow, okay? I'm tired and London's had a big day. She seems wiped out already."

"Fair enough," I said.

She poured herself a glass. "How did she do at tennis?"

"About the same as everyone else. First day, learning to hold the racket at the proper end, all the basics. There were a couple of girls from the neighborhood, so she seemed happy to be there."

"I think tennis will be good for her. It's a great sport to socialize."

"And the girls look cute in those shorts, I might add."

"Ha, ha. How about art class? And dance?"

"She had fun at art, but as for dance, I don't think she likes it very much."

"Give it time. Once she starts competing, she'll love it."

I wondered who Vivian imagined would be bringing her to the competitions, but kept my thoughts to myself. "Were you able to get a workout in?"

"I squeezed it in at lunch," she answered. "A pretty good one, in fact. I felt great the rest of the afternoon."

"Good for you," I said. "And how was your day?"

"Nothing like last week, that's for sure. Things are a lot calmer in the office. For a few minutes there, I felt like I had time to actually settle in at my desk and take a breath."

I smiled. "My day was pretty interesting."

"Yeah?"

"Have you ever heard of a guy named Joey Taglieri?"

She frowned. "You mean the attorney?"

"That's him."

"I've seen his commercials. They run in the mornings."

"What do you think about them?"

"About what?"

"The commercials."

"I don't really remember much about them. Why?"

I told her what we'd talked about and my thoughts in the aftermath.

"Are you sure you want to do that?" she asked, sounding skeptical.

"What do you mean?"

"Don't you think that it's kind of lowbrow? Lawyer commercials? Didn't Peters stop taking on attorneys because other clients didn't approve?"

"Yeah, but it's not as though I've got any other clients to worry about. I just want to get something going, you know? And he clearly spends a lot on advertising."

She nodded and took a sip of her wine. "Yeah, okay. If that's what you think is best."

Not exactly a ringing endorsement, but because she seemed to be in a better mood than she had been lately, I cleared my throat. "Have you found a day care center for London yet?"

"When have I had the chance?"

"Would you like me to start getting some recommendations?"

"No," she said, sounding put out. "I'll do it. It's just . . ."

"Just what?"

"Do we really have to sign her up now? She'd have to give up piano and tennis and art, and you've been able to get her everywhere she needs to be so far."

"They have activities at day care."

"I'm just saying that with her being so upset on Saturday night, I'm not sure it's such a good idea. School's going to be starting in a few weeks anyway."

"It's not a few weeks," I said, doing a quick calculation. "It's *five* more weeks."

"And this is about our daughter. What's best for her. Once school starts, you'll have plenty of time to concentrate on your business. Just keep doing what you're doing and when you have a meeting, drop her off at your mom's house."

"My mom can't watch London every day. She told me she has other things to do."

"She said that? Why didn't you tell me?"

Because you pretty much ignored me all week, nor did you ask about my work at all. "This isn't about my mom, Vivian. I was trying to talk to you about day care."

"I *hear* you. I *get* it. You think ditching your daughter with a bunch

130

of strangers is a good idea so you can be free to do what you want instead."

"I didn't say that."

"You didn't have to. It amounts to the same thing. You're being selfish."

"I'm not being selfish."

"Of course you are. She's our daughter. She's struggling."

"One time," I said. "She had a temper tantrum because you were out of town."

"No. She was upset because her entire world has changed, and now you want to make it even worse. I can't understand why you think it's such a great idea to dump her. Don't you like spending time with her?"

I felt my jaw clench and I exhaled slowly, trying to keep my voice steady.

"Of course I do. But you said I would have to watch her for a week, two at the most."

"What I also *said* was that I wanted to do what's best for our daughter! I haven't had the time to find the right place, and now by the time I do find it and get her signed up, school will be about to start and what would be the point?"

"She'll still need a place to go after school lets out," I said.

"I'll talk to London about it, okay?"

"You'll talk to London about day care?"

"I assume that you haven't. I have no idea how she'd feel about it."

"She's five years old," I said. "She doesn't know enough to know what to think about day care."

"Mommy? I'm hungry."

I turned and saw London in the doorway of the kitchen. Vivian glared at me and I knew we were both wondering how much she'd heard.

"Hey sweetheart," Vivian said, immediately lightening her tone. "Dinner will be ready in a few minutes. Want to help me set the table?"

"Okay," London said, and Vivian moved to the cupboard. She and London set the table; I served and brought the food over.

After London had taken a few bites, she smiled at me.

"Dinner is really good, Daddy."

"Thanks, sweetheart," I said, feeling my heart warm just a little.

My marriage with Vivian might be a little shaky at present and my business going nowhere fast, but at least, I thought to myself, I was learning how to cook.

It didn't make me feel any better.

CHAPTER 10

Moving Forward

When I was a kid, summers were the most glorious time of life. Because my parents believed in hands-off, free-range parenting, I'd usually be out the door before ten and wouldn't return until dinner. There were no cell phones to keep track of me and whenever my mom called a neighbor to ask where I was, the neighbor was often just as clueless as to her own child's whereabouts. In fact, there was only one rule as far as I could tell: I had to be home at half past five, since my parents liked to eat dinner as a family.

I can't remember exactly how I used to spend those days. I have recollections in snapshot form: building forts or playing king of the hill on the high part of the jungle gym or chasing after a soccer ball while attempting to score. I remember playing in the woods, too. Back then, our home was surrounded by undeveloped land, and my friends and I would have dirt-clod wars or play capture the flag; when we got BB guns, we could spend hours shooting cans and occasionally shooting at each other. I spent hours exploring on my bicycle, and whole weeks would pass where I'd wake every morning with nothing scheduled at all.

Of course, there were kids in the neighborhood who didn't lead that sort of carefree existence. They would head off to camp or participate in summer leagues for various sports, but back then, kids like that were the minority. These days, kids are scheduled from morning to night, and London was no exception, because parents demanded it.

But how did it happen? And why? What changed the outlook of parents in my generation? Peer pressure? Living vicariously through a child's success? Résumé building for college? Or was it simply fear that if their kids *were allowed to discover the world on their own, nothing good would come of it?*

I don't know.

I am, however, of the opinion that something has been lost in the process: the simple joy of waking in the morning and having nothing whatsoever to do.

"What's the problem with the commercials?" Joey Taglieri asked, repeating my question to him. It was Tuesday morning, tennis lesson number two. Still angry at me from the night before, Vivian had left that morning without speaking to me.

"The problem is they're boring," he said. "It's just me, talking to the camera in an overstuffed office. Hell, I fall asleep watching them and they cost me a fortune."

"How would you make them different?"

"When I was a kid, my family lived in Southern California for a few years when my dad was still in the Marines. Hated it there, by the way. So did my mom. As soon as he retired, my family moved back to New Jersey. Both my parents were from there. You ever been to New Jersey?"

"I think I flew out of Newark a couple of times."

"That doesn't count. And don't believe all that crap you see on reality TV about Jersey either. It's a great place. I'd raise my daughter there if I could, but her mom's here and even if she's a coldhearted shrew, she's pretty good as a mom. But anyway, back to Southern California. There was this car dealer named Cal Worthington. Ever heard of him?"

"Can't say that I have."

"Old Cal Worthington had the greatest commercials of all time. Every commercial would introduce him and his dog Spot—except that Spot was anything but a dog. Spot might be monkey or a lion or elephant or whatever. There was even a killer whale once. Old Cal had a snappy little jingle that was impossible to forget, with a refrain that went, *Go see Cal, go see Cal, go see Cal.* Hell, I was eight years old and didn't give a crap about cars and I wanted to go to the dealership just to meet the guy and maybe see a few exotic animals. *That's* the kind of commercial I want."

"You want elephants in your commercials? And killer whales?"

"Of course not. But I do want something that people remember, something that makes some injured guy in a Barcalounger sit up and say to himself, 'I gotta see *that* guy. I want *him* to represent me.'"

"The problem is that legal commercials are regulated by the bar."

"Don't you think I know that? I also know that North Carolina generally falls on the advertising-is-free-speech side when it comes to regulations. If you're in advertising, you should know that, too."

"I do," I said. "But there's a difference between coming across as a professional and competent attorney that you can trust, and a low-class ambulance chaser."

"That's exactly what I said to the idiots who made the commercial. And still, they came back with something that's best described as *let's put the viewers into a coma.* Have you even seen them?"

"Of course I have. And actually, they're not that bad."

"Yeah? What's the office phone number then?"

"Excuse me?"

"The office phone number. It's there on the screen the whole time. If the commercials were so great, what's the number?"

"I don't know."

"Bingo. And that's the problem."

"They probably remember your name."

"Yeah. And that's another problem. Taglieri isn't exactly the most southern of names, you know, and that might turn some people off."

"There's not much you can do about your name."

"Don't get me wrong. I'm proud of my family name. I'm just noting another problem I have with the commercials. There's too much of my name and not enough of the phone number."

"Gotcha," I said. "What do you think about other forms of advertising? Like billboards, websites, Internet ads, radio ads?"

"I don't know," he said. "I haven't much thought about it. And I only have so much money to spend."

"That makes sense," I said, suspecting that any more questions would do more harm than good. On the court, I watched London trying to volley with another girl, but there was more chasing after tennis balls than actual volleys.

"What does your wife do?" Joey asked into the silence.

"She works in PR," I said. "She just started a new job for one of the big developers around here."

"None of my wives worked. Of course, I work too much. Opposites attract and all that. Did I mention that you should always have a prenup?"

"Yes."

"It allows for none of the financial torture that those of the fairer sex like to inflict."

"You sound jaded."

"On the contrary. I love women."

"Would you ever get married again?"

"Of course. I'm a big believer in marriage."

"Really?"

"What can I tell you? I'm a romantic."

"So what happened?"

"I tend to fall in love with the crazy ones, that's what happened."

I laughed. "I'm glad I don't have that problem."

"You think so? She's still a woman."

"And?"

I had the sense Joey was trying to read me. "Hey," he finally said, "as long as you're happy, then I'm happy for you."

On Wednesday night after dance class, London was predictably glum as she crawled into the car.

"Tonight, since Mom's away, how about we have pizza for dinner?"

"Pizza isn't good for you."

"As long as you don't eat it all the time, it's fine. When was the last time you had pizza?"

She thought about it. "I can't remember. When is Mommy getting home again?"

"She'll be home tomorrow, sweetie."

"Can we call her?"

"I don't know if she's busy, but I'll send a text okay?"

"Okay," she said. In the backseat, she seemed smaller than usual.

"How about we go out for pizza anyway, just you and me? And after that, we'll stop and get ice cream?"

Though she didn't say yes, she didn't say no either, and we ended up at a place that made a decent thin-crust pizza. While we were waiting, Vivian called using FaceTime, and after that, London's mood began to lift. By the time we hit Dairy Queen she was chatting away happily. She spent most of the ride home talking about her friend Bodhi and his dog Noodle, and how he'd invited her over to his house so he could show her his light saber.

My first thought was that my daughter was far too young to be shown any boy's light saber; the next thought, which came an instant later, was that it was likely one of the playdates that Marge had suggested I set up, and that the light saber wasn't a metaphor but an actual play sword inspired by the *Star Wars* movies.

When we got home, London ran up the stairs to see Mr. and Mrs. Sprinkles and though I expected her to stay up there for a while, she appeared in the living room a few minutes later.

"Daddy?"

"Yes, sweetheart?"

"Can we go bike riding again?"

I stifled a groan. I was tired and wanted nothing more than to stay glued to the couch.

"Of course we can," I said instead, and as I stood, I suddenly remembered that Vivian had said that she'd wanted to watch London ride her bike the night before, but she must have forgotten.

Right?

London made three turns on her own. Wobbly, but she was able to regain her balance, and even during the other turns, I had to help less than I'd had to before. On the straightaways, I'd barely touched her bicycle at all. Because she was growing more confident, she rode faster, and by the end of our session, I was panting and sweating, my shirt soaked through.

"How about you take a bath upstairs while I take a shower downstairs?" I suggested. I wasn't sure what to expect. The last time Vivian was out of town hadn't gone so well.

Tonight she simply nodded. "Okay, Daddy."

I cleaned up and by the time I reached her room, London was sitting on the bed in her pajamas, the brush and bottle of detangling spray beside her. After the detangler worked its magic and I was finished with her hair, I propped myself against the headboard.

I read *Two by Two* along with a few other books. I kissed London goodnight, and as I was about to turn out the light, I heard her voice again.

"Daddy?"

"Yes?"

"What's day care? I heard you and Mommy talking about it."

"Day care is place where kids go when their moms and dads work, so that grown-ups can make sure you stay safe."

"Like a house?"

"Sometimes. But other times, it's in a building. They have toys and games and activities, and a lot of kids really like it because there's always something fun to do."

"But I like being with you and Mommy."

"I know you do. And we like being with you, too."

"Mommy doesn't. Not anymore."

"Of course she does. She loves you very much. She just has to work."

"Why does she have to work?"

"Because we need money to live. Without money, we couldn't buy food or clothes or toys or even Mr. and Mrs. Sprinkles."

She seemed to think about that. "If I give them back to the pet store, can Mommy stop working?"

"No, sweetheart. It doesn't work that way." I hesitated. "Are you okay, sweetie? You seem kinda sad."

"Mommy's gone again. I don't like it when she's gone."

"I know you don't, and I know she'd rather be here with you, too."

"When you were working, you always came home."

"Our jobs are different. She sometimes has to work in different cities."

"I don't like it."

I don't either, I thought. But there wasn't much I could do about it. Changing the subject, I put my arm around her. "You were so great riding your bike today."

"I was going super fast."

"Yes you were."

"You could barely keep up."

"Daddy could use more regular exercise. But I'm glad you enjoy it."

"It's fun going fast."

"Is it more fun than...piano lessons?" I asked, wiggling her slightly as I said the final two words.

She giggled. "Yes."

"Is it more fun than...tennis?"

"Yes."

"Is it more fun than...dance?"

"Yes."

"Is it more fun than...art?"

"Yes," she giggled. "But it's not more fun than Bodhi."

"Bodhi! Biking is WAYYYY more fun than Bodhi."

"No it isn't. Bodhi's WAYYYYY MORE fun."

"No, no, no."

"Yes, yes, yes." She giggled. "And I want to go to his house!"

By then, I was giggling, too. "Oh, no," I said. "I think you're WAYYYY too little to go over to BODHI'S house."

"No, I'm not. I'm BIG!"

"I don't know..."

"Yes, yes, yes. I'm big enough to go to Bodhi's house."

"Okaaaay," I said, "I guess I can ask his mom about that."

She beamed before putting her arms around my neck.

"I love you, Daddy."

"I love you, too, baby girl."

"I'm not a baby."

I squeezed her tight. "You'll always be my baby."

After turning out her lights and thinking I'd reached the point where I couldn't keep up with London any longer, I went to the garage and rolled my bicycle out of the garage. I'd had it for years and like London's had been, it was more neglected than damaged. I cleaned and oiled it, added WD-40 to the sprockets, and filled the tires before giving it a test ride.

Good enough, I thought, and heading inside, I perched my computer on the kitchen table. Pulling up YouTube, I watched a dozen different Cal Worthington commercials, thinking Taglieri had been right; the jingle was snappy and old Cal always had his dog Spot, which was always an exotic animal. The spots were memorable, but the whole thing came across as hucksterism at its finest. It's no wonder a kid would want to meet the car dealer, but I wasn't so sure that it would inspire the confidence necessary to land clients as an attorney.

I watched Taglieri's commercials again. Afterward, I jotted the number on a pad of paper, and matched the numbers to the letters, wondering if I could come up with a word or two to make the phone number more memorable. Nothing leapt immediately to mind with the number he had, but if he added a second toll-free number, there might be something I could do. I thought first of simply spelling his last name, but there were eight letters and seven numbers, so that wouldn't work, even if people could remember how to spell Taglieri, which was doubtful. I might be able to do something like W-I-N-4-Y-O-U or T-A-G-I-S-I-T or maybe even B-U-L-L-D-O-G, but none of those seemed exactly right. I hoped something better would come to me.

While I knew Taglieri's business would benefit from other forms of advertising, I focused first on the commercials because I knew it was a language he'd understand. How, then, to make them better—and different enough—to entice him to make the switch? I spent the next couple of hours jotting down various ideas until they began to solidify: Ditch the office and the suit; instead, let's show Taglieri outside the courthouse, in a sweater, looking neighborly, like someone who really cares. Similar script, but more…familiar and casual in mood and tone.

Definitely different, but then again, I wasn't sure it was quite up to the level of Cal Worthington either. Maybe it was because I was tired, but even as I continued to tinker with various slogans and ideas for images, my mind kept wandering to the ludicrous. You wanted raw hucksterism? How about you dress up in a superhero outfit and crash through doors to take on the evil insurance executives? Or how about I drape you in an American flag with images of bald eagles to show how trustworthy you are? Or maybe I'll have you do cool things, like break through blocks of wood like a karate expert, to show how you're ready to do whatever it takes to win?

As the images rolled through my mind, I found myself occasionally laughing, even if I couldn't imagine ever using them. Creativity and originality were fine, but people who were injured didn't want slapstick. They wanted experience and tenacity and trust, and I was struck by the notion that instead of trying to do all of that in a single commercial, it might be possible to capture those ideas individually in a series of commercials…

To me, it seemed right, and I felt my heart thump in my chest. I wondered if Taglieri would be interested in something like that. And if I could persuade him to sit down for a pitch, I knew I'd need to lay out the idea for at least two or three commercials. The first would be reminiscent of what he was doing now, but the second and third ones?

They had to be different and while one would be short, the other should feel like a special event, the kind of commercial that would only run every now and then, the kind that almost tells a story…

I could feel the gears turning, the beginning of an idea, and I continued to develop it over the next couple of hours, bits and pieces coming together.

As to the third commercial—a short one, using humor and focusing on a single theme—the idea leapt to mind just as I was shutting down the computer. Like magic, I was struck with yet another idea a few minutes after that, the creativity beginning to flow.

Feeling good about myself, I turned out the lights an hour later and though it took a while for me to fall asleep, once I was out, I slept better than I had in weeks.

"So you're saying that you want to take your pitch on a test drive, and I'm the sucker you've chosen?"

It was Thursday morning; Joey had dressed down today, in shorts and a T-shirt, just like me. And still, he was sweating through his shirt.

"I wouldn't phrase it that way."

"You know I'm a busy man, right? I don't know if I can handle any more business."

That was a new reason for rejection and I wasn't sure what to say. He must have seen my expression because he laughed.

"I'm kidding. I gotta get as many people as I can to walk into my office so I can find those nuggets that actually pay the bills. I've got three associates and three paralegals, and that means the bills are high. My specific area of law has become a volume business these days, even if it means sifting through all the nutjobs for a surefire winner. I need people calling the office and walking through that door."

"That's why I'm talking to you. I can help."

"How long would it take you to put something together?"

"I've already got some general ideas," I admitted. "It wouldn't take long at all to finalize everything."

He looked me over. "All right. Monday afternoon. One o'clock. I'm in court the rest of the week, and the week after that."

I couldn't fathom waiting that long, even if it meant that I'd be buried in work the next three days.

"One o'clock it is," I agreed.

"Just remember, though."

"What's that?"

"Don't waste my time. I hate when people waste my time."

That afternoon, knowing the presentation had to be as informative as possible with far more specific detail than the ones I'd done last week, I went to work. Though I was going to present a plan that offered a broad campaign in a variety of media, I started with the commercials because it seemed to be Taglieri's main area of interest. My first step was to start with the script and after the first drafts were complete, I began to cut and paste together generic images I pulled from the Internet, so Taglieri would be able to follow the flow of the commercials in the way I imagined. While I worked, London was content to play with her Barbies, but I worked from the kitchen table, so I could keep an eye on her.

Vivian rolled in a little past five. I gave her a quick rehash of my day before she spent some time with London and made dinner. It was only after I got London in bed that Vivian and I were able to get some alone time. I found her on the couch, flipping through a magazine, a nearly empty glass of wine on the end table beside her.

"Did she go down okay?"

"She was tired. Only a couple of books tonight."

"How's your work going?"

"There's a way to go, but I'll get it done."

"I noticed when I pulled in that you fixed up your bicycle."

"I want to be able to ride with London."

"She said that the two of you went riding again."

"She rode. I ran and almost died. Hence the repairs on my bike. She's getting pretty good. I can't keep up with her anymore."

"She's got a lot of energy."

"Yes she does."

She turned a page. "I was able to make some calls to day cares while I was out of town."

"Really?" I asked, feeling a mixture of astonishment and relief, along with a stab of guilt I hadn't expected. Our previous discussion of the matter had led me to believe she'd never call at all. "When did you have the time?"

She nodded. "When Walter was meeting with Senator Thurman. But it was just a preliminary call. I didn't schedule any appointments though because I wasn't sure about my travel schedule next week."

"You're traveling next week, too?"

"I think so. But I'm not sure what days yet."

"When do you think you'll find out?"

"I'm hoping by tomorrow, but who knows? I'll let you know as soon as I know."

I didn't know how Spannerman could believe that scheduling last-minute overnights was fair to employees, but then again, my experience of him told me that he probably didn't care.

"What did the day cares say?"

"I didn't speak to them very long. I just wanted a sense of some of the activities they offer, how many kids are there, things like that."

"Did you feel comfortable with them?"

"They seemed okay. The people I talked to were conscientious, but even they told me that we couldn't get a real sense of the places unless we actually visited."

"Makes sense," I said. "How was your trip, by the way?"

"Productive. In addition to the senator, Spannerman met with two different representatives, and our lobbyist. Now that the PAC has more funding, it's a lot easier to meet with the people we need to."

"That's not a surprise."

She shrugged. "So you had pizza last night, huh? And ice cream?"

"I figured she'd enjoy it. She wasn't in the best mood after dance."

"She'll like it more once she starts competing. That's when I started to like it."

"You used to dance?"

"I've told you that before."

Not that I could remember. "How long did you dance?"

She continued to flip through the magazine. "I don't know. Two or three years? What does it matter?"

"It doesn't. I was just making conversation."

"It's not a big deal. My teacher was nowhere near as good as London's. I wish she would have been. I probably would have kept at it longer." She reached for her glass. "Would you mind getting me another half a glass of wine? I'm exhausted and I really want to be able to sleep tonight. Especially since I promised to make up for our date night."

"Yeah," I said, glad she remembered. "Sure."

I rose from the couch and went to the kitchen, returning with a half a glass. By the time I got there, Vivian had turned the television to a reality show, and though we sat together for another hour, she retreated into silence, content to watch her show and flip through the magazine, as if I weren't there at all.

Friday morning, and as soon as I woke, my thoughts flashed to the presentation. I was out of bed minutes later, and as I'd done the day before, I worked from the kitchen table until it was time to head to art class. While London was painting, I parked myself at the coffee shop, and lost in thought, I didn't notice the passage of time. The next thing I knew, London's class was over.

Oops.

I gathered my things and walked quickly to the studio, feeling relief when I spotted London and Bodhi in the corner, heads together. I was about to call out to her when I saw Emily watching me with an amused expression.

"Hi, Russ."

"Oh, hey Emily. You're still here?"

She smiled, looking relaxed. "I saw you in the coffee shop a few minutes ago, and you looked pretty intense with whatever you were working on. When you didn't show up, I thought I'd wait until you got here to make sure London was okay."

"You didn't have to do that," I said.

"No worries. Believe me, my son was thrilled that you're late."

"Where is he?"

"My son?" She motioned in London's direction. "He's talking with your daughter."

I suppose I should have seen the resemblance; now that I knew, I could see it clearly. "Bodhi's your son?"

"Small world, huh?" As we watched them, she went on. "They're so cute at this age, aren't they? They're just so . . . innocent, you know?"

"I was thinking the same thing."

"No hamsters today?"

"Was I supposed to bring them?"

She laughed. "Not that I know about. But Bodhi loves Mr. and Mrs. Sprinkles. Ever since she brought them, he's been asking me if we could get some hamsters, too."

"Sorry. If it makes you feel any better, London wants to play with Noodle. And see Bodhi's light saber."

"Don't get me started on the light saber. Bodhi brings that thing everywhere. He started to cry when I wouldn't let him bring it into church last weekend. How's your work coming?"

"It's going well. I'm hoping to finish this weekend. How's your painting?"

"It's been hard to get back into the rhythm. Tough couple of years, I guess."

"Makes sense," I agreed. "I haven't been able to swing by the gallery to see your work yet."

"I didn't expect you to. I'm guessing that between work and London, you're on the go pretty much every day. London's schedule is packed. Dance, piano, art, and now tennis." When she saw my expression, she went on. "What can I tell you? Bodhi talks about her all the time. He wants a playdate."

"So does London, but frankly, I'm not even sure how to go about setting up something like that."

I sensed her amusement. "It's not that complicated, Russ," she said. "We talk about it. As in, what's your schedule like? Do you have any time on Monday afternoon? Can London come over?"

As soon as she said it, I knew it would be perfect. But...

When I didn't answer, she went on. "Do you have something else planned?"

"No," I answered, "it's not that. Actually, I'm supposed to have a presentation at one o'clock."

"Then it's perfect. I can pick her up here and bring her to the house. I'll feed her lunch and let the two of them hang out until you come by to get her."

"Isn't that almost like babysitting? Since I'll be off working?"

"That's called a happy coincidence. Let's plan on it, okay?"

"Are you sure? It feels like I'm taking advantage of you."

She laughed. "You haven't changed much, have you?"

"What do you mean?"

"You worry too much about things you shouldn't. You don't think that if I had something to do, I wouldn't find someone to watch Bodhi?"

"Thank you," I said. "That'll help me out a lot."

"I'm happy to do it, and Bodhi will be thrilled. Of course, he's going to be super excited all weekend, so I'll have to deal with that. And speak of the devil, here they come."

I watched the two of them scampering toward us.

"Mom?" Bodhi asked. "Can we go to Chick-fil-A for lunch?"

"Sure," Emily answered.

I felt London tug on my sleeve. "Daddy? Can we go, too?"

"You want to go to Chick-fil-A?"

"Please?" she pleaded.

I sensed Emily waiting for an answer, but I couldn't tell whether she was happy or bothered by the idea that I might join them.

"Yeah," I said. "We can go."

Chick-fil-A was bustling. London and Bodhi ran off toward the climbing play area while Emily and I made small talk in line. After picking up our order, we called the kids over and they wolfed down their food before rushing back to the climbing area.

"I like coming here because it helps Bodhi get some of his energy out. He's been a little rambunctious ever since his dad left. His dad isn't around much and it's been hard on him."

"I'm sorry to hear that," I said.

"It is what it is. There's not much I can do about it."

"Is there a way to talk to your ex into spending more time with him?"

"I don't see how. He moved back to Australia last April. Of course, he's coming in the week after next and he'll be in town until the third or fourth week of September. Some big project or whatever, and he said he'd like to see Bodhi as much as possible. Which is great, but it'll throw Bodhi's schedule out of whack until then, and after that, I have no idea when he'll be back. I have no idea how Bodhi's going to handle his dad leaving again." She shook her head. "I'm sorry. I swore to myself that I wasn't going to be one of those women who talk non-stop about their ex."

"Sometimes it's hard not to, especially when it comes to kids."

"I know you're right, but it still gets boring. Hell, I get bored hearing myself talk about it." She folded her hands on the table in front of her. "So how about you tell me exactly what you're working on. You were completely zoned in when I saw you."

"It's a presentation for a prospective client. An attorney, and it's kind of a big deal for me. My business hasn't exactly taken off the way I wanted it to."

"I'm sure he'll love your ideas."

"How would you know that?"

"Because you're smart and creative. You always were. They're your gifts."

"I always thought you were the creative one."

"That's why we got along as well as we did." She shrugged. "Well, until the end, anyway."

"How does this painting thing work?"

"You mean as a profession? Or how did I get started?"

"Both. I knew you were passionate about painting, but you told me you thought you'd end up getting your master's and teaching somewhere."

"I just got lucky. After you and I broke up, I went a little crazy there for a while and all I did was paint. I took all the hurt and angst I was feeling and somehow got it down on various canvases. By the end, they were stacked in my parents' garage, and I had no idea what to do with all of them. I wasn't even sure any of the paintings were any good. A little while after that, I met David and life moved forward, and eventually, I heard about this festival of the arts in Greensboro. I decided on a whim to rent a booth and even before I finished setting everything up, I met a gallery owner. He examined all my work and agreed on the spot to bring in some of my work. Within a month, it had sold out."

"That's amazing," I said.

"Like I said, I was lucky."

"It's more than luck. But it makes me feel bad."

"Why?"

"Because I was the cause of all that hurt and angst. What I did to you is still one of my biggest regrets and I'm sorry."

"You already apologized for that a long time ago," she responded.

"I know. But still."

"Guilt is a wasted emotion, Russ. That's what my mom tells me, anyway. Besides, I could have probably handled it better, too."

"You handled it fine."

"If you say so. What I can say is that my career wouldn't be where it is without that experience. And my marriage wouldn't have lasted as long as it did, either. Let's just say I had to learn to forgive."

"David had an affair?"

"Not just one. Many."

"Why did you stay?"

She nodded toward Bodhi. "Because of him. David may have been a terrible husband, but he was also Bodhi's hero. Still is, I'm sure." She paused before she shook her head. "And there I go again, talking about my ex."

"It's all right."

She was quiet for a moment. "You know what the hardest thing is about being divorced? It's like I'm not even sure what it means to be a single, independent adult. I pretty much went from you to David, and now here I am, with no idea what I'm supposed to be doing. Between work and Bodhi, it's not like I have time to hang out in bars or go to parties. And frankly, that's never been my style anyway. It's just that..." I could see a trace of sadness in her expression as she searched for the right words. "It isn't the life I ever imagined. Half the time, I feel like a stranger in my own skin."

"I can't imagine what it would be like to be single."

"I don't like it. But believe me, the other option is sometimes even worse."

I nodded, unsure what to say. In time, she sighed and went on. "I'm just glad I'm able to work from home. Otherwise it would have been harder on Bodhi than it already is."

"He seems like a happy child to me."

"Most of the time, he is. But every now and then, he melts down."

"I think that's true of every child. Even London can throw a mean temper tantrum."

"Yeah?"

I told her about the previous weekend. When I finished, Emily wore an uncertain expression.

"Wait a minute. When Vivian got home, she didn't take London to the blueberry farm?" she asked.

"She said it was too hot so they went to the mall instead. London didn't seem to mind. I think she was happy because her mom was home. She's still getting used to the idea that Vivian is working while I take care of her."

"From what I can tell, you're doing a good job with her."

"I'm not so sure. Half the time, I feel like I'm faking it."

"So do I. That's normal."

"Really?"

"Of course. I love Bodhi, but it's not like I wake up excited about bringing him to the dentist or helping him clean his room or running him here and there. That's normal. It's the stuff of parenting."

"I still feel like I'm not doing enough. Yesterday and this morning, I worked and pretty much left her on her own. I mean, I was there and kept an eye on her, but it's not like I spent meaningful time with her."

"Don't be so hard on yourself. I'm sure she was fine. And you'll get better at the whole balance between work and parenting thing. Look at today. You successfully set up your first playdate."

That I did. "Thanks," I said. "I'll pick her up from your place as soon as I'm done."

"Sounds great."

"Of course, you're forgetting something."

"What's that?"

"You're going to need my address, aren't you? And my phone number?" She reached for her phone. "Give me your number and I'll text you the info."

I gave it to her just as the kids reached the table.

"Hi, Mom. We're done," Bodhi announced.

"Did you have fun?"

"We climbed to the top."

150

"I saw that. You're a great climber. And guess what? London is coming over on Monday to meet Noodle."

Both of their faces lit up. "Really? Thanks, Mom! Can she bring Mr. and Mrs. Sprinkles?"

When Emily looked to me, I raised my hands. "It's your call. But they have a travel cage."

"Why not?" Emily answered. "I'm sure Noodle will just love that."

I laughed before we said our goodbyes, and as London and I began walking to the car, I felt a twinge of unease at the thought that I'd had lunch with Emily, something I hadn't done with Vivian in a long time, and that the conversation had seemed anything but forced.

But I was probably making too much of it, wasn't I?

CHAPTER 11

And Then There Was One

*E*mily had told me that guilt was a wasted emotion, but I'm not so sure about that. I understood the point she was making—that it does nothing to change the past—but guilt was a tool my mom used effectively as she raised Marge and me. "Clean your plate—there are starving people in the world" was a common expression, especially when Mom served up leftover surprise, which was an accurate description of the dish. Whatever was left over in the fridge at the end of the week was either tossed together in a stew or covered with lasagna noodles and Marge and I would wonder how teriyaki beef and fettuccini chicken could possibly be paired in a way that didn't make us gag. Some other common ones—"If you really cared about this family, you'd take out the garbage," and, "Maybe one day you'll love your mom enough to sweep the back porch"—all had the effect of making my shoulders cave in and wonder how I could be such an awful child.

My mom felt no guilt whatsoever about using guilt as a tool to control us, and sometimes, I wish could be more like that. I wish I could simply forgive myself and move on, but then again, if I really wanted to change, why didn't I? Once, when London was still a young toddler, I brought her to a trail just off the park. We didn't walk long or far, but at the halfway point, I could tell she was getting tired and I pointed out a stump where she could rest.

Seconds later, I heard her cry out, and then all at once she was screaming wildly in obvious pain. I scooped her into my arms in a mad panic, trying to figure out what on earth was happening when I spotted a few ants on her leg.

But they weren't simply ants. They were fire ants, ants with both jaws and stingers, and wildly aggressive. They swarmed, biting and stinging, leaving welts, and while I swatted at the ants, even more kept appearing. They were in her clothes, in her socks, even in her shoes. In that instant, I put her down and started ripping the clothes from her body as fast as I could, even her diaper. I swatted and brushed, getting stung countless times in the process and rushed my screaming child as fast as I could to the car.

I didn't know what to do. This, like so many things, was Vivian's area of expertise, and I drove like a wild man for the five minutes it took me to reach home. I carried London into the house and Vivian took over immediately, her tone sharp with me but soft with London. She brought London into the bathroom and applied rubbing alcohol to the already swelling stings, gave her an antihistamine, and started applying cold washcloths to the affected area.

Perhaps it was the efficiency and confidence she showed that finally ended London's hysterics. Meanwhile, I felt like a passerby on a city street, in the aftermath of a horrible accident, amazed that Vivian had known exactly what to do.

In the end, there was no long-term damage. I went back to the park and disposed of London's clothes in a trash bin, since the ants were still swarming over them. The swelling lingered for a day or two but London was soon back to her normal self. She doesn't remember the event—I've asked her—and while that makes me feel better, I still experience guilt when I think back on that awful day. And guilt serves to teach me a lesson. I'm now cautious about where London sits whenever we're in the woods or in the park, and that's a good thing. She's never been swarmed by fire ants again.

Guilt, in other words, isn't always wasted. It can keep us from making the same mistake twice.

After lunch at Chick-fil-A with Emily, I spent the afternoon working. Wanting to get a sense of how much Taglieri was spending, I spoke to a friend in sales at the cable company. It turned out that Taglieri was paying premium rates and had too many poor slots, a bummer for him but a godsend to me. After that, I touched base with the head of the film crew I intended to use. We'd worked together in the past, and we went over the kinds of shots I wanted, as well as the projected cost.

All that information was jotted on a pad of paper for easy retrieval when I needed to add it to the presentation. After that, I continued to perfect the scripts and tweaked a few more of the generic images I'd pulled together; by that point, my outline for two of the commercials was nearly complete.

I was in a good mood as date night approached, despite having to bring London to dance with the evil Ms. Hamshaw. Vivian made it home at a reasonable hour, and after we got London to bed, we ate dinner by candlelight and ended up in the bedroom. And yet, there was less magic than I hoped for; it wasn't until Vivian started on her third glass of wine that she began to relax and while I know that the honeymoon period of any marriage eventually comes to an end, I suppose that I'd always believed that it would be replaced by something deeper, a *two-of-us-against-the-universe* bond or even genuine mutual appreciation. For whatever reason—maybe because I sensed a continuing distance between us—the night ended with me feeling vaguely disappointed.

On Saturday morning, Vivian took advantage of her *Me Time* before spending time with London the rest of the day. It gave me the quiet time I needed to focus on other areas of the presentation: an updated website, Internet advertising, billboards and sporadic periods of radio advertising. I added in projected costs for everything over the course of a year, including vendors' fees and my own, along with a slide showing Taglieri's projected savings.

I worked on Sunday as well, finishing up on Sunday afternoon, and wanted to go through it with Vivian. But for whatever reason, she seemed to be in no mood to listen or even talk to me, and the rest of the evening unfolded in the same stilted way that seemed to be becoming our norm. While I understood that our lives had recently veered in directions neither of us could have anticipated, I found myself wondering not whether Vivian still loved me, but whether she even liked me at all.

On Monday morning before London woke, I wandered into the master bathroom while Vivian was applying mascara.

"Do you have a minute?"

"Sure. What's up?"

"Are you upset with me? You seemed irritated last night."

"Really? You want to do this now?"

"I know it's probably not a good time..."

"No, it's not a good time. I have to leave for work in fifteen minutes. Why do you always do this?"

"Do what?"

"Try to make me the bad guy."

"I'm not trying to make you the bad guy. After I finished the presentation, you barely spoke to me."

Her eyes flashed. "You mean because you pretty much ignored me and London all weekend?"

"I wasn't ignoring you. I was working."

"Don't make excuses. You could have taken a break here and there, but instead, you did what you wanted to do. Just like always."

"I'm just trying to say that it seems like you've been angry with me for a while now. You barely spoke to me on Thursday night either."

"Oh, for God's sake. I was tired! Don't try to make me feel bad for it. Have you completely forgotten about date night? Even though I was tired on Friday night, too, I got all dressed up and we had sex because I knew you wanted it. I'm tired of feeling like I never do enough."

"Vivian—"

"Why do you always have to take things so personally?" she demanded, cutting me off. "Why can't you just be happy with me? It's not like you're perfect either, but you don't see me coming in and complaining about the fact you can't even support your family anymore."

Her words made me flinch. What did she think I'd been trying to do all weekend? But she didn't want an answer. Instead, she walked past me without a word, grabbed her workout bag and stormed from the house, the front door slamming behind her.

The sound must have awakened London, because she came down the stairs a couple of minutes later and found me sitting at the kitchen table. She was still in her pajamas, her hair puffing out on the side.

"Were you and Mommy fighting?"

"We were just talking," I said. I hadn't yet recovered from Vivian's outburst and felt sick to my stomach. "I'm sorry if the door was too loud."

She rubbed her nose and looked around. Even groggy, I thought she was the most beautiful little girl in the world. "Where is she?" she finally asked.

"She had to go to work, sweetie."

"Oh," she said. "Do I have tennis this morning?"

"Yes," I said. "And art class with Bodhi. We have to remember to bring your hamsters."

"Okay," she said.

"How about a hug, baby girl?"

She came over and wrapped her arms around me, giving me a squeeze.

"Daddy?"

"Yes?"

"Can I have Lucky Charms?"

I held my daughter close, thinking how much I'd needed a hug. "Of course you can."

Taglieri wasn't in the bleachers that morning; in his place, I saw a woman I presumed was ex number three because she walked past me with Taglieri's daughter. I'm not sure what I expected—bleached blond hair, maybe—but she seemed to blend in well with the other mothers.

I brought my computer with the intention of rehearsing my presentation but I found it hard to concentrate. My mind kept circling back to the cutting words Vivian had spoken and while I may have worked all weekend, her reaction to it struck me as out of proportion and completely unfair. I wished again that I could make her happy, but I wasn't, and her expression as I'd stood before her made that clear.

It wasn't simply her anger at me that I'd witnessed, after all.

I'd also seen, and heard, her contempt.

"Are you okay?" Emily asked.

I'd walked into the art studio and London made a beeline toward

156

Bodhi, holding Mr. and Mrs. Sprinkles in their carry-cage. As I watched her, Emily must have seen something in my expression, but I didn't want to tell her about Vivian and me. It seemed wrong somehow.

"I'm okay. It was kind of a rough morning."

"I can tell," she said. "How can we turn that frown upside down?"

"I have no idea," I answered. "A million dollars might help."

"Can't do that," she said, "but how about a Tic Tac? I think I have some in my purse."

Despite my mood, I cracked a grin. "I'll pass. But thanks."

"We're still on for today, right? Bodhi's been talking about it since he woke up."

"Yeah, we're on."

"Are you ready for your presentation?"

"I hope so," I said. I shifted the laptop from one hand to the other, thinking it felt strangely heavy. "Actually, I'm more nervous than I thought I would be. Taglieri would be my first client, and I haven't had a chance to even rehearse my pitch yet. When I was at Peters, there was always someone around who'd listen."

"Would it help if you ran through it with me? I know I'm not in advertising, but I'd be happy to lend an ear."

"I can't ask you to do that."

"You didn't. I'm volunteering. I have some free time. And besides, I've never heard an advertising pitch before. It'll be a new experience for me."

Though I knew she was offering to be nice, I felt the need to go over it, if only so I wouldn't continue to replay the argument.

"Thanks," I said. "I'll owe you."

"You already owe me. Playdate, remember? Not that I'm keeping score."

"Of course not."

We strolled to the coffee shop, got our drinks and sat at a table. First, I walked Emily through a few slides on the PowerPoint that spoke to the power of advertising, another few slides showing breakdowns of advertising dollars in the legal world, and still more that profiled a few other legal firms in Charlotte, and their estimated revenues. From there, the presentation emphasized the power of using a broader advertising strategy, across multiple platforms, to increase awareness, and a mockup of the kind of user-friendly and up-to-date website that would be far more effective. I then showed a sampling of various legal commercials, along with Taglieri's, emphasizing the lack of differentiation. Finally I went over the slides that showed how I could not only create an overall advertising campaign—and film three commercials—but also save him money.

She pointed to the computer. "Do you always do this much work beforehand?"

"No," I said. "But I think this is the only shot I'll have with this guy."

"I'd hire you."

"You haven't seen the commercials yet."

"You seem more than competent already. But, okay, show me."

I took a deep breath and showed her the outline for the two commercials I'd be pitching, the first somewhat similar to what he was already doing.

My idea was to open with two photographs of auto accidents, a photo of a construction site, and another of a warehouse. Off screen, Taglieri is speaking: *"If you've been injured in an accident or on the job, you need help from an expert."* Taglieri appears next, walking slowly in front of the courthouse, wearing a cardigan and addressing the camera.

"My name is Joey Taglieri and my specialty is helping people who are injured. It's what I do best, and I'm on your side. Consultations are free and there's no cost until I get you the money that you deserve. I've won millions of dollars for my clients, and now I want to help you get your life back. Let me fight for you. Call..."

There was a toll-free number followed by I-N-J-U-R-E-D, and Emily furrowed her brow. "I like that he's outside and not in an office," she offered.

"It makes him more approachable, don't you think? I also wanted to make sure the phone number was memorable."

"And you said you have a second commercial?"

I nodded. "This one has a different feel," I offered.

It opened with everyday images of Charlotte—both places and people—while Taglieri spoke off camera in a calm voice.

"Welcome to another day in the Queen City. Tourists come to experience the sights and sounds and smells, but our best attractions aren't our barbecue, or our racetrack, or our sports teams, or our lakes and trails, or our skyline. It's our people. Our community. Our friends and families and coworkers and neighbors who make this place feel like home. And when one of them is injured on the job, a stranger at an insurance company, maybe someone who can't even find Charlotte on the map, will do everything he or she can to deny coverage, even if lives are ruined in the process. To me, that's just plain wrong."

From there, the camera shifts to Taglieri, wearing a shirt and tie, but no jacket.

"I'm Joey Taglieri, and if you've been injured and need some help, give me a call. After all, we're neighbors. I'm on your side and we're in this together."

When it was finished, I tapped the keyboard, shutting down the screen. "What do you think?"

"Very folksy."

"Too folksy?"

"Not at all," she said. "And it's definitely original."

"Is that good or bad?"

"He'll be blown away."

"I just don't want to waste his time. He hates when people waste his time."

"He told you that?"

"Yes."

"At least he's honest. I like that."

As I walked into the law offices of Joey Taglieri, my nerves were still jangling and I had to force my hands not to shake. I'd just finished running through most of the presentation and the first of the commercials—I held the second commercial and financials in reserve—and when I finished, I waited for Joey to say something. Anything. Instead, he continued to stared at the final image.

"Is that phone number available?"

"As of last Friday, yes. And it's the kind of number that people will remember."

Taglieri nodded. "I like the number, so that part's a definite. And I get how the other kinds of advertising will help. But I can't say that the commercial really grabs me."

I nodded, knowing he'd feel that way. "After hearing what you said about Cal Worthington, my concept is less about having *one commercial* than a *series of commercials*. At the same time, I didn't want to go too far out on a limb. The reason personal injury attorneys use commercials like these is because they do work."

"A series of commercials? Won't that be expensive?"

I pulled up the slides outlining the estimated costs that I'd put together.

"Upfront, there will certainly be additional costs, but over the course of a year, you'll not only save money but get a lot more in return. Not only more commercials, but more extensive advertising, in a variety of ways."

He zeroed in on the line that showed how much he was spending and pointed toward it. "How did you know how much I was paying?"

"I'm good at my job," I said.

I wasn't sure what he thought about my answer. In the silence, he fiddled with a pen on his desk. "What would be your plan, then? How would you begin?"

"I'd get to work on the website and Internet advertising, especially search platforms, so you'll have better exposure there. Simultaneously, we'd schedule filming for the first two commercials. We'll also get the voice-over done. I'm almost certain that I can have the first one airing by October, when the new website is ready. That dovetails perfectly with the timing for Internet advertising and search prioritization. The second commercial will be ready for the holiday season, and I'm confident it'll be something that people remember. But you'll be the judge of that."

"All right. Let's see your idea."

I showed him. Afterward, he leaned back in his chair and rubbed his jaw. "I don't know what I think," he said. "I've never seen anything like it."

"That's the point. It forces you to remember it because it makes you think."

"It doesn't have much of a sales pitch."

"No, it doesn't, but it keeps your name out there. I'm thinking we should follow that up with a couple of billboards in January. Two fantastic ones are coming available around then, and I'd like to lock them up if you're in agreement. And then, of course, there are the third and fourth commercials. Like the first commercial, those will air year-round, one starting in October or November depending on filming schedules, and the other in January, rotating after that. They're shorter, single theme, and humorous."

"Let's see what you have."

"I didn't put together any slides for them."

"Why not?"

"You're not my client yet."

He seemed to think about that. "How about you give me a hint?"

"It would focus on your experience."

I had the sense that the meeting had become more important to him than he'd anticipated, always a good sign.

"I'll need a bit more than that."

"All right," I said. "But only for one of them. Imagine a little girl, around eight years old, sitting at a legal desk surrounded by law books, including one that says 'Personal Injury.' She's scribbling on a yellow legal pad, looking harried, and reaches over to the phone and says into the speaker, *Dolores? Can you bring me another chocolate milk?* At that point, the screen fades to black, and words appear as if being typewritten onto the screen.

"When you've been injured on the job and need help with your medical bills, you don't want a lawyer who's new on the job. You want a lawyer with experience. You want someone who's won millions of dollars for his clients. You want Joey Taglieri."

When I finished, Joey began to grin. "I like it."

I nodded without responding. I'd learned over the years that saying nothing was often the best thing I could do when it came to a client who was considering pulling the trigger.

No doubt, Joey knew that, too, because he leaned back in his chair again. "You should know that I've checked into your background," he said. "After you talked me into this meeting, I called your old boss."

I felt my chest constrict. "Oh," I said.

"He was vague, as bosses always are, but he said that you went out on your own a couple of months ago. You told me you had your own firm, but you didn't mention that you just started it."

I felt my mouth go dry "My firm might be new, but I've been in advertising for thirteen years."

"He also suggested to me that instead of talking to him, it would probably be better if I called to get recommendations or opinions from your current clients."

"Oh," I said again.

"Do you think I could do that? Contact some of your other clients?"

"Uh... Well..."

"That's what I thought you might say. If I were to guess, my suspicion is that you don't have any other clients as of yet. So after I spoke to your boss, I drove by your office this weekend. Turns out I recognized the place. A former client of mine owns the place. It's not exactly the kind of office that inspires confidence."

I forced myself to keep my voice steady. "For the most part, I meet clients at their place of business. And if you want to talk to previous clients, I can probably get you some names. I've worked with dozens of clients in the Charlotte area."

"I know that, too," he said, raising his hand. "I called a few of them already. Three of them, to be exact. They're still with Peters and they weren't thrilled at the idea of talking to me until I told them I had no intention of telling Peters anything about it."

"How did you...?"

When I trailed off, he finished the question for me. "Know who to contact? You're good at your job and I'm good at mine. But anyway, each of them said you were terrific. Very creative, very hardworking, and very good at what you do."

"Why are you telling me this?"

"Because I want you to know that while I'm not thrilled with the idea of being your first, and only, client, I've been trying to convince myself that it probably means you'll have more time to work on my campaign. Frankly, I'm not sure I've gotten there yet. But after seeing what you've done, I'll admit that I'm impressed with the thought process you put into all this."

He stopped there and I took a deep breath.

"What exactly are you saying?"

With my head spinning after the meeting with Taglieri, I drove to Emily's house. Had it not been for the navigation system on my phone, I never would have been able to find it. Though not far from my home, I'd never detoured through that particular neighborhood, and the main access road wasn't particularly well marked. The lots were heavily wooded and the homes were midcentury modern, with large windows, cedar plank siding, and main levels that rose and fell with the topography.

After pulling up the drive, I followed a curving walkway that passed over a koi pond and led to the front door. When Emily opened the door, I was struck again by the warmth of her smile.

"I didn't expect you so soon," she said. "For some reason, I thought your presentation would take longer. Come on in."

If the argument with Vivian made it hard to concentrate and the meeting with Taglieri left my head spinning, then stepping into the home of a recently divorced woman with whom I'd shared a bed made the day seem even more surreal. It felt wrong somehow, inappropriate, and I reminded myself that I'd simply come by to get my daughter. It was no different than picking her up from my mom's, but even so, the feeling that I was doing something illicit only intensified as Emily motioned toward the stairs.

"The kids are up in the playroom with Noodle. They finished lunch about half an hour ago so they haven't been up there that long."

I nodded, making sure to maintain distance between us. "Did they have a good time?"

"They've had a great time," she said. "They've been laughing a lot. I think your daughter is in love with the dog."

"That doesn't shock me in the slightest," I said. "How did Noodle do with the hamsters?"

"He sniffed the cage for a few seconds and that was about it."

"Good." I put my hands in my pockets, the voice inside my head continuing to whisper that I shouldn't be here, that my presence in Emily's home was inappropriate. Turning away from Emily, I surveyed the room. With an open floor plan and shaded sunlight streaming through large windows along the rear of the house, it was comfortable and eclectic, with odds and ends scattered throughout the room, the home of an *artist*. On the walls, I spotted a handful of large paintings that I assumed she'd done.

"You have a beautiful home," I said, trying to keep the conversation innocuous.

"Thank you," she said, sounding far more at ease than I was feeling. "I've actually been thinking about selling the place. There's too much maintenance, and a couple of the rooms are in serious need of renovation. Of course, I've been saying that ever since David moved out. I'm sorry it's such a mess."

"I didn't notice," I said. "Are those some of your paintings?"

She moved closer to me, not too close, but close enough that I was able to catch a whiff of the honeysuckle shampoo she used. "Some of my older work. I've been wanting to trade a few of them out for some more recent paintings, but that's been on the back burner, too."

"I can understand why the gallery owner loves your work."

"They remind me of when I was pregnant with Bodhi. They're darker and less textured than a lot of what I do now. Moodier, too. Of course, I was sick as a dog for months when I was pregnant, so maybe that has something to do with it. Hold on a second." She walked toward the staircase. "Bodhi? London?" she called out. "Are you still okay?"

In chorus, I heard their answer. "Yes!"

"Your dad's here, London."

Footsteps pounded overhead and I caught sight of my daughter peeking through the railings. "Daddy? Can I stay longer? Bodhi has an extra light saber and it's red! And we're playing with Noodle!"

I looked toward Emily. "It's fine with me," she said with a shrug. "She's keeping Bodhi busy and happy, which makes my life easy."

"Maybe a few more minutes," I called up. "But we can't stay long. Remember that you have dance tonight."

"With Ms. Hamshaw?" Emily asked. When I nodded, Emily went on. "I've heard some pretty interesting things about her. And by 'interesting,' I mean not particularly good."

"I'm not sure London enjoys it all that much," I admitted.

"So pull her out."

With Vivian, such things aren't always that easy, I thought to myself. In the silence, Emily hooked a thumb toward the kitchen. "Would you like some sweet tea while you wait? I just made a pitcher."

I heard the voice in my head again, this time telling me to politely decline, but instead, I found myself saying, "Sounds good."

I followed her toward the breakfast table in the kitchen; the hamster cage was on the floor in front of French doors that led to the backyard. Off to the side, I saw another room, obviously her studio. There were paintings stacked along the walls and another on an easel; there was an apron draped over the battered desk, along with hundreds of containers of paint.

"This is where you work?"

"My studio," she said, pulling out the pitcher of tea. "It used to be a screened porch, but we glassed it in when we bought the house. It's got perfect light in the morning."

"Is it hard to work at home?"

"Not really. But I've always painted at home so I don't know any different."

"How does that work with Bodhi?"

She poured the tea into the glasses, added ice to both, and brought them to the table. "I work in the mornings before we really get going for the day, but even after that, it's not too bad. If I get the urge to paint, he'll head upstairs and play or watch TV. He's gotten used to it. "

She took a seat and I followed her lead, still feeling far too self-conscious. If Emily felt the same, she didn't show it.

"How did it go with Taglieri?"

"It went well," I said. "He hired me. For the entire campaign I proposed."

"That's great!" she cried. "Congratulations! I knew you'd nail it. You've got to be thrilled."

"I don't think I've had time to really process it yet."

"It'll sink in soon enough, I'm sure. Are you going to celebrate tonight?"

I remembered Vivian's behavior that morning. "We'll see."

"He's your first client. You have to celebrate. But before that, I want to hear how it went. Walk me through it."

Recapping the events distracted me from my discomfort, and when I recounted how Taglieri had called Peters and the things he'd said, she put her hands to her mouth, her eyes wide.

"Oh, that's terrible! Did you just shrivel up?"

"It wasn't pleasant, that's for sure."

"I think I would have died."

"That's pretty much exactly how I felt. I think he just wanted to see me squirm."

"Lawyers will do that," she agreed. "But still, that's great. I couldn't be any happier for you."

"I appreciate that. It feels like I got the monkey off my back, you know?"

"I know exactly how you feel. I can remember the first time I found out that one of my paintings had sold in the gallery. At the time, I was certain I'd never be able to make a living with my art, and I kept expecting the owner to call me and tell me that a mistake had been made and when he finally did call with good news, I was so afraid to hear what he might say that I let my voicemail pick it up."

When I laughed, she went on. "So what's next? How does it work in your world?"

"I'll get a contract to him tomorrow and as soon as he signs it, I'll get to work. There's scouting, scheduling, getting permits, and working with my tech guy on the website. Camera and sound crews to call, agencies, rehearsals…filming is always a major production."

"Can you do all that while you're watching London?"

I hadn't even begun to think about it, but replied, "I'm going to have to. But we're trying to find the right day care."

"I know. London told me at lunch. She doesn't want to go. She said that it was pointless since she was starting school soon anyway."

Pointless? That sounded more like Vivian's word than my daughter's. "She said that?"

"It amazed me, too. But then again, she seems a lot more mature than Bodhi."

I took a long pull from the glass, wondering what else Vivian had said to London about day care. "Other than that, London was okay?"

"She was perfect. Your daughter is very sweet. She loves Noodle, by the way. She wants to bring her home. I told her that I'd have to ask you."

"We're good with the hamsters." I held up a hand. "I couldn't handle a dog in addition to everything else going on. I'm thinking of giving up sleep for a while."

She smiled, looking almost wistful. "London mentioned that you taught her to ride a bike."

"I did."

"I keep wanting to do that for Bodhi, but I'm afraid I won't be able to keep him from falling over. I think I'll need to hit the gym first and develop some upper-body strength. In all my spare time, I mean."

"Kids are definitely time consuming."

"I know," she said. "But I wouldn't change it for the world."

She was exactly right, I thought, finishing my glass.

"Thanks for this. I'd hate to take any more of your time and we really should go."

"I'm glad London came over. I got to know Bodhi's best friend a little better."

I rose from the table, grabbed the hamster cage, and followed Emily to the door. When I called for London, she and Bodhi trotted down the steps, followed by a small poodle.

"Noodle the poodle?" I asked.

"Bodhi named him," she said.

"I'm ready," London announced. "Noodle is sooooooo cute, isn't he, Daddy? Can we go to the pet store? I want to see if they have a dog like Noodle."

"Not today," I said. "Unfortunately, Daddy's got some work to do. Say goodbye to Miss Emily, okay?"

She gave Emily a hug. My daughter would voluntarily hug anyone; I'd seen her hug the mailman and old women at the park. She also hugged Bodhi, and as we made our way to the car, I felt her slip her hand into mine.

"Miss Emily is really nice. She let me have marshmallow fluff on my peanut butter sandwich."

"That sounds tasty. And I'm glad you had fun."

"I did. Can Bodhi come over to my house next time?"

I wondered how Vivian would feel about that.

"Please?"

"We'll have to make sure it's okay with his mom, okay?"

"Okay. And you know what?"

"What?"

"Thanks for bringing me over. I love you, Daddy."

Vivian's edginess was still evident when she got home from work, at least when it came to me, but by then, I can't say it caught me off guard. It wasn't until later that evening, as I sat beside her on the couch that I finally saw the flicker of a smile. It vanished as quickly as it had come, but I'd known her long enough to understand that the cold shoulder was probably more like the produce drawer in the fridge as opposed to the freezer.

"I've got good news," I said.

"Yeah?"

"I got my first client today. I'll be dropping off the contract tomorrow."

"With that lawyer you were telling me about?"

"That's the one. I know you weren't too keen on the idea that I'd be working with attorneys, but I'm excited about it. We'll be shooting four different commercials and there's a lot of other media, too."

"Congratulations," she said. "When does all this start?"

"As soon as he signs. I have a guy who'll start the website and Internet stuff right away, but before we can film, there's a lot of preliminary work. We probably won't do any filming until the end of August."

"That's perfect," she said.

"Why's it perfect?"

"Because London will be in school then."

"And?"

"And I called the day cares again today and I don't think it's going to work out. My top two choices," she said, mentioning their names, "won't have any openings until school starts. And the third option, which *might* be able to start her earlier won't know for sure until next week. And after that, the intake process requires at least a couple of weeks, before she can actually attend. By then, we're coming up on the middle of August, but it also means she'd only be there for a week or so before school starts."

"Why on earth would it take so long?"

"Because all these places do interviews along with credit and background checks, which is exactly the kind of security I'd need to feel comfortable."

"Do you want me to call? See if there's anything they can do to speed up the process?"

"You can," she said with a shrug. "I don't think there's much they can do about waiting lists though."

"Maybe we should look into a nanny."

"That would still take at least a couple of weeks, and they're also expensive. And what would we do when school starts? Fire her?"

I wasn't sure. What I did know was that had she started looking for day care when she first landed the job, the story might have been different.

"I guess you're saying that I'm going to have to keep watching London, huh?"

"I certainly can't, and besides, you've done it so far. It didn't stop you from landing your first client."

"There's a lot of prep work I'm going to have to do."

"I don't know what else we can do. Especially with what's going on with work."

"You mean travel?"

"Not entirely. And that reminds me…I have to go to Atlanta on Thursday and won't be back until Friday evening."

"There goes date night."

She rolled her eyes. "I told you I'd be traveling this week, so don't make it a bigger deal than it is. But, since it's obviously important to you, I'm hoping to be home at a reasonable hour, so we can still have date night, okay?"

"Deal," I said.

"Men," she said with a shake of her head. "Anyway, what I was trying to say was that something else is brewing at work. Something big. Aside from the executives, no one else at the company knows. So don't say anything."

"Who would I tell?"

"I don't know. Small talk with your clients? Marge? Your parents?" She sighed. "Anyway, the reason I'm going to Atlanta is because Walter is planning to move our corporate headquarters to his offices there. He wants me to oversee the process."

"You're kidding."

"He's been talking to me about it since I started, but he finally made up his mind. He's going to let the rest of the employees know next week."

"Why's he moving the office?"

"He says that the coastal building restrictions in North Carolina have gotten ridiculous, so he's decided to focus on developments in Georgia and Florida. Which makes sense, if you think about it. And he's also been thinking about running for office one day, and he'd rather do that in Georgia. That's where his family is from, and his dad used to be a representative there."

I could care less about Walter and his plans, I thought. "What does that mean for your job?"

"I'll be okay. He already told me not to worry."

"So you'll work in the Charlotte office?"

"I don't know," she said. "Walter and I brainstormed a bit, but like I said, he didn't make any decisions."

"You're not thinking that we might have to move?"

"I hope not."

I hope not? I didn't like the sound of that.

"I don't want to move," I responded.

"I know. We're thinking that I'll be able to split time between here and there."

Split time? "What does that mean?"

"I don't know, Russ," she said, exasperation creeping into her tone. "Until the move, I'm guessing that Walter and I will have to be in Atlanta two or three days a week. After that, who knows?"

"Just you and Walter?"

"Why would the other executives have to go?"

I wasn't sure I liked her answer.

No, scratch that. I *definitely* didn't like her answer.

"And there will be other travel as well?"

"Probably."

"I'd hardly ever see you. London wouldn't see you."

"That's not true and you know it," she flared. "It's not like I'm getting deployed overseas for six months at a stretch. Lots of couples have to deal with commuting between cities. Besides, Walter's the boss, not me. What am I supposed to do?"

"You could always quit," I offered. "And maybe get something part-time?"

"I don't want to quit. I really like what I do and Walter's a great boss. Not to mention the fact that we can't afford to give up my salary, can we? Since you only have one client?"

The way she underscored that it was my fault that we'd been thrust into this predicament in the first place upset me. And maybe it was my fault, a thought that only increased my agitation. "When is all this supposed to be happening?"

"Sometime in September. That's why we're going to Atlanta this week. To make sure the office will be ready in time."

September was six weeks away. "I don't see how it's possible to move everyone that quickly."

"It's really just the executives who will have to move. There will be layoffs in Charlotte, but it's not like everyone is getting fired. We still have a lot of developments in North Carolina in various stages of construction. As for Atlanta, it's mainly about hiring more people. From what I've heard, the offices already have more than enough room."

"I don't know what to say."

"There's not much to say until I know more."

"I don't understand why you didn't mention all this until now."

"I didn't mention it because nothing was certain until today."

Had someone told me in advance that on a day that I landed my first client, Vivian would have work-related news with even greater potential impact on our lives, I would have said they were crazy. Which shows how much I know.

"All right," I said. "Keep me informed."

"I always do," she said. "On another note, London told me that she had a playdate with Bodhi today?"

"While I was doing my presentation," I said. "She had a good time. She talked about Noodle the poodle all afternoon."

"Bodhi's the son of your ex-girlfriend, right? Emily?"

"Yeah, that's her."

"I've heard some people in art class talking about her. They said she was pretty bitter about her divorce."

"Divorce can be hard," I said, remaining noncommittal.

"London also said that you had lunch with her last week."

"I took London to Chick-fil-A. But yes, Emily was there, too."

"You probably shouldn't have lunch with her again. Or go to her house, even for a playdate. That's how rumors get started."

"What kind of rumors?"

"You know exactly what rumors I'm talking about. She's divorced and you're married and on top of that, she's an ex-girlfriend? It doesn't take Einstein to figure out what people would start saying."

Yes, I thought, I knew exactly, and as I sat beside my wife, I wondered how such a great day could end with me feeling as bad as I did.

"Emily, huh?" Marge asked over lunch a few days later. We were at my house; Vivian had gone to Atlanta earlier that morning, and I'd picked up the signed contract from Taglieri—and my first check as a business owner!—right after London's piano lesson. I'd also locked up the phone number, which was critical. Marge, however, had no interest in talking about those things. "How is sweet Emily doing?"

On the back porch, London was making a mess with the finger paints Marge had brought with her.

"Don't make this into something that it isn't. London had a playdate."

"That the two of you set up on an earlier date at Chick-fil-A."

"It wasn't a date."

"Maybe you should be standing in front of the mirror when you say that. But you didn't answer my question."

"I already told you. She's still getting used to being divorced, but other than that she's doing well."

"I always liked her."

"I know. You've said that before."

"And I can't believe you told Vivian about it."

"I didn't. London did."

"So you weren't going to tell her?"

"Of course. I don't have anything to hide."

"Too bad. Everyone needs some excitement now and then."

At my expression, she burst out laughing, which led to a coughing fit. I watched as she pulled out an inhaler and took a puff.

"What's that?"

"My doctor thinks I have asthma, so he prescribed this. I have to puff this stupid thing twice a day now." She slipped the inhaler back into her pocket.

"Did he prescribe horn-rimmed glasses and a pocket protector, too?"

"Ha, ha. Asthma can be pretty serious, you know."

"I was kidding," I said. "If you remember, I had it as a kid. Allergy induced. Whenever I was anywhere near a cat, my chest would lock up like a vise."

"I remember, but you're changing the subject. What I was saying is that I know how much you love Vivian. And I'm sure that you've already learned your lesson when it comes to the pitfalls of cheating. Who was that with again? Oh, that's right. Emily. Which, is of course, the subject at hand."

"Do you sit back and consciously plan these conversations? So you can maximize your enjoyment at my expense?"

"It just comes naturally," she said. "You're welcome."

I laughed. "Before I forget—don't say anything to Vivian about the fact you know about the headquarters moving to Atlanta. I wasn't supposed to tell anyone."

"I'm your sister. I don't count."

"She specifically mentioned you."

"I can believe that. But okay, since we're in the trading secrets mode, it's my turn. Liz and I are thinking about having a baby."

I broke into a grin. "Really?"

"We've been together long enough. It's time."

"Are you thinking of adopting or..."

"We're hoping that one of us will be able to get pregnant. I know I'm getting up there in years so I'm thinking it'll be Liz, but who knows? Of course, she's only two years younger than I am. Anyway, we have an appointment with a specialist and I guess we're both going to get checked out from top to bottom to see if it's even a possibility. If not, then we'll think about adoption, or maybe even sign up to be foster parents."

"Wow," I said. "This is serious. When are you starting the process?"

"Not until November. There's a wait list for this particular specialist. Supposedly, he's one of the best in the country and it seems like everyone our age, or having problems, wants to see him." Noting my goofy grin, she asked, "What?"

"I was just thinking that you'll be a great mom. Liz too."

"We're excited."

"When did all this happen?"

"We've been talking about it for a while."

"And you never told me?"

"It's not as though we'd made any decisions about it. It was just something that came up every now and then. But that biological

174

clock kept ticking, and lately, it's been getting pretty loud for both of us. I woke up the other morning to chimes."

"Have you told Mom and Dad?"

"Not yet. And don't you tell them either. I would rather we find out whether it's even possible for either of us to get pregnant first or whether we'll go the adoption route. I keep envisioning the doctor telling me that my uterus is covered in cobwebs."

I laughed. "I'm sure you'll be fine."

"That's because I, unlike you, exercise. Of course, my cough isn't making it easier, but I force myself to go to the gym."

"You're still coughing?"

"Too much. Supposedly, even after the cold is better, your lungs can take six weeks to heal."

"I didn't know that."

"Neither did I. But the point is, unlike you, I'm still dedicated to my health."

"I don't have time to work out."

"Of course you have time. You can go first thing in the morning. That's when all the moms do it."

"I'm not a mom."

"I hate to break it to you but lately? You kind of are."

"You always know exactly what to say to make me feel better."

"I call 'em like I see 'em. And you and I both know a little exercise wouldn't hurt you. You're looking a little soft these days."

"I'm in shape."

"Of course you are. If round is a shape, I mean."

"You're a real peach, you know that?"

On Friday morning, I stood in front of the mirror, thinking that maybe Marge had a point about starting to exercise again. But not, unfortunately, today.

I had things to do, and while I watched London and brought her to art class, I spent the rest of my time putting together a time line for Taglieri's campaign, with the thought that day care was most likely off the table.

Much of it I could do from home; getting the permits, scouting locations, and getting appropriate releases meant time in and out of the car and lots of driving. As long as I spread it out over a period of days, I didn't think London would be too bothered by it at all.

When I'd spoken to Vivian, I'd said as much to her. I could hear the relief in her voice and for the first time in years, we spent more than half an hour on the phone simply talking. I'd missed that, and I had the sense that she'd missed it, too, and even though she ended up arriving home a little later than she'd wanted, she laughed and smiled, even flirted with me, and in the bedroom, she was both sexy and passionate, something I'd been craving, something that left me certain that she still cared for me.

In the morning, her good mood persisted. Before she left for yoga, she made breakfast for London and me, and asked if we were planning to visit my parents.

"If you are, can you wait for me? I'd like to come."

When I assured her we would, she kissed me goodbye and I felt the light flicker of her tongue against my lips. In the ensuing glow—and with my mind flashing back to the night before—I had no doubts as to the reasons I'd married her in the first place.

While we waited for Vivian to return, London and I went to the park, where we followed a nature trail that led to the golf course. Years ago, an Eagle Scout fulfilling his service project had mounted small plaques near various trees listing both their common and scientific names. At each of them, I read the information to London and would point out the bark or the leaves, pretending I knew far more than I did. She would repeat the words—*Quercus virginiana* or *Eucalyptus viminalis*—and even though I knew I'd forget pretty much everything by the time I returned to the car, while on the trail I felt a little smarter than usual.

But London *stayed* smart. Back home, I made sandwiches and while we were eating on the back porch, she pointed to a massive tree in the backyard. "That's a *Carya ovata*!" she exclaimed.

"That one?" I asked, not bothering to hide my amazement.

She nodded. "Shagbark hickory."

"How do you know?"

"Because you showed me," she said, gazing up at me. "Remember?"

Not even slightly, I thought. To me, it had reverted to being a tree. "I think you're right."

"I am right."

"I trust you."

She took a drink of milk. "When's Mommy getting home?"

I checked my watch. "Pretty soon."

"And then we're going to Nana and Papa's?"

"That's the plan."

"I want to bake today. Cupcakes again."

"I'm sure Nana will love that."

"Will Auntie Marge and Auntie Liz be there?"

"I hope so."

"Okay. I'd better bring Mr. and Mrs. Sprinkles. I'm sure they'll want to say hi."

"I'm sure."

She chewed her sandwich. "Hey Daddy?"

"Yes?"

"I'm glad I get to stay with you."

"What do you mean?"

"Mommy told me that I'm not going to day care. She said you could work and take care of me at the same time."

"She did?"

She nodded. "She told me this morning."

"She's right, but you might have to be in the car with me while I get my stuff done."

"Can I bring my Barbies? Or Mr. and Mrs. Sprinkles?"

"Of course," I said.

"Okay. It'll still be fun then."

I smiled. "I'm glad."

"When you were little, did you go to day care?"

"No. Auntie Marge watched me."

"And Auntie Liz?"

"No. Auntie Liz wasn't around yet."

"Oh," she said. She took another couple of bites of her sandwich, her head turning from side to side as if taking in the world one sense at a time. I watched her, thinking about how beautiful she was, not caring whether I was biased at all.

"Daddy! There's a giant bird in the tree!" she cried. When she pointed, I spotted the bird. It was chocolate brown with white head feathers glowing in the sunlight. As I stared, it spread its wings before tucking them back in.

"That's a bald eagle," I told her in amazement. In all the years I'd lived in Charlotte, I'd only seen one twice. I was struck by a sense of wonder, a recurring theme during our weeks together. Staring at my daughter, I suddenly understood how much had changed between London and me. Because I'd become comfortable in my role as the primary caregiver, London had become more comfortable with me, and all at once, the thought of being separated from her for hours on end once school began made my heart ache in a way I hadn't expected. That I loved London had never been in question; what I now understood was that I liked her, too, not only as my daughter, but as the young girl I'd only recently come to know.

It might have been that thought, or maybe it had something to do with how the week had gone, but whatever the reason, I felt unusually tranquil, almost entirely at peace. I'd been down and now I was heading back up, and though I acknowledged that the feeling might be a fleeting one—I was old enough to know that much—it was as real as the sun. Watching London's rapt expression as she stared at the eagle, I wondered if she would remember this experience, or if she knew how I felt about our newfound closeness. But it didn't really matter. It was enough to feel it myself and by the time the eagle flew away, I held on to the image, knowing it would stay with me forever.

CHAPTER 12

Bad Weather on the Horizon

In February 2004—I'd been out of college for almost two years, and
had been seeing Emily almost as long—I went to visit my parents on the
weekend. Already, the habit of seeing them had been firmly established
by then. Normally, Emily would join me, but for reasons lost to time, she
couldn't make it that weekend and I was on my own.

When I arrived, my dad was working on my mom's car, not the Mustang. His head was under the hood and I saw that he was adding a quart
of oil.

"Glad to see you're taking care of your better half's car," I said, half joking, to which my dad nodded.

"Have to. Gonna snow this week. I already have the winter survival
kit in the backseat. I wouldn't want your mom to have to get it out of the
trunk in case she gets stuck on the roads."

"It's not going to snow," I said. The temperature was already springlike;
I was wearing a T-shirt and had actually debated wearing shorts to their
house.

He squinted at me from under the hood. "Have you been watching the
weather?"

"I heard something about it on the radio, but you know weather guys.
They're wrong more often than they're right."

"My knees say it's going to snow, too."

"It's almost seventy degrees!"

"Suit yourself. I'm going to need some help wrapping the pipes after I
finish up here. You'll be around to pitch in like the old days?"

My dad, I should say, had always been that type of guy. If a hurricane was expected to hit the Carolina coast, my dad would spend days clearing debris from the yard, moving things to the garage, and closing up the shutters, despite the fact Charlotte was nearly two hundred miles from the coast. "You weren't around when Hugo hit in 1989," he would tell Marge and me. "Charlotte might as well have been Dorothy's farmhouse. Whole city practically blew away."

"Yeah, I'll be here," I said to him. "But you're wasting your time. It's not going to snow."

I went inside and visited with my mom for a while; when my father came in and motioned toward me an hour later, I knew what he expected. I helped without complaint, but even when I watched him start to work on his own car, I didn't take his cautions to heart. And even if I had, I wouldn't have had the slightest idea what might be included in a winter-survival kit. That's what I told myself later, anyway, but the real reason I wasn't ready for what came next was that, at that age, I thought I was smarter than he was.

As late as Tuesday afternoon, the temperature was still inching toward sixty degrees; on Wednesday, despite the clouds rolling in, the temperature nearly hit fifty and I'd forgotten completely about my dad's warning. On Thursday, however, the storm smashed into Charlotte with a fury: It began to snow, lightly at first, and then more heavily. By the time I was driving to work, the snow was accumulating on the highways. Schools were closed for the day, and only half the people made it to the agency. The snow continued to fall, and when I left work in midafternoon, the roads were nearly impassable. Hundreds of motorists ended up skidding off the highway, myself included, amidst a snowfall of more than a foot in a city with only a few snowplows available. By nightfall, the city of Charlotte had come to a standstill.

It took nearly five hours for a tow truck to arrive and pull me out. Though I wasn't in danger—I'd brought a jacket, had half a tank of gas and my heater was working—I kept thinking about the differences between my dad and me.

While I blithely hoped for the best, my dad was the kind of guy who always expected and prepared for the worst.

August brought with it sweltering temperatures and high humidity broken by the occasional afternoon thunderstorm, but the weeks leading up to London's first day of school felt entirely different than the previous weeks, if only because I was actually *earning an income.*

Despite being scheduled every single minute of the day, I felt less stressed than I had since starting my business. I worked with the tech guy for everything tech related, scouted locations and got the releases I needed, talked with the head of the film and sound crews, picked up the permits, talked to an agent at the local casting agency, signed a contract for the billboards, and locked in a great deal for television advertising. All that in addition to finalizing the rehearsal and shooting schedule for the first two commercials and overseeing the casting session for the third commercial, all of which would take place the same week London began school.

Despite those things, I still got London to and from her activities, went bike riding, received a million hugs and kisses, and even got her piano and art classes rescheduled once school began. Tennis camp came to an end right around the time we attended an open house at the school, where London had a chance to meet her new teacher. There, she learned that Bodhi would also be in her class, and I was able to visit with Emily for a minute. Since her ex had been in town, her schedule had been unpredictable and I hadn't seen her much since our playdate. I introduced her to Vivian—my wife's demeanor could best be described as distant, but with a warning—and understood that I better keep such visits with Emily to a minimum or there were going to be *problems.*

Vivian spent two or three nights a week in Atlanta, and when at home, she continued to blow warm and cool. That was better than the hot and cold I'd been experiencing, but the excitement of the date night toward the end of July wasn't repeated, and the endlessly shifting temperature of my wife's moods left me both excited and nervous about seeing her whenever the SUV pulled up in the drive.

If there was any other change to my routine during that period, it had to do with exercise. The day after I'd really looked at myself in the mirror, I took Marge's advice and on the first Monday of the month, I set the alarm forty minutes earlier. I donned a pair of running shorts and commenced a slow trudge through the neighborhood, one in which I was passed by every jogging mother, two of whom were also pushing strollers. Years ago, I'd been able to jog five or six miles and feel refreshed when I finished: after a mile and a half on day one of my new regime, I practically collapsed on the front porch rocker. It took me more than an hour to feel like myself again. Nonetheless, I did it the following morning, and the morning after that, a streak that hasn't been broken. By the second week of August, I added push-ups and sit-ups to my routine, and my pants became steadily looser as the month wore on.

London had improved enough on her bike to allow me to ride beside her, and on the day after the open house at school, we traversed the neighborhood together, even racing for an entire block. I let her win, of course. After stowing our bikes back in the garage, I gave her a high-five, and we ended up drinking lemonade on the back porch, hoping to see another bald eagle while the sun began its descent.

But even though we didn't, I suspected I'd long remember that day, if only because it, too, was perfect in its own way.

"Don't you think she already has enough clothes for school?" I asked Vivian. It was the Saturday before school was supposed to start, and because Vivian had arrived home late from Atlanta the night before, we'd agreed to put off date night until tonight.

"I'm not getting clothes," Vivian said as she finished dressing in the bathroom. She'd already been to yoga and the gym, and had showered; it was one of those mornings of frantic activity for her. "I'm getting school supplies. Backpack, pencils, erasers, and some other things. Did you even check the school website?"

I hadn't. In all frankness, the thought hadn't even crossed my mind. I had, however, received and paid the bill for the first semester tuition, which put another dent in the savings.

"I thought we were going to Mom and Dad's."

"We are," Vivian answered. "This isn't going to take that long. Why don't you head over and we'll meet you there?"

"Sounds good," I said. "Are you in Atlanta again this week?"

It was a question I'd begun to ask regularly.

"I leave Wednesday and there's a dinner on Friday night that I can't miss, but we're flying back afterward. I really hate that I'm missing most of London's first week at school."

"There's no way you can get out of it?"

"No," she said. "I wish I could, but I can't. Do you think she'll be mad at me?"

"If you were missing her first day, it might be different, but she'll be okay." I wasn't completely certain about that, but I knew it was what Vivian wanted to hear.

"I hope you're right."

"Speaking of school," I went on, "the tuition bill arrived and I've been meaning to ask you about your paychecks."

"What about my paychecks?"

"Have you received any yet?"

She slung her purse over her shoulder. "Of course I've received my paychecks. I don't work for free."

"I haven't seen any deposits into our checking or savings account."

"I opened another account," she said.

I wasn't sure I'd heard her right. "Another account? Why?"

"It just seemed simpler. So we could keep track of our budget and your business expenses."

"And you didn't tell me?"

"Don't make this into a bigger deal than it is."

But it IS a big deal, I thought, still trying to make sense of it. "Our savings account is getting a little low," I said.

"I'll take care of it, okay?" She leaned in and offered a quick kiss. "But let me get going with London so we can get to your parents' at a decent time, okay?"

"Yeah," I said, wondering if my wife had wanted to make my head spin. "Okay."

"That definitely falls into the *that's-very-interesting* category," Marge opined.

"I just don't know why she didn't even mention it."

"Hello? That's pretty easy. It was because she didn't want you to know."

"How was I not going to know? I'm the one who writes the checks."

"Oh, she knew you'd find out. Eventually. And that when you did, you'd sit back trying to figure it out."

"Why would she want to do that?"

"Because that's what she does. She likes to keep you guessing. She's always been that way."

"No, she hasn't," I said.

"Liz?" Marge asked.

"I'd rather not get involved," Liz said, holding up a hand. "I'm off the clock. Now, if you'd like to know a wonderful Italian marinara recipe, or if you have some insights into safaris, count me in."

"I appreciate that, Liz. I've heard Botswana has some fabulous safaris."

"I would love to go one day. That's my dream trip."

"Can we get back on topic please?" Marge said. "We have something very *interesting* going on."

"Rhinos are interesting," I said. "Elephants, too."

Liz put a hand on Marge's knee. "We really should try to schedule a safari in the next couple of years. Don't you think that would be fabulous?"

"I don't like when you take his side when he tries to change the subject."

"He didn't just try. I think he did a pretty good job. I saw an advertisement for a place called Camp Mombo. It looked amazing."

"I think you should definitely try to find a way to go," I said. "It's one of those once-in-a-lifetime things."

"Would both of you please return to the subject at hand?"

Liz giggled at Marge's obvious frustration. "Every couple has their own style of communication and they often speak in shorthand. Unless I know the subtext, I wouldn't know what to think about it."

"See?" Marge offered. "She agrees with me that it's fishy."

"No, she didn't. She didn't say anything."

"That's just because you couldn't read her subtext."

"Seriously," I said to Liz later, "why do you think Vivian didn't tell me that she'd opened another bank account? I know you're off the clock, but I'd really like to understand what's going on."

"I'm not sure I can tell you what's going on. My guess would be as good as yours."

"But if you had to guess?"

She seemed to think about what to say. "Then I'd say that it was just like she said and that it was no big deal. Maybe she simply wants her own account so she can see exactly how much she's contributing and it makes her feel better about herself."

I thought about that. "Have you had clients who've done things like this? Other wives?"

Liz nodded. "A few times."

"And?"

"Like I said, it can mean different things."

"I know you're trying to be diplomatic here, but I'm at a loss. Is there anything you can tell me?"

Liz took her time before answering. "If there's one common thread that underlies situations like these, it's generally anger."

"You think Vivian's angry with me?"

"I don't spend a lot of time with Vivian, and when I do, it's usually when we're here with the whole family. There's only so much one can learn in a setting like this. But when people are angry, they often behave in ways that are dictated by that emotion. They can do things they ordinarily wouldn't do."

"Like open a secret bank account?"

"It's not secret, Russ. She told you about it."

"So she's . . . not angry?"

"I think," she said, "that you'd be in a better position to answer that than I am."

Another hour passed, and there was still no sign of Vivian or London. Marge and Liz had gone for a walk around the block while Dad had settled in front of the television to watch a ball game. I found my mom in the kitchen, dicing potatoes as a large pot of stew simmered on the stovetop, the aroma already tantalizing. She wore a bright orange apron that I vaguely remembered buying for her.

"There you are," she said. "I was wondering when you'd finally get around to visiting with your old mom."

"Sorry," I said, leaning in to give her a hug. "I didn't mean to offend."

"Oh, hush. I was kidding. How are you? You look like you've lost weight."

I liked that she'd noticed. "Maybe a little."

"Are you eating enough?"

"I've started jogging again."

"Yuck," she said. "I don't understand how anyone can like jogging."

"What are you making? It smells great in here."

"It's a French country stew. Joanne gave me the recipe and I thought I'd give it a try."

"Liz probably has a great recipe."

"I'm sure she does. But Joanne beat her to punch."

"Do I know Joanne?"

"From the Red Hat Society. You probably saw her when you picked up London at lunch that day."

"Was she the one wearing the red hat? And the purple blouse?"

"Ha, ha."

"How are those fine red-hatted ladies doing?"

"They're wonderful, and we have so much fun together. Last week after lunch, a few of us went to a lecture at the college given by an astronomer. Did you know that they've recently discovered an earth-sized planet that orbits another sun? And that the planet is the same distance from the sun as Earth? Which means there could actually be life on that planet."

"I didn't know that."

"We talked about it at our next meeting."

"Because you want to be the first group to welcome the aliens with red hats if they ever visit?"

"Why are you teasing me? It's not nice."

I chuckled. "I'm sorry, Mom. I couldn't resist."

She shook her head. "I don't know where you got the idea that teasing mothers is a good thing. You certainly didn't learn it from me."

"That's true," I said. I motioned to the onion sitting beside the chopping block. "Do you need me to help with that?"

"You're volunteering in the kitchen?"

"I've been doing quite a bit of cooking lately."

"SpaghettiOs from a can?"

"Now who's teasing who?"

Her eyes sparkled. "Just trying to keep up with my children. But no, I don't need any help. Thank you, though. Is your father watching the game, or is he still in the garage?"

In the family room, I saw the flicker of the television screen.

"The game," I answered.

"I had a dream about him a couple of days ago. Or at least, I think it was about him. It was one of those dreams where everything was foggy, so I couldn't see very well. But he was in the hospital with the cancer."

"Hmmm."

"Anyway, there were all these beeping machines around him and *Judge Judy* was on the television. The doctor was from India I think, and there was a giant stuffed animal on the bed beside your dad. A big, purple pig."

"Hmmm," I said again.

"What do you think it means? The purple pig, I mean?"

"I really couldn't tell you."

"Did you know my grandmother was psychic? She used to have premonitions, too."

"I thought you said it was a dream."

"The point is that I'm worried about him."

"I know you are. But the doctor said he was fine. He hasn't been short of breath again, has he?"

"Not that I've noticed. And if he has, I'm sure he wouldn't tell me."

"I'll ask him, okay?"

"Thank you," she said. "Where are Vivian and London?"

"They're grabbing some last-minute school supplies. They should

187

be here pretty soon. London's first day is Tuesday, by the way. I don't know if you'd like to come, but you're welcome to."

"Your dad and I will both be there," she said. "It's a big day for her."

"It is," I admitted.

My mom smiled. "I can remember your first day of school. You were so excited but after I walked you to the classroom, I remember going back to my car and crying."

"Why were you crying?"

"Because it meant you were growing up. And you were so different than Marge. You were always so much more sensitive than she was. I worried about you."

I wasn't sure I was happy about being described as more sensitive than my sister but I suspected my mom probably wasn't entirely wrong about this.

"It turned out okay. You know I always liked school. I just hope London will, too. We went to the open house and she met her teacher. That seemed to go okay."

"She'll be fine. She's smart and mature and really sweet. Of course, I'm biased."

"That's a good thing."

"I'm just glad that you're not angry with me."

"Why would I be angry with you?"

"Because I wasn't able to watch London whenever you needed it."

"You were right," I said. "It wasn't your responsibility. But let's just say I developed a whole new level of respect for single mothers."

"It's been good for London, too. She's changed a lot this summer."

"You think so?"

"Of course she has. You're just too close to see it."

"How has she changed?"

"The way she talks about you, for starters. And how much she talks about you."

"She talks about me?"

"Lately, she talks about you all the time. It's, 'Me and Daddy went bike riding,' or 'Daddy played Barbies with me,' or 'Daddy took me to the park.' She never used to do that."

"That's pretty much been my life these days."

"It's been good for you, too. I've always thought that your dad could have benefited from knowing how the other half lives."

"But then he wouldn't be the big, gruff guy that Marge and I came to fear."

"Hush," she says. "You know he loves you both."

"I know," I said. "As long as I don't talk to him too much while the ball game's on. Of course, Marge and London can talk the whole time and there's no problem."

"That's because Marge knows the game better than you do, and London will get up from his lap and bring him a beer. Why don't you try that?"

"I'm too big to sit in his lap."

"You're such a comedian today. There are a couple of beers in the fridge. Why don't you grab two, and see what happens. He likes visiting with you."

"I know exactly what's going to happen."

"Oh, don't let him scare you. Just remember—he can sense your fear."

I laughed as I walked to the fridge, certain that I had the best mom in the world.

"How are you, Dad?"

I held an open bottle of beer toward him. "For you," I said. Fortunately, I'd timed it perfectly with a commercial, which he'd already muted.

"What are you doing?"

"I brought you a beer."

"Why?"

"Why? Because I thought you might want one?"

"You're not going to ask if you can borrow some money, are you?"

"No."

"Good. Because the answer's no. It's not my fault you quit your job."

My father, the King of Blunt. I took a seat on the couch beside him. "How's the game going?"

"Braves are losing."

I brought my hands together, wondering what to say next. "How are things, Dad? Plumbing business going okay?"

"Why wouldn't it be?"

I don't know, I thought. *Because you make me nervous sometimes?* I took a drink of my beer. "I told you I landed my first client, right?"

"Yep. The attorney. Italian guy."

"I'll be filming a couple of commercials next week. I also have to meet with some child actors, so I can film a third commercial, too."

"I don't like lawyer commercials."

"You don't like any commercials, Dad," I said. "That's why you mute them."

He nodded in agreement while the silence grew between us, the only sound my mother's humming from the kitchen. He scratched at a corner of the label from the bottle, figuring it was probably polite to ask a question. "How's Vivian?"

"She's doing well," I said.

"Good," he said. At that point, the game came back on and my dad reached for the remote control. The mute went off and a peek at the box score showed that the Braves were down by three runs with four innings left to go.

"We should head to a Braves game one day. You and I."

He scowled at me. "Are you gonna keep talking all day, or will you let me enjoy the game in peace?"

"I think you've scared him, Dad," Marge said, collapsing on the couch beside my dad. She and Liz had returned from their walk.

"What are you talking about?"

Marge pointed toward me. "He's perched over there like he's afraid to move a muscle."

My dad shrugged. "He was talking and talking, like one of them windup dolls."

"He'll do that," Marge agreed. She nodded toward the set. "What's the score?"

"Four to four now, bottom of the eighth. Braves are coming back."

"Have they brought in their relief pitcher?"

"In the seventh inning."

"Who is it?"

My dad mentioned a name I didn't recognize. "That's a good choice," Marge noted. "I really like his slider but his changeup is good, too. How's he doing so far?"

"Lot of pitches. He's having to work it."

"Do you remember the days when we had Maddux, Smoltz, and Glavine?"

"Who doesn't? That was one of the best rotations ever, but this year..."

"Yeah, I know. Down year. But at least they're not the Cubs."

"Can you imagine? Over a hundred years since they've won it all. Makes the Curse of the Bambino seem ridiculous, especially considering the last few years."

"Who do you think will win it all?"

"I don't care, as long as it's not the Yankees."

"I'm thinking the Mets might pull it off."

"As good a guess as any," he agreed. "They're playing good ball. Royals, too, and they've got some serious offense this year."

As he answered, Marge sent a lazy wink in my direction.

Eventually, Marge and I joined Liz on the back porch. From the living room, sounds of the game drifted outside.

"I was never a baseball fan," I said to my sister. "I ran track in high school."

"And now you're jogging with the mamas. Don't ever let anyone tell you that you let your raw athleticism go to seed."

I turned toward Liz. "Does she talk to you like this?"

"No," Liz answered. "If she does, she knows I won't feed her. Besides, you're an easy target."

"I was just trying to say that I don't think Dad would have wanted to talk to me, even if I did know as much about baseball as you do."

"Don't feel bad about it," Marge shrugged. "You might not know baseball, but I'm sure Dad can't name every Barbie accessory either, so you've got that going for you."

191

"That makes me feel so much better."

"Oh, don't be so thin-skinned. Dad won't talk to me when he's in the garage. That's your place, not mine."

"Really?"

"Why do you think I bothered learning anything about the Braves? He probably wouldn't talk to me at all unless he was asking me to pass the mashed potatoes while we were eating."

"Do you think that he and Mom talk the way they used to?"

"After almost fifty years? I doubt it. There's probably not much left to talk about. But hey—it clearly works for them."

"Daddy!" I heard from the kitchen, and I saw London was skipping in my direction. She was wearing a dress that could have been worn on the red carpet and holding a soft lunch box emblazoned with an image of Barbie. Another item to add to my vast knowledge of Barbie accessories, Marge was no doubt thinking. "Look what I got!" London said, raising it for me to see. "It fits into my Barbie backpack, too!"

"That's great, sweetheart. It's really pretty."

She hugged the three of us while we all took turns admiring her lunch box.

"Are you excited about school?" Marge asked.

London nodded. "I start Tuesday."

"I know," Marge said. "Your dad told me. He said that you met your teacher, too."

"Her name is Mrs. Brinson," London said. "She's really nice. She said that I might be able to bring Mr. and Mrs. Sprinkles to show-and-tell."

"That would be great," Marge said. "I'm sure the other kids will love them. Where are they now? Did you bring them?"

"No. They're at home. Mommy said it was too hot to leave them in the car while we were shopping."

"She's probably right. It's pretty hot today."

"Are you hungry?" I asked London.

"Mommy and I had lunch not too long ago."

So that's where you were. "Did you see Nana in the kitchen?"

"She says we're going to make pudding-in-a-cloud in a couple of minutes. It's a snack, though, so it won't ruin my dinner. And then we're going to plant some flowers."

"That sounds fun. How about Papa?"

"I sat in his lap for a little while. His whiskers were itchy when he kissed me. He liked my lunch box, too."

"I'll bet he did. Did you watch the game with him?"

"Not really. We talked about Mr. and Mrs. Sprinkles and he told me that he missed them. And then we talked about school and my bike, and he said he wanted to watch me ride it sometime. Then he told me that when he was little, he used to ride his bike all the time. Once, he said he rode it all the way to Lake Norman and back."

"That's a long way," I said, not doubting it for a minute. It sounded like something my dad would have done. Just then, Vivian emerged from the house.

I stood and gave my wife a kiss; Marge and Liz offered hugs before taking their seats again. Vivian sat down, too.

Vivian straightened London's dress. "I think Nana's waiting for your help in the kitchen, sweetie."

"Okay," London said, scampering off and vanishing inside. When the door closed behind her, I turned toward Vivian, aware that I was still bothered about her separate bank account, but it wasn't the time or place to let her know how I felt. I forced myself to smile and pretend nothing was wrong at all.

"How did it go today?"

"You wouldn't believe what a pain it was." Vivian sighed. "It took forever to find the right backpack. They were sold out almost everywhere, but we finally got lucky at the last place we went. It goes without saying that the stores were packed. It was like everyone in Charlotte had the same idea and waited until the last minute to grab school supplies. Which meant, of course, that I had to get London a bite to eat because she was starving by the time we finally finished."

"Shopping isn't for the faint of heart," Marge observed.

"At least it's done," Vivian said. She turned from Marge to Liz, focusing somewhere in between them. "How are things going with you two? Any trips planned?"

Marge and Liz both enjoyed traveling; in the years they'd been together, they'd visited over fifteen different countries.

"Next weekend, we're going to Houston to see my parents," Liz answered. "In October, we're off to Costa Rica. Right after London's birthday."

"Wow... What's in Costa Rica?"

"It's more of an adventure trip. Zip-lines, rafting, hiking through the cloud forest, and we'll see the Arenal volcano."

"Sounds like fun."

"I hope so. And then in early December, we'll be going to New York City. There are some shows we want to see, and I hear the 9/11 Memorial Museum is really moving."

"I love New York around the holidays. I never thought I'd miss it when I left, but every now and then, I find myself wondering why I ever left in the first place."

We left because we were getting married. I didn't say that, but Liz— being Liz—probably sensed my agitation and like me, wanted to keep things cordial. "There's no other city quite like it, is there?" she said. "We always enjoy our trips there."

"If you need help getting dinner reservations anywhere, let me know. I can call my old boss and I'm sure he can pull some strings."

"Thank you. We'll keep that in mind. How's the office move to Atlanta going?"

"It's going. For whatever reason, I've been put in charge of the logistics, and it's been a lot more work than I imagined. I have to be in Atlanta for a couple of days at the end of the week."

"But you'll be at school on London's first day?"

"I wouldn't miss it."

"I'm sure that will make London very happy. Is there an official move-in date yet? For Atlanta, I mean?"

"Sometime in mid-September, I'm guessing. It's really going to be an incredible office. It's right on Peachtree, with amazing views. And Walter has been setting up some of the executives with temporary corporate apartments, so that's made things a little easier, too."

"Will you be using one of the apartments?"

"I suppose it depends on how much time I'll actually have to spend there."

It depends?

Before I could figure out what *that* meant, Liz went on. "But you'll be able to mainly work out of Charlotte, right?"

"That's the hope, but who knows for sure? This week, I'm in Atlanta three days, but Walter is toying with the idea of eventually running for governor. Not next year, but in 2020. But between his real-estate developments and his PAC and now this, don't be shocked if I have to be there four days a week."

"That's a lot of nights in a hotel."

"If I'm there that much, I'd probably take Walter up on his offer for a corporate apartment."

"Seriously?" I finally interjected, unable to help myself.

"What can I tell you? Liz is right about hotel living."

"I'd rather you not have an apartment in Atlanta," I said, wondering why I was just finding out about this now, instead of in private.

"I know you don't," she said. "Do you think I want that?"

I didn't respond, because I wasn't quite sure I knew the answer.

"Why would he want to be governor?" Marge asked, interrupting my thoughts. "He already has all the money and power he needs."

"Why not? He's been successful in everything he's done. He'd probably be a great governor."

Even as Vivian was talking, I was still thinking about the bank account and the apartment. Marge probably was, too, based on her expression. Liz, meanwhile, was a master at keeping conversations on neutral ground. "It sounds to me like he'll be keeping you very busy over the next few years," Liz said.

"I'm busy all day, every day already."

"And you enjoy it," Liz said.

"I do. I really missed working, and it's an exciting place to work. I feel like I'm finally getting back to being the real me, if that makes any sense."

"It makes all the sense in the world," Liz agreed. "I tell my clients that meaningful work is essential for good mental health."

"Being a stay-at-home mom is meaningful, too," I pointed out.

"No question about it," Liz said. "I think everyone would agree with the idea that staying at home to raise a child is meaningful and important." Then, to Vivian: "Has it been hard being apart from London?"

"I know she misses me," Vivian answered. "But I think it's important that she sees me working outside the home. The last thing I want is for her to think that women should aspire to being barefoot, pregnant, and in the kitchen as a life's goal."

"When were you ever barefoot and pregnant in the kitchen?" I interjected.

"It's a figure of speech, Russ," she said. "You know what I mean. And frankly, it's been good for Russ, too. I think he has a lot more respect for what my life was like for five years."

"I always had respect for what you did," I said, tired of feeling like I had to continually defend myself. "And yes, you're right that watching London takes a lot of energy. But I'm also working, too, and trying to balance both has been the difficult part."

Vivian's eyes narrowed for an instant, her dislike for my comment obvious. She turned her attention to Marge again. "How are things with you? Work going okay?"

It was the kind of innocuous question that defined their relationship—a question that meant nothing and kept conversation superficial.

"Like they say, whenever we want to liven up the office party, we invite a couple of funeral directors."

Despite myself, I smiled. Vivian didn't.

"I don't know how you do it," Vivian said. "I can't imagine staring at numbers all day and dealing with the IRS."

"It's not for everyone, but I've always been good with numbers. And I enjoy helping my clients."

"That's good," Vivian said. She added nothing else and the four of us descended into silence. Marge picked at her fingernail while Liz adjusted the hem of her shorts. It didn't take a genius to understand that the levity that had been present all afternoon evaporated as soon as Vivian had taken a seat on the porch. Even Vivian seemed at a loss for words. She stared at nothing in particular before finally, almost reluctantly, focusing on Marge again. "What time did the two of you get here today?"

"Twelve thirty or so," Marge answered. "We got here a few minutes after Russ did."

"Anything exciting happen?"

"Not really. It's just a typical Saturday. Mom's been in the kitchen all day, we went for a walk, Dad started in the garage until the ball game came on. And, of course, I teased your husband for a while."

"Good for you. He needs someone to keep him in line. He's been a little moody these days. At home, it seems like lately, I can't do anything right."

I turned toward her, too startled to speak *again*, and wondering: *Are you talking about me or you?*

Separate bank account. Corporate apartment. A possibility of up to four nights a week spent in Atlanta.

The more I thought about Vivian's *Saturday Surprises*, the more I began to suspect that she brought it all up here because she knew I wouldn't argue with other people around. Of course, once we got home, she'd say that we'd already discussed it, so there was no reason to go over it again; if I even tried, I was doing so because I wanted to start an argument. It was a win-win situation for her and left me no recourse at all, but what bothered me even more than the blatant manipulation was that Vivian didn't seem to be troubled at the prospect of spending more days apart than we spent together. What would that mean for us? What would that mean for London?

I wasn't sure. I had no desire to leave Charlotte, but if push came to shove, I would. My marriage was important to me—my *family* was important to me—and I would do whatever it took to keep us together. As for my company, it wasn't as if I was firmly established in Charlotte, and if the possibility of a move was on the horizon, I might as well start searching for clients in Atlanta, assuming I had some sense of what Vivian's upcoming schedule might be. The whole thing was still so vague though, so uncertain.

And yet…if I suggested the possibility of moving the family, I wasn't sure how Vivian would respond. Would she even want that? I felt as though Vivian and I were sliding on ice in opposite directions, and the more I tried to hold on to her, the more determined she seemed to pull away. She had a desire for secrecy that nagged at me and while I'd assumed that we'd support each other in our employment challenges, I couldn't shake the feeling that Vivian had little enthusiasm for that kind of mutual reliance. Instead of she and I against the world, it felt like Vivian against me.

Then again, perhaps I was making too big of a deal about all of this; maybe I was too argumentative and focused too much on her faults, not her strengths. Once London was in school and we adapted to our respective work schedules, things might not appear so bleak, and our lives would be on the upswing again.

Or maybe they wouldn't.

Meanwhile, as I was pondering these things, Vivian was discussing various shows in New York with Marge and Liz. She went on to recommend that they visit a rooftop bar on Fifty-Seventh Street with a view of Central Park that not too many people knew about; I could remember taking Vivian on lazy Sunday afternoons, back when I used to believe I was the center of her world. How long ago that suddenly seemed.

Just then, London emerged carrying two servings of pudding-in-a-cloud, handing one each to Liz and Marge; she followed that with servings for Vivian and me. Despite my inner turmoil, the sight of London's excitement couldn't help but make me smile.

"This looks delicious, sweetheart," I said. "What's in it?"

"Chocolate pudding and Cool Whip," London answered. "It's like a soft Oreo cookie and I helped Nana make it. She said it won't ruin my appetite because it's just a snack. I'm going to go eat mine with Papa, okay?"

"I'm sure he'll love that." Taking a quick bite, I commented, "Very tasty. You're a great chef."

"Thank you, Daddy," she said. To my delight, she leaned in for a quick hug before heading back into the house, no doubt headed for my dad's lap with a couple more desserts.

Vivian had seen London hug me and while she offered a benign smile in response, I wasn't sure what, if anything, she felt about being left out. As soon as London closed the door, Vivian put her dessert on the table, sugar being the enemy and all. Not so with me, Marge, or Liz. Marge was on her second spoonful when she spoke again.

"You've got a big week ahead. London starting school, Vivian traveling, and you're filming commercials, right? When does that start?"

"We have rehearsal on Wednesday afternoon, and we'll film on Thursday and Friday, then a couple of days the following week. I also have a casting session next week."

"Busy, busy."

"I'll be okay," I said, realizing I actually meant it. With London in school, I had eight free hours to work, which seemed like all the time in the world compared to the life I was leading now. I took another bite of the dessert, feeling Vivian's gaze on me.

"What?" I asked her.

"You not going to eat all of that, are you?" Vivian asked.

"Why shouldn't I?"

"Because we'll be having dinner in an hour. It's not good for you. Or your waistline."

"I think I can handle it," I said. "I'm down six pounds this month."

"Then why try to put it back on?" Vivian asked.

When I didn't respond, Liz cleared her throat. "How about you, Vivian? Are you still going to the gym and doing yoga at that place downtown?"

"Only on Saturdays. But I work out at the office gym two or three times a week."

I blinked. "There's an office gym?"

"You know that. You've seen me bringing my gym bag to work. I wouldn't have time otherwise. Of course, it sometimes also ends up being a working session depending on which executive is there."

Though she didn't mention a name, I had a sinking feeling that by executive, my wife actually meant Walter, which, if true, struck me as the cruelest *Saturday Surprise* of all.

By then, I was downright glum. Vivian and Marge continued their superficial conversation while I pretty much tuned out, my thoughts exploding like fireworks between my ears.

London and my mom emerged from the house, both of them wearing gardening gloves. London had clearly borrowed a pair from my mom, since they seemed about three sizes too large.

"Hey sweetie!" I called out. "Time to do some planting?"

"I have gloves, Daddy! And Nana and me are going to make the flower bed soooo pretty!"

"Good for you."

I watched as my mom lifted a shallow plastic tub containing twelve smaller plastic pots, marigolds already in bloom. London grabbed two trowels, and my mom listened attentively while London chattered away nonstop on their way to the flower bed.

"Have you ever noticed how good Mom is with London?" Marge asked. "She's patient, cheerful, and fun."

"You sound a little bitter when you say that," Liz observed.

"I am," she said. "It's not like Mom ever planted flowers with me. Or showed me how to make pudding-in-a-cloud. Nor was she patient, cheerful, or fun as a general rule. When she spoke to me, it was because she had some chores she wanted me to do."

"Are you open to the idea that your memories may be selective?" Liz asked.

"No."

Liz laughed. "Then maybe you should simply accept the notion that she likes London more than she ever liked you or Russ."

"Ouch," Marge said. "That's not very therapeutic."

"I wish London would get to see my parents more often than she does," Vivian remarked. "It makes me sad that she doesn't have the same kind of relationship with them. Like she's missing out on getting to know my family."

"When was the last time they were here?" Liz asked.

"Thanksgiving," Vivian said.

"Why don't they come and visit this summer?"

"My dad's company has been involved in a huge merger and my

mom doesn't like to travel without him. I suppose I could bring London to them, but these days, when would I have the time?"

"Maybe that will change when things settle down," Liz suggested.

"Maybe," Vivian said, a frown suddenly appearing as she watched London digging while my mom put the flowers into the ground. "If I'd known London would be planting flowers, I would have brought a change of clothes. Her dress is practically new, and she'll be upset if she can't wear it again."

I doubted that London cared as much as Vivian. London probably couldn't remember half of the dresses she owned, but my thoughts were interrupted by a sudden, piercing scream from London, the sound of pain and fear...

"OW, OW, OWWW!!! It HURTS! DADDY!!!!"

Instantly, the world splintered into disjointed images; I felt myself rising, the chair flung out behind me...Liz and Marge turning their heads, shock in their expressions...Vivian's mouth in the shape of an O...My mom reaching for London...London beet red and crying, shaking her hand, her face contorted...

"IT HURTS, DADDY!!!"

I bolted off the porch toward her, adrenaline coursing through my system. As soon as I reached her, I scooped her into my arms.

"What's wrong? What happened?"

London was sobbing too hard to answer, her screams drowning out her ability to answer, her hand held away from her body.

"What's wrong? Did you hurt your hand?"

Mom's face was white. "She was stung by a bee!" she called out. "She was trying to swat it off her hand..." Vivian, Liz, and Marge were beside us as well. Even my dad had appeared in the doorway and was hustling toward us.

"Was it a bee?" I asked. "Did a bee sting you?" I tried to reach for London's hand, but she was frantically waving it, convinced the bee was still attached.

Vivian quickly took hold of London's arm, even as London continued to scream. She rotated it, finally focusing on the back of London's hand.

"I see the stinger!" she shouted at London. London continued to flail, oblivious, as Vivian went on. "I have to get it out, okay?"

Vivian gripped London's arm tighter. "Hold still!" she demanded. Using her fingernails, it took a couple of attempts to loosen the stinger, but then with a quick pull, the stinger was out. "It's out, sweetheart," she announced. "I know it hurts," she soothed, "but it'll be okay, now."

No more than fifteen seconds had passed since I first heard London begin to scream but it seemed far longer. London was still crying, but she struggled less and her screams had begun to subside as I held her. Her tears dampened my cheek as everyone pressed in around her, trying to comfort.

"*Shhh . . .*" I whispered, "*I've got you now . . .*"

"*Are you okay?*" Marge asked, stroking London's back.

"*That must have hurt, you poor thing . . . ,*" Liz added.

"*I'll get the baking soda . . . ,*" my mom announced.

"*Come here, baby,*" Vivian said, reaching for London. "*Let Mommy hold you . . .*"

Vivian's arms snaked around London, but all at once, London buried her face in my neck.

"I want Daddy!" London said, and when Vivian started to lift her, I felt London squeeze even harder, nearly choking me, until Vivian finally relented.

I carried London back to my chair and took a seat, listening as her cries gradually diminished. By then, my mom had mixed baking soda and water, forming a paste, and brought it to the table, along with a spoon.

"This will help the swelling and take away some of the itch," she said. "Do you want to watch me put it on, London?"

London pulled away from my neck, watching as my mom applied the paste to her skin.

"Will it sting?"

"Not at all," my mom answered. "See?"

London was back to sniffling by then and when my mom was finished, London brought her hand closer. "It still hurts," she said.

"I know it does, but this will make it feel better, okay?"

London nodded, still examining her hand. I brushed away her tears with my finger, feeling the moisture on my skin.

We sat at the table for a while making small talk, trying to distract London and watching for an allergic reaction. None of us expected one—neither Vivian nor I were allergic, and London hadn't been allergic to the fire ants—but since it was London's first bee sting, no one knew for sure. London's breathing seemed normal and the swelling didn't worsen; when we turned the conversation topic to Mr. and Mrs. Sprinkles, London even seemed to temporarily forget her pain, if only for a few seconds.

Once we knew that London was fine, I recognized that all the adults had overreacted. Our panic, our rush to soothe, the way we'd fussed over her in the aftermath, struck me as a bit ridiculous. It wasn't as though she'd broken an arm or been hit by a car, after all. Her screams of pain had been real, but still...*she'd been stung by a bee.* As a kid, I'd probably been stung half a dozen times and when it happened the first time, my mom hadn't made paste from baking soda and water, nor had she held me in her arms to comfort me. If memory serves, my mom simply told me to go wash the stinger off and my dad said something along the lines of, "Stop crying like a baby."

When my mom finally asked if London would like another spoonful of chocolate pudding, she hopped off my lap and gave me a kiss before following my mom into the kitchen. She held her hand out in front of her like a surgeon who'd just prepped for an operation. I said as much out loud, eliciting a laugh from Marge and Liz.

Vivian, however, didn't laugh at all. Instead, her slitted gaze seemed to accuse me of a crime: *betrayal.*

CHAPTER 13

Crime and Punishment

I was twelve years old and Marge was seventeen when she came out of the closet, or whatever the politically correct way to say it is these days. Marge wasn't conscious of being politically correct back then; it just sort of happened. We'd been hanging out in her bedroom and the subject of the homecoming dance at the high school came up. When I asked why she wasn't going, she turned toward me.

"Because I like girls," she said abruptly.

"Oh," I remembered saying. "I like girls, too." I think part of me vaguely suspected that Marge might be gay, but at that age, everything I knew about sexuality and sex pretty much came from murmured conversations in school hallways or the occasional R-rated movie I'd watched. Had she told me a year later, when I would wedge my bedroom door shut with a shoe to have some privacy practically every day, I don't know how I would have reacted, although I suspect it would have been a bigger deal. At thirteen—middle school—anything out of the ordinary is considered the Worst Thing Ever, sisters included.

"Does that bother you?" she asked, suddenly engrossed in picking at her cuticle.

It was only when I looked at her—really looked—that I understood how anxious she was about telling me. "I don't think so. Do Mom and Dad know?"

"No. And don't say a word to them. They'll freak out."

"Okay," I said, meaning it, and it was a secret that stayed between us, until Marge sat my parents down at the dining room table the following year and told them herself.

That doesn't make me noble, nor should you infer much about my character at all. Even though I sensed her anxiety, I wasn't mature enough to understand the full gravity of what she'd told me. When we were growing up, things were different. Being gay was weird, being gay was wrong, being gay was a sin. I had no idea of the internal struggles Marge would face, or the things people would eventually say behind her back—and sometimes even to her face. Nor am I arrogant enough to believe I can fully understand them even now. The world to my twelve-year-old brain was simpler and whether my sister liked girls or boys frankly didn't matter to me at all. I liked and disliked her for other reasons. I disliked, for instance, when she'd pin me on my back, her knees on my arms, while she scoured my chest bone with her knuckles; I disliked when Peggy Simmons, a girl I liked, came to the door and she told her that "He can't come to the door because he's in the bathroom, and he's been in there a long, long time," before asking Peggy, "Do you happen to have any matches?"

My sister. Always doing right by me.

As for liking her, it was really pretty simple. As long as she wasn't doing something dislikable, I was more than happy to like her. Like younger siblings everywhere, I had a bit of hero worship when it came to Marge, and her revelation didn't change that in the slightest. As I saw it, my parents treated her like a young adult while they treated me like a child, both before and after she told me. They expected more from her, whether around the house or in taking care of me. I'll also admit that Marge made my own path to adulthood smoother than it otherwise would have been because my parents had always been there, done that with Marge first. Surprise and disappointment, after all, often go hand-in-hand when it comes to raising children, and fewer surprises usually meant less disappointment.

When I snuck out one night and took the family car? Marge did it years before.

When I had too many drinks at a high school party? Welcome to the club.

When I climbed the water tower in our neighborhood, a popular teenage hangout? That was already Marge's favorite place.

When I was a moody teen who barely spoke to either my mom or dad? Marge taught them to expect that, too.

Marge, of course, never let me forget how much easier I had it but to be fair, it often led me to feel like an afterthought in the family, which wasn't easy either. In our own ways, we each felt a bit slighted, but in our private struggles, we ended up leaning on each other more and more with every passing year.

When we talk about it nowadays—what she went through—she downplays how hard it was to come out to others, and it makes me admire her all the more. Being different is never easy, and being different in that way—in the South, in a Christian home—seemed to strengthen her resolve to appear invulnerable. As an adult, she lives in a world defined by numbers and spreadsheets, calculations. When she speaks with others, she tries to hide behind wit and sarcasm. She deflects intimacy with most people and while we're close, I wonder if my sister sometimes found it necessary to hide her emotional side, even from me. I know if I asked her, she would deny it; she would tell me that if I wanted sensitivity, I should have asked God for a different sister, the kind of sister who carried a Kleenex at the ready on the off-chance a sad song began playing on the radio.

Lately, I've found myself wishing that I'd impressed upon her that I saw the real her, that I've always loved who she was. But as close as we are, our conversations seldom reach those depths. Like most people, I assume, we talk about the latest goings-on in our lives, hiding our fears like a turtle tucking its head back into its shell.

But I've also seen Marge at her lowest.

It had to do with a girl named Tracey, her roommate. Marge was a junior in college at UNC Charlotte, and while she didn't hide her sexuality, she didn't flaunt it either. Tracey knew from the very beginning but it never seemed an issue. Often together, they fell into a close and natural friendship the way college roommates often do. Tracey had a boyfriend back home and after the breakup Marge was there to pick up the pieces. Eventually, Tracey noticed that Marge was attracted to her and didn't discourage the feeling; she even speculated that she might be bisexual but wasn't exactly sure. Then, one night, it happened. Marge woke in the morning feeling like she'd discovered the part of her that had been missing; Tracey woke, even more confused, but willing to give the relationship a try. They were discreet *at Tracey's insistence, but that was fine by Marge, and over the next few months, Marge fell even more deeply in love. Tracey, on the other hand, began to pull away and, after returning home for spring break that year, told Marge that she and her boyfriend had reconciled and that she wasn't sure she and Marge could remain friends. She told her that she would be moving into an apartment that her parents had rented, and that what she and Marge had shared was nothing but experimentation. It had meant nothing to her.*

Marge called me just before midnight. She was drinking and babbling, telling me bits and pieces of the story and slurring that she wanted to die. I'd just gotten my driver's license and somehow, I knew exactly where to find her. I raced to the water tower and spotted her car parked beneath it. I made the climb and found my sister sitting near the edge, her legs dangling. There was an open bottle of rum beside her, and it was immediately clear that she was beyond drunk and practically incoherent. When she saw me, she scooted closer to the edge.

Speaking quietly, I was able to convince her to let me come closer; when I finally reached her, I put my arm around her and inched her back from the ledge. I held her as she sobbed, remaining at the top of the water tower until it was nearly dawn. She begged me not to tell our parents and after I promised, I drove her back to her dorm room and put her in bed. When I got home, my parents were livid—I was sixteen and had been out all night. They grounded me for a month, and I lost driving privileges for another three months after that.

But I never told them where I'd been, or how devastated my sister had been that night, or what might have happened to her, had I not shown up. It was enough to know that I'd been there for her, that I'd held her in my arms when she'd needed it the most, just the way I knew she would for me.

Needless to say, after dinner with my family, Vivian and my postponed date night didn't happen. Vivian wasn't in the best of moods by the time we got home. Neither was I.

Sunday morning began in a lazy fashion, one that allowed for a third cup of coffee after a five-mile run, my longest run in nearly ten years. London was watching a movie in the family room and I was reading the paper on our back patio when Vivian stepped outside.

"I think London and I need a *Mommy and Me* day," Vivian announced.

"A what?"

"You know, girl stuff. We'll get all dressed up and get a manicure and pedicure, maybe have her hair styled, things like that. Kind of a mini-celebration before her first day of school, where we're not having to rush around like crazy like we did yesterday."

"Is any place open on Sunday?"

"We'll find something," she said. "I could use a good mani-pedi, too."

"Does London even know what a mani-pedi is?"

"Of course she does. And it'll be good to have some alone time with her, you know? I've been working so much lately. And it'll give you a break, too, to do whatever you want. Goof around, work, whatever."

"When do I ever goof around?"

"You know what I mean," she said. "Anyway, I have to go help her pick out some clothes. I want to get all dressed up and make it special."

"That sounds like a very girly day," I agreed. "I hope the two of you have a good time."

"We will."

"How long do you think you'll be out?"

"Oh, I don't know. It depends. We might not be back until dinner if London wants to have lunch. I want the day to sort of play out in a relaxed sort of way. Who knows? Maybe she'll want to see a movie."

Forty-five minutes later, they were out the door, and I had the place to myself. These days, it wasn't all that common, but I'd grown so used to rushing from here to there that I wasn't even sure what I should do. Because everything was pretty much arranged with Taglieri, there wasn't really anything in the way of work, and other than a few dishes to place in the dishwasher, the house was tidy. I'd finished my workout and the paper and I'd visited with my family most of the day before, all of which left me wandering the house aimlessly after I'd been on my own for less than an hour. Something was missing—or rather, someone—and I realized that what I really wanted to do if I'd had the option was to ride bikes through the neighborhood with London, the two of us together on a wonderful lazy Sunday afternoon.

Vivian and London didn't return home until nearly seven and I ate both lunch and dinner alone.

I would have loved to have been the kind of guy who'd gone to the gym or meditated, or spent the afternoon reading a biography of Teddy Roosevelt, but the low-key day led to a low-key energy level without a tinge of self-improvement ambition. I ended up spending the day surfing the Internet, one click leading to the next, whatever caught my interest. I read about a giant jellyfish that had washed up on the beaches of Australia, the ongoing travails of various countries in the Middle East, the impending extinction of gorillas in central Africa, and the "Ten Best Foods to Eat to Reduce Belly Fat Fast!"

If there was anything about the surfing to be proud about, it was that I didn't read a single item about any celebrity. It wasn't enough to make me hitch up my pants and walk a bit taller, but it was something, right?

Vivian and London were both weary by the time they came home, but it was a good kind of weary. London showed me her fingernails and toenails and told me that they'd seen a movie and gone shopping, in addition to eating. After her bath, I read to her as usual, but she was yawning steadily before I turned the final page. I kissed her, inhaling the scent of the baby shampoo she still preferred to use.

By the time I was downstairs, Vivian was in her pajamas and sitting in the family room, holding a glass of wine. The TV was on—some show about housewives, most of whom seemed emotionally unstable—but Vivian was more chipper than usual. She chatted about her day, gave me a coy expression when I made a suggestive comment and we ended up in bed.

It wasn't exactly a planned date night, but I was happy nonetheless.

On Tuesday morning, London's first day of school, Vivian and I walked with her through the parking lot, toward the classroom building. When I asked if she wanted me to hold her hand, she hooked her thumbs under the straps on her backpack.

"I'm not a little girl anymore," she said.

Yesterday, Vivian and I had received an email from the teacher saying that the first day could be traumatic for some children and that it was best not to linger over goodbyes. A quick kiss or pat on the back and let the teacher lead them into the classroom, the email instructed. We were discouraged from standing by the door and watching, or gazing through the classroom windows for too long. We were warned against letting our children see us cry, no matter how emotional we might feel, because that might heighten our child's anxiety. We were given the phone numbers of the school nurse, and told that the school counselor would be available in the lobby, if any parents wanted to discuss what they were feeling about their child heading off to school. I wondered if my parents had ever received a letter like that when Marge or I started school and laughed aloud at the thought.

"What are you laughing about?" Vivian asked.

"I'll tell you later. It's nothing."

Up ahead, I saw my mom and dad, waiting by the car. Dad was in his plumber's outfit, which consisted of a blue button-up short-sleeved shirt with the company logo, jeans, and work boots. My mom, thank God, was sans apron or a red hat; she *blended*, which I appreciated even if London didn't care.

London saw them and started running. My dad scooped her up as she jumped. He called her Pumpkin, which I'd never heard before. I wondered if it was new or if I was completely oblivious.

"Today's the big day," my mom said. "Are you excited?"

"It's going to be fun," London said.

"I'm sure you'll love it," my mom assured her.

My dad kissed London on the cheek as he lowered her to the ground.

"Will you hold my hand, Papa?" London asked.

"Of course I will, Pumpkin."

London walked ahead with my dad while Vivian told my mom a bit about the email we'd received from the teacher. My mom frowned in confusion.

"They have a counselor for the *parents?*"

"She works for the school," Vivian explained. "Some parents might be nervous or upset. I'm sure she'll nod and listen and tell them they'll be fine. It's no big deal."

"Are you nervous?"

"No. I feel a trace of sadness, like it's the end of an era, but that'll pass I'm sure."

"Well...good."

We entered the lower school building and as I watched mothers and their children entering the classroom two by two, I thought of the story of Noah's ark, London's favorite book. I expected to see Emily and Bodhi but didn't spot them; I wondered if she'd already come and gone or hadn't yet arrived.

Not that it mattered, of course. We stood in line with other parents and children who were heading toward the kindergarten class; sets of two by twos both in front and behind us. The line moved quickly and when we were at the door, Vivian took charge, joining my dad and London.

"Okay, sweetie. Give Papa and Nana a kiss, okay? Then it's my turn."

London did as she was told, kissing both my parents before kissing Vivian.

"Your dad will pick you up, but I want to hear all about school when you get home. And remember, you have piano today at four, okay? I love you."

"I love you, too, Mommy."

The teacher was smiling. "Well, hello London. Good to see you again. Are you ready for a fun day?"

"Yes, ma'am," London replied, and with a gentle hand on her back, Vivian scooted London forward while the teacher made room for her to pass. As cautioned, we didn't linger at the door or windows, though I was able to spot London standing at a low table littered with felt of different shapes and sizes. Kids were stacking them, making designs. Still no sign of Bodhi, but London didn't seem fazed.

It was only when we were making our way back to the car that I registered what had happened.

"I didn't have a chance to kiss her goodbye."

"That's okay. You'll see her after school." Vivian shrugged.

"Do you want to swing by the lobby to see the counselor?"

"Not a chance," she said. "I'm already late for work. Walter is probably pacing his office, waiting for me."

While London was in school, I reconfirmed all aspects of filming before meeting with the head of the camera crew. We reviewed the schedule, along with the footage that was needed—especially for the longer commercial, which had more than a dozen different shots and would need three days—and made sure we were on exactly the same page. After that, I also cold-called the offices of half a dozen plastic surgeons, and lined up two meetings for the following week.

Not bad for a day's work, and when I went to pick up London, I waited in a queue that stretched down the street. Unlike the drop-off, pickup was more chaotic and time consuming, and it took twenty minutes before London finally got in the car.

"How was your first day of school?" I asked her, slowly pulling out and watching her reflection in the rearview mirror.

"It was fun," she said. "The teacher let me help her read *Go, Dog. Go!* at story time. Some of the kids don't even know their letters yet."

"They'll catch up," I said. "I don't think I was reading when I went to kindergarten."

"Why not?"

"My parents didn't read to me too much. They probably assumed I'd learn to read when I was in school."

"Why didn't they read to you?"

"I don't know. Maybe they were too tired."

"Mom reads to me when she's tired. And you read to me when you're tired."

"People are just different, I guess. Hey, by the way, did Bodhi ever show up at school?"

"Yes and we get to sit at the same table. He's really good at coloring."

"That's great. It's nice to sit by someone you already know."

By then, the school was receding in the distance. "Daddy?"

"Yes?"

"Can we go to Dairy Queen before piano? Since I went to school today?"

Noting the time, I did a quick calculation. "I think we can squeeze that in."

The stop for ice cream meant that we arrived at the piano teacher's house with only a few minutes to spare. London had been on the go for eight hours, nine by the time the lesson was over, and that didn't count the time it had taken her to get ready for school. She was going to be exhausted by the time we got home.

While London practiced, I took a walk through the neighborhood. My knees were a bit achy from the regular jogging but not too bad. I had just set out when I heard my cell phone ringing. Marge.

"How did London do on her first day?" Marge asked without preamble.

"She had a good time," I answered. "Her friend Bodhi was there."

"Yeah? How about Bodhi's mom?"

"I didn't see her," I said. "We were gone by the time she and Bodhi got there."

"Thank God," she said. "Otherwise, poor Emily might have been melted by Vivian's laser-beam death stares."

"Aren't you supposed to be working instead of picking on my wife?"

"I'm not picking on her. If anything, I'm on her side. I mean if Liz started hanging out with her ex, who also happened to be a terrific, beautiful, recently separated woman, I'd be trying to annihilate her with my laser-beam stares, too."

"What is it with women?"

"Oh please. Don't even go there. Are you kidding? I'm sure you just love hearing her bring up *Walter* in every conversation. Even I was getting tired of his name."

"She works for him," I said, trying to downplay it. "It's normal."

"Yeah? What's my boss's name?" When I didn't answer, she went on. "And who cares if they work together, exercise together, travel together, and fly on the private jet together, right? And what does it matter if she mentions her billionaire boss's name more than she mentions yours? You're so evolved that you're above feeling even the slightest tinge of jealousy."

"Are you trying to get a rise out of me?"

"Not at all," she said. "But I do want to know how the rest of your

213

weekend went, after you left Mom's. I take it you didn't bring up the *new-bank-account* or *apartment-in-Atlanta* things?"

"No. Saturday night ended up being pretty quiet. We went to bed early. We were all tired. And on Sunday, I had a break actually." I told her a bit about Vivian and London's day.

"Like I didn't see *that* one coming," Marge offered.

"What are you talking about?"

"Did you notice the way she was staring at you after London was stung by the bee?"

I remembered exactly but didn't want to say it. Instead: "She was just upset that London was hurt."

"Nope. She was upset because London went running to you and not her to comfort her. Liz noticed it, too."

I remembered thinking the same thing and said nothing.

"So what does she do?" Marge went on. "She spends all day with London on Sunday, and then rushes London into the classroom before you had a chance to kiss her goodbye."

"How do you know about that?"

"Because Mom called and told me. She thought it was odd."

"You're crazy," I said, suddenly feeling suddenly defensive. "You're reading too much into it."

"I might be," she admitted. "I hope I am."

"And stop talking about Vivian like that. All of you need to stop dissecting everything she does. She's been under a ton of pressure these last few weeks."

"You're right," she said. "I was out of line. I'm sorry." There was a pause. "What are you doing now?"

"Are you trying to change the subject?"

"I'm doing my best. I've already apologized."

"London's at her piano lesson. I'm on a walk. I figured I'd burn a few more calories before dinner."

"Good for you," she said. "You look thinner in the face by the way."

"You can't really tell yet."

"Oh yeah you can. This last weekend, I was like . . . wow."

"You're just trying to butter me up so I don't stay mad at you."

"You never stay mad at me. You're such a people pleaser, you'll

214

probably hang up worried that my feelings were hurt because you called me out."

I laughed. "Goodbye, Marge."

The thing is, as unhappy as I was about Marge's assessment of Vivian, I couldn't shake the notion that there may have been more than a grain of truth in it. The only event that didn't fit neatly into Marge's theories was our amiable Sunday night, but even Vivian's unexpected warmth could have been explained by the feeling that she'd reaffirmed her undisputed primacy in London's life.

On the other hand, that was crazy. So what if London had run to me after being stung by a bee? My feelings wouldn't have been hurt if she'd instead run to Vivian; people in healthy marriages didn't fall prey to such petty power struggles. Vivian and I were a team.

Weren't we?

I sensed instantly that Vivian wasn't in a pleasant mood when she returned from work, and when I asked about her day, she launched into a story about how the CFO had just submitted her two-week resignation, which threw the company into sudden upheaval.

"Walter was absolutely furious," she said on her way to the master bedroom. She went into the closet and began removing her work clothes. "And I can't say that I blame him. Just last week, she'd formally agreed to move to Atlanta. She even used it to negotiate a relocation fee bonus—which she already collected—and now she suddenly informs us that she's taken a new job? People are always trying to take advantage of Walter, and I watch it happen all the time. I'm so sick and tired of it."

There's that name again, remembering Marge's needling. Not *once* but *twice*.

"I'm sure she's doing what he thinks is best for her family."

"You didn't let me finish," Vivian snapped. In her bra and panties, she shimmied into a pair of jeans. "It turns out she's also been recruiting other executives to follow her to the new company, and there are rumors that a few other executives are actually thinking about it. Do you know how much damage that could do to Walter's company?"

Third time's a charm. "Sounds like a rough day."

"It was awful," she said, grabbing a white T-shirt. I couldn't help noting how stylish Vivian was, even when dressing down. "Of course, what that means to me is that because of this new wrinkle, I'm probably going to have to spend even more time in Atlanta, at least for a while anyway."

That part I heard clearly. "More time than four days?"

She held up her hands and drew a long breath. "Please don't add to an already awful day. I know you're upset. I'm upset, too. Just let me go spend some time with London and we'll talk about it later. I want to hear how her first day went and unwind and maybe have a glass of wine, okay?"

By then, she was already on her way to see London.

While they were in the family room, I made a quick dinner; chicken, rice, glazed carrots, and a salad. When it was ready, they came to the table. Vivian was still distracted and tense. London, meanwhile, kept up a steady stream of chatter—how she and Bodhi played hopscotch at recess, that Bodhi was a really good jumper, and countless other details of her exciting day at school.

After dinner, I cleaned the kitchen while Vivian went upstairs with London. Despite the late hour, I called Taglieri to speak to him about the rehearsal tomorrow and make sure he'd reviewed the script. The one thing I'd learned from clients is that the more familiar they were with the script, the more successful they were at integrating other directions.

By the time I got off the phone, I could hear the sound of shouting upstairs. I hurried up the steps, stopping in the doorway of London's bedroom. Vivian was holding a damp towel; London, in her pajamas, had wet hair and her cheeks were streaked with tears.

"How many times have I told you *not* to put the wet towels into the hamper?" Vivian demanded. "And this dress shouldn't have gone in the hamper in the first place!"

"I said I'm sorry!" London shouted back. "I didn't mean it!"

"Now everything is going to smell mildewed and some of the stains have probably set."

"I'm sorry!"

"What's going on?" I demanded.

Vivian turned toward me, her expression livid. "What's going on is that your daughter's new dress is probably ruined. The one she wore on Sunday."

"I didn't do it on purpose!" London said, her face crumpling. Vivian held up her hand, her lips a grim line.

"I know you didn't. That's not the point. The point is, you put a dirty dress into the hamper with your new dress, and then you put *wet towels* on top of them. How many times have I told you to let the towels dry over the side of the tub before you put them in the hamper?"

"I forgot!" London cried. "I'm sorry!"

"It was my fault," I interjected, the wet-towel rule clearly new to me. I'd never seen Vivian and London yell at each other like this before. The sight brought back memories of the night London and I had argued. "I just tell her to put anything dirty in the hamper."

"The truth is that she knows what to do!" Vivian snapped before directing her attention to London. "Right?"

"I'm sorry, Mommy," she said.

"I'll bring them to the dry cleaner tomorrow," I volunteered. "I'm sure we'll be able to get the stains out."

"That's not the point, Russ! She doesn't have any respect for the things I've bought her, no matter how many times I tell her!"

"I said I'm SORRY!" London screamed.

One thing I knew for sure: Vivian was way too angry and London way too tired for something like this to continue.

"How about I finish up here?" I offered. "I can get her in bed."

"Why? So you can tell her that I'm overreacting?"

"No, of course not—"

"Oh, please. You've been undermining me ever since I went back to work," she said, "but okay, fine. I'll leave the two of you alone." She started for our bedroom before facing London again. "I'm very disappointed that you don't care enough about me to listen," she said.

I saw the angst on London's face as soon as Vivian left and my first thought was to try to make sense of how cruel Vivian had sounded. I should have responded but Vivian was already down the steps and London was crying so I stepped farther into the room and took a seat on the bed. I opened my arms. "Come here, baby girl," I whispered and London came toward me. I put my arms around her and pulled her close, feeling her body continue to shake.

"I didn't mean to ruin my dress," she whimpered.

"I know you didn't. Let's not worry about that right now."

"But Mommy's mad at me."

"She'll be okay in a little while. She had a rough day at work and I know she's really proud that you did so well in school today."

Her cries gradually began to subside, diminishing to sniffles. I wiped her tears away with my finger.

"I'm proud of you, too, Pumpkin."

"Papa calls me that, not you."

"Maybe I can call you that, too."

"No," she said.

Despite her sadness, I smiled. "Okay. Maybe I'll call you . . . Donkey."

"No."

"Butterbun?"

"No," she said. "Call me London."

"Not even baby girl? Or sweetie?"

"Okay," she nodded, her head shifting against my chest. "Mommy doesn't love me anymore."

"Of course she does. She'll always love you."

"Then why is she moving away?"

"She's not moving away," I said. "She just has to work in Atlanta sometimes. I know you'll miss her." As I held my daughter, I ached for the little girl who was no doubt as confused as I was by what was happening to our family.

It took more than the usual number of stories before London was able to finally settle down enough to go to sleep. After kissing her on the cheek, I went downstairs and found Vivian pulling items from the closet.

"She's ready for a kiss if you want to head up."

Vivian grabbed her cell phone and walked past me, placing the clothes she'd removed on the bed in the master bedroom. There were two open suitcases, each of them already half packed and there were far more outfits than necessary for a three-day trip. There were business suits and workout clothes, casual wear and dresses more appropriate for dinner dates. I wasn't sure why she was packing so much. Did she not intend to come home this weekend? Surely she would have mentioned that already... but then I realized that there was no reason to believe that. I would learn what was up when she wanted me to know. As I stared at the half-packed suitcases, the phrase *corporate apartments* leapt again to mind. Though I'd felt hollowed out when I'd been with London only moments ago, the emptiness had now been replaced with knots.

I couldn't bear staring at the clothes any longer so I went to the kitchen and debated whether or not to pour myself a drink before deciding against it. Instead, I stood before the sink and absently stared at the backyard. The sun had gone down not long before, the sky still clinging to the last vestiges of daylight, and the moon had not yet risen. The resulting sky—a fast-fading twilight—struck me as strangely foreboding.

I felt a growing understanding emerging along with a creeping sense of fear. The more I thought about my wife, the more I accepted the notion that I no longer had any idea what she was thinking. About London, about me. About us. Somehow, despite the years we'd been together, she'd become a stranger to me. Though we'd made love only two nights earlier, I wondered if was because she loved me or because it was a habit, a lingering residue of the years we'd spent together, more physical than emotional. But that option, as heartbreaking as it felt to me, was better than the alternative—that she'd made love to me as a distraction, because she was doing or planning something even worse, something I didn't even want to imagine.

I told myself that it wasn't true and even if she was vacillating when it came to her feelings toward me, she would always want what was best for our family.

Wouldn't she?

I didn't know, but then I heard Vivian speaking in a low voice as she descended the stairs. I heard her say the name *Walter* and she told him to hold on; I knew that she didn't want me to know she was on the phone. I heard the front door open and close. Though I shouldn't have, I crept toward the living room. The drapes were closed, the living room already dark, and I stood behind the curtains, gazing through the opening between the fabric and the glass. I was spying on my wife, something I had never imagined doing before, but the rising fright made it feel as though my free will had vanished. I knew it was wrong, even as I was craning my neck and shifting the curtain—and by then it was too late to stop.

I could not hear much until Vivian laughed, a joyful sound, one that I hadn't heard in what seemed like years. But it wasn't simply the laugh that startled me; it was the way she smiled and the light in her eyes, the giddiness she radiated. Gone was the Vivian who'd come home surly from work or snarled at London; the irate Vivian who'd been in the master bedroom was nowhere to be seen.

I had seen that expression on Vivian's face before in moments of undiluted happiness, often having to do with London. But I'd also glimpsed it when we were alone, back when I was younger and still single and courting a woman I'd met at a cocktail party in New York.

Vivian looked like she was in love.

By the time Vivian reentered the house, I was in the den. Afraid of what I might say, I avoided speaking with her. I didn't want to spend time with her and I forced myself to review Taglieri's script, the words meaning nothing at all, even as I read them.

I felt her move behind me, but only for an instant. I heard her footsteps recede to the master bedroom, where I knew she planned to fill both suitcases until they were nearly bulging.

I stayed in the den for an hour, then another, and finally a third hour. Vivian finally came back to check on me. I think she was caught off-guard by the fact that I hadn't sought her out. The last she knew, I'd been comforting a crying London, and because she knew me, she assumed I would try to discuss the incident.

Now, though, like she'd done so often to me, I'd left her wondering what was going on.

"Are you coming to bed?"

"In a little while," I answered without turning around. "I still have some work to do."

"It's getting late."

"I know," I said.

"I shouldn't have yelled at London the way I did. I apologized when I tucked her in."

"I'm glad," I said. "She was upset."

She waited. I still didn't turn. She continued to wait but I added nothing more.

"Okay, whatever," she finally said with a sigh. "Goodnight."

"Goodnight," I whispered, but even as I said it, I had begun to wonder whether that really meant goodbye.

Thirteen days passed before I learned the truth.

I went to the agency the following day and found the perfect young actress for the commercial I envisioned; that commercial would film later in September, once a chunk of the editing on the first two had been completed. I rehearsed with Taglieri and we shot the commercial outside the courthouse the following day, and completed the voice-over for the second commercial. We filmed the second commercial, and the following week, I made the presentations to the two plastic surgeons. I left one of those meetings thinking I had a chance to land my second client, and went to work on a more detailed proposal.

As my first step, I immersed myself in the doctor's website and studied the direct mailings he'd done in the past. They'd been designed by his office manager and they were all over the board when it came to the themes we'd discussed—safety, professionalism, improved self-image, and limited recovery time—and I had no doubt I could design a more cohesive campaign. After that, I reviewed a dozen websites for plastic surgeons around the country and touched base with my tech guy, getting a rough estimate of the costs.

From there, I got started, and I spent two full days putting my ideas into the kind of presentation that I thought was necessary for his business.

The hours I wasn't working were devoted to London and taking care of the house. And the laundry. And the yard. And the hamsters. I brought London to and from school, piano, and dance—Vivian took her to art class on Saturday—and we rode our bikes on six separate days. By that point, London had grown confident enough on the final ride to let go of the handlebars for a couple of seconds on a flat and straight stretch of roadway.

We celebrated with lemonade on the back porch while we again looked for bald eagles.

As for Vivian, she returned on Friday evening, and spent most of the weekend with London. She was polite to me, but seemed intent to keep the two of us at a distance. I went to visit my parents on my own, and when she left on Monday morning, she brought along with her two more bulging suitcases. By then, the only things left in her closet were the clothes she seldom wore. She told me that she would be using one of the corporate apartments, but by then, I'd expected her to say exactly that.

She was gone all week. She FaceTimed with London every night at six and occasionally she tried to prod me into conversation. I couldn't do it. She got angry with me about it on Tuesday and Thursday, and hung up on me when I still wouldn't rise to the bait.

She came home on Friday afternoon at the start of Labor Day weekend, catching me slightly off-guard. Actually, part of me was shocked to see her at all, even though I didn't want to admit that to myself. London was thrilled. Vivian picked her up from school and took her to dance, then eventually got London ready for bed. She told me when it was my turn to go up, and I read four stories, staying upstairs longer than I had to, because I was afraid to face Vivian alone.

But she said nothing that frightened me. Though date night was off the table—even I wasn't in the mood—Vivian was strangely pleasant, making small talk, but I wasn't in the mood for that either.

Saturday and Sunday were quiet days. Vivian spent nearly all her time with London—just the two of them—while I worked out, cleaned the house, reviewed the footage for the commercials and made some notes, and visited my parents. I avoided Vivian because by then, I was afraid of what she was going to tell me.

On Monday, Labor Day, Marge and Liz had a barbecue at their place. Vivian, London, and I spent most of the afternoon there. I didn't want to go home because I knew what would happen once we did.

I ended up being right. After I read to London and shut off the lights, Vivian was sitting at the dining room table. "We should talk," she began. Her words are mostly a jumble to me even now but I caught the major points. It just happened, she said; she hadn't mean for it to happen. She'd fallen in love with Walter. She was moving to Atlanta. We could talk next week, but she was traveling to Florida and Washington, D.C., and besides, I probably needed time to sort through what she'd told me. She didn't see the point in arguing about it; it had nothing to do with me; things just happen. She was leaving tonight, too. She'd told London that she would be working out of town again, but hadn't told London yet that she was leaving me. It was easier that way, for now, but we'd talk about London when emotions weren't so fraught. And, she added, she wouldn't be staying the night.

The private jet, she said, was waiting.

CHAPTER 14

Shock

When I was in college, my friends and I used to go out on the weekends, which typically began Thursday around three and concluded upon waking late on Sunday morning. One of the guys I hung out with most—a guy named Danny Jackson—shared the same major and we ended up in many of the same classes. Given NC State's sizable student population, it seemed to me that the class-scheduling gods must have decided that we needed to see more of each other.

Danny was as easygoing a guy as I ever met. Born and raised in Mobile, Alabama, he had a very pretty older sister who was dating the punter for the Auburn Tigers, and he never said a bad word about his parents. He seemed to imply they were pretty cool as far as parents went and they must have passed that on to him, because I felt the same way about him. Whatever I wanted to do—grab a burger at two in the morning, or swing by a frat party or watch a ball game at the local sports bar—Danny was always up for it. Whenever we met up, we'd find ourselves picking up our conversation in the same spot we'd left it, even if it had been weeks since we'd seen each other. He drank PBR—he swore it was the best beer in the world, as evidenced by the blue ribbon—and while he would often drink enough to acquire a buzz, he had an automatic slow-down switch in his head that pretty much prevented him from ever becoming drunk. Which was quite a contrast with the rest of the college population—for them, getting smashed seemed the entire point of drinking.

One Saturday night, Danny and I were out with a few other guys at one of the more crowded college bars. With finals looming, most of us were a bit anxious, which of course we tried to downplay. Instead, we drank as we usually did—a bit past buzzed—all except Danny, whose slow-down switch had flipped to the "on" position.

He got the call a little past eleven; I have no idea how he even heard the ring over the noise in the bar. But he did, and after glancing at the screen, he got up from the table and went outside. We thought nothing about it. Why would we? Nor did we consider it amiss when he walked past our table after coming back inside and made a beeline for the bar.

I watched him wedge himself between some people, vying for the bartender's attention. It took a few minutes before he received his drink, but when he turned, I saw that he'd ordered a cocktail—a very tall glass of something golden brown. He wandered off toward another area of the bar, as if he'd forgotten us entirely.

Of everyone there, I was probably his closest friend, so I followed him. By then, he was leaning against the wall near the restroom. As I approached, he took a huge swallow from his glass, finishing nearly a third of its contents.

"What do you have there?" I asked.

"Bourbon."

"Wow. That's a pretty big glass."

"I told them to fill it," he said.

"Did I miss the contest where Pabst got second place, not first?"

It wasn't particularly funny and I don't know why I said it, other than that the way he was acting was making me nervous.

"It's what my dad drinks," he said.

For the first time, I noticed his shell-shocked expression. Not the effect of alcohol. Something else.

"Are you okay?" I asked.

He took another long drink. By then, the glass was half empty. It had to be at least four, maybe five shots. Danny was going to be drunk, maybe very drunk, in a very short while.

"No," he said. "I'm not okay."

"What happened? Who called?"

"My mom," he said. "It was my mom who called." He pinched the bridge of his nose. "She just told me my dad died."

"Your dad?"

225

"He was in a car accident. She found out just a few minutes ago. Someone from Highway Patrol came by the house."

"That's . . . awful," I said, truly at a loss for words. "Is—is there anything I can do? Can I bring you to your place?"

"She's getting me a ticket to fly home tomorrow. I don't know what I'm going to do about finals, though. Will they let me retake them next week?"

"I don't know, but that's the last thing you should be thinking about right now. Is your mom okay?"

It took him a long time to answer. Instead, he seemed to be staring into the distance.

"No," he said. He gulped at his drink, finishing it. "She's not. I need to sit down."

"Sure," I said. "Let's go."

I led him back to the table. Despite the alcohol he'd consumed, he didn't seem affected at all. Instead, he sat quietly, adding nothing to the conversation. He didn't mention the death of his father to anyone else at the table, and an hour later, I drove him back to his apartment.

He went home on Sunday, just as he'd told me he would. And though we were friends, I never saw or heard from him again.

"Hold on," Marge said. After I dropped London off at school on Tuesday morning, she'd come straight to my house, where we sat at the kitchen table. "So she just . . . left?"

"Last night," I said.

"Did she at least say she was sorry?"

"I don't remember." I shook my head. "I can't even . . . um . . . I mean . . . I . . ."

I couldn't keep my thoughts straight; my roiling emotions—shock and fear, disbelief and anger—had me veering from one extreme to the next. Though I knew I'd done it, I couldn't remember driving London to school only a few minutes earlier; the drive had been consigned to nothingness.

"Your hands are shaking," Marge said.

"Yeah . . . I'm okay." Trailing off, I took a long breath. "Shouldn't you be at work? I can scramble up some eggs."

Marge would tell me later that I got up from the table and went to the fridge; as soon as I pulled it open, I must have decided I needed coffee instead. I went to the coffee cabinet and then realized I should probably get cups out for Marge and me first. But I must have thought I still needed coffee so I set the cups beside the coffeemaker. She watched as I went to the fridge and pulled out the eggs before returning them to the same location. She said I then wandered to the pantry and came out with a bowl and . . .

"How about I make breakfast?" she suggested, rising from the table.

"Huh?"

"Have a seat."

"Don't you need to go to work?"

"I've decided that I'm taking the day off." She reached for her cell phone. "Sit down. I'll be back in minute. I just have to tell my boss."

As I took my seat, I was struck anew by the realization that Vivian had left me. That she was in love with her boss. She was gone. I watched Marge open the door to the back patio.

"Where are you going?"

"I'm going to call my boss."

"Why are you calling your boss?"

Marge stayed with me all day. She picked up London from school and also brought her to and from her piano lesson. Liz came by after her last appointment, and together they not only made dinner, but kept London entertained and helped her get ready for bed. It wasn't often that her aunties came by to play, and London was over the moon from the extra attention.

Again, it would be Marge who would tell me this. Like the drive to school, I wouldn't be able to remember it. The only thing I really remember was watching the clock and waiting for Vivian to call, something she never did.

The next morning, after sleeping less than three hours, I crawled out of bed feeling almost hungover, with all my nerves on edge. It was a

227

monumental effort to shower and shave, something I'd neglected the day before. Nor had I eaten much—only a few bites at breakfast and dinner—but the thought of food was inconceivable.

Marge handed me a cup of coffee as soon as soon as I entered the kitchen, then started loading a plate. "Take a seat," she said. "You need something in your stomach."

"What are you doing here?"

"What does it look like? I came by this morning to make sure you had something to eat."

"I didn't hear you knock."

"I didn't," she said. "After you went to bed, I borrowed your house key. I hope you don't mind."

"It's fine," I said. Raising the mug, I took a sip but the coffee tasted wrong, *off* somehow. Despite the tantalizing aromas, my stomach remained knotted. Nonetheless I pulled out my chair at the table and plopped down. She set a plate in front of me, piled high with eggs, bacon, and toast.

"I don't think I can eat," I offered.

"Too bad," she said. "You're going to eat, even if I have to tie you to the chair and feed you myself."

Too worn out to argue, I forced down a few bites; strangely, every bite seemed a little easier than the last, but I still finished less than half of it.

"She left me."

"I know," Marge said.

"She didn't want to try to work it out."

"I know."

"Why? What did I do wrong?"

Marge took a puff from her inhaler, buying time, and fully aware that casting blame or heaping criticism on Vivian would only heighten my emotional turmoil.

"I don't think you did anything wrong. It's just that relationships are hard, and both people have to want them to work."

As true as the statement was, I felt no relief when she said it.

"Are you sure you don't want me to stay with you today?" Marge asked.

"I can't ask you to take another day off," I said. Eating seemed to have had a mildly stabilizing effect on my emotional state. I still wasn't great, mind you. Not even close. The emotional surges may not have been the tidal waves of yesterday, but they were still in the rogue wave category, the kind that sank the *Andrea Gail* in the film *The Perfect Storm*. I felt wildly off balance, but hoped that I could still handle the basics. Get London to school and back. Dance class. Order pizza for dinner. I knew I wouldn't have the mental or emotional energy for anything else; even reading the paper or vacuuming were way beyond my capabilities. My goal was simply to stay upright and take care of my daughter.

Marge didn't seem convinced. "I'm going to call and check on you today. More than once."

"Okay," I agreed, but I knew there was part of me that was afraid to be alone. What if I simply broke into pieces as soon as she left? Or shattered, like the rest of my world.

Vivian had left me.

She was in love with someone else.

I was a terrible husband, worthless, and I had failed.

I disappointed her one too many times, and now I was alone.

Oh, my God, I thought, as soon as Marge closed the door behind her. I'm alone.

I'm going to end up dying alone.

While London was at school, I walked. I paced from one end of the house to the other and back again; I walked the streets of my neighborhood for hours. Questions about Vivian smashed into one another like endless battering rams. Was she in Atlanta or in another city? Was she taking the day off to set up the apartment or at the office? I wondered what she was doing—I imagined her using an earpiece as she spoke on the phone in a corner office, or hurrying down the hall carrying a stack of papers, the office I envisioned shifting from sleek and modern to stuffy and formal. I wondered whether Spannerman was with her; I wondered whether she was laughing beside him or at her desk with her head in her hands. I checked my cell phone constantly, hoping to hear from her, watching for texts or missed calls. I brought the phone everywhere. I wanted to hear her voice telling me that she'd made a mistake and that she wanted to come home. I wanted her to tell me that she still loved me. I wanted her to ask me to forgive her, and in my heart, I knew that I wouldn't hesitate. I still loved her; the thought of life without her was incomprehensible.

All the while, I continued to wonder what I had done wrong. Was it quitting my job? Was it that I'd gained a little weight? Was it that I had worked too much, prior to quitting my job? And when did things start going wrong? When did I become disposable? How could she leave us? How could she leave London? Did Vivian intend to take her to Atlanta?

The final question was the worst of all, too much to contemplate, and after finally returning to the house, I was exhausted. I knew I should nap, but as soon as I lay down, my mind began to race. Marge called three times, and I realized I had yet to tell my parents what had happened, but I still didn't want to believe it.

I wanted this to be a dream.

In midafternoon, I picked up London while my internal storm continued to rage. She asked for ice cream, and though the request felt impossibly taxing, I somehow made it to Dairy Queen. I also, somehow, got her to dance class on time.

I went for a walk while London was at class. I'm not a strong man. I paced to the end of the strip mall. When I reached it, tears had begun to blur my vision and all at once, I was standing by myself with shoulders heaving, my face in my hands.

"When's Mommy coming home?" London asked me. There was a box of pizza on the table and I set my slice of pizza aside. I'd finished half of it. "I don't know, sweetheart. I haven't talked to her," I said. "But as soon as I find out, I'll let you know."

If she thought my answer odd, she didn't show it. "Did I tell you that Bodhi and me found a baby turtle at recess?"

"A baby turtle?"

"We were playing freeze tag and I found it over by the fence and he was so cute. And then Bodhi came over and he thought it was really cute, too. We tried to feed it grass, but it wasn't hungry, and then all the other kids came over and the teacher came over, too. And we asked if we could put it in a box and bring it into the classroom and the teacher said yes!"

"That sounds exciting."

"It was! She got a pencil box and she put the turtle in it, and then we all walked with her while she brought it into the classroom. I think the turtle was scared because it kept trying to get out but it couldn't because the box was too slippery on the sides. And then we wanted to name it but the teacher said that we probably shouldn't because she was going to let it go."

"She didn't want to keep it?"

"She said that it probably missed its mommy."

I felt a lump in my throat. "Yeah. That makes sense."

"But me and Bodhi named him anyway. We decided to call him Ed."

"Ed the turtle?"

"We also thought about calling him Marco."

"How do you know it's a boy turtle?"

"We just know."

"Oh," I said and despite the torment of the last couple of days, I found myself smiling.

It didn't last.

While I was putting the remains of the pizza into ziplock bags, Vivian called. When I saw her photograph on the screen of my phone, my heart suddenly hammered in my chest. London was in the family room watching television and I stepped out the kitchen door, onto the back patio. I steeled myself before connecting the call.

"Hey there," I said, trying to sound like everything was normal between us when actually, nothing was normal at all. "How are you?"

She hesitated. "I'm okay. How are you?"

"It's been a little strange here," I said. "But I'm holding up. Where are you now?"

She seemed to debate whether or not to answer. "I'm in Tampa," she finally admitted. "Is London around? Or is she already in the bath?"

"No, not yet. She's in the family room."

"Can I talk to her?"

I steadied my breathing. "Before I put her on the phone, don't you think we should talk?"

"I'm not sure that's a good idea, Russ."

"Why not?"

"Because I don't know what you want me to say."

"What I want you to say?" I repeated. "I want you to give us another chance, Vivian." I ignored the deafening silence on her end. "I still feel like I don't know what's really going on. How can we make this work? We can go to counseling."

Her voice was tight. "Please, Russ. Can I just talk to London? I miss her."

Don't you miss me? Or are you with Walter right now?

The thought came unbidden, bringing with it the image of my wife calling from a hotel suite, Walter watching television in an adjoining area, and it was all I could do to step back inside the house and call to my daughter.

"Your mom's on the phone, London. She wants to say hi."

I couldn't help but eavesdrop on the conversation, even when London wandered toward the family room. I heard her tell Vivian about her day—she also told Vivian about the turtle—and say *I love you;* I heard her ask when Vivian was coming home. Though I didn't hear the answer, I could tell by London's expression that she didn't much like the answer. *Okay, Mommy,* she eventually said. *I miss you, too. We can talk tomorrow.*

Vivian knew I generally turned my phone to airplane mode when I went to bed, and old habits dying hard, I did so again that night. In the morning, after turning it back on, I saw that Vivian had left two voicemails.

"I know you wanted to talk and we will, but only when we're both ready. I don't know what else I can tell you. I want you to know that I didn't plan for this to happen, and I know how much I've hurt you. I wish it wasn't this way, but I don't want to lie to you either.

"I'm mainly calling about London. Right now, it's insanely busy at work with the transition and Walter's PAC and all the traveling. We still have the DC leg, and we're flying up to New York this weekend. And since I'm traveling so much, it's probably best if London stays with you for a while. I want to get settled in here first and get her room set up, but I haven't had time to start either of those things. Anyway, I think it's important that you don't tell London what's going on yet. She's already stressed with school and I know she's got to be exhausted. Besides, I think this is something we should do together. Hold on. Let me call you right back. I don't want your voicemail to cut me off."

The second voicemail picked up where she'd left off.

"I spoke with a counselor today about the best way to tell London, and she said we should stress that we think it's best if we just live apart for a while, without mentioning separation or divorce. And obviously, we should both emphasize that it doesn't have anything to do with her and that we both love her. Anyway, we can discuss it more in person, but I wanted to let you know that I'm trying to do what's best for London. We'll also have to talk about when it might be a good time for her to come to Atlanta." She paused. "Okay, I think that's it. Have a good day."

Have a good day?

Was she kidding? Sitting on the edge of the bed, I replayed the voicemails several times. I think I was searching for something—anything—to suggest that she still cared about me in the slightest, but if it was there, I didn't hear it. I heard a lot of what she wanted, cloaked in terms that were ostensibly all about London's well-being, and the subterfuge infuriated me. While I was thinking about it, my cell phone rang.

"Hey there," Marge said, her tone sympathetic. "Just calling to check in on you."

"It's not even seven in the morning."

"I know, but I was thinking about you."

"I'm . . . kind of angry, actually."

"Yeah?"

"Vivian left a couple of messages," I said. I paraphrased as best I could.

"Oh, boy. That's what you woke up to? Not exactly a cup of delicious coffee, is it? Speaking of which, I'm on your street and about to pull in your driveway. Unlock your front door."

I left the bedroom and padded downstairs. By the time I got the door open, Marge was already getting out of the car, holding a pair of Styrofoam cups.

Watching her walk up the drive, I noted she was already dressed for work. "I can make coffee here," I said.

"I know. But I wanted to lay my eyeballs on you. Did you get any sleep last night?"

"Maybe four or five hours."

"I didn't sleep much either."

"Liz keeping you up late?"

"No," she said. "Just worried about you. Let's go inside. Is London up yet?"

"Not yet."

"How about I get her ready while you enjoy your coffee?"

"I'm not incompetent."

"I know," she said. "Actually, you're the opposite. You're holding up a lot better than I would be in your shoes."

"I doubt that."

Surprising me, she reached out to touch my cheek, something I could never remember her doing before. "I haven't had to talk you down from a water tower, have I?"

Thanks to the coffee and Marge's early morning help, I felt a bit better than I had the day before when I drove London to school. She chattered away in the backseat about her dream—something about a

frog that kept changing colors every time it hopped—and her innocent cheer was exactly what I needed.

Back at home, I forced myself to put on my running gear. I hadn't
run since Vivian's announcement—the first days I'd missed since
I'd started back up—and I hoped that the physical exertion would
leave me feeling more like myself. On the run I was fine despite adding a couple extra miles, but by the time I'd finished my shower, I
found myself thinking about Vivian again. The fury I'd felt earlier had
diminished, replaced by an overwhelming sadness.

It was almost too much to bear, and knowing I couldn't face yet
another day like the two I'd just weathered, I had to do something.
Anything. My desire to work was zero, but I forced myself to go to my
den. As soon as I took a seat at the desk and saw a photo of Vivian,
I knew that staying at home wasn't going to work. There were too
many reminders here; too many reasons for the emotional train to
start steaming again.

It was time, I thought, to visit my office.

Packing up my computer, I went to the office I'd rented. The shared
receptionist was startled to see me, but reported as usual that I had no
messages. For the first time, I honestly didn't care.

I unlocked my office. Nothing had changed since I'd last been
here—it had been weeks—and there was a thin sheen of dust on my
desk. I set my computer on it anyway and opened my email.

Dozens of messages, most of them receipts for automatic bills or
spam. I deleted as much as I could and filed the bills in the appropriate folders, until I was left with the emails containing links to the
footage for the commercials. With the presentation for the plastic
surgeon already complete, it was Taglieri's turn. I reviewed the notes
I'd taken the weekend before; of the six takes we'd made in front of
the courthouse, three were definite no-gos. Of the three that were
workable, I eventually whittled that down to two. Of those, I thought
he was better in the beginning in the second take, and better at the
end in the first take. With a little editing—I had basic software on
my computer—I'd be able to put those two sections together. There's
nothing quite like movie magic.

Even better, I *liked* him in the footage we'd shot, and I was sure that others would as well. He came across exactly the way I hoped—honest, competent, and likable—but more than that, he looked *good* on camera. Maybe it was the natural lighting, but it was a vast improvement over his previous commercials.

The footage for the second commercial was much more complicated. There were a lot of different scenes shot from varying angles—and a particularly gorgeous scene of a meadow with grazing horses—along with many different people, and that multiplied the way the commercial could eventually play out. Knowing it would take more time and energy than I'd be able to summon, I decided to simply work on the first commercial.

The software I used wasn't commercial grade, but that was okay; I'd already spoken to the best freelance editor in town, and slowly but surely I got to work. At lunch, I had to force myself to finish a bowl of soup I'd picked up from the deli, then went back to editing until it was time to pick up London from school.

It had not been an easy day. Whenever my concentration waned—even for a second—the emotional turbulence, and questions, would return. I'd get up from my desk and pace; other times, I would stand near the window, feeling as my chest grew tight and hands began to shake in what seemed to be an airless office. I would feel—*deeply feel*—my own loss in a way that made me believe there was no reason to go on.

But inevitably, because distraction was my only hope of salvation, I would return to the desk and try to lose myself in the service of Taglieri.

"What you're experiencing is normal," Liz assured me on the back patio later that night, after I told her what I was going through. She and Marge had shown up at my house yet again after work. Marge had brought Play-Doh and was sitting on the floor with London while they sculpted various items.

"You've suffered a profound shock. Anyone would be upset."

"I'm worse than upset," I admitted. "I can barely function."

While Liz and I had talked hundreds of times, it was the first time

I ever felt that I *needed* to talk to her. The day had left me spent. I wanted nothing more than to run away or find a dark, quiet place to hide, but with London, I couldn't do that. Nor did I think it would help; after all, I would carry my thoughts with me wherever I went.

"But you told me you went to work," she said. "You got London to and from school and piano. And she's eaten."

"I picked up fast food on the way home."

"That's okay. You've got to learn to be gentle with yourself. You're handling this about as well as anyone could. Especially the way you're dealing with the emotions."

"Did you not hear anything I told you?"

"Of course I did. And I know it feels unbearable, but believe it or not, the fact that you're letting yourself feel the emotions instead of suppressing them is a good thing. There's an old saying that goes like this: *The only way out is through.* Do you understand what that I mean by that?"

"Not really. But then again, my brain doesn't seem to be working all that well. The next time I look at the commercial I edited together, I'll be depressed at what a terrible job I did."

"If it's that bad, you'll fix it, right?"

I nodded. I had to fix it. Because Vivian had opened her own bank account, it was up to me to cover all the bills, including, I assumed, the mortgage.

"Good. And that will be another step forward. And as to what I meant earlier—too many people think that suppressing emotions— or avoiding them—is healthy. And sometimes it can be, especially after the passage of time. But in the immediate aftermath of a trauma-tizing event, it's often better to simply allow the feelings to surface and to experience them fully, while reminding yourself that the feeling will pass. Remind yourself that you're not your emotions."

"I don't even know what that means."

"You're sad now, but you're not a sad person and you won't always be sad. You're angry now, but you're not an angry person, and you won't always be angry."

I thought about what she'd said before shaking my head. "I just want to stop the emotions from being so intense. How do I do that?"

"Keep doing what you're doing. Exercise, work, take care of London. In the end, it's just going to take time."

"How much time?"

"It's different for everyone. But every day, you'll feel a little less vulnerable, a little stronger or resolute. If you thought about Vivian every five minutes today, maybe next week, you'll think about her once every ten minutes."

"I wish I could snap my fingers and be done with it."

"You and everyone else who experiences something like this."

Later that night, after London had FaceTimed with her mom and had gone to bed, I continued to sit with Marge and Liz. For the most part, Marge was content to listen.

"In your experience," I asked, "do you think she'll come back?"

"I've seen both situations, honestly," Liz answered. "Sometimes, what someone thinks is love is just infatuation and after the shine wears off, they decide they've made a mistake. Other times, it is love and it lasts. And still other times, even if it is infatuation, the person comes to the conclusion that the love they felt for the first person is no longer there."

"What should I do? She won't even talk to me."

"I don't know that there's anything you can do. As much as you might want to, you can't control another person."

I wanted a drink, I wanted to forget and simply not care, if only for a little while, but even though there was beer in the refrigerator, I held off because I feared that once I started drinking, I wouldn't stop until the fridge was empty.

"I don't want to control her. I just want her to want to come back."

"I know you do," Liz said. "It's clear that you still love her."

"Do you think she still loves me?"

"Yes," Liz said. "But right now, it's not the same kind of love."

I turned toward Marge. "What happens if she wants London to move to Atlanta with her?"

"You fight it. Hire a lawyer and make a case that she should stay with you."

"What if London wants to go?" I felt the pressure of tears beginning to form. "What if she would rather be with her mom?"

At this, Marge and Liz were silent.

Friday, I took London to and from school and dance, but otherwise buried myself in work like the day before. I was barely surviving. I remembered that fourteen years earlier, on a horrible day I would never forget, the Twin Towers collapsed.

Then came the weekend. Liz's suggestions had become a mantra: work out, work, take care of London and though I wouldn't be heading into the office, I nonetheless wanted to follow her advice.

I woke early and ran seven miles, my longest run in years. I forced myself to eat breakfast and then fed London. While she relaxed, I finished my edits on the first commercial and started working on the second one. I brought London to art class, continued to edit while she was there, and learned that London had made a vase. She carried it to the car gingerly, careful not to bang it on anything.

"We have to bring this back next week so that I can paint it," London told me. "I want to paint yellow flowers on it. And maybe some pink mouses."

"Mouses?"

"Or a hamster. But hamsters are harder to paint."

I had no idea why that would be, but what do I know?

"Okay. Flowers and mouses," I said.

"Pink mouses."

"Even better," I agreed. "Are you ready to head to Nana's?"

I helped her into the car, knowing that it was time to tell my parents that Vivian had left me. Because Marge wanted to stay with me while I shared the news, Liz took it upon herself to take a walk with London. I called my father in from the garage, and he took a seat next to my mom.

I spilled it all in a single rush of words. When I finished, it was my dad who responded first. "She can't leave." He frowned. "She's got a kid."

"I should call her," my mom interjected. "She's probably going through a phase."

"It's not a phase. She told me she was in love with him. She's got her own place now."

"When is she coming back?" my mom asked. "If she comes next weekend, your dad and I will be out of town. We're going to visit your uncle Joe in Winston-Salem. It's his birthday."

My dad's younger brother by a couple of years, Joe was a mechanic who'd never married but had, over the years, gone through one long-term girlfriend after the next. Growing up, he was the cool uncle, and I can remember wondering why he'd never married. Now, I suspected he might have been onto something.

"I don't have any idea when she's coming back," I answered.

"The work must have been too stressful," my mom said. "She's not thinking right."

"How is she going to see London?" my dad asked.

"I don't know, Dad."

"Doesn't she want to see London?" my dad pressed.

"I should really call her," my mom fretted.

"You're not going to call her, Mom," Marge said. "This is their business. I'm sure that Vivian will be back to see London. And even though she hasn't told Russ when that might be, I'd guess it'll be within the next week or so. In the meantime, it's probably not the best time to pepper Russ with a ton of questions or to start making plans. As you can imagine, it's been a pretty rough week for him."

"You're right," my mom suddenly said. "I'm sorry. It's just such a shock, you know?"

"It's okay, Mom," I said. I watched my dad rise from the couch and walk to the kitchen.

"How are you holding up?" my mom asked.

I ran a hand through my hair. "I'm doing the best I can."

"Is there anything I can do? Do you need help with London?"

"No," I said. "I'm doing okay with that. It's not so hard, now that she's in school."

"Why don't I bring over some dinners for the week? Would that help?"

I knew she felt like she needed to do something. "That would be great," I said. "London likes your cooking a lot more than she likes mine."

I felt a tap of cold glass against my shoulder. My dad had a beer in each hand and was holding one out. "For you," he said. "I'm in the garage if you want to talk."

When I wandered out to the garage twenty minutes later, my dad motioned for me to sit on a stool while he took a seat on a toolbox. I'd brought out a second beer for both of us; there was something on my mind—something I hadn't mentioned to either Marge or Liz—and I wanted his perspective.

"I don't know if I can do this," I said.

"Do what?"

"Be a single father. Take care of London. Maybe it would be better if London went to live with Vivian in Atlanta."

He cracked open the beer I'd brought him. "I take it you want me to tell you that I'm in agreement with you."

"I don't know what I want."

"That's not your real problem. Your real problem is that you're afraid."

"Of course I'm afraid."

"That's what parenting is all about. Doing the best you can while being terrified of screwing up. Kids can turn hair gray faster than anything else, if you ask me."

"You and Mom weren't afraid."

"Of course we were. We just never let on, is all."

I wondered whether that was true. "Do you think I should fight for London like Marge said? If it comes to that?"

My dad scratched at the jeans he was wearing, leaving a streak of grease. "I think you're a damn good father, Russ. Better than I ever was, that's for sure. And I think London needs you."

"She needs her mom, too."

"Maybe. But the way you've been taking care of her? I know it wasn't easy, but you just got up and did it, and she's a happy little girl. And that's what being a dad is all about. You do what needs to be done and love your kid the best way you can. You've been doing that and I'm real proud of you." He paused. "Anyway, that's what I think."

I tried to recall whether he'd ever said anything like that to me before but knew that he hadn't.

"Thanks, Dad."

"You're not going to cry are you?"

Despite everything, I laughed. "I don't know, Dad."

"Why are you crying?"

I wiped at a tear I hadn't known was there. "It doesn't take much these days."

CHAPTER 15

One Day at a Time

Unlike my friend Danny, I was around to experience my mom's angst as one by one, she lost the family with whom she'd grown up. I was thirteen when my grandfather died, eighteen when my grandmother died, twenty-one when the first of her brothers passed away, and twenty-eight when the last one slipped from this world to the next.

In each case, my mom bore the heaviest burden. All four were lingering deaths, with frequent trips to the hospital while poison was administered in the hopes of killing the cancer before it killed them. There was hair loss and nausea, weakness and memory loss. And pain. Always, there was too much pain. Toward the end, there were occasional days and nights spent in the ICU, with my relatives sometimes crying out in agony. My mom was there for all of it. Every night, after work, she would head to their homes or to hospital, and she would stay with them for hours. She would wipe their faces with damp cloths and feed them through straws; she came to know the doctors and nurses in three different hospitals on a first-name basis. When the time came, it was she who helped with funeral arrangements, and I always knew that despite our presence she felt very much alone.

In the weeks and months following that fourth funeral, I suppose that I thought she would rebound in the way she always had before. On the surface, she hadn't changed—she still wore aprons and spent most of her time in the kitchen when Vivian and I visited—but she was quieter than I remembered and every once in a while, I would catch her staring out the window above the sink, isolated from the sounds of those of us nearby. I

243

thought it had to do with the most recent loss; it was Vivian who finally suggested that my mom's grief was cumulative, and her comment struck me as exactly right.

What would it be like to lose one's family? I suppose it's inevitable in everyone's family—there is always a last survivor, after all—but, Vivian's comment made me ache for my mom whenever I would see her. I felt as though her loss had become my loss, and I began swinging by more frequently. I'd drop by after work two or three times a week and spend time with my mom, and though we didn't talk about what she—and I—was going through, it was always there with us, an all-encompassing sadness.

One night, a couple of months into my new routine, I dropped by the house and saw my dad trimming the hedges while my mom waited on the porch. My dad pretended not to have noticed my arrival and didn't turn around.

"Let's take a drive," my mom announced. "And by that, I mean that you're driving."

She marched toward my car and after opening the passenger door, she took a seat and closed the door behind her.

"What's going on, Dad?"

He stopped trimming but didn't turn to face me. "Just get in the car. It's important to your mom."

I did as I was told and when I asked where we were going, my mom told me to head toward the fire station.

Still confused, I did as I was told and when we were getting close, she suddenly told me to turn right; two blocks later, she directed me to take a left. By then, even I knew where she wanted me to go, and we pulled to a stop next to a gate that was bordered on either side by wooded lots. Before us stood the water tower, and when my mom got out of the car, I followed her.

For a while, she said nothing to me.

"Why are we here, Mom?"

She tilted her head, her eyes seeming to follow the ladder that led to the landing near the top.

"I know what happened," she said. "When Tracey and Marge broke up. I know she was brokenhearted and that you met her here. You were still a child, but somehow, you talked her down and brought her back to the dorms."

I swallowed my denials, something easier said than done. Nothing I could say would matter; this was my mom's show.

"Do you know what it's like to think that my daughter might have died here? When she told me, I remember wondering to myself why she hadn't called me or your dad. But I know the answer to that, too. You two share something wonderful, and I can't tell you how proud that makes me. We may not have been the best parents, but at least we raised you both right."

She continued to stare at the water tower. "You were in so much trouble, but you never said anything to us. About where you'd been that night. I wanted to tell you that I'm sorry."

"It's okay," I said.

I saw a deep sadness in her expression as she turned toward me. "You have a gift," she said. "You feel so deeply and you care so much. And that's a wonderful thing. That's why you knew exactly what to do with Marge. You took her pain and made it your own, and now you're trying to do the same thing with me."

Though she trailed off, I knew that more was coming.

"I know you think you're helping, but no matter what you do, you can't take my sadness away. But you are making yourself miserable. And that breaks my heart, and I don't want you to do that. I'm getting through this one day at a time, but I don't have the strength to have to worry about you, too."

"I don't know if I can stop worrying about you."

She touched my cheek. "I know. But I want you to try. Just remember that I've made it through one hundred percent of the worst days of my life so far. Just like your dad, and Marge. And, of course, you have, too. And how we get through them is one day at a time."

Later that night, I thought about what my mom had told me. She was right, of course, but what I didn't know was that as challenging as life had sometimes been, the worst days were still yet to come, and they would be the worst of all.

Nine thousand, three hundred and sixty minutes.

That was how long it had been—well, *approximately*, anyway—since my world turned upside down, and to me, it felt as though I'd been hyperaware of the passage of every single one of them. Every one of these minutes in the past week had passed with agonizing slowness, as I seemed to be experiencing them with every cell in my body, every tick of the clock.

It was Monday, September fourteenth. A week ago, Vivian had left me. I continued to dwell on her obsessively, and the night before, I'd had trouble sleeping. Going for a run helped, but by the time I'd returned, I'd lost my appetite. In the last week, I'd dropped another seven pounds.

Stress. The ultimate diet.

Even as I made the phone call, I think I already knew what I was going to do. I told myself I simply wanted to know where Vivian would be traveling this week, but that wasn't true. When the receptionist at Spannerman answered, I asked to be connected to Vivian and reached a woman named Melanie who identified herself as Vivian's assistant. I didn't know my wife even had an assistant, but apparently there was much I didn't know about her, or maybe, had never known at all.

I was told that Vivian was in a meeting and when Melanie asked my name, I lied. I told her that I was a local reporter and wanted to know whether she would be around this week to speak. Melanie informed me that Vivian would be in the office today and tomorrow, but after that, she would be out of the office.

I then called Marge and asked if she would pick up London from school and later, bring her to dance. I told her that I was going to see my wife, but that I would be home later tonight.

Atlanta was four hours away.

I'm not sure how I imagined my surprise visit might go. In the car, one prediction replaced the next. All I knew was that I had to see Vivian; there was a part of me that hoped the hard-edged exterior she offered to me on the phone would melt away in my presence and we would find a way to salvage our relationship, our family, the life I still wanted to live.

My stomach clenched in knots as I drove, evidence of a simmering anxiety that made the drive more difficult than it should have been. Thankfully, traffic was relatively light, and I reached the outskirts of Atlanta at a quarter to twelve. Fifteen minutes later, with my nerves jangling hard, I found the new Spannerman building and pulled into the parking lot.

I found a space in the visitor section but hesitated before getting out of the car. I didn't know what to do. Should I call her and tell her I was downstairs? Should I enter the building and show up at the reception desk? Or storm past the reception and confront her in the office? The countless variations on our conversation that I had imagined on the drive always began with me sitting across from her at a table in a restaurant, not with the steps that led up to that point.

My mind, I knew, wasn't quite up to par these days.

Vivian would certainly prefer that I call; that way she could perhaps put me off entirely. For that reason, showing up inside seemed preferable, but what if she was in a meeting? Would I leave my name and sit in the waiting room, like a kid who'd been called in to meet the school principal? I wanted to head straight for her office, but I had no idea where it was, and something like that would cause a scene, which might even be worse.

I forced myself from the car as I continued to ponder my choices. All I knew for sure was that I needed to stretch my legs and use the restroom. Spotting a coffee shop across the street, I jaywalked through the stalled traffic to reach the other side. When I left the coffee shop and crossed the street again, I made the decision to call Vivian from the building lobby. That's when I saw them—Spannerman and Vivian in a brown Bentley, getting ready to pull out of the parking lot, onto the street. Not wanting them to see me, I edged closer to the building and ducked my head. I heard the roar of the engine as it finally pulled out, inching its way into traffic.

Even though I didn't have much of a plan in the first place, the little I did have was going up in smoke. Despite the lack of appetite, I supposed I could grab a bite to eat and try to catch up with her in an hour or so, which seemed preferable to waiting around, and I started back to my car.

Pulling out of the lot, I noticed that the traffic had barely moved and I could still see the Bentley about eight cars ahead of me. Beyond it, I saw there was some construction going on; an eighteen-wheeler loaded with steel girders was backing onto a work site and the traffic on the street had ground to a halt.

When the truck cleared the road, traffic started moving again. I followed along, conscious of the Bentley in front of me, watching as it made a right turn. I felt like a spy—or rather, a creepy private investigator—when I took the turn as well, but I told myself that since I wasn't going to confront them at lunch or do anything crazy, it wasn't a big deal. I just wanted to know where they were eating—I wanted to know something about the new life my wife was leading—and that was normal, something anyone would do.

Right?

Nonetheless I could feel my anger growing. Now there was only a single car between us, and I could see them up ahead. I imagined Walter talking and Vivian responding; I pictured the same joyful expression she'd worn when on the phone with him after her argument with London and my anger transformed into feelings of disappointment and sadness at all I had lost.

Why didn't she love me?

They weren't on the road long. They took a left, and then quickly turned into a parking garage beneath a splashy high-rise called Belmont Tower. It had a doorman out front, the kind you see in New York, and I drove on, finally pulling into a restaurant parking lot just up the block.

I killed the engine, wondering if there was a restaurant inside the high-rise. I wondered if it was the location of the corporate apartments. I wondered if this was where Walter Spannerman lived.

Using my phone, I found the information: Belmont Tower was a Spannerman project, and there was also a video link. I clicked it and saw Walter Spannerman boasting about the building amenities; as his final selling point, he proudly announced to viewers that he'd chosen to live on the top floor.

I stopped the video, but like a man choosing to march unassisted to his own execution, I stepped out of the car and made for Belmont Tower. I signaled to the doorman when I was close and he approached.

"It's a beautiful building," I said.

"Yes, sir. It really is."

"I was wondering if there's a restaurant in the building? Or a dining club for the tenants?" I said.

"No, there isn't. However, the building has a relationship with La Cerna next door. It's a five-star restaurant."

"Are there any apartments for rent?"

"No, sir."

I put a hand in my pocket. "Okay," I said. "Thanks for your help."

A few minutes later, dazed at the idea that Vivian had most likely gone with Spannerman to his penthouse, I was in my car and on my way back to Charlotte.

I arrived half an hour after London got back from school and when I opened the door, she came running.

"Daddy! Where were you?"

"I had to work," I said. "I'm so sorry I couldn't pick you up."

"That's okay. Auntie Marge was there. She drove me home." She put her arms around me. "I missed you."

"I missed you, too, baby."

"I love you."

"Ditto," I said.

"What does *ditto* mean?"

"You say 'ditto' when you want to say the same thing. You said I love you, so I said ditto, meaning I love you."

"That's neat," she said. "I didn't know you could do that."

"It's just a crazy world, isn't it? Did you learn anything fun in school?"

"I learned that spiders aren't insects. They're called arachmids."

"You mean arachnid?"

"No, Daddy. Arachmid. With an M."

I was pretty sure she was wrong, but she'd figure it out eventually. "That's cool."

"It's because insects have six legs and spiders have eight legs."

"Wow...you're pretty smart, you know that?"

"But I still don't like spiders. I don't like bees anymore either. Even though they make honey. But butterflies are pretty."

"Just like you. You're pretty, too. Prettier than any butterfly," I said. "Can I go say hi to Auntie Marge for a minute?"

"Okay. I have to check on Mr. and Mrs. Sprinkles. Did you remember to give them water?"

Oops.

"No, I didn't. But they had plenty yesterday. I'm sure they're okay."

"I'll go make sure."

I kissed her cheek and put her down. She ran toward the steps and vanished from sight. Marge, I noticed, had been watching us from the kitchen.

"You're a good dad, you know that?" she said when I reached her.

"I try. How was she?"

"You mean in the hour I've had her? I had to drive her home *and* get her a Popsicle. And then, Mom showed up with a ton of food and I had to deal with that, too. I put some in the refrigerator and some in the freezer, by the way. Let's just say that you really owe me for this one. I'm exhausted. What a day! I'm not sure I can take any more."

My sister had a flair for sarcastic melodrama, obviously. "I didn't think I'd be back so soon."

"Neither did I. And when you did get home, I thought you'd resemble a pile of mashed potatoes. What happened? Was she even there?"

"I saw her," I said. "Well, kind of." I told her what had happened. While I spoke, she poured two glasses of ice water and handed one to me.

"Can I ask a question?"

"Go ahead."

"Why didn't you just wait for her?"

"After they went to Spannerman's place, I realized I didn't want to see her after that."

"Because?"

"She was…with *him*. Probably at his penthouse or whatever. And…"

"And what? She left you. She told you she was in love with him. You do know she's sleeping with him, right?"

250

"I know that," I said. "I just don't like to think about it...I don't *want* to think about it."

Marge offered a sympathetic expression. "That makes you perfectly sane."

I hesitated, realizing I was utterly exhausted. "What am I going to do?"

"You're going to take care of yourself. And you're going to continue to be a good father to London."

"I mean about Vivian."

"For now, let's just worry about you and your daughter, okay?"

I never should have gone to Atlanta.

On Tuesday, I tried to bury myself in work on Taglieri's commercial, but it was hard to stay focused and I thought endlessly of Vivian. I would see her in the Bentley, Spannerman in the seat beside her; whenever I imagined her expression, it was the same one I'd seen on the patio.

Those images haunted me, bringing with them a sense of inadequacy. Of inferiority. I hadn't simply been rejected; I'd been replaced by someone wealthier and more powerful, someone who had the ability to make Vivian laugh and smile in a way that I could not.

She had left me, not for reasons of her own, but because of me.

I said as much to Marge on the phone the following day, and when she wasn't able to talk me out of funk, she and Liz showed up at my home after work. It was Tuesday night and I'd fed London one of the meals my mom had made; as soon as they walked in the door, Marge and London headed off to watch a movie in the family room while Liz and I sat on the back patio.

I recounted everything that had happened and the way I'd been feeling. When I was finished, Liz brought her hands together.

"What did you think would happen if you talked to Vivian?"

"I guess I was hoping that she'd make the decision to come back. Or at the very least, we'd discuss how we could work it out."

"Why? Has she given you any indication that she wants to come back? Or try to work it out?"

251

"No," I admitted. "But she's my wife. We've barely spoken since she left."

"I'm sure that the two of you will have a sit-down when she's ready. But I can't promise that you'll like what she tells you."

It wasn't that hard to read between the lines. "You don't think she'll come back, do you?"

"I'm not sure my opinion is any better than anyone else's. Or that it's even relevant."

"You're right. It's not relevant. But you've seen situations like this before, and you know Vivian. I'd still like to know what you think."

She exhaled. "No," she finally said. "I don't think she's coming back."

I wanted numbness; I didn't want to feel or think about Vivian, but it seemed that the only time I could find oblivion was in the hours that London was in school, when I buried myself in work. On Wednesday, I continued to bury myself in Taglieri's second commercial before finally sending it off to the editor for polishing and finalizing. After that, I worked on the presentation for the surgeon on Thursday afternoon. I was proposing a different campaign than I'd recommended for Taglieri—a much higher online presence and user-friendly website, a heavy emphasis on patient testimonials on video, direct mail, social media, and billboards—and even though I was far less than a hundred percent during the presentation, I left the meeting the following day with a handshake agreement knowing I'd landed my second client. Like Taglieri, he'd committed to a year of services.

With those two clients, I realized that I'd replaced nearly half of my previous salary, not counting bonuses. It was enough to meet my monthly obligations with a few trims here and there, and made it significantly easier when I picked up the phone and canceled our joint credit cards.

I let Vivian know via text.

Vivian called me later that night. Since my ill-advised adventure in Atlanta on Monday, I'd allowed London to answer the phone as soon as I saw Vivian's image pop up on the screen. London let me know that Vivian would be calling me back later. As she headed up the stairs to get ready for bed, I wondered whether she'd figured out that things had changed between her mother and me, or that we were no longer going to be a family.

While I waited for her call, I didn't want to get my hopes up, but I couldn't help it. I would imagine hearing her apologize or say that she was coming home, and yet, like the turbulence of my emotions, those thoughts would be replaced with the memory of what Liz had told me, or that the only reason Vivian was calling was because I'd canceled the credit cards, and she wanted to let me know how angry she was.

The push and pull left me exhausted, and by the time the phone finally did ring, I had little emotional energy to expend, no matter what she might say.

I let the phone ring four times before finally connecting the call.

"Hi," I said. "London said you'd be calling."

"Hi, Russ," she said. Her voice was calm, as if nothing had changed between us at all. "How are you?"

I wondered if she really cared or was simply being polite; I wondered why I felt the need to try to read her, instead of letting the call simply unfold.

"I'm fine," I forced out. "You?"

"I'm okay," she said. "London sounds like she might be coming down with a cold."

"She didn't say anything to me."

"She didn't to me, either. I could hear it in her voice, though. Make sure she's taking her vitamins and maybe get her some orange juice in the morning. She'll probably need some children's cold medicine, too."

"How can she get a cold? It's almost ninety degrees outside."

"She's in school. New kids, new germs. It happens in every school at the beginning of the year."

"All right," I said. "I'll have to run out to get some orange juice and the medicine, but she's been taking her vitamins."

"Don't forget," she said. "And anyway, I was calling for a couple of reasons. First, I'm coming to Charlotte this weekend. I really miss

London and if it's okay with you, I'd like to spend some uninterrupted time with her."

But not me.

"Of course," I said, keeping my voice steady. "She'd love that. She misses you, too."

"Good. Thank you." I could hear her relief and wondered why she'd anticipated any other reaction. "But here's the thing. I don't think it's a good idea for me stay in a hotel. I think that would be very strange for her."

I frowned. "Why would you stay at a hotel? You can stay at the house. We have a guest room."

"I think she'd notice if I slept in the guest room. Even if she doesn't notice, I don't think we should put her in the position where she asks the three of us to do things together. I would really like it to be just the two of us, for her sake. So she doesn't get confused."

"What are you saying?"

"Would you mind staying with your parents? Or maybe with Marge and Liz? On Friday and Saturday night?"

I could feel my blood pressure spike.

"You're kidding, right?"

"No, Russ. I'm not. Please. I know I'm asking a lot, but I don't want to make things any harder on London than they already are."

Or maybe, I thought, *you'd rather it not be any harder on you.*

I let the silence crackle between us.

"Yeah," I finally said. "I guess I can ask Marge. My parents are going to be out of town."

"I'd appreciate it."

"Remember that London has dance on Friday night, and then art class on Saturday morning, so you probably won't have time to do yoga."

"I've always put my daughter first, Russ. You know that."

"You've been a great mom," I conceded. "Oh, for art class, you'll need to bring the vase she made last week. This weekend, she'll be painting it."

"Where is it?"

"I put it in the pantry. Top shelf, on the right."

254

"Got it," she said. "Oh, one last thing."

"Yes?"

"I was wondering if you had time for a late lunch tomorrow. Around one thirty? We need to talk before I have to pick up London from school."

Despite everything, I felt my heart skip a beat at the thought of sitting across the table from her. Of seeing her.

"Of course," I said. "Where?"

She named a place we both knew, a place we'd eaten many times before. Including, once, on our anniversary.

I hung up the phone, wondering if it was an omen.

"Of course you can stay with us," Marge said into the receiver. I'd just returned from the grocery store and was putting the orange juice into the refrigerator before calling her. "You'll have to promise not to walk around in your droopy underwear or drink your coffee at the table without a shirt on, though. In fact, don't even pack any droopy underwear, okay?"

"Do you even know me?"

"Of course. Why do you think I'm pointing these things out?"

"I promise."

"We won't be around on Saturday, though. You'll be on your own. A friend of ours is having a housewarming party."

No wife, no London, no parents, and now, no sister to see on the weekend. I wondered when the last time was that I was utterly on my own, figuring it had been years since something like that had happened.

"No worries. I have work."

"I'll still call you, just to make sure you're okay. But back to Vivian. Are you sure lunch is such a good idea?"

"Why wouldn't it be?"

"Whenever someone says 'we need to talk,' it's never a good thing."

"Believe me when I say I'm not expecting much."

"I'm glad," she said. "You remember what Liz said, right? She's not going to tell you that she wants to come back."

255

"Liz told you what we talked about?"

"Of course not," she said. "But I know you, and it's not too hard to figure out what you might ask her. And because I know her, I also know what she told you. It's not as though the two of us haven't had a million discussions about what's going on. It's been a hot topic around the old homestead these days."

"There are better things for the two of you to discuss than my marriage."

"And you'd be right ninety-nine percent of the time," she said. "But lately? We're definitely in that pesky one percent."

"What else are you saying to each other?"

"We talk about how much you're hurting, and that we don't know what to say or do to make it better. You're such a good man, such a good father. It isn't fair."

I couldn't help but choke up a bit. "You don't have to worry about me."

"Of course I do. Big sister, remember?"

I hesitated. "Do you think Vivian is struggling?"

"I'm sure she is. You can't do what she did and not feel at least a little bit of guilt. But I'm not sure she dwells on her feelings the way you do. My sense is that you two are just wired differently."

That made sense. But... "I still care about her," I offered. "She's been a wonderful wife."

Marge breathed into the receiver. "Are you sure about that?"

Vivian had been right about London; when she woke Friday morning, her voice had a raspy edge to it and on our way out the door, she began wiping at her nose. I wondered how long it would take for the medicine to kick in.

After drop-off, I tossed some clothes in a duffel bag and drove to the office. Still no phone calls for the Phoenix Agency, but on the upside, the receptionist was getting used to my presence and had even started saying, "Good morning, Mr. Green."

I spent most of the morning working with my tech guy. Together, we discussed and made decisions on the overall plan, then moved toward discussions of Internet prioritization, targeted banner ads, and a social media campaign. We spent almost three hours together and by the end, I felt like he had more than enough work to keep him busy for a couple of weeks, as did I.

Once that was done, I sent confirmation emails regarding the third commercial I'd film for Taglieri the following Friday, then left a message for the surgeon asking for the names of patients who might be willing to provide on-camera testimonials.

As I worked, I noticed the tension in my shoulders and back seemed to be intensifying, and it dawned on me that I was nervous at the thought of seeing Vivian. Despite her betrayal, despite asking me to make myself scarce all weekend, I wondered if I would meet with a Vivian who was willing to try to work things out. While I knew that Marge and Liz were trying to keep me grounded in reality with what to expect, the heart wants what it wants. Hope might leave me crushed in the end, but losing all hope somehow seemed even worse.

I ended up leaving the office at half past noon, and arrived at the restaurant fifteen minutes early. I'd made reservations and the waiter led me to a table near the window. Most of the other tables were already occupied. I ordered a cocktail, hoping that it would keep me calm. I wanted to approach the lunch in the same way I had the phone call, but as soon as Vivian entered the restaurant, I held my breath, releasing it only when she approached the table.

Dressed in jeans and a red blouse that accentuated her figure, she looked effortlessly chic as always. She propped her sunglasses on her head and offered a quick smile as I stood. When she was close, I wondered whether or not to kiss her on the cheek, but she didn't give me the opportunity.

"Sorry for being late," she said as she sat down. "I had trouble finding a place to park."

"Friday at lunch is always busy here. I think a lot of people are getting an early start to the weekend."

"I'm sure," she said. She pointed to my cocktail, which was nearly finished. "I see you're doing the same thing."

"Why not? I'm a free man this weekend."

"Maybe so, but you still have to drive."

"I know."

She deliberately unfolded her napkin, taking her time, and avoiding my gaze. "How's work?"

"Better. I landed another client. Plastic surgeon."

"I'm glad it's working out for you. Oh, by the way, did you remember to give London some medicine?"

"I did. And orange juice."

"And she knows I'm picking her up today, right?"

"Yes," I said. "And the guest room is ready to go, too."

"Would you care if I slept in the master bedroom? I'll change the sheets first, obviously."

"No, I don't mind. We're still married."

I thought I saw a flash of exasperation but it vanished as quickly as it had come.

"Thanks," she said. "I just want London to have a nice weekend."

"I'm sure she will."

She turned toward the window, taking in the street, then seemed to remember something. Reaching for her handbag, she pulled out her phone and tapped in the code. She tapped a button, used her finger to scroll, and tapped another couple of times. She scrolled some more. In the silence, I took another drink, finishing the cocktail. Finally, setting the phone aside, she offered a pinched smile.

"Sorry. Just checking up on work. I was on the phone for almost the entire drive to Charlotte."

"How was the drive?"

"With the weekend on tap, traffic was heavy. And we didn't get in until late last night. We flew in from Houston, and the night before that, we were in Savannah. I can't tell you how happy I am to have a relaxing weekend on tap."

I tried to ignore the word *we*. It was better than *Walter*, but it still stung. I said nothing and Vivian reached for the menu. I couldn't remember a conversation with Vivian that ever felt more stilted.

"Have you decided what you're going to have?" she asked.

"I'll probably just order some soup. I'm not that hungry."

She looked up and for the first time, she seemed to really see me. "You've lost weight," she observed. "Are you still jogging?"

"Every morning. And I'm down almost fifteen pounds." I didn't tell her that much of the weight loss was both recent and due to her, since my appetite was largely nonexistent.

"You can see it in your face," she said. "You were getting some jowls, but they're almost gone now."

It was odd, I thought, how she could offer a compliment while still getting in a dig at the same time. I wondered whether she was still working out with Spannerman, and whether she ever mentioned to him that he had jowls. Probably not.

"Have you decided what you're going to do this weekend with London?" I asked.

"Not really. It's kind of up to her, obviously. I want to spend a lot of time doing what she wants to do." She perused the menu. It didn't take long; even I knew she was going to order a salad and the only question was which one she'd want. Soon after she set the menu aside, the waiter appeared at the table. She ordered an unsweetened iced tea and an Asian salad; I ordered a bowl of the vegetable beef. When the waiter left, Vivian took a sip from her water, then traced her finger through the condensation. Like me, she seemed to be at a loss for words, the elephant in the room being what it was, intended to say.

"So," I said, finally. "You said you needed to talk to me?"

"It's mainly about London," she said. "I've been worried about her. She isn't used to me being gone so much. I know it's been hard for her."

"She's doing okay."

"She doesn't tell you everything. I just wish there was a way I could be with her more."

I could have pointed out that she could come home, but she probably already knew that. "I can imagine," I offered.

"I've been talking to Walter and given the amount of travel I have ahead of me in the next few months, there's just no way that I can bring her to Atlanta just yet. I'm still out of town three or four nights a week and I haven't even had time to get her room set up or even begin looking for a nanny."

I felt a surge of relief but wanted to make sure I'd heard her right. "So you're saying that you think it's best if London stays with me?"

"Only for a while. I'm not abandoning my daughter. And you and I both know that daughters need their moms."

"They need their dads, too."

"You'll still be able to see her. I'm not the kind of mother who would keep her child from seeing the father. And you and I both know that I was the one who raised her. She's used to me."

Her child. Not, I noticed, *our* child.

"It's different now. She's in school and you're working."

"Be that as it may," she said, "I wanted to talk to you about what's going on right now, okay? And even though I'm traveling a lot, I still want to be able to see her as much as I possibly can. I wanted to make sure that you didn't have a problem with that."

"Of course not. Why would you think I'd have a problem with it?"

"Because you're angry and hurt, and you might want to try to hurt me back. I mean, you didn't even call to talk to me about canceling the credit cards. You just up and did it. You do know you should have called first, right? So we could discuss it?"

I blinked, thinking about the secret bank account she'd set up. "Seriously?"

"I'm just saying you could have handled it better."

Her chutzpah was staggering and all I could do was stare at her. The waiter arrived with her iced tea, and as he set it on the table, her phone rang. Checking the screen, she stood from the table.

"I've got to take this."

I watched her walk from the table and head outside; from my seat, I could see her, though I forced myself to look away. I munched a couple of ice cubes until the waiter came by with a basket of bread and some butter. I nibbled on that, absently listening to the drone of conversations around me. In time, Vivian returned to the table.

"Sorry," she said. "That was work."

Whatever, I thought. I didn't bother responding.

The waiter brought our food, and she dressed her salad before dicing it into bite-sized portions. The aroma of the soup was tantalizing, but my stomach had locked down. The small amount of bread had taken up all the room. I nonetheless forced myself to take a bite.

"There's something else I think we need to discuss," she said finally.

"What's that?"

"What we're going to say to London. I was thinking that we should probably sit down with her on Sunday, before I leave."

"Why?"

"Because she needs to know what's going on, but in a way that she can understand. We need to keep it as simple as possible."

"I don't know what that even means."

She sighed. "We tell her that because of my job, I'll have to live in Atlanta and that she's going to stay with you for a while. We explain that no matter what happens, we both love her. It's not really necessary to go into long explanations, and I don't think that's a good idea anyway."

You mean like explaining that you're in love with another man?

"I can talk to Liz. She might be able to give me some dos and don'ts."

"That's fine, but be careful."

"Why?"

"She's not your therapist. She's your sister's partner. I assume she's taken your side in all this, and wants you to believe that I'm the bad guy."

But you are the bad guy!

"She wouldn't do that."

"Just make sure," she warned. "I also don't think it's a good idea to tell her what's happening between you and me. It would be better if she gets used to the two of us being apart first. Then it won't come as such a shock when we do tell her."

"Tell her what?"

"That we're getting divorced."

I set my spoon aside. Though I suspected she'd say the word eventually, in the here and now, it still shocked me to hear it aloud.

"Before we start talking about divorce, don't you think it might be a good idea for the two of us to talk to a therapist? To see if there's any way to salvage what we have?"

"Keep your voice down. This isn't the time or place to talk about this."

"I am keeping my voice down," I said.

"No you're not. You can't hear yourself when you get angry. You're always loud."

I pinched the bridge of my nose and took a deep breath. "All right," I said, forcing myself to speak even more quietly. "Don't you want to even try to make it work?" I could barely hear myself above the din of the lunch crowd.

"You don't have to whisper," she retorted. "I was just asking you to keep your voice down. People could hear you."

"I got it," I said. "Stop changing the subject."

"Russ..."

"I still love you. I'll always love you."

"And I just told you that this isn't the time or place for this! Right now, we're here to talk about London and why she should probably stay here for the time being and what we are going to say to her on Sunday night. We're not here to talk about us."

"Don't you want to talk about us?"

"I can see that trying to have a normal conversation with you wasn't a good idea. Why can't we discuss things like adults?"

"I *am* trying to talk to you."

She took a bite of her salad—she'd barely eaten any to that point— and then placed her napkin on the table. "But you never listen! How many times do I have to tell you that this isn't the time or place to talk about you and me? I said it nicely, I thought I was being clear, but I guess you had other ideas. So for now, I think it's best if I probably leave before you start yelling at me, okay? I just want to have a pleasant weekend with my daughter."

"Please," I said. "You don't have to leave. I'm sorry. I wasn't trying to upset you."

"I'm not the one who's upset," she said. "You are."

With that, Vivian rose from the table and strode for the exit. When she was gone, I sat in shock for a couple of minutes before finally signaling for the waiter to bring the check. Rehashing the conversation, I wondered whether I really had been too loud, or whether it had been an easy excuse for Vivian to bring the lunch to an early conclusion.

There was, after all, no reason for her to stay.

Not only was she in love with another man, as far as the weekend went, she'd gotten everything she'd wanted from me.

CHAPTER 16

❋

The Sun Also Rises

I liked Liz as soon as I met her, but I'll admit that I was amazed that my parents felt the same way. While they accepted the fact that Marge was gay, I often sensed that they weren't exactly comfortable with the women Marge dated. There was a generational aspect to it—they'd both grown up in an era in which alternative lifestyles were typically kept in the closet—but it also had to do with the kind of women that Marge originally seemed to favor. They struck me as a bit on the rough side and were often prone to profanity in casual conversation, which had a tendency to make both my mom and dad go red in the face.

Marge told me that she'd met Liz at work. Accounting offices, I think most would agree, aren't your usual pickup joints, but Liz had recently joined a new practice and was in need of an accountant. Marge happened to have an opening in her afternoon schedule, and by the time Liz left the office, they'd made arrangements to meet for a glass of wine before dropping by an art opening in Asheville.

"You're going to an art gallery?" I remember asking Marge. We'd met at a bar after work, the kind of place with neon beer signs and the slightly rancid smell of too many spilled drinks. At the time, it was one of Marge's favorite watering holes.

"Why wouldn't I go to an art gallery?"

"Maybe because you don't like art?"

"Who says I don't like art?"

"You did. When I tried to show you some pictures of Emily's art, you said—and I quote—'I don't like art.'"

264

"Maybe I've matured in the past few years."

"Or maybe Liz just blew your socks off."

"She's interesting," Marge admitted. "Very smart, too."

"Is she pretty?"

"What does that matter?"

"I'm just curious."

"Yes. She's very pretty."

"Let me guess. The art opening was her idea?"

"As a matter of fact, it was."

"Does she drive a motorcycle? And favor leather jackets?"

"How would I know?"

"What does she do?"

"She's a marriage and family therapist."

"You don't like therapists either."

"I didn't like my therapists. Well, the last one was okay, but I didn't much like the others. Of course, there were a few years there where I was pretty angry, and I'm not sure I would have liked any therapist."

"Have you told Liz about your anger issues?"

"That's all in my past. I'm not like that anymore."

"Good to know. When can I meet her?"

"It's a little early, don't you think? We haven't even gone out yet."

"All right. So after you do go out, when can I meet her?"

It ended up being a little less than two weeks. I invited the two of them over to my apartment, and grilled a few steaks on my pint-sized patio. Liz brought dessert, and the three of us split a bottle of wine. It took me all of thirty seconds to feel at ease with Liz, and it was clear that she already cared deeply for my sister. I could see it in the attentive way she listened whenever Marge spoke, her easy laughter, and how attuned she seemed to Marge's hidden, emotional side. When it finally came time for them to leave, Marge pulled me aside.

"What do you think of her?"

"I think she's fantastic."

"Too fantastic for me?"

"What are you talking about?"

"I don't totally get what she sees in me."

"Are you kidding? You're awesome. You had her laughing all night long."

Marge didn't seem convinced but she nodded anyway. "Thanks for having us over. Even if you did burn the steaks."

"They were purposely charred," I explained. "It's supposed to add flavor."

"Oh, it did. Burned is often the goal of world-class chefs."

"Goodbye, Marge," I said. "And you're welcome."

"Love you."

"That's only because I put up with you."

Marge didn't introduce Liz to my parents until another month had passed. It was a Saturday afternoon, and within minutes of her arrival, Liz disappeared into the kitchen to help my mom, the two of them chatting as if they were old friends. My dad sat with Marge, watching a ball game. I was sitting with them too, not that either of them seemed to notice.

"What do you think, Dad?" Marge asked during one of the commercials.

"About what?"

"Liz," Marge said.

"She seems to be getting along with your mom pretty well."

"Do you like her?"

My dad took a sip of his beer. "It doesn't matter what I think."

"You don't like her?"

"I didn't say that. What I said was that it doesn't matter how I feel about her. The only thing that really matters is how you feel about her. If you know why you like her and she's good enough for you, then she'll be good enough for your mom and me."

Then the game came back on, and my dad descended into silence. All I could think was that my dad was, and always will be, one of the smartest men I've ever known.

After my lunch with Vivian, I went back to work, but my thoughts were jumbled and I felt out of sorts. The feeling intensified as three o'clock came and went, and I began to feel the loss of London's company. As important as it was for London to spend time with Vivian, I wasn't convinced that I had to be invisible the entire weekend for their time together to be meaningful. I wondered why I hadn't protested more strongly when Vivian had suggested it, but deep down, my problem was me. I knew I still wanted to please her and as much as that suggested a flaw in my character, that flaw was exacerbated by the obvious: If I hadn't been able to please her before, why on earth would I think I was able to please her now?

It was, I think, the first time I realized the depth of that particular problem. Even I had trouble making sense of it. Logically, I knew it was both ridiculous and unlikely—why, time after time, did I continue to try?

I wished I could be another person. Or, better yet, I wished I could be a stronger version of me and I wondered whether I needed professional help. I wondered if professional help would change anything. Knowing me, I'd end up trying to please my therapist.

It's been said that parents always screw up their kids and since I'd been a people pleaser for as long as I can remember, it logically flowed that it was all my parents' fault. Why then, I wondered, did I feel the need to visit them so regularly? Why did I try to visit with my dad during ball games, or tell my mom that her meals were delicious?

Because, I thought to myself, *I wanted to please them, too.*

I finally left the office a little after five and drove to Marge's. I told myself that I would keep talk about Vivian to an absolute minimum—even I was tired of her—a goal that lasted all of twelve seconds. I whined my way through dinner and Marge and Liz were supportive as always. If I was a broken record, they were too, and while they assured me repeatedly that I would be okay, I still wasn't sure whether to believe them.

They dragged me to a movie and we had our pick of the late-summer blockbusters still lingering in theaters. We chose something fun—one of those stories with flawed heroes battling really evil bad guys intent on destroying the planet, and lots of action—but even so, it was hard for me to relax and enjoy it. I found my thoughts drifting to how Vivian and London had spent the afternoon and what they'd had for dinner; I wondered if my wife was sitting in the family room and flipping through a magazine after London had gone to bed. I wondered whether she'd called Spannerman, and if so, how long they'd talked.

After the movie, I tried to do some reading. My sister had a few books in the spare bedroom, but trying to lose myself in a novel was impossible. I gave up and turned out the light, and spent hours tossing and turning before finally falling asleep.

I woke two hours before dawn.

At a quarter to eleven on Saturday morning, my cell phone rang. I'd already jogged, showered, had coffee with Marge and Liz, and started to put together the questions for the patient testimonials. It is easy to accomplish a lot when one wakes up in what feels like the middle of the night.

When I pulled the phone from my pocket, I saw it was Vivian and I hit the magic button.

"Hello?"

"Hi, Russ. Are you busy?"

"Not really," I said. "I'm at my sister's. What's up? Is London all right?"

"She's fine. But I forgot to bring the vase to art class, and I was wondering if you might swing by the house and bring it here. I'm almost at the studio and if I turn around and go back, she's going to be really late."

"Yeah," I said. "No problem. I'll be there as quick as I can."

I hung up the phone and grabbed my keys. I'd placed them in a basket on the table by the door.

Behind me, I heard Marge call out: "Where are you going?"

"Vivian called. I need to bring London the ceramic vase she made last week."

"Then you better get to it, seal."

"Seal?"

"She commands and you comply. If you're lucky, maybe she'll toss a fish at you."

"It's for London, not Vivian," I snapped.

"Keep telling yourself that."

Though I was annoyed by her comment, it passed in the rush to get to my house, and then to London's class. Marge lived ten minutes away; if I hit more green lights than red, I'd be there shortly after class started.

I wondered, absently, whether London had told Vivian about the yellow flowers and pink mouses. I smiled. *Mouses.* It had sounded so cute coming from her, I just didn't have the heart to correct her. I wanted to see my daughter, even if only for a few seconds. Though it had only been a day, I missed her.

I got home, grabbed the vase, and was fortunate to hit one green light after another, the Man Upstairs obviously understanding the urgency of my mission.

I pulled into the lot and spotted Vivian standing outside the studio. When I parked, she was already approaching my car, motioning me to roll down the window.

I did and passed the vase to her.

"Thanks," she said. "Let me get back in there."

I felt myself deflating like an old balloon. "Before you go—did you two have a good time yesterday?"

She was already backing away. "We had a terrific time. I'll call you tomorrow to let you know what time you should come over to the house."

"Can you send London outside so I can say hi?"

"She can't," she said. "They've already started painting," she said. She turned and vanished into the studio without another word and I thought to myself that seals were actually lucky.

At least they got a treat.

I didn't want to return to Marge's right away. Vivian's demeanor put me in a pissy mood, one intensified by the fact that I hadn't slept much. Caffeine, I thought. I needed caffeine, and I pulled in a few doors down from the studio and parked in front of the coffee shop. No doubt Vivian would rather I had gone somewhere else for an iced tea on the off chance that *London might see me!* But in a rare turn, I told myself that I didn't care whether she might get angry or not. I actually wanted her to be angry with me.

Maybe, I thought, that was the first step in correcting my need for Vivian's approval. After all, Marge had been right about my reasons for racing to the studio earlier; even after yesterday's lunch, I'd still wanted Vivian's approval, not London's. If there was anything positive to come out of it, it was that I realized that Vivian was making it easier for me to *not* want her approval; why try when it simply wasn't possible? And if she happened to give it, I doubted whether that would change anything.

I pushed through the door, wondering if this was the first step in fixing this particular character flaw of mine when I heard my name being called out.

"Russ?"

I recognized the voice and spotted Emily waving from a table, a newspaper spread before her, a glass of tea on the table. With her luxurious hair curling in the heat and a casual, low-cut T-shirt tucked into faded jeans shorts and sandals, she was beautiful in an earthy, natural way. The sight of her made my irritation melt, and I realized that she was the very person I'd wanted to see, even if I hadn't been consciously aware of it. "Oh, hey Emily," I responded, unable to suppress a smile. Instead of getting in line, I found myself heading toward her table, almost on autopilot. "Long time, no see. How are you?"

"I'm good," she said with a genuine smile. "My schedule's been crazy for the past few weeks."

Mine, too, I thought. "What's been going on?"

"I had to finish some pieces for the gallery, but David's been in town, too. And that meant a whole lot of running around."

"You mentioned that he'd be around. How much longer is he staying?"

"It's his last weekend. He'll be flying back to Sydney on Tuesday."

As she spoke, I caught the glint of reflected light in her hazel eyes, triggering memories that seemed to make the years roll backward. I motioned toward the counter and the words were out before I could stop them. "Will you be here for a few minutes? I was thinking about getting some iced tea."

"I'll be here," she said. "The raspberry tea is fantastic."

I went to the counter and ordered; I took her advice and when it was ready, I brought my glass to the table. She'd just finished folding up the paper, making room, as I took a seat.

"Anything interesting in the paper?"

"A lot of bad stuff. It gets old. I wish there were more stories about good things."

"That's why they have the sports section."

"I suppose. But only if your team wins, right?"

"If they lose, I skip the sports section."

It wasn't particularly funny, but she laughed anyway. I liked that. "What's been going on with you?" she asked. "I haven't seen you in forever."

"I wouldn't even know where to start."

"Did you film those commercials like you wanted? For the lawyer?"

"I did. They're being finalized in the editing room now, and the first one will hopefully air in about two weeks. I'm filming another one for him next week. And I also signed a plastic surgeon as a client."

"Is he any good? In case I need his services?"

"I hope so," I said. "But you don't need any work done."

"Good answer," she said, "even if it's not true. And congratulations on the new account. I know you were worried and I'm glad it's working out for you."

"I'll need another few clients before I breathe a sigh of relief, but I do feel like I'm finally on the right track."

"And you've lost some weight, I notice."

"Fifteen pounds."

"Did you want to lose weight? Because I didn't think you needed to lose any in the first place."

I couldn't help comparing her response to Vivian's, when she'd mentioned my jowls.

"I'm still a few pounds from where I want to be. I've started running again, doing push-ups, all that good stuff."

"Good for you. I can tell it's working. You look great."

"You, too," I said. "So...what have you been up to? You said you had to finish some gallery pieces?"

"I've been working nonstop. For some reason, virtually all of my pieces at the gallery sold in just a few days last month. Different buyers, different states. I don't know why. Maybe it has something to do with the cycle of the moon or whatever, but the gallery owner called me and asked if I had more work to display. Long story short, I had a bunch of partially completed paintings, and I decided to try to finish them. I completed eight, but the others . . . they are going to take more time. I've spent a lot of time staring or repainting or adding different media . . . it's like they're trying to tell me what they should end, but for some reason, I'm just not able to hear all of them."

"They do wonderful things with hearing aids these days."

"Really," she said, feigning wonder. "I didn't know that. Maybe that's the answer."

"It's about as much help as I can offer. I'm not an artist."

She laughed. "How was London this morning? Bodhi couldn't wait to see her. I'd say he has a crush on her, but he's too young for something like that."

It would have been easy to lie and say something innocuous, but sitting across from Emily, I didn't want to.

"I don't actually know how she was. She was with Vivian this morning."

"Then what are you doing here?"

"Vivian forgot to bring the vase she was supposed to paint. I had to bring it to her."

"Yeah," Emily nodded, "I heard about that project as soon as I got there. We weren't here last week, so I guess Bodhi will be making his vase today. He's in there with David right now and I guess they're kind of on their own."

"I suppose I should ask why you're here, then."

"I brought Bodhi. David met us here. He's been staying at one of those extended-stay hotels since he's been in town. Which is fine for him, but Bodhi doesn't sleep well at that place, so Bodhi's at my house every night. Which has meant a lot of back and forth since David's been in town. On the plus side, I've had plenty of time to work, since David's spending a lot of time with him. Trying to make as many memories as possible, I guess. Like today, they're going go-karting after they finish up here."

"That's a good thing, isn't it?"

"Of course," she said, with less enthusiasm than I'd expected. "What David doesn't understand is that it's going to make it that much harder for Bodhi when he leaves again. Bodhi was finally getting used to him not being around and I'm going to have to help pick up the pieces."

"Did you tell him that?"

"How can I? Even though he wasn't a good match for me, he's actually a pretty loving dad. And he's also not a bad person. He made it possible for us to stay in the house and for Bodhi to be able to go to the right school. He was more than generous in our divorce settlement."

As she said the word *divorce*, I thought about the conversation Vivian and I had at lunch and I must have flinched.

"I'm sorry," Emily said quickly. "I really am doing my best not to talk about David. I don't know why his name seems to enter every conversation."

"It's not that," I said. I clutched my glass of iced tea with both hands. "Vivian left me."

Emily mouth widened into an O. "Oh my God," she finally breathed. "That's awful. I'm not sure what else to say."

"There's not much you can say."

"Are you sure you're not just taking some time apart? Like separation?"

"I don't think so. At lunch yesterday, she said we were getting divorced. And she wants us to sit down and talk to London tomorrow night."

"What happened? I mean, does it bother you if I ask? You don't have to answer, obviously."

"She's in love with her boss, Walter Spannerman. And she's now living in Atlanta."

"Oh, boy."

Now, there was an understatement. "Yeah."

"How are you doing?"

"Okay sometimes, not so well at other times."

She nodded, her expression soft. "I understand exactly what you mean. When did all this happen? And again, you don't have to tell me if you'd rather not."

I thought about it before taking a sip of my tea. Though I'd talked endlessly with Marge and Liz, I still felt the need to process it verbally. I'm not sure why, other than that people cope in different ways, and for me, I had to talk. Reprise. Question. Wonder. Whine. Repeat. Repeat. Repeat. My sister had been more than patient with me since Vivian had left, but I felt bad that I'd needed her ear to the extent I had. Same with Liz. And yet, I still felt compelled to process; I felt an overwhelming desire to go through all of it once more.

"I'd like to tell you about it, but I'm not sure even where to start," I said. I stared out the window. Emily leaned across the table.

"What are you doing this afternoon?" she asked.

"No plans," I said.

"Do you want to go for a walk? Or at least get out of here?"

"A walk sounds great."

I followed Emily, even though I wasn't sure where she was going, other than it was in the general direction of her place. In time, she turned onto a private drive that led to a private country club, with a membership fee that was a bit out of my league. She pulled into a shady spot not far from the practice putting green, and I parked beside her.

"This okay?"

"A golf course?"

"It's a gorgeous walk. I'm out here three or four times a week. Usually in the mornings."

"I take it you're a member."

"David loved to golf," she said.

We stepped onto the cart path and began making our way down one of the lush green fairways. As I took in the surroundings, I realized Emily had been right. The fairways and greens were immaculate and generously lined with dogwoods, magnolias, and live oaks. There were neatly trimmed azalea bushes and ponds that sparkled beneath blue skies; a steady breeze kept the temperature tolerable.

"What happened?" she asked, and over the course of the nine or ten holes we traversed, I told her everything. Maybe I shouldn't have; maybe I should have been more reticent, but once the flow of words started, I seemed unable to stop. I talked and talked, answering Emily's questions whenever they came up. I told her about our marriage and the early years with London, I told her how important it had been to me to make Vivian happy, my never-ending desire to please her. I spoke about the last year, and went into detail describing what an emotional basket case I'd been since Vivian had walked out the door. As I spoke, I was alternately confused and sad, enraged and frustrated, but mainly, I was still at a loss. I felt like someone who thought he'd known the rules of the game he'd been playing, only to learn that the wrong rules had been placed in the box.

"I appreciate you listening," I said as I came to the end of my sorry tale.

"I was glad to," she said. "I've been through it, too. And I get it. Believe me. The year that David moved out was the hardest year of my life," she said. "And yes, the first couple of months were excruciating. All day, every day, I wondered whether I'd done the right thing by telling him to go. And after that, I'm not saying that I was Mary Poppins. It took probably another four or five months before I began to feel a little bit like my old self again some of the time. But by then, I also kind of knew that Bodhi and I were going to make it."

"How are you now?"

"Better," she said. She cracked a wry smile. "Well, most of the time. It's strange, but the more time passes, the less I can remember the bad things while the good memories still linger. Before Bodhi, we used to lie in bed on Sunday mornings and have coffee and read the paper. We didn't even talk that much, but I still recall how comfortable those mornings felt. And like I said, David was always a good father. It would be so much easier if I forgot the good stuff instead."

"It sounds like it was really hard."

"It can be awful. Arguing about money is often the worst part. When money's involved, it can get vicious."

"Was it like that for you?"

"No, thank God. David is more than fair with alimony and child support, and we couldn't make it if he weren't. It doesn't hurt that his family is as rich as Midas and he earns a lot of money, but I also think he felt guilty. It's not that he's a bad guy, he's just not a particularly good husband, unless you don't mind constant philandering."

"I can see how that might be a problem for some."

I felt her eyes drift toward me. "She might come back, you know. Sometimes they do."

I reflected on Friday's lunch, and the way she'd acted when I handed off the vase. I remembered what Liz had told me.

"I don't think so."

"Even if she realizes she made a mistake?"

"I still don't know that she'd want to come back. I get the sense that she's been unhappy with me for a long time. I tried to be the best husband and father I could be and it never seemed to be enough."

"You sound like you're not sure whether I'll believe you."

"Do you?"

"Of course. Why wouldn't I?"

"Because she left me."

"That was her decision. And it says less about you than it does about her."

"I still feel like a failure."

"I can understand that. I felt the same way. I think most people do."

"I'm not sure Vivian does. She doesn't seem to care at all."

"She cares," Emily said. "And she's hurting, too. Walking away from a marriage isn't easy for anyone. But she's also in love with someone new, and that's a big distraction. She isn't thinking about the two of you as much as you are. Which means she's not hurting as frequently as you are."

"I think I need a distraction."

"Oh, yeah, that's exactly what you need. Maybe some midtwenties, cheerleader type, right? Or an aerobics teacher? Or maybe a dancer." When I raised an eyebrow, she shrugged and went on. "Those were David's preferences. Of course, if push came to shove, he'd sleep with anyone."

"Sorry."

"I'm not. He's not my problem anymore," she said. "He's dating someone back in Sydney. He told me he's actually thinking about marriage."

"Already?"

"It's his life," she shrugged. "If he asked me, I'd tell him that he

276

should probably give it more time, but he didn't ask so I didn't offer. And besides, we're divorced. He can do what he wants."

I put a hand in my pocket as I walked beside her. "How can you do that? Not let it bother you, I mean. When I think about Vivian and Walter, I get so angry and it hurts. I can't disengage."

"It's still too new," she said. "But as tough as I sound and as much as I meant what I said about David, it still hurt when he told me. No one likes to feel they're easily replaced. For a long time, even though I told people that I wanted David to be happy after we'd separated, what I really wanted was for him to sit at home like a hermit, feeling awful about himself and grieving for everything he lost."

I imagined Vivian like that. "That sounds good. How can we convince them to do that?"

She laughed. "If only it were that easy, right? Exes are never easy. Last weekend, he actually hit on me."

"Seriously? What about his girlfriend?"

"She didn't come up. And I'll admit that there was a minute or so where I considered going through with it. He is handsome, and we used to have a good time together."

"How did it happen?"

"Alcohol," she said and I laughed.

"Anyway, he'd been out all day with Bodhi and when he brought Bodhi home, Bodhi went right to bed. I was having a glass of wine and I offered him one. One glass led to the next and he was being his regular charming self, and the next thing I knew, his hand was on my knee. I knew what he wanted and…"

I waited as she collected her thoughts. She looked over at me.

"I knew it was a terrible idea, but I still liked the way he made me feel. It's crazy, but that's how it was. It's been a long time since I felt desired and attractive. Part of it's my own fault, of course. It's not like I've really put myself out there in the last year and a half. I've gone on a few dates and the guys were nice, but I figured out pretty quickly that I wasn't ready to start another relationship. Which meant that when they called a second time, I always put them off. Sometimes, I wish I were the type of person who could sleep around without feeling guilty or like I'm a tramp, but I'm not wired that way. I've never had a one-night stand."

"Wait, I thought there was this guy in college once..."

"That doesn't count," she said with an airy wave. "I have erased that evening from my memory, so it never happened."

"Ah," I said.

"Anyway, David started to kiss my neck, and part of me was thinking *Oh, why the hell not?* Fortunately, I came to my senses. On the plus side, he handled the rejection gracefully. No temper tantrums, no argument. Just a shrug and sigh, like I was the one who was really going to be missing out." She shook her head. "And I can't believe I just told you all that."

"It's no big deal. If it makes you feel better, I probably won't remember it. The tornado of emotions I'm living in is wreaking havoc with my memory."

"May I ask a question?"

"Go ahead."

"What about London?"

"That's more complicated," I admitted. "For now, Vivian thinks it's best that London stay with me since she's traveling so much and hasn't had time to get her place set up. But she was pretty clear that after that, she wants London to move to Atlanta."

"How do you feel about that?"

"I don't want her to go...but I also know that she needs her mom."

"What does that mean?"

"I don't know. I guess it's something we'll be discussing. To be honest, I don't know anything about this entire process."

"Have you spoken to an attorney yet?"

"No," I said. "She didn't mention divorce until yesterday. And before that, I was in no condition to do much of anything."

By then, I could see the clubhouse in the distance. I wasn't sure how far we'd walked, but we'd been out there for over an hour. My stomach gurgled.

Emily must have heard it. "Are you hungry? Why don't we grab a bite to eat?"

"I don't think we're dressed for the country club."

"We'll sit in the bar area. It's casual. It's where golfers end up after they finish their rounds."

As much as the walk with Emily had felt *necessary*, having lunch—just the two of us, at the club—made me feel as though I was crossing a boundary of sorts. I was still married. Vivian and I weren't even legally separated. Hence, this was wrong.

And yet...

The other side of the equation was obvious, even to me. What would Vivian say to me if she found out? That I was crossing a line? That rumors would start?

I cleared my throat. "Lunch sounds great."

The clubhouse was imposing and somewhat stuffy on the outside, but the interior had been recently renovated and was lighter and airier than I'd expected. Windows lined two of the walls, offering a spectacular view of the eighteenth hole. I spotted a foursome making their way to the putting green as Emily pointed to a table in the corner, one of the few that wasn't already occupied.

"How about over there?" she said.

"Fine."

I followed her to the table, my eyes drifting lower to the once-familiar contours of her legs, glad she was in shorts. They were tan and lean, the kind of legs that had always caught my eye.

After we sat, she leaned across the table. "I told you we wouldn't be underdressed. That group just came in from the tennis courts."

"I didn't notice," I said. "But good to know."

"Have you ever eaten here?"

"Once, in the dining room. Jesse Peters has a membership here and we met with a client."

"I see him every now and then. Or used to anyway. I would catch him staring at me."

"That sounds like him."

"Oh, if you're interested, the burger here is out of this world," she said. "The chef actually won a burger competition on one of those shows on the Food Network. It comes with some amazing sweet potato fries."

"I haven't had a burger in a long time," I said. "Is that what you're getting?"

"Of course."

I couldn't help noting that Vivian would never have ordered a burger, nor would she have approved if I'd ordered one.

The waitress came by with menus, but Emily shook her head. "We're both getting the burgers," she said. "And I'd like a glass of Chardonnay."

"Make it two," I said, surprising myself. Of course, the whole afternoon had been bewildering to that point, but in a good way. Emily, I noticed, was gazing out the window, toward the putting green before she turned back to me.

"I guess our children are done with art class by now. What do you think London is doing?"

"Vivian probably took her out to lunch. As for what's next, I have no idea."

"Didn't she tell you?"

"No," I said. "Our lunch on Friday was a little tense, so we didn't get around to discussing their plans."

"They were tense with David, too, for a long time. It's just a hard and awful thing for anyone to live through, even if it has to be done. And only people who've gone through it can understand how terrible it really is."

"That's not very encouraging," I said.

"It's true, though. There's no way I could have made it without the support of some really good friends. I probably talked to both Marguerite and Grace on the phone two or three hours a week—maybe more, in the beginning. And what was strange was that prior to my divorce, I wasn't particularly close to either of them. But I ended up leaning on them, and they were always there to prop me up when I needed it."

"They sounds like lifesavers."

"They are. To this day, I'm not sure why they were there for me the way they were. And I'm guessing that you'll probably need the same thing—two or three people that you can really talk to. It was strange—I thought that my sister Jess or Dianne, who was probably my best friend at the time, would be my stalwarts. But it didn't work out that way."

280

"What do you mean?"

"It's hard to describe, but Marguerite and Grace always knew how to say the right thing at the right time, in just the right way. Jess and Dianne didn't. Sometimes, they offered advice I didn't want to hear, or they questioned whether I was doing the right thing when what I really needed was reassurance."

Considering this, I wondered who I would lean on. Marge and Liz, obviously, but they sort of counted as one person. I already knew my mom would get too emotional, and my dad wouldn't know what to say. As for friends, it dawned on me that I didn't really have any. Between work and my family, I'd let most of my friendships wilt on the vine in the years since London was born.

"Marge and Liz have been great," I said.

"I figured they would be. I always liked Marge."

The feeling is mutual, I thought.

The waiter delivered two glasses of wine. Emily reached for her glass. "We should make a toast," she said. "To Marge, Liz, Marguerite, Grace, Bodhi, and London."

"The kids, too?"

"Bodhi was the real reason I didn't fall apart. Because of him, I couldn't. It'll be the same with London."

I knew she was right as soon as she said it. "All right. But then, I feel like I have to put you in there, too. You've been pretty supportive so far."

"And you can always call me any time."

We fell into small talk then. I told her about London, while she spoke about Bodhi; she told me about some of the places she'd traveled in the years since we'd last seen each other. Perhaps because we'd already spoken exhaustively about Vivian and David, their names didn't come up, and for the first time since Vivian had walked out the door, the anxiety I'd been feeling seemed to dissipate entirely.

The burgers eventually arrived and we each ordered a second glass of wine. The burger, as she'd predicted, was among the best I'd ever had. It was stuffed with cheese and topped with a fried egg, but because my recent lack of appetite had made my stomach shrink, I couldn't eat more than half.

Our plates were cleared, but we lingered at the table, finishing our wine. She told me a story about Bodhi giving himself a haircut, laughing aloud when she showed me the picture on her cell phone. He'd lopped off, nearly down to the roots, an inch-wide chunk of hair in what used to be his bangs. His forehead shown through like a gap between teeth, but what made the photo priceless was his grin.

"That's great," I laughed. "How were you?"

"Initially I was upset, not only about his hair but that he'd gotten hold of the scissors in the first place. When I saw how proud of himself he was, though, I started to laugh. The next thing I knew, we were laughing together. Then I grabbed my phone. Now, this photo is framed and sits on my bedside table."

"I'm not sure how I would have reacted if London had done that. And one thing I can say for sure: Vivian would not have laughed."

"No?"

"She wasn't a big laugher." In fact, I couldn't remember the last time I'd heard her laugh.

"Even with Marge? Marge used to crack me up all the time."

"Especially with Marge. They don't really get along that well."

"How is that possible? Does she still tease you?"

"Mercilessly."

Emily laughed again and I was reminded of how much I had always liked the sound of her laugh, melodic and genuine at the same time.

"You know what?" she said. "This day turned out a lot better than I thought it would. If you hadn't come along, I don't know what I'd be doing. Probably staring at my paintings in frustration. Or cleaning the house."

"I'd probably be working."

"This is way better."

"Agreed. Would you like another glass?"

"Of course," she said. "But I won't. I have to drive. But go ahead if you want one."

"I'm fine, too. What are you doing tonight?"

"Like you, I'll be hanging out with my sister. You remember Jess? She and Brian invited me to dinner."

"That sounds fun."

"Mmm...not so sure. I sometimes wonder if Brian thinks I'm putting ideas in Jess's head. Like about getting divorced."

"Are they having troubles?"

"All married couples have troubles now and then. It kind of goes with the institution itself."

"Why is marriage so hard?"

"Who knows? I think it's probably because people get married without knowing who they really are in the first place. Or how they're crazy."

"Are you crazy?"

"Of course. And I don't mean crazy-crazy. I mean, in the way that everyone is. One person might be too sensitive to perceived slights, or another might get really angry when they don't get their way. Another shuts down or holds grudges for weeks. That's what I'm talking about. We all do things that are unhealthy in relationships, but I'm not sure people recognize that unless they're really self-aware. And when you consider that each partner brings his or her own set of issues, it's a miracle that any marriages last the duration."

"That's a little pessimistic, don't you think? Your parents have been married forever. Mine have, too."

"But are they happy with each other? Or are they together out of habit? Or because they're afraid to be alone? In the coffee shop earlier, I was watching this older couple a few tables over. They may have been together for fifty years, but I don't think they said a single word to each other."

I thought about my parents, remembering that Marge and I had wondered the same thing.

"Do you think you'll ever get married again?"

"I don't know," she said. "Sometimes I think I want to, but other times, I think I'm happy being alone, too. And with Bodhi, it's not as though I have a lot of energy to devote to finding a new life partner. What I can say is that I'm a lot clearer on the kind of person that I want if it ever comes to that. I've decided to be very picky."

I was quiet, suddenly returning to Vivian, bringing with her an almost physical weight. "I don't know what's going to happen with Vivian. And I still don't know why she was so unhappy with me."

"Maybe she was just unhappy. And maybe she just thinks she's happier with someone new, but sustained happiness isn't something someone else can deliver. It comes from within. That's why there are antidepressants; that's what people hopefully learn in therapy."

"That's very Zen."

"It took me a while to finally accept that David's philandering wasn't about me, or whether I was pretty enough, or affectionate enough. It was about David's need to prove to himself that he was desirable and powerful—and the way he did that was by sleeping with other women. In the end, I know I did my best to make our marriage work, and I know that's all I can ask of myself." She reached across the table and put her hand on my arm. "The same goes for you, too, Russ."

When she removed her hand, the warmth and comfort of her touch lingered, a physical affirmation of her words.

"Thank you," I managed to say.

"You're welcome. And I mean it. You're a good guy."

"You don't know me that well anymore."

"Actually, I think I do. You're pretty much the same guy you always were."

"And I blew it with you."

"You made a mistake. I know you didn't do it to hurt me. And again, I've forgiven you. You still need to forgive yourself."

"I'm working on it. But you're kind of making it hard, since you're being so nice about it."

"Would you rather I be cruel and vindictive?"

"If you were, I'd probably crumble."

"No you wouldn't. You're stronger than you think."

We'd finished our wine and by unspoken agreement, we rose from the table. A glance at my watch showed that we'd spent nearly three hours together, which didn't seem possible.

We started toward the exit and made our way to our cars. "Remember what I said about finding a couple of good friends to lean on. You're probably going to need them."

"Are you volunteering?"

"I already did, remember? And I hate to tell you this, but if my experience is any guide, it's probably going to get worse before it gets better."

"I can't imagine how it can get worse."

"I hope for your sake that it doesn't."

I reached for her door, opening it for her. "Me, too."

"Rewind and start from the beginning," Marge said. "You went for a long walk and then had lunch with Emily? And you drank wine?"

She and Liz had gotten home a few minutes earlier. On the way, they'd called, asking what I wanted for dinner. They were planning to pick up Mexican takeout and when I told her that I wasn't hungry, Marge said she'd pick something for me anyway. In the to-go box was a burrito the size of a softball, along with rice and refried beans. Marge and Liz had both ordered taco salads. and we took our seats at the table.

"Yeah," I said. "What's the big deal?"

Marge paused and took a puff from her inhaler before smirking. "Let's just call it an act two twist I never saw coming."

"Really?" Liz asked between bites. "They did have that date at Chick-fil-A, remember?"

"Would you stop with the date talk? We walked. We talked. We had lunch."

"That's what a date is. But fine. My question is whether you think you'll call her again."

"Her son Bodhi is London's best friend. If we have to set up a play-date, I might have to."

"That's not what I meant."

"I know what you meant." I said. "I have no interest in dating anyone. Right now, I can't imagine wanting to date ever again."

What I didn't say was that even though I didn't want to date, I didn't much like the concept of being alone, either. What I wanted was for Vivian and me to go back to what we had before. I wanted to rewind and start over.

Marge seemed to read my mind. "Have you heard from Vivian? About what time you can go home tomorrow?"

"Not yet. I'm going to call London later. I figure she'll tell me then."

Marge pointed to the burrito. "You're not eating."

"I wouldn't be able to finish this if I were stranded on a desert island for a month."

"Why don't you at least try a bite?"

I did as she asked; while it was tasty, I was still full from the hamburger, and I turned toward Liz. "Did you learn any Mexican recipes in your class?"

Liz nodded as she poked at her salad. "A few. I could have made you something, but I was feeling kind of lazy. And I would have had to run to the store."

"Do you have some easy and healthy recipes? Meals that London would enjoy?"

"Plenty. Do you want me to pick a few favorites?"

"Would you? I want to keep things normal, but I'm not very experienced in the kitchen. I do want to keep London on a good schedule, though. Which includes dinner."

"I'll have some recipes for you by tomorrow."

"I appreciate it," I said. "How was the housewarming party?"

"It was a lot of fun," Liz said. "The house is very stylish. Even though our friends just moved in, they had all their paintings hung. It was actually pretty impressive."

Automatically, I wondered whether they owned any of Emily's. I wondered, too, how Emily's night with her sister Jess was going. Under Marge's scrutiny, I forked another piece of the burrito.

"Today was the first time I didn't think about Vivian every waking minute."

Marge offered a thoughtful expression. "What was that like?"

"Strange," I said. "But I think it was good for me. I don't feel quite as anxious now."

"You're already beginning to heal, Russ," Marge said to me. "You're stronger than you think."

I smiled, remembering that Emily had said exactly the same thing.

After dinner, I dialed Vivian using FaceTime, and she answered on the second ring.

"Hey there," she said, "London and I are cuddled up watching a movie. Can she call you back a little later?"

"Hi, Daddy!" I heard London call out. "Nemo and Dory are with the sharks!"

"Yeah, sure," I said. "Did you two have a good time today?"

"We had a lot of fun," Vivian said. "She'll call you back, okay?"

"I love you, Daddy!" London shouted. "Miss you!"

The sound of her voice made my heart ache.

"That's fine," I said. "I'll be around."

I carried my phone with me while I helped Marge and Liz in the kitchen; I kept it on the table beside me when Marge brought out the Scrabble board. Liz, I learned, took the game seriously, and she was good. By the end, she'd outscored both my sister and me combined, but the game was a lot more fun than I remembered.

It was almost enjoyable enough, in fact, to make me forget the fact that London didn't call back.

Almost, but not quite.

In the morning, I received a text from Vivian. *Can you come by at six thirty? Let me know if that works for you.*

It struck me as kind of late, especially since she had to drive back, but I wasn't going to point that out. She was trying to spend as much time with London as she could, but because I was still annoyed that I hadn't had a chance to talk to London, I put my phone aside without responding. I didn't text her back until almost two in the afternoon.

My run that morning was nearly eight miles and when I got home, I did a hundred push-ups. Only when I'd showered did my irritation begin to wane.

Liz put together a small recipe book of about fifteen recipes, most with no more than six different ingredients. Afterward, she showed me how to meal plan, and we went to the grocery store to stock up on everything I would need.

Though Marge and Liz would disagree, I nonetheless felt a bit like a third wheel, and after lunch, I hopped in the car and drove to the bookstore. I had never been a big reader, but I found myself wandering to the relationship section of the bookstore. There were a few shelves of books about coping with divorce and I thumbed through all of them before finally selecting a few. When I was checking out, I was sure that the clerk would read the titles before glancing at me with pity, but the teenage girl with pink hair behind the register simply scanned the books before shoving them into a bag and asking me whether I'd like to pay in cash or with credit.

Afterward, I decided to swing by the park, on the off chance that London would be there. If she was, I wasn't sure whether I would intrude, but I wanted to see her. It occurred to me that I was behaving like an addict who was suffering from withdrawal, but I didn't care.

When I got to the park, there was no sign of Vivian and London. I pulled in anyway. With the temperatures cooling off a bit this weekend, there were more kids there than usual. I took a seat on the bench and opened one of the books. I began to read, at first because I thought I should, but after half an hour, because I wanted to.

What I learned was that Marge, Liz and Emily had been right. Though it may have felt otherwise, what I was going through wasn't unique. The emotional swings, the self-blame, the circular questions and sense of failure were par for the course when it came to most divorces. But reading about it, as opposed to simply hearing it, made it seem more real somehow, and by the time I finally closed the book, I felt a little better. I thought about returning to Marge's, but instead I spotted a boy who resembled Bodhi and I reached for my phone.

When Emily picked up, I rose from my seat, inexplicably nervous. I walked toward the fence that lined the perimeter.

"Hello?"

"Hey there," I said. "It's me, Russ."

"What's going on? You doing okay?"

"I'm fine," I said. "Just missing London and had to get out of the house. How are you doing?"

"About the same. David and Bodhi are at the movies right now. I

288

think they're going out for pizza later. Which means that I've been staring at my paintings again."

"Have you deciphered the whispers yet?"

"Working on it. What have you been up to today?"

"I ran eight miles. Felt pretty good, too. I hung out with Marge and Liz, went to the bookstore. Now, I'm just killing time and thought I'd call to say thanks for yesterday."

"My pleasure. I had a great time," she said.

I felt a strange sense of relief at that. "How was dinner with your sister last night?"

"She and her hubby had been arguing before I got there. Though they kept it mostly in check, I still noticed a lot of glaring and heard more than half a dozen deep sighs. It was kind of like a stroll down memory lane, what with David and all."

I laughed. "That sounds awful."

"It wasn't pretty. But Jess called this morning to apologize. And then, right after, she launched into yet another story about how Brian seemed intent on antagonizing her."

We continued to chat while I circled the park, and more than once, I caught myself smiling. I had forgotten how easy Emily was to talk to, how intently she listened, and how freely she volunteered information about herself. She never seemed to take too much too seriously, a trait she had always possessed but now felt seasoned by maturity. It made me wish I could be more like her.

After forty minutes, we finally ended the call. Like yesterday, the time seemed to pass effortlessly. As I walked back to my car, I wondered why Vivian and I hadn't been able to talk with the same ease, and by allowing her name to slip into my consciousness I felt another burst of frustration that I hadn't been able to speak to London. Preventing my daughter from talking to her mother was something I'd never done, not since Vivian had walked out the door. Emily, I thought to myself, would never do something like that, and as I slid into the car, I found myself thinking about how naturally beautiful Emily was—no makeup masking skin with a slightly olive undertone, no expensive highlights or collagen fillers.

She was more beautiful now, I thought to myself, than she'd been when we'd dated.

Emily, I realized, had sounded happy to hear from me, and I couldn't deny that it made me feel better. People pleasing is best when it happens easily, after all, and where I constantly felt like I was struggling to please Vivian, it seemed that with Emily, all I had to do was be me, and that was more than enough.

And yet, as much of a distraction as Emily had been, I hadn't been lying to Marge or Liz. As an old friend—and an attractive one at that—it was understandable that I'd enjoyed spending time with Emily and it probably made sense that I'd called her. I felt comfortable with her, just as I always had. What it didn't mean was that I was ready—or even interested—in a relationship. After all, healthy relationships required two well-adjusted people, and at the present time, I wasn't enough for her.

I said as much to Marge before I left for home, but she just shook her head.

"That's Vivian's voice you're hearing in your head," she said to me. "If you saw yourself the way everyone else does, you'd know what a catch you really are."

I arrived at the house at half past six and hesitated at the door, wondering if I should knock. It was ridiculous, of course, and the fact I felt that way led to a growing sense of frustration, one that was directed more at myself than at Vivian. Why did I still care so much about what she thought?

Habit, I silently heard myself answer, and I knew that habits could take a long time to break.

I opened the door and stepped inside, but there was no sign of London or Vivian. I heard sounds coming from upstairs and I moved toward the steps when Vivian rounded into view, holding a glass of wine. She beckoned to me, and I followed her into the kitchen. Glancing around, I noticed pans and plates piled in the sink, and neither the stove nor the counters had been wiped. There was half a glass of milk and a placemat that still sat on the table, and I knew in that moment that she had no intention of cleaning the kitchen before she left.

I felt as though I no longer knew her, if I ever did.

"London's upstairs in the bath," she said without preamble. "I told her that I'd come and get her in a few minutes because we needed to talk to her. But I thought we should get on the same page first."

"Didn't we already cover this on Friday?"

"Yes, but I wanted to make sure you remembered."

Her comment felt like an insult. "I remember."

"Good," she said. "I also think it'll be easier for London if I take the lead."

Because you don't want her to know about Walter, right?

"This is your show," I said.

"What's that supposed to mean?"

"Just what I said," I said. "You're making all the decisions. You've yet to ask what I might want."

"Why are you in such a cranky mood?"

Was she serious? "Why didn't you have London call me back last night?"

"Because she fell asleep. Not ten minutes after you called, she was sound asleep on the couch. What was I supposed to do? Wake her up? You see her every day. I don't."

"That was your choice. You're the one who walked out."

Her eyes narrowed and I thought I saw in them not simply anger but hatred. She kept her voice steady. "I was hoping we'd be able to behave like adults tonight, but it seems pretty clear that you have different plans."

"You're trying to blame all this on me?"

"I just want you to hold yourself together while we talk to our daughter. The other option is to make it as painful as possible for her. Which would you prefer?"

"I would prefer not to be doing this at all. I would prefer you and I had an honest discussion about salvaging our marriage."

She turned away. "There's nothing to talk about. It's over. You should be receiving the settlement agreement this week."

"Settlement agreement?"

"I had my attorney put it together. It's pretty standard."

By *standard*, I'm sure it stipulated that London was living with her in Atlanta, and I felt my insides twist. All at once, I didn't want to do this; I didn't want to be here. I didn't want to lose my wife and daughter, I didn't want to lose everything, but I was nothing but a bystander, watching my life unravel in ways that seemed entirely beyond my control. I was exhausted and when the nausea finally passed, my body felt as it might dissolve.

"Let's just get this over with."

London handled it better than I thought she would, but then again, it was clear to me London was so exhausted that her attention seemed to wander. Add in her runny nose, and I had the sense that what she really wanted was to go to sleep.

As I'd expected, Vivian omitted much of the truth and kept the conversation so short that I found myself wondering why she'd deemed it so critical in the first place. By the end, I suspected London had no idea that anything was actually changing between Vivian and me; she was as used to Vivian traveling as I was. The only time she became upset was when it came time for Vivian to leave. Both she and Vivian were in tears as they hugged goodbye in the driveway, and London's sobs grew worse as Vivian finally pulled away.

I carried her inside, my shirt growing damp in spots from her tears. Her bedroom smelled like a farm; in addition to cleaning the kitchen, I would have to clean the hamster cage. I gave London some additional cold medicine, put her in bed. She scooted closer to me and I slipped my arm around her.

"I wish Mommy didn't have to leave," she said.

"I know it's hard," I said. "Did you have a good time this weekend?" When she nodded, I went on. "What did you do?"

"We went shopping and watched movies. We also went to the petting zoo. They had these cute goats that fall over onto their sides when they get scared, but I didn't scare them."

"Did you go to the park? Or ride your bike?"

"No. I rode the carousel at the mall, though. I rode a unicorn."

"That sounds fun."

She nodded again. "Mommy said you have to remember to clean the hamster cage."

"I know," I said. "The cage is kind of smelly tonight."

"Yeah," she said. "Mommy didn't want to hold Mr. or Mrs. Sprinkles because they were smelly, too. I think they need a bath."

"I don't know if hamsters can take baths. I'll find out."

"On the computer?"

"Yes."

"The computer knows a lot of stuff," she said.

"It sure does."

"Hey, Daddy?"

"Yes?"

"Can we go bike riding?"

"How about we give it a couple of days, until you feel better. You also have dance class, remember?"

"I remember," she said without enthusiasm.

Trying to keep her slightly improved mood from going downhill, I brightened. "Did you get to see Bodhi this weekend?"

"He was in art class. I painted my vase."

"With yellow flowers? And pink mouses? Can I see it?"

"Mommy took it with her. She said it was really pretty."

"I'm sure it was," I said, trying to hide my disappointment. "I wish I could have seen it."

"Do you want me to make you one? I can. And I think I can paint my mouses even better."

"I'd love that, sweetie."

I cleaned the hamster cage and the kitchen; though I hadn't noticed earlier, I also had to straighten up the family room. Barbies and their accessories had been strewn about, blankets needed to be folded and returned to the appropriate chest, and a half-eaten bowl of popcorn had to be emptied into the trash before being washed and dried. Remembering I still had dinners my mom had prepared, I moved a few Tupperware containers from the freezer to the refrigerator. I also unloaded the groceries I'd picked up with Liz and Marge earlier.

Later, I crawled into bed and caught the scent of perfume, one that I knew Vivian had been wearing. It was light and flowery but otherwise unknown to me, and I knew I'd never sleep. I stripped the bedding and put clean sheets on the bed. I wondered if she'd intended any message by leaving behind dirty sheets or a messy house. It might have been anger, but I didn't think so. My gut was telling me that she no longer cared how I might feel because she no longer cared about me at all.

CHAPTER 17

Moving Forward and Backward

When I was dating Emily—before I did something stupid—we spent the first week of July in Atlantic Beach, North Carolina. With two other couples, we'd rented a house close enough to the water that we could hear the waves breaking in unrelenting rhythm. Though we'd split the rent three ways, it was still a stretch for all of us, so we'd brought coolers packed with food we'd purchased at the grocery store. We planned to cook instead of going out to restaurants, and as the sun started to go down, we'd fire up the grill and start our feast. In the evenings, we'd drink beer on the porch to the sound of the radio, and I can remember thinking that it was the first of many such vacations Emily and I would end up taking together.

The Fourth of July was particularly special. Emily and I woke before the others, walking the beach as the sun began to rise. By the time everyone got out of bed, we'd set up our spot on the beach, complete with a steamer I'd rented to cook the scallops and shrimp that had been unloaded at the docks only a few hours earlier. We supplemented the seafood with corn on the cob and potato salad, and set up an inexpensive volleyball net. When our friends finally joined us, we spent the rest of the day in the sun, kicking back, wading in the surf, and coating ourselves with sunscreen.

There was a carnival in town that week, set up in the main traffic circle near the beach, about a quarter mile from where we were staying. It was one of those traveling carnivals, with rickety rides, overpriced tickets, and games that were almost impossible to win. There was, however, a Ferris wheel, and half an hour before the fireworks were supposed to start, Emily and I ditched the group and climbed aboard the ride. I figured we'd have plenty of time to rejoin our friends afterward, but as fate would have it, the ride broke down just as Emily and I reached the apex.

While stalled at the top, I could see workers tinkering with either the engine or the generator; later, I saw someone race off, only to return carrying a large and obviously heavy toolbox. The ride operator shouted up to us that he'd have the ride working again shortly, but warned us not to rock the carts.

Though the day had been sweltering, the wind was gusting, and I slipped my arm around Emily as she leaned into me. She wasn't frightened, nor was I; even if the engine was fried, I was sure there was some sort of manual hand crank they could use to eventually unload everyone. From our vantage point in the sky, we watched people as they moved among the carnival booths, and stared at the carpet of house and streetlights that seemed to stretch for miles. In time, I heard the familiar thwump of a firework being launched from a barge off shore just before sparkling fingers of gold and green and red expanded across the sky. Wow, Emily breathed, something she repeated throughout the hour and a half we remained stuck on the Ferris wheel. The wind was pushing the scent of gunpowder down the beach, and as I pulled Emily closer I remember thinking that I would propose to Emily before the year was up.

It was around that time that our friends finally spotted us. They were on the beach, people in miniature, and when they figured out that we were stuck, they began to whoop and point. One of the girls shouted up to us that if we planned on spending the night up there, we should probably order a pizza.

Emily giggled, before growing quiet.

"I'm going to pretend that you paid the workers down there to stall the Ferris wheel on purpose," she finally said.

"Why?"

"Because," she said, "for as long as I live, I don't think another Fourth of July will ever measure up to this one."

On Monday morning, London woke with a red nose and continuing sniffles. Though she wasn't coughing, I debated whether to send her to school, but when I suggested as much, she began to fuss.

"The teacher is bringing in her goldfish today, and I get to feed him! Plus, it's coloring day."

I wasn't sure what coloring day entailed, but it was obviously a big deal to her. I gave her some cold medicine at breakfast, and she skipped off to class. I noticed when dropping London off that the teacher had a cold too, which made me feel better about my decision.

On my way back to the car, I caught myself wondering what Vivian was doing and immediately shoved the thought away. *Who cares?* I reminded myself, but more important, I had a commercial to film later that week and another client I needed to impress.

At the office I was swamped with work. I confirmed everything I needed to film Taglieri's third commercial on Friday. I touched base with the tech guy for the plastic surgeon, and even managed to meet with an animal trainer who claimed to have just the dog I needed to film the fourth commercial for Taglieri. We set a date for filming on Thursday of the following week.

Which meant, fortunately, that I didn't have time to think about Vivian much at all.

The settlement agreement was delivered via FedEx on Tuesday afternoon. It also came via email, but I couldn't bring myself to read either version. Instead, I called Joey Taglieri and asked if he would look it over. We agreed to meet at an Italian restaurant not far from his office the following day.

I found him at a booth in the corner, the table topped with a red and white checkered tablecloth and a manila folder lying on a pad of yellow legal paper. He was drinking a glass of mineral water and when I sat, he slid a piece of paper toward me, along with a pen. "Before we get into this, you need to sign a retainer agreement. I told you that I don't do family law anymore, but I can make an exception for you. I can also recommend some attorneys, including the guy who handled my second divorce, but I'm not sure how much they'll be able to help you for reasons I'll get to in a moment. The point is, no matter who you choose, everything you tell me will be covered by attorney-client privilege, even if you ultimately decide to work with someone else."

I signed the retainer agreement and slid it back to him. Satisfied, he leaned back. "You want to tell me what happened?"

I told the same story I had to Marge and Liz and my parents and Emily. By then, I felt as though I'd told the story a hundred times. Taglieri jotted notes along the way. When I finished, he leaned back and said, "All right, I think I got it. I also reviewed the document, and I guess the first thing that you should know is that it looks like she intends to file for divorce in Georgia, not North Carolina."

"Why would she do that?"

"Georgia and North Carolina have different laws. In North Carolina, a couple has to be legally separated for a year before divorce can be granted. That doesn't mean you have to live in separate places, but both of you have to understand that you're separated. After the year is up, one of you files for divorce. The other side then has thirty days to file an answer, but that can be sped up a bit, at which point you get on the court calendar. When your time comes, divorce is granted. In Georgia, there is no *separated for a year* requirement. There is, however, a *residency* requirement. Vivian can't file for divorce until she's been a resident of the state for six months, but after that, it can be granted in thirty days, assuming everything has been worked out between the two of you. In essence, because she's been living in Atlanta since September eighth—or maybe even before that—she'll be able to obtain a divorce next March or April, instead of next year around this time. In other words, she cut six months off the process. There are a couple of other differences concerning fault and no fault that I doubt will pertain to you. I'm guessing she'll file no fault, which essentially means the marriage is broken."

"So she's in a rush to dump me, huh?"

"No comment," he said with a grimace. "Anyway, that's one of the reasons I've decided to offer my services if you want them. I passed the bar in Georgia as well as North Carolina—go Bulldogs!—while the attorneys I used for my divorce haven't. In other words, it's either work with me, or get an attorney in Georgia. Also, I made some calls this morning… apparently, Vivian's attorney is a real piece of work. I've never dealt with her, but she has the reputation of being a bully who likes to wear down the other side until they just throw in the towel. She's also very selective when it comes to clients, so my guess is Spannerman pulled some strings to get her to agree to represent your wife."

"What do I do? I have no idea where to start."

"Just what you're doing right now—you've retained legal counsel. And trust me, nobody knows what to do in the beginning unless they've been through it before. Long story short, in Georgia, there are documents that will have to be filed, everything from disclosure statements, marital settlement agreements, to an affidavit regarding custody. Her attorney will probably press to have everything ready by the six-month mark, so there's going to be a lot of back-and-forth between counsel."

"What about the settlement agreement she sent?"

"That's essentially a contract between the two of you. It covers alimony and property division, things like that."

"What about London?"

"That's where it can get tricky. The courts retain the right to make decisions regarding custody, visitation, and child support. Now, the two of you *can* come to an agreement and the court will take that into account, but they're not bound by it. If it's reasonable, though, the court will usually go along with what the two of you decide. Because London is so young, she won't have much of a say at all. That's probably for the best."

I suspected he'd have to go over all of this again. "What did Vivian want?"

Taglieri reached into the folder and pulled out the agreement. He began to flip through the pages. "As far as property division goes, for the most part, she wants half. That's half the equity in the house, half the money in your banking and investment accounts, half of your retirement. She wants the SUV and half of the value of the contents of the house, in cash. She also wants an additional chunk of change, which I'm guessing is half the total you invested in your business."

I suddenly felt as though I'd been donating blood for a week. "Is that all?"

"Well, there's also alimony."

"Alimony? She earns more than I do right now and she's dating a billionaire."

"I'm not saying she'll get it. I suspect she'll use it, along with the rest of the proposed property division, as leverage to get what she really wants."

"London."

"Yeah," he said. "London."

After my meeting with Taglieri, there was no time to return to the office. Instead, I drove to the school and got there early; I was at the front of the car line. I was looking over the separation agreement—it crowded out all other thoughts—when I heard a tapping on my window.

Emily.

She was wearing tight faded jeans with tears at the knees, along with a formfitting top, and the sight of her made something lift inside me. Opening the door, I stepped out into the sunlight.

"Hey there," I said. "How are you?"

"I feel like I'm supposed to ask you that question. I've been thinking about you the last few days and wondering how Sunday night went."

"It went as well as something like that could, I guess. Vivian did most of the talking."

"How's London doing?"

"She seems all right. Other than the fact that she's still getting over a cold."

"Bodhi, too. He just came down with it yesterday. I think more than half the class is sick right now. It's like a leper colony in there." She seemed to study me for a moment. "Other than that, how are you holding up?"

"So-so," I admitted. "I had to meet with an attorney today."

"Oh, yuck," she said. "I hated that part of it."

"It wasn't a lot of fun," I said. "It still feels like a dream, like it's not really happening. Even though I know that it is."

She looked straight at me and as she held me in her sights, I was struck by the length of her eyelashes. Had they always been that long? I found myself struggling to remember. "Did you have your questions answered?" she asked.

"I wasn't even sure what questions to ask. That's what I was looking over in the car. Vivian sent a proposed separation agreement."

"I'm not a lawyer, but if you have questions, you can call. I might not be able to answer all of them, of course."

"I appreciate that," I said. I could see more cars pulling into line, a steady flow now. As far as I could tell, I was the only male in the pickup line. As I faced Emily, I suddenly heard Vivian's voice in my head—*rumors!*—and wondered if any of the mothers in the car line were watching us. Automatically, I took a slight step backward and slipped my hand into my pocket. "Did David leave for Australia?"

She nodded. "Yesterday evening."

"Was Bodhi upset?"

"Very. And then, of course, he wakes up sick as a dog."

"And no word when he'll be back?"

"He said that he might be able to visit for a few days around Christmas."

"That's good."

"Sure. If he actually shows. He said the same thing last year. He's good at saying things. The problem is, he's not always so good at follow-through."

I wondered where London would be this Christmas. I wondered where I would be.

"Uh-oh," she said, tilting her head. "I said something wrong, didn't I? You sort of drifted off there."

"Sorry. I was just thinking about some of the things the lawyer said to me today. It looks like I might have to sell the house."

"Oh, no. Really?"

"I'm not sure there's another option. It's not as though I have enough cash on hand to simply pay Vivian off."

That was putting it mildly; if I gave in to all her demands, I'd be flat broke. Add in alimony and child support, and I wasn't even sure whether I could afford a two-bedroom apartment.

"It'll all work out," she said. "I know it's sometimes hard to believe, but it will."

"I hope so. Right now, I just want to . . . escape, you know?"

"You need a break from all this," she said, putting her hands on her hips. "Why don't you guys come with Bodhi and me to the zoo in Ashboro this Saturday?"

"What about art class?"

"Puh-lease." She tossed a length of her thick hair over her shoulder. "The kids can skip a day. And I know Bodhi would be thrilled. Has London ever been there?"

"No," I said.

The directness of her offer was disarming and I struggled to come up with a response. Was she asking me on a date? Or was this more about Bodhi and London?

"Thanks," I said. "I'll let you know." By then, I could see teachers beginning to congregate near the door, students assembling by classroom. Emily noticed it too.

"I should get back to my car," she said. "I don't want to hold up the line. It takes them long enough as it is. Good seeing you, Russ." She waved.

"You, too, Emily."

I watched her walk away, trying to decipher the meaning of her invitation, but as she drew farther away, I felt the distinct urge to see more of her. I might not be ready and it might be too soon, but I suddenly wanted that more than anything.

"Hey Emily," I called out.

She turned.

"What time are you thinking of leaving?"

When we got home London was feeling a little better, so we went for a bike ride. I let her take the lead, following along as we traversed the streets of the neighborhood. Her biking ability was improving with every ride. I still had to caution her to move to the side of the road when a car approached, but kids on bicycles were a common sight in the neighborhood, and most drivers gave us a wide berth.

We rode for an hour. Once home, she ate a snack and went upstairs to dress for dance. It seemed to take forever, and after a while I went up to check on her. I found her sitting on the bed, still wearing the same outfit she'd worn earlier.

I took a seat beside her. "What's wrong, sweetie?"

"I don't want to go to dance tonight," she said. "I'm sick."

Her cold hadn't adversely affected her bike ride, so I knew something else was going on. Namely, that she didn't like dance class or Ms. Hamshaw. And who could blame her?

"If you're too tired or still feeling sick, you don't have to go."

"Really?"

"Of course not."

"Mommy might get mad."

Your mom left us, I thought. But I didn't say that.

"I'll talk to her. If you're sick, you're sick. But is there something else going on?"

"No."

"Because if there is, you can tell me."

When she added nothing else, I put my arm around her. "Do you like going to dance?"

"It's important," she said, as if reciting a sacred rule. "Mommy used to dance."

"That's not what I asked. I asked if you like it."

"I don't want to be a tree."

I frowned. "Honey? Can you tell me a little more about what's going on?"

"There's two groups in my class. One group is going away to dance at the competition. They're the good dancers. I'm in the *other* group. We have to dance, too, but only for our parents. And I have to be a tree in the dance that we're doing."

"Oh," I said. "And that's bad?"

"Yes, it's bad. I'm just supposed to move my arms when the leaves grow and fall."

"Can you show me?"

With a sigh, she got up from the bed. She made a circle with her arms above her head, her fingertips touching. Then, separating her arms, she wiggled her fingers as she lowered her hands to her side. When she finished, she took a seat beside me on the bed again. I wasn't quite sure what to say.

"If it makes you feel any better, you were a very good tree," I finally offered.

"It's for the bad dancers, Daddy. Because I'm not good enough to play the frog or the butterfly or the swan or the fish."

I tried to imagine what those animals would be doing and how the dance would unfold, but what was the point? I figured I'd see it soon enough.

"How many other girls are trees?"

"Just me and Alexandra. I wanted to be the butterfly and I practiced really hard and I know all the moves, but Ms. Hamshaw said that Molly gets to be the butterfly."

In the world of a five-year-old, I supposed this was a very big deal.

"When is the show?"

"I don't know. She told us but I forgot."

I made a note to check with Ms. Hamshaw. Before or after class, obviously, so I didn't offend or disrupt her.

"Do you want to go to the zoo this weekend? With me and Bodhi and Miss Emily?"

"What?"

"The zoo. Miss Emily and Bodhi are going. She invited us, but I don't want to go if you'd rather not."

"A real zoo?"

"With lions and tigers and bears. Oh my."

She furrowed her little brow.

"Why did you say 'Oh my'?" she finally asked.

"It's from a movie called *The Wizard of Oz.*"

"Have I seen it?"

"No," I said.

"What's it about?"

"It's about a girl named Dorothy. Her house gets picked up by a tornado and she lands in a place called Oz. She meets a lion and a tin man and a scarecrow, and they try to find the wizard so she can go back home."

"Is there a bear and a tiger in the movie, too?"

"Not that I can recall."

"Then why does the girl say it?"

That's a good question. "I don't know. Maybe because she was afraid she might run into them."

"I'm not afraid of bears. But tigers are scary. They can be really mean."

"Yeah?"

"I learned that when I watched *The Jungle Book*."

"Ah," I said.

"Is Mommy going to come to the zoo, too?"

"No," I said. "She's working."

She seemed to consider that. "Okay," she said. "Since Bodhi's going, we can go, too."

When Vivian FaceTimed later that evening, I noticed she was dressed as though she were about to go out to dinner, no doubt with Spanner-man. I said nothing to her about it, but as she visited with London, the thought stewed in the back of my mind.

Eventually London wandered back to me, holding out the phone. "Mommy needs to talk to you."

"Okay, sweetie," I said, taking it. I waited until she was gone before raising the screen.

"What's up?" I asked.

"I wanted to let you know that I'm going to be out of town this weekend and it might be hard to reach me."

Every part of me wanted the details, but I forced myself not to ask. "Okay."

She had apparently expected me to press for more information, as my single-word answer seemed to throw her off. "All right," she went on after an awkward pause. "Anyway, I'll definitely be in Charlotte to see her next weekend, and I'd like to stay in the house again."

"Without me," I said. I tried hard not to appear wounded.

"I'm thinking about London here, so yes, without you. And, of course, her birthday is two weekends after that, and I'd like to do the same thing. Stay in the house, I mean. Her birthday's on a Friday, but I want to put together a birthday party with her friends on Saturday. You should obviously come to her party, but after that, it would probably be best if you let us have the rest of the weekend to ourselves."

"It's her birthday weekend," I protested. "I'd like to spend time with her, too."

"You're with her all the time, Russ," she said, raising her chin.

"She's in school. And at her activities. You might think I get a lot of downtime with her, but I don't."

She gave an annoyed sigh. "You get to see her every night. You get to read to her. You get to see her every single morning. I don't."

"Because you left," I said, enunciating slowly. "Because you moved to Atlanta."

"So you'd keep me from seeing my daughter? What kind of father are you? And on that subject, you shouldn't have let her miss dance class today."

"She has a cold," I said. "She was tired."

"How is she supposed to improve if you keep letting her miss class?"

The accusatory tone made my back stiffen.

"This is first one she missed. It's not the end of the world. Besides, I don't think she even likes dance class."

"You're missing the point," Vivian said, narrowing her eyes at me. "If she wants a bigger role the next time they have a show, she can't miss classes. You're setting her up to be disappointed again."

"And my point was, I don't think she'll care, since she doesn't like dance in the first place."

I could see her chest rise and fall, a flush creeping up past the neckline of her black cocktail dress. "Why are you doing this?"

"What am I doing now?"

"What you always do! Finding fault, trying to pick a fight."

"Why is it that when I tell you what I think or offer an opinion that's different than yours, you accuse me of trying to pick a fight?"

"Oh, for God's sake. I'm just so sick and tired of your crap, I can't even tell you."

With that, she disconnected the call. It bothered me more than it should have, but I noted with grim satisfaction that it bothered me less than it would have had we still been together. In fact, it bothered me less than it would have yesterday. Perhaps that was progress.

306

At work for the next two days, I hopped from one project to the next, just like earlier in the week. I touched base with the patients that the plastic surgeon had recommended, and scheduled times on October sixth to get them on camera—that was going to be a long day.

On Friday I filmed the third commercial, making sure to place the camera below desk level so we could shoot the young actress from below. This way, her age was emphasized to comic effect.

The takes were so good that even members of the camera crew laughed. Perfect.

That evening, I brought London to dance class as usual.

Despite a clear lack of enthusiasm, she'd come downstairs dressed in her outfit and reminded me that we shouldn't be late.

I didn't ask again whether it was something she wanted to do; I'm sure that Vivian had rebuked London just as she had me, and I had no desire to put London in an awkward position. I, more than anyone, knew how guilty Vivian could make someone feel.

Seeing her sitting on the couch in the family room with her shoulders slightly caved in, I took a seat beside her.

"What would you like to do after dance?" I asked.

"I don't know," she mumbled.

"Because I was thinking that maybe, just maybe, you and I could..."

I stopped. A couple of seconds passed before she looked over at me. "What could we do?"

"It's nothing," I said. "Never mind."

"What is it?"

"Well, the thing is, you might not want to do it..." I pretended to lose interest.

"Tell me!" she pressed.

I forced out a long exhale. "I was thinking that since Mommy isn't here, maybe you and I could have a date night."

London knew all about our date nights, even if she wasn't aware of all that transpired between Vivian and me.

Her expression was one of wonder. "A date night? Just you and me?"

"That's what I was thinking. After dance, we can get dressed up, and cook dinner together, and then after that, we could either color or do some finger painting or maybe even watch a movie. But only if you want to," I said.

"I want to."

"You do, huh? What do you want to eat?"

She brought a finger to her chin. "I think I want chicken," she said, and I nodded.

"That sounds delicious. That's just what I wanted, too."

"But I don't want to finger paint. It might get on my dress."

"How about coloring? I'm not very good, but I can try."

She beamed. "It's okay that you're not very good, Daddy. You can practice."

"That sounds like a great idea."

For the first time since I'd started ferrying London to and from her activities, she was in a good mood on the way to dance, though the class had nothing to do with it. Instead, I listened to a constant stream of ideas about what she could wear that evening. She debated which dress to wear, and whether to pair it with a sparkly hairclip or bow, and what shoes would match best.

Once inside, Ms. Hamshaw motioned for her to proceed to the floor, but she suddenly turned around and ran back to envelop me in a hug before dashing to the door. Ms. Hamshaw evinced no reaction, which I supposed was as much as she could offer in the way of kindness.

While London was in class, I ran to the grocery store and picked up the makings for dinner. Knowing that we had an early morning the following day—we would meet at Emily's at eight—I opted for a rotisserie chicken from the deli, canned corn, sliced pears, applesauce from a jar, and clear grape juice. If we started eating at half past six, she could still be in bed close to her normal bedtime.

What I hadn't factored in was that five year-olds can take a long time to get dressed for date nights with their dads. At home after class,

London raced up the stairs and forbade me to help. I went to my closet and got dressed up as well, even donning a blazer. I prepared dinner, which took all of five minutes, and then set the table, using our good china. Candles completed the picture once I poured the grape juice into wine glasses. Then I leaned against the counter to wait.

I eventually moved to the table and sat.

After that, I wandered to the family room and turned on ESPN.

Every now and then, I would walk to the stairs and call up to her; she would insist that I stay downstairs, that she was still getting ready.

When she finally descended the stairs, I felt a prick of tears behind my eyes. She'd chosen a blue skirt along with a blue and white checkered top, white stockings and shoes, and a matching blue hairband. The grace note was the imitation pearl necklace she'd put on. Whatever my reservations about Vivian's frequent shopping expeditions with our daughter, even London knew that she'd made an impression.

"You look beautiful," I said, rising from the couch. I shut off the television.

"Thank you, Daddy," she said as she carefully approached the dining room table. "The table looks really nice."

Her attempt to be as adult-like as possible struck me as almost unbearably adorable.

"I appreciate that, sweetie. Would you like to eat?"

"Yes, please."

I went around the table and pulled out her chair. When she was seated, she reached for her glass of grape juice and took a sip. "This is very tasty," she said.

I served and brought the plates to the table. London carefully spread her napkin in her lap and I did the same.

"How was school today?" I asked.

"It was fun," she said. "Bodhi said he wants to see the lions tomorrow at the zoo."

"I do, too. I like lions. But I hope they don't have any mean ones like Scar." I was referring, of course, to the villain in the movie *The Lion King*.

"They won't have any lions like Scar, Daddy. He's just a cartoon."

"Oh," I said. "That's right."

"You're silly."

I smiled as she daintily picked up her fork. "I've heard that."

After dinner, we colored. London happened to have a coloring book that featured zoo animals, and we spent an hour at the kitchen table, creating animals that could only have existed in rainbow-filtered worlds.

Though she'd only been in school for a few weeks, I noticed that her coloring had improved. She was able to stay inside the lines, and had even taken to shading various parts of the pictures. Gone were the smears and squiggles of only a year ago.

My little girl was slowly but surely growing up, which for some reason made my heart ache in places I didn't know even existed.

CHAPTER 18

———— 🦋 ————

It's Not a Date

A month after I graduated from college, I attended the wedding of a former fraternity brother named Tom Gregory in Chapel Hill. Tom was the son of two physicians, and his bride-to-be, a waifish brunette named Claire DeVane, had a father who owned fifty-six Bojangles' restaurants, fast-food places specializing in fried chicken and biscuits. The business might not have the elite ring associated with investment banking, but it minted money, and as a wedding gift, Claire's father had already given the couple a mini-mansion, along with a Mercedes convertible.

The wedding was, of course, a black-tie affair. I'd just started work at the Peters Group and had yet to receive my first paycheck; it went without saying that I was usually broke. While I had enough money to rent a tuxedo, I had to crash at another fraternity brother's place. His name was Liam Robertson, and he was about to start law school at UNC. Though he was also from Charlotte, we'd never been particularly close—he was the kind of guy who took delight in abusing the pledges and fed Jell-O shots with Everclear to freshman girls—but Alpha Gamma Rhos stick together.

To that point, I'd worn a tuxedo only once in my life. I'd rented a navy blue tuxedo for my senior prom in high school and the photo of me and my prom date graced the mantel of the fireplace at my parents' house until I married. That tuxedo, however, had a clip-on bowtie, while the tuxedo I'd rented for the wedding had one that I actually had to tie.

Unfortunately Liam Robertson had no more idea of how to tie the thing than I did, and as our departure time drew near, I'd already made half a dozen failed attempts. It was at that point that the front door to Liam's house flew open and Emily walked in.

I'd seen her before but had never been introduced. She and Liam had grown up in the same neighborhood and were supposedly just friends. Nonetheless, she was going to the wedding as Liam's date—"so she can put in a good word for me in case I meet someone." As soon as I saw her, I did a double take.

It wasn't the Emily I'd seen in Liam's company before, the Bohemian with long skirts and Birkenstocks, usually sans makeup. Instead, the woman who stood before me was sheathed in a cocktail dress with a plunging neckline and high-heeled black pumps, an elegant look accentuated by tasteful diamond studs in both ears. The mascara she wore called attention to her striking eye color, and her lips, accentuated with red lipstick, were full and rich. Her hair fell in rippling waves well past her shoulders.

"Hey Emily," I heard Liam shout. "Russ needs help getting dressed!"

"Nice to see you, too, Liam," she said sardonically. "And yes, thank you. I appreciate the compliment."

"You look great, by the way," Liam added.

"Too late," she muttered under her breath as she glided toward me.

"He's always been clueless," she observed, almost to herself. "I take it you're Russ?"

I nodded, trying not to ogle.

"I'm Emily," she said. "Technically, I'm Liam's date, but not really. He's more like a self-absorbed younger brother to me."

"I heard that!" Liam shouted.

"Of course you did. But only because I was talking about you."

Their easy familiarity made me feel like a bystander, despite the fact that our faces were now only inches apart.

"What have we got here?" she said, wrestling the bowtie free before draping it around my neck again. I noticed that she was only a little bit shorter than I and was wearing a heady floral scent.

"I appreciate this," I said. "How do you know how to do this?"

"I had to help my dad when I was growing up," she said. "He never quite got the hang of it either. It always ended up crooked."

She tugged and adjusted the bowtie, her long fingers doing secret things out of eyesight. Our faces were so close it made me feel as though I was

312

about to kiss her, and I thought again how beautiful she was. My eyes were drawn to her lips, then to the line of her neck. Her dress was cut low in the front, revealing a tiny lace bow at the front of her bra.

"Like what you see?" she teased.

I felt myself flush as I hastened to stare straight ahead, like a cadet at the Citadel. She smiled.

"Men," she said. "You're all the same."

I continued to stand at attention, silent as she finished. Then, with a gentle tap to my chest with both hands and a wink, she went on. "But since you're kind of cute, I'll forgive you."

When I pulled into Emily's driveway the following morning, I immediately spotted her loading a small cooler into her SUV.

Getting out of the car, London scampered toward her and gave her a hug.

"Where's Bodhi?" I heard my daughter ask.

"He's in his room," Emily said. "He's picking a couple of movies to watch on the way. Do you want to go up and help him?"

"Yes ma'am," London said, racing toward the front door before vanishing inside.

Emily watched her go before turning toward me. She was dressed in shorts and a sleeveless top, and she'd tamed her hair into a ponytail. Despite the casual *mom-at-the-park* wardrobe, she seemed to glow with health and vitality. I couldn't stop staring at her thick hair and unblemished skin.

"Ma'am?" she asked, referring to London, when I was close.

"She's very polite," I said, hoping my scrutiny wasn't too obvious.

"I like it," she said. "I've tried that with Bodhi, but it's never seemed to take." With the kids in the house, she seemed as youthful as the girl I once knew, giving rise to an internally disorienting sense of time warp.

"It should be fun today," I commented. "London's been excited about it."

"Bodhi, too," she said. "He wants London to ride with us."

"That's fine," I said. "I can follow."

"You'll ride with us, too, dingbat. There's no reason for both of us to have to drive, and there's no way I want to be trapped with those two without assistance. Besides, it'll take us two hours to get there, and this baby," she said, nodding at the SUV, "can play DVDs for the kids."

Her playful ribbing transported me back to the first time I'd ever spoken to her, and how nervous I'd been.

"You want me to drive?" I offered.

"Unless you'd rather be in charge of the snacks. Of course, that means bending and twisting and unwrapping food every few minutes."

I remembered my dad's comment about family trips.

"No, I'm good," I said. "It's probably better if I drive."

Before we had even left the neighborhood, Bodhi asked if they could watch *Madagascar 3*.

"Let's wait until we get on the highway," Emily said over her shoulder.

"Can I have a snack?" Bodhi asked.

"You just had breakfast."

"But I'm hungry."

"What do you want to eat?"

"Goldfish," he demanded.

Vivian had never allowed that particular treat into our home, but it was a staple of my own childhood.

"What's a Goldfish?" London asked.

"It's a cheesy cracker shaped like a fish," Emily said. "It's really good."

"Can I have one, Daddy?"

My eyes flicked to the rearview mirror and I wondered what London was thinking about the fact that I was up front with Emily and not her mom, or whether it mattered to her at all.

"Of course you can."

The drive to the zoo passed quickly. In the backseat, the kids were happily engrossed in the movie, but since they were within earshot, we didn't mention Vivian or David. Nor did Emily and I touch on our shared past. Instead, I told her what I'd been doing at work, and she talked about her paintings and the fact that she had a show coming up in mid-November, which meant she'd be busier than usual until then; we also caught up on our respective families, the conversation and laughter flowing easily, as though we'd never lost contact with each other.

Yet despite our familiarity, the outing still felt new and a little strange. It wasn't a date, but it wasn't something I could have envisioned even a month ago. I was on a road trip with Emily, kids in tow, and though I initially expected to feel a vague sense of guilt, I didn't. Instead, I found myself glancing at her in quiet moments and wondering how David could have been so stupid.

And, of course, why I'd been so stupid, so long ago.

"They're going to be exhausted," Emily predicted, shortly after we arrived at the zoo. Since we parked, they'd raced each other from the parking lot to the ticket booth, and once inside, to the water fountain and back, then ricocheted back to the gift shop. London, I was proud to note, must have inherited some of those track-and-field genes because to my eyes they ran neck and neck. London and Bodhi were studying the gift shop racks as we ambled toward them.

"I'm already exhausted, just watching them."

"Did you get your run in this morning?"

"Just a short one. Four miles or so."

"Better than me. Hoofing it around here will be my exercise for the day."

"How do you stay so fit?"

"Pole dancing," she said. At my startled expression, she laughed.

"You'd probably like that, wouldn't you?" She nudged my shoulder. "I'm kidding, you dork. But you should have seen your expression! It was priceless. I do try to make it to the gym a few times a week, but mainly, I was blessed with good genes and I watch what I eat. It's easier than having to exercise all the time."

"For you, maybe. I like eating."

London skipped toward me as we entered the shop.

"Daddy, look! Butterfly wings!" she cried, holding up a pair of lacy, semi-translucent wings, large enough for her to wear.

"Very pretty," I said.

"Can we get them? In case I get to be the butterfly at the dance?"

For Ms. Hamshaw, with the kids who didn't make the cut for the competition. The performance in which London was supposed to be a tree.

"I don't know, sweetie...," I said.

"Please? They're so pretty. And even if I'm not the butterfly, I can wear them today and make the animals happy. And I can show them to Mr. and Mrs. Sprinkles when I get home."

I wasn't so sure about that, but I checked the price, relieved that they weren't exorbitant. "You really want to wear these today?"

"Yes!" she pleaded, bouncing up and down. "And Bodhi wants the dragonfly wings."

I felt Emily's gaze on me and I turned toward her. "It might make them easier to spot if they run off," she pointed out.

"All right," I said, "but just the wings, okay?"

"And only if you put on sunscreen," Emily added.

Unlike me, she'd remembered to bring some. Oops.

After paying, I helped London slip the wings on. Emily did the same with Bodhi. Spreading enough lotion on their skin to enable them to slither through tiny pipes, we watched as they ran off again, with their arms outstretched.

The zoo was divided into two major areas: North America and Africa. We visited North America first, wandering through various exhibits and marveling at everything from harbor seals and peregrine falcons, to alligators, muskrats, beavers, a cougar and even a black bear. In each case, the kids reached the exhibit before we did and by the time Emily and I arrived, they were usually anxious to move on. Fortunately the crowds were light, despite the glorious weather. The temperature was mild, and for the first time in months, the humidity didn't feel oppressive. Which didn't, however, stop the kids from asking for Popsicles and sodas.

"Whatever happened to Liam?" I asked Emily. "I haven't heard from him in ten years. Last I heard, he was practicing law in Asheville and he was already on his second marriage."

"He's still practicing law," she said, "but his second marriage didn't last either."

"She was a cocktail waitress, too, right? When they met?"

"He has a type," she said, with a smile. "No question about it."

"When was the last time you heard from him?"

"Maybe seven or eight months ago? He heard I was getting divorced and he asked me out."

"He wasn't one of the nice guys you never called a second time?"

"Liam? Oh, God no. We'd known each other growing up, but you know—he's always been a little too into himself for my taste. And in college, we hung out more out of habit than actual friendship. And by habit, I mean he came on to me at least once a semester, usually when he was drinking."

"I always wondered why you tolerated him," I mused.

"Because my parents were friends with his parents and lived across the street from each other. My dad thought he had his act together, but my mom saw right through him all along, thank God. The point is, it had more to do with the fact that he was always there. On campus, at home. Back then, I hadn't developed the ability to just cut people off. Even if they were jerks."

"If it wasn't for him, though, we'd never have met."

She smiled wistfully. "Do you remember when you asked me to dance? At the wedding?"

"I do," I said. It had taken more than an hour for me to work up the courage, even though Liam had by then zeroed in on a woman who would later become wife number one.

"You were afraid of me," she said with a knowing grin.

I was acutely aware of how close she was; up ahead, London and Bodhi were walking beside each other as well, and I flashed on the book I read nightly to London. The four of us walking two by two, because no one should have to walk alone.

"I wasn't afraid," I clarified. "I was embarrassed because you'd caught me ogling when you helped me with my bowtie."

"Oh stop...I was flattered and you know it. We've been over this before—I'd asked Liam about you, remember? He said that you were too nerdy for me. And not handsome enough. And not rich enough. Then he hit on me again."

I laughed. "It's coming back to me."

"Do you stay in touch with friends from college?" She squinted as if trying to recall faces. "We used to see your buddies pretty regularly when we were together."

"Not really," I said. "Once I got married and London came along, I sort of lost track of most of them. You?"

"I have a few friends from college and a handful that I knew growing up. We still talk and get together but probably not as much as we should. Like it did with you, life just got busy."

I noticed the lightest spray of freckles across her cheeks and nose, so faint as to be invisible in anything but perfectly angled, autumn sunlight. I didn't recall her having those fifteen years ago; they were another surprising feature of this once-familiar Emily. For a moment I wondered what Vivian would think if she saw Emily and me together right now.

Suddenly the whole situation struck me as surreal—me with Emily at the zoo with the kids, Vivian in Spannerman's arms somewhere else. How had things come to this? And where had my life taken this unforeseen U-turn?

Emily's hand on my arm startled me out of my reverie.

"You okay?" She studied me. "You went away there for a second."

"Yeah, sorry." I tried for a smile. "Sometimes it just hits me at random moments...how odd and inexplicable it all is, I mean."

She was silent for a moment, letting her hand fall away. "It's going to be that way for a while," she said, her tone soft. "But if you can, try to let whatever comes, come, and whatever stays, stay. And whatever goes, just let it go."

"That's beyond me right now."

"'Right now' being the operative words. You'll get there."

A dull ache of missing Vivian stirred within me then, but it didn't linger. It was a rabbit punch, without the strength of an uppercut, and I understood that it was due to Emily. Given the choice, I realized that it was better to spend the day with a fun and compassionate friend than a wife who seemed to despise me.

"It's been a long time since I did something like this," Emily reflected. When I looked at her inquiringly, she continued. "Hang out with a friend of the opposite sex, I mean ... it was before David, that's all I know. It might have even been before you and I were together. Why is that?"

"Because we were married."

"But I know other married people who have friends of the opposite sex."

"I'm not saying that it can't happen," I conceded. "It's just that it can get tricky and I think most people know that. Human nature being what it is, and given how hard marriage is, the last thing any spouse needs is an attractive alternative. It can make the other party look bad."

She made a wry face. "Is that what I'm doing?" she asked. "No—don't answer. That was inappropriate." She smoothed some stray hairs into her ponytail. "It's not my intent to make anything worse between you and Vivian."

"I know that," I said. "Then again, I'm not sure you could make it any worse. For all I know, she's off in Paris with the guy right now."

"You don't know?"

"The only time we spoke this week was when she told me she wanted to see London two of the next three weekends, including her birthday weekend, then yelled at me for allowing London to miss dance class. She also said it would be 'hard to reach' her, whatever that means. And that I should sleep at Marge's or my parents when she's in town, because she wants the house. Oh, and that she's sick of my crap."

Emily winced.

"It wasn't my favorite phone call," I admitted.

"But you know she shouldn't get to see London every single weekend. Nor should you have to leave the house."

"She says she wants to make it easier for London."

"It sounds to me like she just wants what she wants."

"That, too," I said. "But at the same time, I can see her point. It would be disruptive for London to have to stay in a hotel when her mom's in town."

"Her life has already been disrupted," Emily pointed out. "Why can't she just sleep in the guest room?"

"She thinks that might confuse London."

"So suggest that she go to bed after London is asleep and then set an alarm so she's awake before London. When you're together, just be cordial to one another. I know it's hard when emotions are high, but it's not impossible. And it's better than you getting kicked out of your own house every time she comes to visit. That's just wrong and you don't deserve to be treated that way."

"You're right," I acknowledged, but I was already dreading the argument that would inevitably ensue. More than anyone, Vivian knew how to hurt me when she didn't get her way.

"When we met in the coffee shop that first time, I told you that I'd seen you dropping off London, remember?"

"I remember."

"What I didn't say is that I watched you for a while. I saw the way you are with her, the way she hugged you and told you she loved you. It's obvious to everyone that you are the apple of that girl's eye."

Inexplicably, I felt myself blush with pleasure. "Well, I'm pretty much the only parent she has right now..."

"It's more than that, Russ," she interrupted. "For little girls, their first love should always be their dad, but that isn't always the case. When I saw you two saying goodbye that day, I was struck by how loving and close you seemed. Then I recognized you, and I just knew I had to say hello. So I followed you."

"Come on..."

"Scout's honor," Emily said, making the Boy Scout sign. "You know me. I live by my instincts. Artist. Remember?"

I laughed. "Yeah," I said, meeting her determined gaze and feeling flattered, although for what reason I wasn't sure. "I'm glad you did. I don't know what kind of shape I'd be in right now if you hadn't. You've been a big help to me."

"Yep, that's what I do," she said with a playful "aw shucks" grin.

"You know what's strange?"

"What's that?"

"I don't have any memories of what you were like when you were angry. I can't even recall any serious fights between us. So tell me: Do you get angry?"

"Of course! And I can be scary," she warned.

"I don't believe you."

"Then don't ever test it. I'm like a grizzly bear and jackal and great white shark all rolled into one." She gestured at our surroundings. "I thought animal metaphors would be appropriate. Since we're here at the zoo, I mean."

After viewing the animals of North America and the aviary, the four of us had lunch. Despite a steady stream of snacking during the previous four hours, Bodhi managed to finish a plate of chicken nuggets and fries, along with a chocolate milkshake. London consumed about a third as much, but for her that was a lot. Neither Emily nor I were hungry, both of us opting for a bottle of water.

"Can we go see the lions now?" Bodhi asked.

"Not until we put on more sunscreen," Emily answered, and the kids popped out of their seats. Again, Emily slathered them up.

"You're very good at remembering that. I forget every time."

"You never saw David's extended family. They lived in the Outback—like the Outback, Outback—and you could have measured the depth of their wrinkles with a wooden ruler. A lot of people here get too much sun, but seeing those relatives at our wedding really made an impression on me. I barely leave the house without sunscreen these days."

"That's why you have the skin of a twenty-year-old."

"Ha! Nice try! But a lovely thought nonetheless."

I was tempted to explain that I was sincere, but opted instead to start gathering our food trays.

"Who's ready to head to Africa?" I asked.

I admit that I found the Africa part of the zoo more to my liking. Growing up, I'd seen alligators in the Cape Fear River, muskrats and beavers, all sorts of birds—including that majestic bald eagle—and even a bear. When I was a kid in Charlotte, across the street from my elementary school, a bear was spotted crossing the road and eventually ended up in the branches of an oak tree. It was a juvenile bear and while the sighting was definitely uncommon, everyone knew that bears weren't really that rare in North Carolina. The largest black bear on record, in fact, was killed in Craven County. The point is, the animals of North America that we'd seen earlier didn't strike me as terribly exotic.

Never once, however, had I spotted a zebra or giraffe, or a chimpanzee; I'd never come face-to-face with baboons, or elephants either. Maybe I'd seen them at the circus—my family went to the circus every year when it was in town—but seeing the animals in a setting that was somewhat reminiscent of the wilds of Africa was enough to make even the kids stop and stare for a while. Handing London my phone, she took more than a hundred photos, which added to her excitement.

Because we took our time, we didn't finish up at the zoo until late afternoon. By the time we trekked back to the car, the kids were trailing behind us.

"It's like the tortoise and the hare," I said to Emily.

"Except the hares back there probably ran three times as far as we walked."

"Well, at least they'll sleep well."

"I just hope that Bodhi doesn't fall asleep in the car. If he naps for two hours, he'll be awake until midnight."

"I didn't think about that," I said, suddenly concerned about London's schedule as well. "Kind of like remembering to bring sunscreen. Or bringing snacks for the trip. Obviously, I'm a work in progress when it comes to child rearing on my own."

"We're all works in progress," she said. "It's the definition of being a parent."

"You seem to know what you're doing."

"Sometimes," she said. "Not always. This week when Bodhi was sick, I couldn't decide whether to baby him, or treat his cold like an everyday occurrence."

"I know how my parents would have reacted," I said. "Unless I was bleeding profusely or had broken bones protruding from my skin or a fever high enough to fry my brain, they would have shrugged and told me to tough it out."

"And yet, you turned out just fine. Which means that maybe I was too soft on Bodhi. Maybe he'll learn to like being sick because it gets him special treatment."

"Why is it so hard to be a really good parent?"

"You don't have to be a really good parent," she said. "All you have to do is be good enough."

As I pondered her words, I realized why my parents and Marge had liked Emily so much. Like them, Emily was wise.

CHAPTER 19

Finding My Own Way

*I*t was the wedding in Chapel Hill that cemented my resolve to see Emily again. By the time the cake had been cut and the bouquet had been tossed, Emily and I had danced to more songs than I could keep track of. When the band took a break, we stepped out on the balcony for a breath of fresh air. Above us, a big orange moon hung low in the sky, and I could see Emily staring at it with the same sense of wonder I felt.

"I wonder why it's orange," I mused aloud. To my surprise, I heard Emily answer.

"When the moon is low in the sky, the light scatters because it has to pass through more layers of the atmosphere than when it's overhead. By the time the light reaches our eyes, the blue, green, and purple parts of the spectrum have scattered, leaving only yellow, orange, and red visible to us."

"How do you know that?" I marveled, turning to her.

"My dad explained it to me every time we saw one of these," she said, nodding at the glowing orb hovering over the horizon. "I guess over time, it just stuck."

"I'm still impressed."

"Don't be. If you ask me anything else about the night sky other than the location of the Big Dipper, I wouldn't be able to help you. For instance, I know that one or two of those stars out there are probably planets, but I couldn't tell you which ones they are."

Scanning the sky, I pointed. "That one over there, right above the tree? That's Venus."

324

"How do you know?"

"Because it's brighter than the stars."

She squinted. "Are you sure?"

"No," I admitted and she laughed. "But my dad told me that. He used to wake me in the middle of the night so the two of us could watch meteor showers."

A nostalgic smile crossed her face. "My dad did that with me, too," she said. "And whenever we went camping, he'd stay up with Jess and me for hours, and we'd watch for falling stars."

"Jess?"

"My older sister. Do you have any siblings?"

"I have an older sister, too. Marge." I tried to picture Emily as a girl, with her family. "I'm having a hard time imagining you camping."

She knitted her brows. "Why?"

"I don't know," I said. "I guess maybe because you strike me as more of a city girl."

"What does that mean?'

"You know . . . coffee shops, poetry readings, art galleries, joining protests, voting socialist."

She laughed. "One thing's for sure—you don't know me at all."

"Well," I said, gathering my courage, "I'd like to know you better. What do you like to do for fun?"

"Are you asking me out on a date?"

Her gaze left me feeling a bit flustered. "If your idea of fun is skydiving or shooting apples off my head with a bow and arrow, then the only reason I'm asking is for the sake of conversation."

"But if it's dinner and a movie . . ." She arched an eyebrow.

"That's more my style."

She brought a hand to her chin and slowly shook her head. "No . . . dinner and a movie is just too . . . clichéd," she said finally. "How about a hike?"

"A hike?" Eyeing her stiletto heels, I had trouble picturing her outdoors, communing with nature.

"Yeah," she said. "How about Crowders Mountain? We can follow the Rocktop Trail."

"I've never been there," I said. In fact, I'd never heard of it.

"Then it's a date," she said. *"How about next Saturday?"*

I looked at her, suddenly wondering whether I'd asked her out or if she'd asked me, or even whether it really mattered. Because I could already tell that Emily was extraordinary, and I knew without a doubt that I wanted to get to know her better.

On Sunday, when I had spare time, I worked on the third commercial and shipped it off to the editor, which took less time than I thought it would. It had to take little time, since the rest of my day was spent with London.

It may not be politically correct to say, but the fact that London was going to school made my life better, too. As much as I loved my daughter, Sunday wore me out and I was looking forward to heading to work, if only because it seemed somehow easier than entertaining a five-year-old for sixteen straight hours.

My good mood, however, ended even before I got to the office on Monday morning. I'd just dropped London off when I fielded a call from Taglieri, asking if it was possible for me to swing by his office.

Half an hour later, I was sitting across from him in his office. His jacket was off and his sleeves were rolled up; on his desk were messy piles of what I assumed to be ongoing cases.

"Thanks for making time this morning," he said. "I connected with Vivian's attorney on Friday. I wanted to get a sense of her and see if there was a way to make all of this proceed as smoothly as possible."

"And?"

"Unfortunately, she was exactly as billed. After hanging up, I went to her firm's website because I had to see what she looked like. During our call I kept picturing an ice statue instead of a real person. I mean, she was subzero."

His description conjured up a number of future scenarios, none of them particularly good for me. "What does that mean?"

"It means it's probably going to be harder for you than it should be, depending on how forcefully you intend to fight."

"I don't care about the money as much as I care about London. I want joint custody."

"I hear you," he said, raising his hand. "And I know that's what you want. But I'm not even sure what that means. Vivian's living in Atlanta and because she wants residency in Georgia, she's not coming back here. My question to you is whether you're willing to move to Atlanta."

"Why do I have to move? My house is here. My family is here. My job is here."

"That's my point. Even if you received joint custody, how would that work? It's not like you'd have the chance to see London very much. Which is why, I assume, Vivian is asking for sole custody, as well as physical custody. She's willing to grant you visitation..."

"No," I said, cutting him off. "That's not going to happen. I'm her father. I have rights."

"Yes, you do. But we both know that courts tend to favor women. And Vivian's attorney is telling me that Vivian was the primary care-giver until only a few months ago."

"I worked so she could stay at home!"

Joey raised his hands, even as his voice adopted a soothing cadence. "I know that," he said, "and I don't think it's fair either. But in custody battles, fathers are at a real disadvantage. Especially in situations like these."

"She's the one who moved out. She left us!"

"According to Vivian's attorney, it was because you left her with no other choice. You were no longer able to support the family and you'd drained a big chunk from the savings account. She was forced to get a job."

"That's not true! Vivian took the job because she wanted to. I didn't make her do anything..."

Taglieri fixed me with a sympathetic look. "I believe you. I'm on your side, Russ. I'm just relaying some of the things Vivian's attorney said to me. By the way, that woman may be an ice queen and a bully, but I'm not afraid to take her on. She's never had to go toe-to-toe with the Bulldog, and I'm good at my job. I just wanted to update you in person and prepare you for what comes next. This thing is already ugly, and it's probably going to get even uglier over the next few months."

"What do you need me to do?"

"For now, nothing. It's still early. As for the settlement agreement she sent, just pretend it doesn't exist. I'll draft a response for you to look over and I already have some ideas on that. That said, my court schedule is full for the next couple of weeks so you won't see anything from me right away. I don't want you to worry if you don't hear from me. There's always a tendency in these situations to want to get everything done as quickly as possible, but it generally doesn't work that way. What I do want is to touch base with her and have a longer conversation, but even then, there's no reason to rush. Right now, London is still living with you. That's a good thing, and the longer it goes on, the better it is for you. Also keep in mind that Vivian can't file for divorce until next March at the earliest, so we still have time to work out a settlement that's agreeable to both parties. Until then, you might want to check if it's possible for you and Vivian to work something out that's acceptable to both of you. I'm not saying that she'll go for something like that—in fact I doubt that she will—but it's worth a try."

"And if she doesn't want to work something out?"

"Then just keep doing what you're doing with London. Be a good father, spend time with your daughter, make sure London gets to school and eats and sleeps right. I can't stress how important that is. Keep in mind that we can always bring in a psychologist to talk to London and present a report to the court..."

"No," I said, interrupting. "I'm not going to put London in the middle of all this. She's not going to have to choose between her mother and father."

His eyes dropped. "You might not think it's a good idea, but Vivian may insist on it in the hope that it will benefit her case."

"She wouldn't do that," I said. "She adores London."

"It's precisely because she adores London," he said, "that you shouldn't be surprised by anything she's willing to do in order to gain custody."

After the meeting with Taglieri, I was more angry, and frightened, than I'd been since Vivian had walked out the door. In my office at work, I fumed. I called Marge and repeated what Taglieri had said; Marge was as livid as I was. When she referred to Vivian with a term synonymous with female dogs, I echoed the sentiment.

But talking to Marge did little to make me feel better, and in the end, I called Emily and asked if she could meet me for lunch.

Considering how furious I was, I wanted to avoid going to a restaurant. Instead, I asked her to meet me at a park near the house, where there was a scattering of picnic tables. Not knowing what she would want, I ordered two sandwiches from the deli, along with two different kinds of soup. I added some bags of chips to the order, along with two bottles of Snapple.

Emily was already seated at one of the tables when I pulled into the gravel lot. Parking beside her, I grabbed the food and strode to the table.

I must have looked upset as I approached, because she rose from her seat and gave me a quick hug. She was wearing shorts, a peasant blouse, and sandals, similar to what she'd worn when we'd walked the golf course together. "I'd ask how you were doing, but it's pretty clear it's a bad day, huh?"

"Definitely a rough one," I admitted, more affected by the feeling of her body against mine than I felt comfortable acknowledging. "Thanks for meeting me here."

"Of course." She sat as I laid out the food on the table and took a seat across from her. Behind us, preschoolers were clambering over a small wooden structure featuring low slides, bridges and swings. Mothers either stood nearby or sat on benches, some fiddling with their phones.

"What's going on?"

I ran through the conversation I'd had with Taglieri. She listened with a frown of concentration, inhaling sharply at the end, her eyes slitted in disbelief.

"Would she really do that? Put London in the middle of a fight between the two of you?"

"Taglieri seemed to think it wasn't just possible. He believes it's probable."

"Oh, boy," she said. "That's terrible. No wonder you're upset. I'd be furious."

"That's an understatement. Right now, I can barely stand the thought of her. Which is strange, because ever since she left, it seems like all I've wanted was to see her."

"It's really hard," she said. "And until you go through it, you can't know what it's like."

"David wasn't like this, was he? You said that he was generous when it came to money and you got custody of Bodhi."

"It was still terrible. When he walked out the door, he was seeing someone, and for the next month, I kept hearing from people I knew who'd seen him out and about with this woman, acting like he didn't have a care in the world. It was totally demoralizing, evidence that ending the marriage and losing me mattered not at all to him. And while he was generous in the end, he didn't start out that way. He talked at first about bringing Bodhi with him to Australia."

"He couldn't do that, could he?"

"Probably not. Bodhi's an American citizen, but even the threat caused me a few weeks of sleepless nights. I couldn't imagine not being able to see my son."

It was a sentiment I could fully relate to.

After lunch, I returned home instead of going back to the office. On the mantel and walls were dozens of photographs, mostly of London. What I hadn't noticed in all the years that I lived there was how many photos of London included Vivian—almost all professionally shot— while only a few candid ones of London and me graced our home.

Staring at them, I wondered how long Vivian had considered me so marginal to my daughter's existence. Perhaps I was reading too much into it—while Vivian was with London, I'd been at work, so of course there were more photos—but why hadn't she noticed and rectified the situation? Why hadn't she tried to memorialize more moments with the three of us, so that London could see for herself that I loved her as much as Vivian did?

I wasn't sure. What I did know was that I didn't want to be constantly reminded of Vivian, which meant some things had to change. With newfound resolve, I walked through the house, removing the photos that included Vivian. I had no intention of throwing them away; I put a number of them in London's room while I stacked others in a box that Vivian could take back to Atlanta with her, stowing the box in the foyer closet. Afterward, I changed into a T-shirt and shorts. Heading to the family room, I began to rearrange the furniture. Couches, chairs, lamps—I even moved a painting from the den to the living room and vice versa. By the time I was done, I couldn't claim that it looked better—Vivian did have good decorating sense—but it definitely looked different. I did the same in the den, moving the desk to an alternate wall, shifting the bookshelf and flipping the location of two paintings. In the master bedroom, I kept the bed in the same place, but moved all the other furniture I could, and then switched out the duvet on the bed for another that I found in the linen closet, one that hadn't been used in years.

In another closet, I found assorted household goods, and I spent a few minutes switching out vases and lamps, along with some decorative bowls. One good thing about Vivian's shopping over the years, I suppose, was that my overstuffed closets held the equivalent of a department store.

As soon as London got home from school, she took in her surroundings with wide eyes.

"It looks like a new house, Daddy."

"A little bit," I admitted. "Do you like it?"

"I like it a lot!" she exclaimed. Though her endorsement made me feel good, I suspected that it never occurred to London not to like it. With the exception of dance class, London seemed to like everything.

"I'm glad," I said. "I didn't move anything in your room."

"You could have moved the hamster cage if you wanted to."

"Do you want me to?"

"They're still kind of noisy at night. They run on that wheel as soon as it gets dark."

"That's because they're nocturnal."

She looked at me like I was crazy. "Of course they're *not turtles*. They're hamsters."

"Nocturnal," I said, slowly enunciating the word. "That means they like to sleep during the day."

"You mean so that they don't miss me while I'm at school?"

I smiled. "Exactly."

She was quiet for a few seconds. "Hey Daddy?"

I loved the way she said those words when she was about to ask me for something, and I wondered how old she would be when it finally stopped. Or if, by then, I'd even notice.

"Yeah, sweetie?"

"Can we go for a bike ride?"

Between my workout that morning and redecorating efforts, I was already exhausted, but *Hey Daddy* won out, as it usually did.

For the first time, I remembered to slather sunscreen on my daughter.

It was, however, the end of September and relatively late in the afternoon, so it probably fell into the category of too little, too late.

London donned her helmet and as soon as I helped her get going—she still couldn't do that part on her own—I hopped onto my bike and pedaled quickly to catch up to her.

While the roads near our house offered wonderfully flat, long stretches, the streets on the far side of the neighborhood had hills. Not big hills, mind you; in my youth, I probably would have considered them boring. I preferred racing down the steepest hills, the kind that made me squeeze the handlebars so tight I'd lose feelings in my fingers, but London and I were different in that regard. The thought of going faster and faster, without pedaling, made London nervous, and so far we'd avoided the hilly roads.

It was the right thing to do, especially early on, but I felt that she'd reached the point where she could handle a shallow downslope, and we rode in that direction.

Unfortunately, the mosquitoes were out in force, and I watched as London slapped at her arm. Her bike wobbled slightly as she temporarily released her grip on the handlebars, but she didn't seem to be in danger of falling. My little girl had come a long way since that first bike ride, and I sped up, pulling beside her.

"You're such a good rider now!" I called out.

"Thank you," she said.

"Maybe we could bring Bodhi for a bike ride sometime."

"He doesn't know how yet. He's still using the training wheels."

As soon as she said it, I remembered Emily telling me the same thing.

"Do you think you're ready to try some hills?"

"I don't know," she said, giving me a sidelong look. "They're kind of scary."

"They're not too bad," I said. "And it's kind of fun to go even faster."

Letting go of the handlebar again, she reached over and scratched at her opposite arm. Again the bike wobbled.

"I think I got stung by a mosquito."

"Probably," I said. "But mosquitoes bite, they don't sting."

"It's itchy."

"I know. When we get back home, I'll put some hydrocortisone cream on your arm, okay?"

We eventually made our way to the hillier section of the neighborhood, pedaling up a gradual incline. The opposite side was shorter and slightly steeper, and when we reached the top, London slowed her bike to a stop and put her feet down.

"What do you think?" I asked.

"It's kind of big," she said, an anxious tremor in her voice.

"I think you can do it," I said encouragingly. "How about we give it a try?"

As a kid, I barely would have considered the slope a hill. Of course, I was remembering something from a quarter century earlier, and in my mind, I had always known how to ride a bike. Perhaps I'd forgotten the uncertainties of being a beginner.

I say this now because of what happened next; I'll also say that had there not been a specific chain of unpredictable events—one leading to the next in a domino effect—then most likely, everything would have been fine. But it wasn't.

As soon as London got the bike moving again, she wobbled and swerved from the middle of the road to the left-hand side. It was a bigger wobble and more of a swerve than I'd seen in a while and she probably would have righted herself, were it not for the car that began to back out of the driveway twenty yards up. I doubted the driver had seen us; hedges surrounded the yard and London was small. Furthermore, the driver seemed to be in a hurry, based on his speed, even in reverse. London locked on to the sight of the car and swerved farther left; simultaneously, she slapped at another mosquito bite. Directly ahead of her loomed a mailbox mounted on a sturdy base.

Her front tire hit the shoulder where the asphalt met the dirt.

"Watch out!" I screamed, as the bike wobbled hard. London tried to get her other hand back on the handlebars but it slipped off the grip. By then, I knew what would happen, and I watched in horror as the front wheel suddenly jerked. London catapulted over the handlebars, her head and upper body smashing into the mailbox with a sickening thud.

I was off my bike and racing toward her, screaming her name even as her front tire continued to spin. I vaguely noticed the look of surprise on the driver's face before I crouched beside London's limp form.

She was facedown, unmoving, utterly silent. Panic flooded every nerve as I gently turned her over.

So much blood.

Oh God, Oh God, Oh God . . .

I don't know whether I was saying the words or hearing them in my mind as my insides turned to jelly. Her eyes were closed; her arm had simply flopped to the ground when I'd rolled her, like she was sleeping.

But she wasn't sleeping.

And her wrist looked as though someone had stuffed half a lemon under the skin.

In that instant, my fear was as all consuming as anything I'd ever experienced. I prayed for a sign that she was still alive, but for what seemed an eternity, there was nothing. Finally, her eyelids fluttered and I heard a sharp intake of breath. The scream that followed was ear shattering.

By then, the driver was gone, and I doubted whether he'd even seen what happened. I didn't have my phone so I couldn't call 911. I thought about rushing to a house—any house—to use their phone to call an ambulance, but I didn't want to leave my daughter. Those thoughts raced through my head in the blink of an eye and she had to get to the hospital.

The hospital . . .

I scooped her into my arms and began to run, cradling my injured daughter in my arms.

I tore through the neighborhood, feeling neither my legs nor my arms, hurtling forward with single-minded purpose.

As soon as I reached our house, I opened the car door and laid London on the backseat. The blood continued to flow from a gaping wound on her head, soaking her top as if it had been dipped in red paint.

I raced into the house to grab my keys and wallet and rushed back to the car, slamming the front door of the house so loudly that the windows rattled. Jumping behind the wheel of the car, I turned the key, my tires squealing.

On the seat behind me, London was no longer moving and her eyes were closed again.

My senses sharpened with adrenaline, I had never been more aware of my surroundings as I edged the accelerator higher. I flew past houses and rolled through a stop sign before gunning the engine again.

Hitting the main road, I passed cars on the left and right. At a red light, I came to a stop, then rolled through, ignoring the sounds of honking horns.

London lay silent and terrifyingly inert.

I made the fifteen-minute drive in less than seven minutes and slammed to a halt directly in front of the emergency room. Again, I cradled my daughter in my arms and carried her into the half-full waiting area.

The intake nurse knew an emergency when she saw one and was already rising as she called out, "This way!" directing me through the double doors.

Rushing her into an examination room, I laid my daughter on the table as a nurse hustled in, followed a moment later by a doctor.

I struggled to explain what had happened while the doctor lifted her eyelids and shone a light at her pupils. His movements were efficient as he barked commands to the nurses.

"I think she was unconscious," I said, feeling helpless, to which the doctor responded tersely with some medical jargon that I couldn't hope to comprehend. The blood was wiped from London's face and her wrist briefly examined.

"Is she going to be okay?" I finally asked.

"She needs a CAT scan," he replied, "but I've got to staunch the bleeding first." Time seemed to slow down as I watched the nurse clean London's face more thoroughly with an antiseptic pad, revealing a half-inch gash directly above her eyebrow. "We can stitch this, but I'd recommend that we get a plastic surgeon in here to do it so we can minimize the scarring. I'll see who's available unless you prefer to call a surgeon you know."

My new client.

I mentioned the doctor's name and the ER doctor nodded. "He's very good," he said before turning to one of the nurses. "See if he can make it here. If not, find out who's on call."

As two more nurses entered with a gurney, London stirred and began to whimper. In an instant, I was at her side, murmuring to her, but her gaze seemed unfocused and she didn't seem to know where she was. Everything was happening so fast . . .

As the doctor started to question her gently, all I could think was that I'd convinced her to ride down the hill.

What kind of father was I?

What kind of father would urge his child into such a risky situation?

I was sure that the doctor was asking himself the same questions when he looked at me. I watched as gauze pads and bandages were plastered on my daughter's head.

"We're going to need to take her now," he said, and without waiting for my response, London was wheeled from the room.

I filled out the insurance paperwork and used the hospital phone to call Marge. She agreed to swing by my house and grab my phone before coming to the hospital; she also said she would call Liz and my parents.

In the waiting room, I sat with hands together and head bowed, praying for the first time in years, praying that my little girl would recover and hating myself for what I'd done.

My dad was the first to arrive; he'd been working a job just a few blocks away, and he strode into the waiting room, his face tight with worry. When I filled him in, he didn't offer or expect a hug; instead, he took a seat in the chair beside me. Or rather, he nearly collapsed into it. I watched as he closed his eyes and when he finally opened them, he couldn't meet my eyes.

I realized then that he was as terrified as I was.

Liz arrived next, then my mom, and finally Marge, who looked paler than usual. Unlike my dad, they all wanted and needed to be held after I shared what I knew. My mom cried. Liz clasped her hands together, as if praying. Marge wheezed and coughed and took a puff of her inhaler.

My dad finally spoke.

"She'll be all right," he said.

But I knew he said it because he wanted to believe it, not because he actually thought it was true.

My client, the plastic surgeon, arrived soon thereafter and I rose from my seat.

"Thank you for coming," I said. "I can't tell you how much this means to me."

"You're welcome. I have kids, too, so I understand. Let me head back and see what I can do."

He disappeared through the double doors.

We waited.

Then waited some more, an agonizing limbo.

In time, the doctors finally appeared.

I tried and failed to read their expressions as they motioned for us to follow them back. Leading us into one of the patient rooms, they closed the door behind us.

"I'm pretty certain she's going to be all right," the ER doctor said without preamble. "The CAT scan showed no signs of any subdural hematomas or other brain injuries. London is fully conscious now and was able to answer questions. She knew where she was and what had happened to her. Those are all good signs."

It felt as though my entire body released a breath I hadn't known it was holding. "That said, she was unconscious for a while, so we're going to keep her overnight for observation. It's just a precaution. In rare cases, swelling can occur later, but I'm not expecting to see that. We just want to make sure. And, of course, she'll have to take it very easy for the next few days. She can probably go back to school on Wednesday, but no physical activity for at least a week."

"How about the gash on her head?"

My client answered. "It was a clean gash. I stitched it on the inside and the outside. There's going to a light scar that may last for a few years, but it should fade over time."

I nodded. "And her arm?"

"It was her wrist," the ER doc answered. "The X-ray didn't show a break, but there's so much swelling we can't be sure. There are a number of small bones in the wrist so there's no way to tell right now whether anything is broken. Right now, we're thinking that it's just a nasty sprain, but you'll have to bring her in for another X-ray in a week or two to be sure. The splint is fine until then."

Unconscious. Scarred. A wrist that may be sprained or worse. The information left me feeling depleted.

"May I see her?"

"Of course," he said. "She's getting a splint put on her wrist right now and will be moved to a private room, but that shouldn't take long. All in all, considering what happened, she was lucky. It's a good thing she was wearing a helmet. It could have been a lot worse."

Thank God Vivian had insisted that I make London wear a helmet, I thought.

Vivian.

I'd completely forgotten to call her.

"How are you feeling, sweetheart?" I asked.

London looked better than when I brought her into the emergency room, but she certainly wasn't the little girl who'd hopped on her bike earlier that afternoon. A large white bandage obscured her forehead and her wrist looked tiny in its bulky splint. Pale and fragile, she appeared as though she were being swallowed by her bed.

My mom and dad, along with Liz and Marge, had crowded into the room, and after the hugs and kisses and tales of worry, I'd taken a seat on the bed beside London. I reached for her good hand and felt her squeeze it.

"My head hurts," she said. "And my wrist hurts, too."

"I know," I said. "I'm sorry, baby girl."

"I don't like sunscreen," she protested, her voice weak. "It made my handlebars slippery."

I flashed on the image of her scratching at the bites on her arms. "I didn't think about that," I said. "We probably don't need too much sunscreen anyway now that the summer is done."

"Is my bike okay?"

I realized I'd left both bikes where they lay. I wondered if someone had removed mine from the road, suspecting that someone had. Maybe even the driver. I was also pretty sure that the bikes would be there until I returned to pick them up; it was that kind of neighborhood.

"I'm sure it is, but if it isn't, we can fix it. Or get a new one."

"Is Mommy coming?"

I really, really need to make that call, I thought.

"I'll find out, okay? I'm sure she'll want to talk to you."

"Okay, Daddy."

I kissed the top of her head. "I'll be right back, okay?"

The rest of my family crowded around the bed while I stepped into the hallway. I made for the elevators, seeking privacy. What I hadn't wanted was anyone in my family—London especially—listening in on a conversation that I was dreading. When I checked my phone, I noticed that Vivian had already called twice, no doubt wanting to speak with London. I connected the call, and felt my stomach begin to clench.

"London?" she asked, picking up.

"No, it's me, Russ," I said. "I wanted to let you know right off the bat that London is fine. I'll put her on the phone in a few minutes, but you should know that she's okay first."

"Why? What happened?" Vivian's fear came through like an electric current.

"We were bike riding and she crashed. She sprained her wrist and cut her forehead, and I had to bring her to the hospital..."

"The hospital?"

"Yeah," I said. "Let me finish, okay?" I drew a breath and launched into a description of what had happened. Surprising me, she didn't interrupt, nor did she raise her voice. But her breathing was ragged and erratic, and when I was done, I could tell she'd begun to cry.

"And you're sure she's okay? You're not just saying that?"

"I promise. Like I said, I'll get you on the phone with her in just a minute. I stepped out of the room to call you."

"Why didn't you call me earlier?"

"I should have and I'm sorry. I was in such a panic that I wasn't thinking straight."

"No, I get it. I...um..." She hesitated. "Hold on a second, okay?"

It was more than a second; I was on hold for almost a minute before she finally came back on the line. "I'm heading to the airport now. I want to be with her tonight."

I was about to tell her that there was no need for her to come, but if our positions were reversed, I know I would have moved mountains to reach London.

"Can I talk to her now?"

"Of course," I said. I walked back down the hallway and entered London's room. Handing over the phone, I watched London press the phone close to her ear, but I could still make out what Vivian was saying.

She never mentioned me; her focus was entirely on London. Toward the end, I heard Vivian ask to speak to me again. This time, I didn't feel the need to leave the room.

"Hey there," I said.

"She sounds good," Vivian said with palpable relief. "Thanks for putting her on. I'm in the car now and should be there in less than a couple of hours."

Thanks to Spannerman's private jet, no doubt. Which was no doubt the reason she'd put me on hold earlier. So she could ask him.

"I'll be here. Let me know when you land."

"Will do."

Vivian texted when she touched down. For a moment I wondered whether my family should stick around, but then I chided myself. London was in the hospital, and they would stay until visiting hours were over. Because that's what family was supposed to do. End of subject.

However, I suspected that my family harbored a natural curiosity regarding Vivian. My parents hadn't seen her for over a month—since the day London started school—and it had been even longer for Marge and Liz. I'm sure they were wondering whether the new Vivian differed from the one they'd known for years. And how, of course, we would all treat each other.

A nurse came in to check London's vitals; the doctor followed and asked London questions again. Though my daughter's voice was weak, she answered them correctly. He told us that he would continue to monitor her condition regularly for the next few hours. When he left, I found a channel on the TV that was showing *Scooby-Doo*. Though London was watching, she looked as though she might soon fall asleep.

Vivian arrived a few minutes later. In faded jeans that were torn at the knees, black sandals and a thin black sweater, she was her usual chic self, though she looked harried.

"Hey everyone," she said, sounding out of breath and distracted. "I got here as fast as I could."

"Mommy!"

She rushed to London, covering her with kisses. "Oh, sweetie... you were in an accident, huh?"

"I have a cut on my forehead."

Vivian took a seat beside London, her eyes gleaming with unshed tears. "I know. Your dad told me. I'm glad you were wearing a helmet."

"Me, too," she said.

Vivian planted another kiss on the top of her head. "Let me say hi to everyone, okay? And then I want to sit with you for a while."

"Okay, Mommy."

Rising from the bed, she approached my parents. Right away, she embraced them, as well as Marge and Liz. I realized later that I'd only ever seen her touch Marge and Liz a few times in my life. To my amazement, she wrapped me in a brief hug as well.

"Thank you all so much for coming," she said. "I know it made London feel better to have you all here."

"Of course," my mom answered.

"She's a tough little girl," my dad pronounced.

"Visiting hours are almost over," Marge said. "So Liz and I are going to take off. We'll let the three of you visit for a while."

"Us, too," my dad nodded. "We'll leave you alone."

I watched as they gathered their things and then followed them into the hallway. Like Vivian, I hugged them all and thanked them for coming. In their eyes, I could see the questions they wanted to ask but didn't. Even if they had asked, I doubt that I would have had any answers.

Returning to the room, I saw that Vivian was perched beside London on the bed. London was telling her about the car that backed out and how the sunscreen had made her handlebars slippery.

"It must have been scary."

"It was very scary. But I don't remember after that."

"You were very brave."

"Yeah, I am." I had to smile at her matter-of-factness. Then: "I'm glad you're here, Mommy."

"I am too. I had to come because I love you so much."

"I love you, too."

Vivian lay down next to London on the bed and slipped her arm around her, both of them watching *Scooby-Doo*. I took a seat in the chair and watched them, relieved, somehow, that Vivian had come. Not simply for London's sake, but because a part of me still wanted to believe in Vivian's goodness, despite all she'd done to me.

Observing the two of them, I did believe in that goodness—and I also noted Vivian's forlorn expression, recognizing how hard it was for her to be separated from London. I sensed her anguish at being so far away when the accident had happened, despite how quickly she'd been able to get here.

I could see London's eyelids drooping, and rising from the chair, I crossed the room and turned out the light. Vivian offered me the slightest of smiles, and I was struck by the melancholy thought that the last time that the three of us had been alone together in a hospital room, London was not yet a day old. On that day, I would have sworn on my life that the three of us would always be united in the love we felt for each other. We were a family then, the three of us together. But it was different now and I sat in the darkness wondering if Vivian felt the loss as deeply as I did.

Midmorning the next day, London was discharged from the hospital. I'd already called the school and the piano teacher, explaining her absence and canceling her lessons for the week. I also let London's teacher know that she shouldn't be active at recess once she returned to school. Thankfully, the nurses had given me some disinfectant wipes to clean the backseat of the car, because I hadn't wanted London to see the bloody mess.

As I signed the discharge papers, I glanced over at Vivian, noticing how tired she looked. Neither of us had slept much; throughout the night, the nurses and doctor had come into the room to check on London, waking all three of us in the process. London, I assumed, would sleep for most of the day.

"I was wondering," Vivian said, sounding uncharacteristically tentative, "if I could come back to the house for a while. So I can spend some more time with London. Would you mind?"

"Not at all," I said. "I'm sure London would like that."

"I'm probably going to need a nap and a shower, too."

"That sounds fine," I said. "When do you have to go back?"

"I'm flying out tonight. Walter and I have to be in DC tomorrow. More lobbying."

"Always busy," I remarked.

"Too busy, sometimes."

I analyzed her comment on the drive home, wondering at the hint of weariness in her tone. Was she just tired, or was the jet-set lifestyle beginning to feel less exciting than it once had?

It was a mistake to try to read meaning into every word, tone, and nuance, I told myself. What had Emily said to me? If it comes, let it come. If it stays, let it stay. If it goes, let it go.

When we reached the house, I carried London inside. She'd already begun to doze off, and I brought her straight up to her bedroom. Vivian followed us up and after I got London tucked in bed, I watched as Vivian went to the guest room. Though I'm sure she noticed that I'd rearranged the furniture, she said nothing to me about it.

My car was too small to load my bike in the trunk, but I squeezed London's bike into the back. Someone had leaned the bikes against the mailbox. I drove London's bike home, put on my running gear, and ran back to the same mailbox. It was while grabbing mine that I saw the blood that had dried on the asphalt and my stomach did a flip-flop. I rode my bike home, went for a run, and took a cooling shower. Both London and Vivian were still sleeping, so I went back to the bedroom for a nap. I drew the shades and slept like the dead.

When I awoke, I found Vivian and London watching a movie in the family room. Though wearing the same clothes she'd arrived in, Vivian had showered, the tips of her hair still wet, and London was curled up next to her on the sofa. On the coffee table were the remains of London's snack—turkey and pear slices—most of which she had eaten.

"How are you feeling, London?"

"Good," she said, without looking up.

"How did you sleep?" Vivian asked.

I was struck by how ordinary she sounded.

"Well. I needed it." I motioned to the plate. "I know London just had a snack, but what are you thinking for dinner? Do you want me to make something?"

"I think it might be easier if we just order something, don't you? Unless you're really in the mood to cook."

I wasn't. "Chinese?"

She squeezed London closer to her. "Do you want Chinese food for dinner?"

"Okay," London said, still absorbed in the movie. The bandage on her head, along with the splint on her arm, made me wince.

Though I wanted to visit with London—part of me wondered whether she was angry with me for what had happened—I didn't want to do anything that might upset the détente that seemed to currently exist between Vivian and me. Instead, I went to the kitchen and ate a banana, then wandered to the computer in the den, trying to lose myself in work but feeling distinctly unfocused. In time, I called the Chinese restaurant and went to pick up the food.

We ate on the back porch, just like old times. Afterward, London took a bath and dressed in her pajamas. As bedtime approached, Vivian and I slipped into our familiar roles—she read first, followed by me. But when I finally came back downstairs, Vivian had already shouldered her handbag and was waiting near the door.

"I need to get going," she said. Did I detect a hint of resignation in her voice? I reminded myself again that it was pointless to read anything into it.

"I figured."

She adjusted the strap of her handbag, as if stalling would help her find the words she needed. "I noticed that you rearranged the house and took a lot of the photos down. The ones that included me, I mean. I was going to say something earlier, but I didn't think it was the right time."

For whatever reason, I didn't want to admit that I'd done so in a fit of anger. But I didn't feel I was wrong, either; I knew I would do the same thing again.

"Like you, I'm just trying to move forward," I stated. "But I put some of the family photos in her room. Because we'll always be her parents."

"Thank you," she said. "That was thoughtful of you."

"I put the other photos in a box if you want to bring them with you. There are some fantastic ones of you and London."

"That would be great."

I went to the closet and retrieved the box; as I held it beneath my arm, her eyes flashed to the photos. I felt acutely, perhaps more than ever, that our era as a couple had really and truly come to an end, and I had the sense she was thinking the same thing.

"Let me get my keys and I'll put this in the trunk," I said.

"I can carry it," she said, reaching for the box. "You don't need to drive me. There's a car waiting out front."

I handed it over. "A car?"

"It's not like we can leave London here alone, right?"

Right, I thought, wondering how I'd overlooked something so elementary. Being around Vivian—a Vivian who reminded me of the woman I had married, the very same Vivian with whom I had no future—seemed to have thrown me.

"All right, then," I said. I put a hand in my pocket. "About this weekend," I started, "and me having to stay at Marge's or my parents'..."

"You don't have to," she said, cutting me off. "I realized today that there's no reason for you to do that. It's not fair to you. I'll just stay in the guest room if that's okay."

"It's fine," I said.

"But you know I still want to spend as much time with London as I can. Just the two of us. I know that may not seem fair, but right now, I really don't want to confuse her."

"Of course," I said. "That makes sense."

She shifted the box beneath her arm and I wondered whether to offer a hug or a kiss on the cheek. As if anticipating my action, she turned toward the door.

"I'll see you in a few days," she said. "And I'll call London tomorrow."

"Sounds good," I said, opening the door for her. Behind her, idling on the street, was a limousine. Vivian started toward it and I watched as the driver quickly exited the car to help her carry the box. He opened the door and put the box on the seat. Vivian waited for him to move aside, then got into the car. I couldn't help thinking that it all seemed as natural as breathing for her—as though she'd always had a car and driver, had always been the lover of a billionaire.

I couldn't see her through the darkened glass of the car and I wondered whether she was watching me, but in the end, I simply turned away. Stepping into the house, I closed the door behind me, feeling strangely sad.

For a moment I hesitated. Then I reached for my phone.

Emily answered on the second ring.

We were on the phone for nearly two hours. Though I did most of the talking, working through my sense of loss, she managed to make me smile and laugh more than once. And every time I wondered aloud if I was a good person, she assured me that I was blameless. I needed to hear that, somehow, and when I finally turned in for the night, I closed my eyes wondering how I'd been lucky enough to rediscover Emily, who was exactly the kind of friend I needed most.

CHAPTER 20

Autumn

I love autumn," Emily said to me. "It 'wins you over with its mute appeal to sympathy for its decay.'"

"Excuse me?"

"I was talking about autumn," Emily said.

"I got that. I'm just trying to understand what you said."

"Not me. Robert Browning. Well, kind of . . . I might have gotten a few words wrong here or there. He was an English poet."

"I didn't know you read poetry."

It was October 2002, a few months after Emily and I had been stuck on the Ferris wheel. It was also less than a few weeks after the Great Mistake, the one involving the woman I'd met in the bar. Marge had already warned me more than once not to say a thing to Emily, but I was still agonizing over my terrible secret.

We were, in fact, on a double date with Marge and Liz. We'd taken a trip to the Biltmore House in Asheville, which was for a long time the largest private home in the world. I'd been there before as a child but had never gone with Emily; it had been her idea to go, and also to invite Marge and Liz. When Emily had begun to quote Browning, the four of us were savoring wine from the Biltmore winery.

"I majored in art, but I had to take other classes, too," Emily pointed out.

"I did, too. But I never took one that included poetry."

"That's because you majored in business."

"Exactly," Marge cut in. "Just because you botched your education, there's no need to put Emily on the defensive."

"I'm not putting her on the defensive. And I didn't botch my education . . . I was just making conversation."

"Don't let him scare you off, Emily," Marge said. "He might be a bit lowbrow, but he's got good qualities, too."

Emily laughed. "I hope so. It's been more than two years. I'd hate to think I've been slumming with him all this time."

"I'm right here," I said to both of them. "I can hear you."

Emily giggled, this time joined by Marge. Liz wore a benevolent expression.

"Don't let them get to you, Russ," Liz said, laying a hand on my arm. "If they keep picking on you, then you and I can go tour the greenhouse, and we'll hold hands and make them jealous."

"Did you hear that, Marge?" I said. "Liz is hitting on me."

"Good luck," Marge shrugged. "I know her type, and you're not it. You've got a little too much of those Y chromosomes for her."

"That's a shame. Because I know a hundred guys who would probably jump at the chance to go out with her."

Marge smiled at Liz. "Of that I have no doubt."

Liz blushed and I caught Emily's eye. In response, she leaned over and whispered in my ear. "I think they're perfect together."

"I know," I whispered back. "I do, too."

Even as I said it, guilt began to eat away at me with renewed fury. Less than a week later, I told her about the Mistake.

Why couldn't I have kept my mouth shut?

"No bruising? No cuts or blood or frantic calls to 911?"

After I dropped London off at school the next day, I found Marge waiting in my kitchen. I'd called her that morning to tell her about my visit with Vivian, but she'd told me to hold off because she wanted the full account in person.

"London's still sore, but she's doing fine."

"I wasn't talking about London. I meant you. Or, I guess I could have been talking about Vivian, too. Depending on how angry she made you."

"It was good," I assured her. "Surprisingly pleasant, in fact."

"What does that even mean?"

"She wasn't angry, and she didn't make me feel like the accident was my fault. She was . . . nice."

"You do understand that it wasn't your fault," she said. "That's why they call them accidents."

"I know," I said, wondering whether I fully believed it.

Marge turned and coughed; when she reached for her inhaler, I noticed that she looked a little drawn.

"Are you okay? You were coughing a lot the other night," I said, frowning.

"Tell me about it. Last week, I spent two days locked in a room with a client who was sick as a dog. Then, swell guy that he was, he called to let me know he had bronchitis."

"Have you seen a doctor?"

"I went by the urgent care over the weekend. The doctor thinks it's probably viral, which means he didn't prescribe anything. I'm just hoping I have it completely behind me by the time Liz and I leave for Costa Rica."

"When is that trip again?"

"The twentieth until the twenty-eighth."

"I wonder what it would be like to have time for a vacation," I mused, feeling a little sorry for myself.

"It's wonderful," Marge shot back. "Whining, on the other hand, is less than appealing. How are you and Emily getting along? Did you tell her what happened to London?"

"I spoke with her last night. After Vivian left."

"Ah."

"What do you mean by 'ah'?"

"You know the old saying: The quickest way to get over someone is to get over someone else."

"Classy."

"Don't blame me," she said. "I didn't invent the expression. And we both know it goes for women, too. As in, the quickest way to get over someone is to get under someone else."

"Emily and I are just friends."

She reached over and gave my shoulder a squeeze. "Keep telling yourself that, little brother."

350

After Marge left, getting to the office was easy, but immersing myself in work was more elusive. While the emotional intensity of the last two days didn't come close to rivaling the days immediately following Vivian's announcement that she was in love with Spannerman, my reserves were low. Too much had happened in too short a time; it hadn't even been a month since all the upheaval began.

Nonetheless, there were things to do. At the top of the agenda was ensuring that the filming of Taglieri's fourth commercial was on track. By the time I reconfirmed everything, I was surprised to see an email from the editor, stating that the editing for the third commercial, the one featuring the child actress, was complete.

Because the third commercial had turned out so well, my instincts were to start airing both the initial one as well as the third, right away. I left a message at Taglieri's office suggesting that, and soon received the go-ahead. As I locked in the schedule with the cable company, I felt a familiar thrill at the thought that *my* work—and *my* company—would soon reach hundreds of thousands of people.

On a less thrilling note, I also left two messages at the dance studio. Ms. Hamshaw had yet to return my call.

London was all smiles when I spotted her at pickup amongst her classmates, and though she walked more slowly than usual to the car, I could tell already that she'd had a good day.

"Guess what?" she said as soon as she climbed into the car. "My teacher let me be her helper today. It was so much fun!"

"What did you do?"

"I got to help her hand out papers and I got to collect them. And I got to clean the whiteboard with the eraser during recess. But then she let me color on it and I got to erase that, too. And I got to wear a badge that said 'Teacher Helper' all day."

"And you could do all that with your sore wrist?"

"I just used my other hand," she said, demonstrating. "It was easy. And at the end of the day, I got a lollipop."

"That sounds like a pretty amazing day. Do you need my help buckling yourself in?" I'd had to do it for her that morning.

"No," she said. "I think I can do it now. I had to learn to do a lot of stuff with one hand."

I watched as she tugged at the seatbelt. Though it took a bit longer than usual, she was finally able to manage.

I pulled out of the lot and was beginning to accelerate on the road when I heard her voice again.

"Hey Daddy?"

My eyes flickered to the rear view mirror. "Yes, sweetheart?"

"Do I have to go to dance tonight?"

"No," I said. "The doctor said that you should probably take it easy this week."

"Oh," she said.

"How was your head today? And your wrist?"

"My head didn't hurt at all. My wrist hurt sometimes but I tried to be strong like Bodhi."

I smiled. "Is Bodhi strong?"

"He's very strong," she said, nodding. "He can pick up everyone in the whole class. Even Jenny!"

I gathered Jenny was big for her age. "Wow," I said. "I didn't know that."

"Do you think I could go over to Bodhi's house? I want to see Noodle again."

I flashed to an image of Emily. "I'll have to ask Bodhi's mom, but if it's all right with her, it's all right with me. Not this week, though—maybe next week, okay? Since you should be resting?"

"Okay," she said. "I like Miss Emily. She's nice."

"I'm glad," I said.

"And it was fun going to the zoo with her and Bodhi. Can I see the pictures I took on your phone?"

I handed my cell phone back to her and she began scanning through the pictures. She reminisced about the animals she'd seen and what they'd been doing, and as she chattered on, I noticed that London didn't mention her mother at all, even though she'd seen Vivian the day before.

London, I realized, had grown accustomed to spending time with me alone, for better or for worse.

Because she'd watched television for much of the day before, I didn't want to park London in front of the electronic babysitter again. At the same time, I had to limit her activity, and we'd already done the coloring thing not too long ago, so I was at a bit of a loss. On a whim, I decided to swing by Walmart on the way home from school. There, I chose a board game called Hoot Owl Hoot! The box explained that the goal of the game was to help the owls fly back to their nest before the sun came up. Each player drew a color card and flew an owl to a color tile on the way to its nest, but if a player drew a sun card, the game moved one step closer to sunrise. All the players won if the owls made it back to their nests in time.

I figured that it was something both of us could handle.

London was thrilled to visit the toy section of the store, and she wandered from one side of the aisle to the other, enthralled by one item after the other. More than once, she pulled an item from a shelf or rack and asked if she could have it; while I was tempted to give in, I didn't. Nearly everything she'd shown me would have held her interest for only a few minutes after we returned home, and her toy box and shelves were already bursting with neglected stuffed animals and knickknacks.

The game ended up being a hit. Because the rules were simple, London got the hang of it quickly, and she was alternately overjoyed or despondent, depending on whether the owls appeared as if they would make it home in time. We ended up playing four games at the kitchen table before she began to tire.

Afterward, I relented when she asked if she could watch TV for a while, and she lay on the couch, yawning. Maybe it was just Vivian's voice harping in the back of my mind, but I felt that I still needed to let Hamshaw know about the accident. Because she hadn't returned my call, however, I felt like I had to do it in person.

I told London about swinging by the studio, loaded her in the car, and spotted Ms. Hamshaw in what I assumed was her glass-walled office. London elected to stay in the car. Ms. Hamshaw had looked over at me as soon as I entered, but took her time before finally making her way over to me.

"London wasn't in class on Monday," she observed, arching an eyebrow in apparent displeasure, before I even had a chance to speak.

"She was in a pretty bad accident on her bike," I said. "I left you a couple of voicemails. She ended up at the hospital. She's recovering, but she won't be in class today or Friday, either."

Ms. Hamshaw's expression did not change. "I'm glad to hear she's all right, but she has a performance coming up. She still needs to attend class."

"She can't. The doctor says she has to take it easy this week."

"Then unfortunately, she can't perform in the recital next Friday night."

I blinked. "Excuse me?"

"London has already missed two classes. If she misses a third, she's not eligible to perform. You may feel that to be unfair, but it's one of the ground rules of the studio. She was informed of that when she signed up."

"She was sick the first time," I said, with dawning incredulity. "On Monday, she was unconscious."

"I'm sorry to hear of her misfortune," Ms. Hamshaw said, sounding anything but. "As I said earlier, I'm glad she's recovering. But rules are rules." With that, she crossed her skinny arms.

"Is this because she needs to practice? She's one of the trees and she showed me what she's supposed to do. I'm sure if she's here next week, she'll have more than enough time to master it."

"You're missing the point." Ms. Hamshaw's mouth was a thin line. "I have rules for the studio because parents and students will always find a reason not to come to class. Someone is sick or a grandparent is visiting or there's too much homework. I've heard every excuse imaginable over the years, but I can't foster a culture of excellence unless everyone shows commitment."

"London's not participating in any competitions," I reasoned. "She hasn't been chosen to do so."

"Then perhaps she should practice more, not less."

I squelched the urge to let Ms. Hamshaw know what I thought of her ridiculous little quasi-military operation, and instead said patiently, "What do you suggest that I do? Since her doctor told us to limit her activity?"

354

"She can come to class and sit in the corner and watch."

"Right now her head hurts and she's exhausted. And on Friday, she'll just be bored if she sits and watches."

"Then she can look forward to the Christmas show."

"Where she'll be a tree again? Or maybe an ornament?"

Ms. Hamshaw straightened, her nostrils flaring. "There are other dancers in her class who demonstrate much greater commitment."

"This is ridiculous," I blurted out.

"That's what people generally say when they don't like the rules."

I brought London home and we ate the leftover Chinese food. Vivian called, and by the time the FaceTime session had ended, London could barely keep her eyes open.

I made the executive decision to skip her bath and got her into her pajamas. I read a short book to her in bed and she was asleep moments after I turned out the light. Descending the stairs, I told myself that I should use the rest of the evening to get some work done, but I simply wasn't in the mood.

Instead, I called Emily.

"Hey there," she said as soon as she answered. "How are things?"

"Not too bad, I guess."

"How's London? Bodhi said she got to be the teacher's helper, so she must be recuperating nicely."

"Yeah, she was pretty excited about that," I said. "And she's fine, really—just a little tired. What did you end up doing today?"

"Worked on one of the paintings for my show. I think I'm getting closer, but I'm just guessing. I could probably work on this one forever and never think it's done."

"I want to see it."

"Anytime," she said. "Thankfully, the other paintings I've started are going well. So far, anyway." She smiled. "How are you holding up? I can't imagine how scared you must have been. I'd probably still be traumatized."

"It was pretty bad," I admitted. "And tonight wasn't so relaxing."

"What happened?"

I replayed my conversation with Ms. Hamshaw.

"So she can't do the recital?" Emily asked when I finished.

"I don't think she was all that excited about it anyway," I said. "I just wish Vivian weren't so hell-bent on having her go there. I don't think London enjoys it at all."

"Then let her quit."

"I don't want another reason to argue with Vivian. And I don't want London in the middle of it."

"Did you ever think that by continually appeasing Vivian, you're just adding fuel to the fire?"

"How do you mean?"

"If you give in every time Vivian gets angry, then she knows that all she has to do is be angry to get what she wants. I mean, so what if she gets angry? What's she going to do?"

She didn't add the question, *Divorce you?* but the obvious truth of her observation startled me. Was that the reason things had started going downhill in the first place? Because I'd never stood up to Vivian? Because I wanted to avoid conflict? What had Marge once said to me?

Your real problem is that you're too damn nice for your own good.

At my silence, Emily went on.

"I don't know if what I said has any bearing. I could be wrong. And I'm not saying this because I *want* the two of you to argue. I'm just saying that you're London's father, and you have just as much right as Vivian when it comes to making decisions as to what is best for London. Lately, you have even more rights than she does, since you're the one who's taking care of her. You're the primary parent these days, not her, but you still seem to trust Vivian's judgment more than your own. To me, London seems like a very happy little girl, so it's clear you've been doing something right."

"So...what do you think I should do?" I asked, trying to digest what she'd said.

"Why don't you talk to London and ask her what she wants to do? And then just trust your instincts."

"You make it sound so easy."

"Other people's problems are always easier to solve. Haven't you learned that yet?" She laughed, a sound at once reassuring and refreshing.

"I have to say, sometimes you remind me a lot of Marge."

"I'm going to take that as a compliment."

"It is."

Emily and I chatted for another hour, and as always, after speaking with her, I felt better. More grounded. More like myself again, and it was enough to spur me to spend an hour on the computer, getting a jump on the next day's work.

In the morning, while London was eating her cereal, I explained what Ms. Hamshaw had said.

"You mean I can't be in the recital?"

"I'm sorry, sweetie... Are you mad you can't dance in the show?"

London's reaction was immediate. "It's okay," she said with a shrug. "I didn't want to be a tree anyway."

"If it makes you feel better, I thought you were a very good tree."

She looked at me as though I had cornstalks growing out of my ears. "It's a tree, Daddy. The butterfly gets to move around. Trees don't."

"Hmmm," I said, nodding. "Good point."

"Do I have to go to dance on Friday?"

"Do you want to go?"

When she shrugged instead of answering, it wasn't hard to read between the lines.

"If you don't want to go, then I don't think you should go. You should only go to dance because you like it and you want to go."

For a moment London studied the floating marshmallows in her bowl of Lucky Charms, and I wondered if she had heard me. Then: "I don't think I want to go anymore. Ms. Hamshaw doesn't like me very much."

"Fine," I said. "You no longer have to go to dance."

London hesitated, and when she looked up at me I thought I

detected a trace of anxiety in her expression. "What's Mom going to say?"

She'll probably get angry, I thought.

"She'll understand," I said, trying to sound more confident than I felt.

After dropping London off at school, I went to the studio, where I met the animal trainer and Gus, a bullmastiff.

The commercial would emphasize *tenacity* and the plan was to have Gus tugging relentlessly on a dog toy. Intercut with the images of the dog would be four screen shots with the following captions:

When you've been injured on the job,
You need a determined and relentless attorney
Call the offices of Joey Taglieri
He won't stop until you get the money you deserve.

Gus the bullmastiff ended up being quite a talented actor, and filming wrapped well before noon.

London wasn't quite as chipper when I picked her up from school as she'd been the day before. Limiting activity and TV required a bit of creativity, and I decided to bring her to the pet store. I needed shavings for the hamsters anyway, but I thought she might enjoy looking at the fish.

There were more than fifty different aquariums; each aquarium had placards that listed the specific types of fish. London and I spent more than an hour moving from tank to tank and naming the various kinds of fish.

It wasn't quite SeaWorld, I'll admit, but it wasn't a bad way to spend a quiet afternoon.

On the way out, she spent some time playing with a few cocker spaniel puppies that were tumbling around in a low pen. They were very cute, and I breathed a sigh of relief when she didn't ask for one.

"That was fun, Daddy," she said as we headed to the car. I had the bag of shavings and hamster food tucked beneath my arm.

"I thought you might like that."

"We should get some fish. Some of them were really pretty."

"Aquariums are even harder to clean than hamster cages."

"I'm sure you could figure it out, Daddy."

"Maybe. But I don't know where we would put the aquarium."

"We could put it on the kitchen table!"

"That's an idea. But where would we eat?"

"We could eat on the couch."

I couldn't suppress a smile. I loved talking to my daughter. I truly did.

On the way home, I swung by the grocery store. Using one of the recipes that Liz had given me, I picked up the ingredients for chicken quesadillas.

I let London pretty much fix dinner on her own. I walked her through each step—and I sliced the chicken after she'd sautéed it—but aside from those things, London did everything herself. She cooked the chicken, added the slices to tortillas, added the grated cheese, and folded the tortillas before putting each one into a pan so it could toast on both sides.

When the meal was ready, she directed me to the table, and I brought over two plates of food, utensils, and two glasses of milk.

"This looks delicious and it smells great," I commented.

"I want to take a picture for Auntie Liz and Auntie Marge. Before you start."

"Okay," I said. I handed my phone to her and she snapped pictures of both plates, then texted them to both.

"Where did you learn how to text?" I asked, amazed.

"Mommy showed me. Bodhi, too. He showed me on Miss Emily's phone. I think I'm old enough for a phone."

"You might be, but I'd rather talk to you in person."

She rolled her eyes, but I could tell she thought it was funny. "You can eat now if you want," she said.

I cut a piece with my fork and took a bite.

"Wow," I said. "This is very tasty. You did a fantastic job."

"Thank you," she said. "Don't forget to drink your milk."

"I won't," I said. I couldn't remember the last time I'd had a glass of milk. It tasted better than I remembered.

"This is amazing," I said. "I can't believe how big you're getting."

"I'm almost six."

"I know. Do you know what you want for your birthday?"

She thought about it. "Maybe an aquarium," she said. "And lots of pretty fish. Or maybe a poodle like Noodle."

Maybe, I thought to myself, spending the day at the pet store hadn't been such a good idea.

After London had gone to bed, I gave Emily a call.

I caught her while she was lying in bed, and as always, we drifted into an easy conversation that was a mixture of reminiscing about our earlier years, and discussing details of our current lives. The call lasted for nearly forty minutes, and when I hung up the phone, I realized that talking to Emily was not only becoming part of my routine, but one of the brightest spots of my days.

On Friday afternoon, Vivian texted that she would be arriving between nine and ten, which was well past London's normal bedtime.

After receiving the text at work, I took a moment to wonder what, if anything, would be expected of me when she arrived, since London might not be awake. Would Vivian finally want to talk? Watch TV in the family room with or without me? Or would she head straight to the guest room? And what was I going to do all weekend?

I tried to repeat Emily's Zen mantra, but it didn't help. Part of me, I knew, was still trying to figure out how to please Vivian.

Old habits die hard.

With dance class off the schedule, I opted for another date night with London, with the idea of keeping her awake until Vivian arrived. I thought bringing her to dinner and a movie would be fun, and I was able to find a kids' movie that would end in time to have us home by nine. After that, London could hop in the bath and put on her pajamas, and with any sort of luck, Vivian would arrive right around then.

I revealed my plans to London when I picked her up from school, and as soon as we got home, she raced up the steps to start getting ready.

"You have plenty of time," I called after her. "We don't have to leave until five thirty."

"I want to start now!" she called back.

She was fully dressed by four and found me in the den, working on the computer, finalizing the still shots I planned to intercut in the dog commercial.

She'd chosen a white blouse, white skirt, and white shoes and stockings, her hair held back with a white headband.

"You look very beautiful," I said, mentally crossing off all Italian restaurants from the list of possible dinner destinations. A single slip and her outfit would be massacred.

"Thank you," she said. "But I don't like the Band-Aid on my forehead. Or my splint."

"I didn't even notice them," I said. "I'm sure you'll be the prettiest girl in the whole restaurant."

She beamed. "When are we going to leave?"

"We still have an hour and a half."

"Okay," she said. "I can go sit in the family room until we're ready."

"You could play with your Barbies," I suggested.

"I don't want to get my dress wrinkled."

Of course.

"What would you like to do?"

"I don't know. But I don't want to get dirty."

I thought about it. "Would you like to play Hoot Owl Hoot! again?"

She clapped her hands. "Yes!"

We played for an hour before I went to change. Like the last time, I donned slacks and a blazer, along with a stylish new pair of loafers. London was waiting for me in the foyer, and, trying to add a bit of ceremony to the occasion, I bowed before opening the door for her.

We had dinner at an upscale steakhouse and after a couple of minutes of adult-like conversation, London slipped back into little girl mode. We talked about Bodhi and her teacher and school and about the kind of fish she wanted in the aquarium.

Afterward, we went to the movie, which left London energized— perhaps it was the Raisinets—and eager to see her mom. Hurrying upstairs when we got back home, she quickly bathed and slipped into her pajamas.

Vivian arrived at the house not long after I'd begun to read. London jumped from the bed and ran down the stairs. I followed, watching as London threw herself into her mother's arms, Vivian's eyes closing in contented delight.

"I'm so glad I got to see you before you went to sleep," Vivian said.

"Me, too. Daddy and me went on a date. We had dinner and we saw a movie and we talked about my aquarium!"

"Aquarium?"

"For her birthday," I said. "How are you?"

"Good. That's a long drive, especially when it starts at rush hour."

I nodded, feeling strangely out of place. I motioned upstairs. "I've already read to her if you want to go up."

She faced London again. "Do you want Mommy to read you a few stories?"

"Yes!" London cried. I watched as the two of them climbed the stairs. And though I was in my house with my wife and daughter, I suddenly felt very much alone.

I retreated to the master bedroom. I didn't want to talk to Vivian, nor did I think she wanted that either. Instead, I read in bed and tried not to think about the fact that Vivian would be spending the night under the same roof.

I fantasized briefly about her sneaking into my bedroom and wondered what I would do. Would I acquiesce with the excuse that we were still married? Or even as a last hurrah? Or would I have the resolve that Emily showed when David had made a pass at her?

I wanted to think I'd be more like Emily, but I wasn't sure I was as strong as she'd been. Nonetheless, I had a feeling that neither of us would be happy afterward. I was no longer a part of her future, and it would only reinforce the hold that Vivian still had over me, despite all she'd done. Moreover, I suspected that I'd feel guilty. Because as I imagined making love to Vivian again, I realized with sudden clarity that what I wanted even more than that was for it to be Emily instead.

In the morning, I rose early and went for a long run. I showered, made myself breakfast and was on my second cup of coffee when Vivian found me in the kitchen. She was in long pajamas, a set I'd bought her for her birthday a couple of years back. She went to the cupboard and pulled out a teabag, then added water to the teakettle on the stove.

"Sleep well?" I asked.

"I did. Thanks. The mattress in the guest room is better than I remembered. But I might just be tired."

"Have you decided what you want to do with London today? After art class, I mean?"

"I don't want to do anything too demanding. She should still take it easy. We could go to Discovery Place, but I want to see what London wants to do."

"I'm going to the office," I informed her. "I want to get as much done for the plastic surgeon as I can, especially since he dropped everything to help London."

"Tell him thank you from me. He did a very good job. I peeked at it last night."

The teakettle whistled and she added hot water to her cup. She seemed to debate whether or not to join me at the table before finally taking a seat.

"There's something I need to tell you," I said. "About dance."

"What about dance?" Vivian took a tentative sip from her steaming cup.

I recapped everything for her, trying to keep it as succinct as possible, including the fact that London wasn't going to be allowed to dance at the recital.

"Huh," Vivian said. "And you told her that London was in the hospital?"

"I told her. It didn't matter. And then London told me straight up that she doesn't want to go anymore. She doesn't think Ms. Hamshaw likes her."

"If she doesn't want to go, then don't make her go. It's just dance."

Vivian gave an elaborate shrug. She spoke without the slightest acknowledgment of her previous insistence that London attend in the first place. There was no reason to bring it up, but it made me wonder whether I'd ever be able to understand what made Vivian tick. And whether I'd ever really understood her at all.

London came downstairs while we were still in the kitchen. She wandered over to the table, still dopey with sleep.

"Hi Mommy and Daddy," she said, giving both of us hugs.

"What can I get you for breakfast?" Vivian asked.

"Lucky Charms."

"Okay, sweetie," Vivian said. "I'll get it for you."

I folded my newspaper and stood, trying to mask my amazement at how easily Vivian had acquiesced to London's request for a sugary cereal.

"Have fun today, ladies," I said.

I spent nearly the entire day on the computer, finalizing everything I could do for the tech aspect of the plastic surgeon's ad campaign, aside from the posting of the patient videos to the website. I forwarded the information to my tech guy and also emailed reminders to the patients about filming on Tuesday.

It was nearly six when I finally looked up. I texted Vivian asking what time London would be going to bed because I wanted to read to her. Vivian answered immediately with the time. Because I'd worked through lunch, I grabbed a sandwich at the deli across street and decided to give Emily a call.

"Am I catching you at a bad time?" I asked, idly cleaning up my desk.

"Not at all," she said. "Bodhi's playing in his room and I was just cleaning the kitchen. How's the weekend going?"

"So far, so good. I was at the office all day. Got a ton of work done. I'm going to head home in a bit to read to London."

"I saw her today when I dropped Bodhi off at art. Vivian, too."

"How'd that go?"

"I didn't stick around to chat," she said.

"Good plan. I'll probably find a way to hide from Vivian after I read to London, too. No reason to press my luck. What are your plans for tonight?"

"Nothing. Finish cleaning the kitchen, watch TV. Maybe have a glass of wine after Bodhi goes to bed."

Unbidden, thoughts of making love to Emily resurfaced, as they had the night before. I pushed them firmly away.

"Do you want some company?" I asked. "After I finish with London? I could swing by for an hour or so. Maybe you can show me that painting you've been working on."

She hesitated and I was certain she was going to say no.

"I'd like that," she said instead.

I made it home just as London was getting ready for bed, and as usual Vivian and I slipped into our familiar roles. She read first, and then I went up to read to London. London chattered on about her day—in addition to art class and Discovery Place, they'd gone to the mall—and by the time I turned out the light, Vivian was already in the guest room with the door closed.

I knocked on the door and heard her voice from the other side.

"Yes?"

"I'm going out for a little bit. I just wanted to let you know, in case London wakes up. I should be back before eleven."

I could almost hear her asking *Where are you going?* in the silence that followed.

"Okay," she said after a moment. "Thanks for letting me know."

Emily had left a note tacked to the door, inviting me in and directing me to the back porch.

I moved quietly through the house, trying not to wake Bodhi. I felt a little like a teenager trying to sneak past my parents, and wondered if the child inside us ever truly left any of us.

Emily was barefoot tonight, in jeans and a red blouse, with her long legs propped against a low bench that lined the porch; a chair had been placed next to her. On the porch table stood an open bottle of wine and an empty glass; she held a half-full glass in her own hand.

"Perfect timing," she said. "I just checked on Bodhi and he's sound asleep."

"London, too."

"I got started without you," she said, raising her own glass. "Help yourself."

I poured and sat next to her. "Thanks for having me over."

"When a friend says he has to hide, my door is open. How is it really, though?"

I considered the question before answering. "We haven't fought, but we haven't seen much of each other, either. It's strange, though. It feels like there's this awkward heaviness in the house."

"Emotions are heavy things," she said. "And it's still early for both of you. How was London when you read to her?"

"She was fine. They had a good day."

"Do you think she knows what's going on yet?"

"I think she knows there's something different, but that's it."

"That's probably a good thing for now. It's hard enough to get through this stage without worrying about your child as well."

I nodded, knowing she was right.

"Do you sit out here a lot?"

"Less than I should—sometimes I forget how pretty it is. I love seeing the stars between all the trees, and the sound of crickets." She shook her head. "I don't know . . . I guess I just get stuck in my routines. Which is why I still haven't gotten around to listing the house yet. I get lazy."

"I don't think you're lazy. We're just creatures of habit." I took a sip of wine, letting a comfortable silence settle between us. Finally, I said, "I feel like I should thank you."

"Why?" I felt her turn toward me, her eyes seeking me out in the darkness.

"For letting me come over. For talking to me on the phone. For the advice you give. For putting up with my confusion and whining. Everything."

"That's what friends are for."

"Emily, we're old friends," I said. "But it's been a long time and it's not like we've been close these past fifteen years. Somehow, though, in just a short time, you've become one of my best friends—again."

I could see the starlight flickering in her eyes. "I read something about friendship once and it stuck with me. It goes like this: Friendship isn't about how long you know someone. It's about who walks into your life, says 'I'm here for you,' and then proves it."

I smiled. "I like that."

"Russ, you sound like you think you're a burden to me. But you're not. Believe it or not, I like talking to you. And I like that we've rekindled our friendship. Aside from Grace and Marguerite, it's just Bodhi and me. And, I don't know...there's something so comforting about our shorthand. Not having to explain everything about who we are and where we come from. We know all that stuff already."

"Guess I'm like an old shoe, huh?"

She laughed. "A favorite shoe...maybe. One that always fit just right and you were never able to replace."

I felt a genuine warmth flowing from her then, and it was such a reassuring sensation—one that I had missed, I realized, in all these uncertain years with Vivian.

"I feel the same, way, Em." I stared at her. "I really do."

She was quiet for a moment, rotating the glass of wine in her hands. "Do you remember than night when we got stuck on the Ferris wheel? The night of the fireworks?"

"I remember," I said.

"I thought you were going to propose to me that night," she said softly. "And when you didn't, I was so...disappointed."

"I'm sorry," I said, meaning it.

"Don't be—it's silly." She waved my apology away. "The point I'm trying to make is that I would have said yes and maybe we would have gotten married. But that also means I wouldn't have Bodhi and you wouldn't have London, and then who would we be? Maybe we would have ended up getting divorced. Or hate each other now."

"I think we could have made it."

Her smile seemed to hold a trace of melancholy. "Maybe. There's no way of knowing. We've both been knocked around enough by life to understand how unpredictable life can be."

I stared at her. "You do know that you continually say things that surprise me and make me think."

"That's because I majored in the humanities, not business."

I laughed, suddenly flooded with gratitude that she'd come back into my life, just when I needed her most.

It wasn't until well past midnight that I finally made it home.

"You were out late last night," Vivian remarked as we crossed paths in the kitchen the next morning. "I thought you said you'd be home by eleven."

Despite the late night, I'd risen early and was ready to start my day by the time Vivian made it downstairs.

"Time got away from me," I offered. I could tell she was curious about where I'd been and what I'd been doing, but it wasn't her business. Not anymore. Changing the subject, I asked, "What time do you think you'll be leaving? Since you have to drive?"

"Six, six thirty? I don't know for sure yet."

"Do you want to have a family dinner before you go?"

"I was going to take London out for an early dinner."

"All right," I said. "I'll be here at six, then."

She seemed to be waiting for me to announce something about my plans for the day. Instead, I went back to sipping my coffee and perusing the paper. When she realized I wasn't going to speak, she finally went back upstairs, no doubt so she could shower and get ready for her day with London.

CHAPTER 21

Clicking on All Cylinders

*E*mily and I saw each other six times before we ever slept together. Our first date after the wedding was the hike she'd suggested; we also went to a concert. We'd had lunch and dinner a few times. By then, I was already falling hard for her, but I wasn't quite sure how she felt about me.

That morning I picked her up early and we drove to Wrightsville Beach. We lunched at a small ocean-side restaurant before strolling to the water's edge. We collected seashells in my baseball cap as we rambled down the beach in the direction of the pier, and I can still picture the way the breeze lifted glinting strands of her hair as she bent down to retrieve a particularly beautiful shell.

We both knew what was coming. I'd arranged for a hotel room for the night, but instead of growing more nervous as the day wore on, she seemed to settle into a state of languid ease. Late in the afternoon, after we checked in, she took a long shower while I lay on the bed, flipping through channels on the television. Afterward, she wandered out wrapped only in a towel to retrieve a change of clothes.

"What are you watching?"

You, I could have said. But instead I answered, "Nothing, really. Just waiting for you to finish in the bathroom so I can shower, too."

"It won't be long," she promised.

It occurred to me that Emily, more than any woman to that point in my life, made me feel comfortable because she always seemed so comfortable with me. I gave her a few minutes before getting up from the bed. By then, she was dressed and applying a little makeup.

"What are you doing?" she asked.

"Just watching you." I met her gaze in the mirror.

"Why?"

"I think watching you put on makeup is sexy."

She turned around and puckered her lips. We kissed and she turned back around.

"What was that for?"

"Once I get my lipstick on, you won't be able to kiss me for a while. Unless you want to wear lipstick, too."

I continued to watch for another minute before heading back to the bed. I plopped down, pleasantly buzzed by her kiss and the promise of the evening to come.

We ate at a bistro overlooking the Intracoastal Waterway, lingering over dinner long after the sun went down. On our way out, we heard music and followed the sound to a bar down the street, where we found a live band playing. We danced until the bar closed, pleasantly weary as we strolled back to the hotel after midnight.

Electricity crackled between us as I unlocked the door and we stepped into our room. The maids had turned down the bed and the lights had been dimmed. I slipped my arms around Emily and pulled her close, feeling the warmth of her body against my own.

I kissed her then, our tongues coming together while my hands slowly began to explore the contours of her body. She gave a shallow gasp and our passion became more intense as I felt her breast through the thin fabric of her dress. Her fingers reached for the buttons of my shirt.

We continued to kiss as she undid them one by one. I lifted her dress and she raised her arms to assist me. I slipped it over her head while my shirt fell to the ground, her skin fiery against my own. Her bra came next, and soon we were naked on the bed and moving together, lost in our own feelings and the mysteries of each other.

It finally happened on Wednesday, and I'll admit that I was as surprised as the receptionist, but I'll get to that. First things first.

On Sunday, Marge and Liz weren't at my parents' when I arrived, and when I called her house, Marge sounded utterly miserable. Coughing, achy, feverish, the whole nine yards. When my mom found out, she decided then and there to make chicken soup, which I was then tasked with delivering to Marge. If possible, she looked worse than she sounded, and joked that even Liz was keeping her distance, since she had clearly been infected with the plague.

Deciding to take my chances, I hugged her anyway, before heading home.

Vivian left around six thirty, after bringing London back from dinner. Her departure was as cordial as the rest of the weekend had been. She asked no questions about my day and I asked no questions about hers; instead we simply wished each other well as she headed out the door. After I put London to bed, I called Emily to ask if she would mind picking up London from school on Tuesday, since I'd be filming all day. Emily assured me that it wouldn't be a problem.

On Monday, Taglieri's new website went live, and the first two commercials began to air. I posted the commercials on his website as well as on YouTube. I worked from home so I could watch the spots as they aired, feeling an almost physical thrill as I watched them. Meanwhile, I worked on templates for direct mail and billboards for the plastic surgeon, getting the messaging right. On Tuesday, I filmed his patients—a very long day, as I'd predicted—and then went to pick up London at Emily's, where we ended up staying for dinner, much to London's delight.

On Wednesday, as I was driving to the office, I received a text from Taglieri asking me to call him and I felt my heart sink. Maybe because the previous weekend had been devoid of drama with Vivian, I felt certain that he was calling with what could only be bad news on the divorce front.

I returned the call right after I parked, standing outside my office. I felt like I needed to be standing when I spoke to him.

"Hi, Joey," I said, trying to keep my voice steady. "I got your text. What's up?"

"My business," he said. "My future bank account."

"Excuse me?"

"You know that new toll-free number? The one you splattered all over those two commercials? The phone's been ringing off the hook. It's crazy. People love that commercial with the kid. They think it's hilarious. And now, we can direct them to the website for basic information. It's incredible. I never would have believed it. My staff is going crazy just trying to keep up."

"You're happy," I said, stunned.

"Damn right, I'm happy. When's that dog commercial going to run? And you need to come up with some more ideas. So put your thinking cap on."

"I can do that," I said.

"And Russ?"

"Yeah?"

"Thanks."

I hung up the phone and strode into the office, feeling like I was six inches taller. When I waved to the receptionist, I watched as she raised her hand.

"Mr. Green? Don't you want your messages?"

"I have messages?"

"Two, actually. They're both from law firms."

Again, I thought of Vivian and wondered if she'd told her attorney to reach out to me directly. If so, I wasn't sure why Vivian hadn't given the lady my cell phone number; as far as I knew, Vivian didn't even know my work number.

But it wasn't Vivian's attorney who'd called. One call was from a firm in Greenville, South Carolina, that specialized in class actions, the other from a personal injury firm in Hickory. In both cases, I was connected immediately to senior partners, each of whom seemed eager to speak with me.

"I like those commercials you're doing for Joey Taglieri, and we were wondering if you would consider coming in to make a presentation about your services."

After hanging up, I let out a whoop of excitement. I just had to tell someone.

I reached for my phone, about to call Marge, but then decided at the last second to call Emily instead.

Floating.

That's how I felt the rest of the week. Like I was floating free of the worries that had been weighing me down for months.

Though it might be only be temporary—what goes up always comes down and all that—I decided I was going to enjoy every single minute, even if I didn't land the two new firms as clients. While it would be great to sign those firms, I received three more calls from lawyers by Friday, making five new potential clients, all of whom had reached out to me. I'd set up presentations with all of them and depending on how many I signed, I thought I might be looking at potentially needing to hire another person, just to keep up.

The Phoenix Agency was officially on its way.

"What are you going to do with all that extra money you'll be making?" Marge said to me over lunch. It was Friday afternoon, and I'd decided to work only a half day as a reward. "Because you happen to have a sister who's in the mood for a new car."

"Wouldn't that be nice?"

"I always knew you'd make it."

"I haven't made it yet," I cautioned. "I still have to make the presentations."

"You're good at that part. You just weren't so good at getting the phone to ring."

I smiled, still on a high. "I'm so excited. And relieved."

"I can only imagine."

"How are you feeling?"

She made a face. "A little better. I'm not coughing too much during the day now, but the nights are still pretty rough. I finally convinced my idiot doctor to prescribe some antibiotics, but I just started taking them yesterday. He said I might not feel any better until Monday."

"That's a bummer."

"It's bad for Liz, too. I kept waking her up, so I've started sleeping in the guest room."

"So Mom's chicken soup didn't work?"

"No. But it tasted good." She pushed her sandwich away. "What are your plans this weekend? Vivian's not coming, is she?"

"She'll be here next weekend. For London's birthday. And I can't imagine London not wanting Bodhi to be there, which means that Emily will probably make an appearance at the party as well."

"And me," Marge said, grinning. "I can't wait to watch."

"Nothing's going to happen. She's been on good behavior lately."

"Hmmm…let's see how long that lasts," Marge said with a skeptical look. "By the way, are you going to Mom and Dad's tomorrow? Liz and I are planning to swing by for a little while, especially since we weren't there last weekend. Since I had the plague, I mean."

"Thank God you haven't given it to Liz," I remarked.

"Yes, especially since she's getting crushed at work. One of the other therapists in her practice group has been on maternity leave since late July."

"Speaking of maternity, when do you and Liz meet with the fertility doctor? Didn't you say sometime in November?"

She nodded. "On the twentieth. The Friday before Thanksgiving."

"What happens if you're both able to have kids? Would you both get pregnant?"

"I'd have the child. I always thought it would be fun to be pregnant."

"Tell me if you're still feeling that way around the eight-month mark. By the time London was born, Vivian was thoroughly sick of being pregnant."

"That's Vivian, and she was younger. I know this will be the only time for me, and I'd make sure to enjoy every minute of it."

"Having a child is going to change your life. It's changed mine, that's for sure."

She looked almost wistful. "I can't wait."

When I picked London up from school, the first thing she asked when she got in the car was whether we were going to have date night again.

"Since it's Friday and Mommy's not here?"

Why not? "That sounds like a terrific idea."

"What should we do?" London asked, already buzzing with anticipation.

"Hmmm," I said. "We could have dinner at home or go out. Or we could go to the real aquarium."

"The aquarium! Can we really go there?"

"Of course. I'm pretty sure it's open until eight o'clock."

"Can we ask Bodhi if he wants to come?"

"You want to bring Bodhi on our date night?"

"Yes. And I can wear my butterfly wings. The ones I got at the zoo. And he can wear his wings, too."

"To the aquarium?"

"For the fish," she said.

I wasn't sure I understood the correlation, but if it made her happy, that was fine with me.

"I can call, but Bodhi might be busy tonight. It's kind of last minute."

"We should try. And Miss Emily can come, too."

I waited until we got home before calling Emily. When I asked about the aquarium, she told me to hold on and then called out to Bodhi.

"Do you want to go to the aquarium tonight? London is going!"

"Yes!" I heard Bodhi shout, before Emily came back on the line.

"I take it you heard him."

"I did," I said.

"What time are you thinking?"

"How about I pick you up in an hour?"

She hesitated. "How about I pick you up? DVDs for the kids, remember? I know it's not that far, but we'll be dealing with rush-hour traffic. Are you okay with doing the driving again?"

"Sure," I agreed.

"Text me the address. And let me start getting the two of us ready. See you in a bit."

"Oh," I said, "London wants Bodhi to wear the wings he got at the zoo."

"Why?"

"I don't know."

She laughed. "It's fine with me. And way better than having him run around with a light saber."

As was becoming her habit, London took a while to get ready for date night. Ultimately she picked a white skirt with lace, a long-sleeved pink top, pink sneakers, and, of course, the butterfly wings.

I'd opted for a more casual outfit: dark pants, dark shirt, and comfortable shoes.

"That's an eye-catching outfit," I said. "You definitely look ready to see the fish."

"I want to get some ideas for my aquarium," she said.

For her birthday, I thought. At least she was making it easy for me, even if I'd end up cleaning the thing.

"Do you want to pick a movie? We'll be riding with Miss Emily again."

"I think we should watch *Finding Nemo*."

"Sounds like a good choice to me."

She found the case and brought it to me. As she was handing it over, I received another message from Taglieri. *Calls still coming in like crazy. You're the man!*

What a great week this was turning out to be. What I didn't know was that it was going to get a whole lot better.

Sea Life aquarium was located in Concord, about fifteen miles north of Charlotte, but the traffic meant it took nearly forty minutes to get there.

Not that any of us minded. I caught Emily up on my recent work triumphs, hinted at Marge and Liz's plans to start a family, and talked about my parents. She shared the latest updates on her family and her paintings for the show. Again, by unspoken agreement, we didn't mention Vivian, David, or our shared past.

At the aquarium, the kids raced from one exhibit to the next, just as they'd done at the zoo. Emily and I trailed behind, keeping an eye on them. As we followed, I couldn't help noticing the glances that

Emily drew from other men. Most of them were with their own families and were circumspect—I'm not sure Emily noticed at all—but I found myself attuned to the way people reacted to her in a way I hadn't before.

We finished our tour of the aquarium, the biggest hits for the kids being the sharks, sea turtles, sea horses, and the octopus. Just as we were stepping out the door onto the promenade, I heard music drifting out of an open door marked as an employee entrance.

The song that was on came to an end, and a radio DJ came on the air, announcing the song coming up: JD Eicher's "Two by Two." I paused.

"Did you hear that, London? There's a song called 'Two by Two.' Just like your favorite book."

"Is it about animals?"

"I don't know," I said. The DJ was still talking and I turned to Emily. "She was supposed to have her recital tonight. She wanted to be the butterfly."

"Right now, I am a butterfly," London announced, letting her wings catch the evening breeze.

"Well, since it's date night, would you like to dance with me?"

"Yes!"

A moment later, the song started, and I took London's hands. By that time, the sun was low in the sky, twilight turning the world sepia colored. Aside from Emily and Bodhi, we had the promenade to ourselves.

I found the lyrics strangely affecting as I danced with my daughter. She swayed and bounced and held my hands, revealing flashes of the young woman she would become, and the innocent girl she still was.

It was, I realized, the first dance I'd ever shared with my daughter, and I didn't know when or if it would happen again. I couldn't imagine dancing with her in a few years—by then, the idea would probably embarrass her—so I lived in the moment and gave myself over to the dance, thankful for yet another wonder at the end of an already unforgettable week.

"That was the most touching thing I've ever seen," Emily said to me as we walked to the car. "I took some photos with my phone. I'll text them to you later."

"It was pretty special," I agreed, still drifting on the melody of the song. "I'm just glad Bodhi didn't try to cut in."

"That wouldn't happen. I asked him to dance, but he said no. Then, he told me he found a snail and he wanted me to pick it up."

"Little boys and little girls are certainly different, aren't they?"

"You get sugar and spice and everything nice," she said, referring to the nursery rhyme. "Meanwhile, I get the snail."

"No puppy-dog tails, though."

"That's only because he couldn't find one."

I laughed. "I'll bet the kids are starving."

"I'm starving, too."

"The real question is whether we let them pick where we eat, or whether we get to pick."

"Just a warning that if we don't find something quickly, Bodhi might start getting cranky. And once that happens, you don't want to be anywhere in the vicinity."

"So . . . Chick-fil-A?"

"Bingo," she said.

Needless to say, the kids were thrilled.

London was still wired when we finally got home, but her energy level started to crash by the time she was in her pajamas. I called Vivian and let London FaceTime with her for a few minutes; afterward, I decided to read *Two by Two*. As I finished, I remembered that Emily had promised to text the photographs of the two of us dancing. Pulling out my phone, I saw that she had, and quickly scrolled through them with London.

"Don't we look good?"

London took the phone from me and stared at the photos.

"You can't see my face because my hair is in the way."

"That's because you were looking at my feet," I said. "That's okay. I was looking at my feet, too."

She continued to scrutinize the images. As she did, I remembered the photos I'd removed from the house and made a mental note to print one of these and have it framed.

London handed the phone back to me.

"What are we going to do tomorrow?"

"There's art class, of course. And after that, we're going to see Nana and Papa. Is there anything else you want to do?"

"I don't know."

"You could help me clean the hamster cage."

"No thanks. It's kind of icky."

Right. Smelly, too, I thought. "Let's see what you're in the mood to do when you wake up tomorrow," I said, tucking the covers around her.

I kissed her goodnight and went back downstairs. I turned on the TV, but the photos that Emily had taken seemed to call to me. I pulled out my phone again and lingered over the images with a smile on my face, more grateful than ever to be the father to such an amazing little girl.

Emily waved as soon as I walked into art class with London the following morning. London ran over to hug her, then went to chase down Bodhi.

"That was fun last night," she said. "I think we're a good team when it comes to keeping the kids entertained."

"Agreed," I said, reflecting that I'd been happily entertained as well. "And thanks for the photos—I'm probably going to get one or two framed. Even with just an iPhone, you clearly have an artist's eye."

"Maybe...or maybe I just sent you the best of the hundred or so I shot," she said with a mischievous smile.

She jerked a thumb in the direction of the strip mall. "You want to grab a cup of coffee while the kids are occupied?"

"I can't think of anything I'd rather do," I said, holding open the door for her. And I meant it.

"It's *the cancer*," my mom insisted. "I just know he has *the cancer*."

Standing in the kitchen, my mom was reprising her usual worries in particularly urgent tones. We'd barely walked in the door after art class when she pulled me aside for a hushed conference.

"Was he having trouble breathing again?"

"No," she said. "But I had the dream about the hospital again last night. Only this time, there was no purple pig. And this time, the doctor was a woman. She was talking about *the cancer*."

"Did you ever think it might just be a dream?"

"Do you have the same dreams twice?"

"I have no idea. I don't remember most of my dreams. But I wouldn't read too much into it unless you've actually noticed something amiss with Dad."

She looked at me with a mournful expression. "*The cancer* sometimes doesn't show many symptoms until it's too late."

"So you're saying that because he feels fine, he might be sick?"

She crossed her arms. "Explain to me why I dreamed it *twice*."

I sighed. "Do you want me to talk to Dad again?"

"No," she said. "But I do want you to keep an eye on him. And if you see something, I'll need your help getting him to the doctor."

"I'm not sure I'd even know what to look for," I protested.

"You'll know it when you see it."

"Did Mom waylay you about *the cancer*?" Marge asked, pouring herself a glass of sweet tea from the pitcher on the table.

I'd just joined her and Liz on the back porch, after sending London off to help my mom in the kitchen. As usual my dad was in the garage, probably lifting an engine out with his bare hands.

"Oh yeah," I said, holding out a glass of my own for Marge to fill. "It's been a few months since she last brought it up, so I guess I should have expected it." I rubbed a hand over my face. "I hope I never get like that."

"Like what?"

"Living in fear all the time."

"She has good reason," Marge said. "*The cancer* knocked off her entire side of the family. Don't you ever worry about it?"

"I don't think I've ever had time to worry about it."

"I think about it," Marge said. "I don't worry, but it does cross my mind from time to time. But I have the sense that if Dad ever starts to develop cancer, the healthy cells will strut over, tap the bad cells on their shoulders, and then proceed to beat the crap out of them." The afternoon sun played across Marge's amused expression, throwing her cheekbones into sharp relief.

"Hey, you're looking good, by the way," I remarked. "You've lost some weight."

"Thanks for finally noticing," said, preening a little bit. "You didn't say anything yesterday."

"I'm paying attention now. Are you on a diet?"

"Of course. I'm going on vacation—meaning, I'll be hitting the beach, and a gal's got to look her best. Besides, with all that running, you were starting to look better than me and I just couldn't have that."

I rolled my eyes and turned to Liz. "And how are you doing, Liz? Marge said you're drowning at work."

"Yeah, I've been covering for another therapist who's been on leave. Lately I spend most of my free time fantasizing about our getaway to Costa Rica. I've even been trying out some Latin American recipes, but Marge won't eat any of it because of the carbs. I keep reminding her that people in Costa Rica aren't as overweight as they are here in US, but to no avail."

"I know my body," Marge countered. "And it helped that I was sick, since my appetite was nonexistent. On a more interesting note, though, did you see the fair Emily today? At art class?"

I pointedly turned to Liz. "Do you know what I like about you?"

"What's that?"

"You don't seem to feel the need to pry into my personal life every time we talk."

"She doesn't have to pry," Marge said. "As a general rule, you blurt out everything you're thinking or feeling without prompting."

Marge probably had a point, but still. I sighed. "I not only saw her today, but we also went to the aquarium last night. With the kids. We're friends, that's all."

"And you probably haven't even noticed how pretty she is, either."

Liz laughed. "Whatever the reason, I'm happy for you, Russ. You seem to be in a much better place these days."

"I am," I said, surprising myself. "I really am."

After Vivian FaceTimed with London, I asked her to call me back to discuss London's upcoming birthday party. When she did, her tone was markedly icier than it had been over the previous weekend.

"I've already made all the arrangements," she said. "I've rented one of those bouncy houses to set up in the backyard, I've set up the catering and I've ordered a Barbie birthday cake. I sent out email invitations as well."

"Uh, okay…," I said, caught off guard by her chilly demeanor. "Can you tell me what time the party is going to start?"

"Two."

Nothing else. She seemed to be trying to make me feel purposely uncomfortable.

"All right," I said slowly. "I assume you sent my parents and Marge and Liz an Evite, but I'll confirm with them just in case." When she didn't answer, I went on. "And you're still planning to stay in the guest room, right?"

"Yes, Russ. I'm staying in the guest room. We've already talked about this."

"Just making sure," I said before she abruptly ended the call.

I let out a long, slow breath. Despite the truce of the previous weekend, it seemed that all bets were off again.

CHAPTER 22

The Eye of the Storm

As a kid, I always loved thunderstorms.

Marge thought I was a kook, but when thunderstorms approached, I would feel an electric sense of anticipation, akin to what my dad felt before the World Series. I would insist on turning out all the lights and would move the armchairs closer to the big picture window in the living room. Sometimes, I would even toss a bag of popcorn into the microwave, and, together, Marge and I would snack while we watched the "show."

In the darkness, we would sit riveted as lightning split the sky in two or flickered in the clouds like strobe lights. During the best storms, the strikes would be close enough for us to feel the static electricity, and I would notice Marge gripping the armrest of her chair. Always, though, we would count how many seconds passed between a flash of lighting and the thunder, tracking the progress of the storm as the center drew near.

In the South, thunderstorms don't usually last very long. Typically, they would pass in thirty or forty minutes, and when the last rumble of thunder faded away we would reluctantly rise from our chairs and turn on the lights, going back to whatever it was we'd been doing before.

Hurricanes were a different story, however. My ever-cautious dad always boarded up the big picture window, so we couldn't watch the full extent of the spectacle. But I remained fascinated by the apocalyptic winds and torrential rain . . . and especially the approach of the eye—that surreal moment when the winds abated entirely and it was sometimes even possible to see blue skies overhead. But the calm is only temporary, for *the back half of the hurricane still lies in wait and with it, sometimes even greater destruction.*

Which, I wonder, is more analogous to life? Or, rather, to my life that terrible year? Was it a series of violent storms, bursting in quick succession? Or was it a single massive hurricane, with an eye that lulled me into believing I'd survived intact, when, in fact, the worst was yet to come?

I don't know.

All I know for certain is that I hope never to experience another year like it, for as long as I live.

London loved her birthday party. The bouncy castle was a hit, she clapped with delight when she saw the cake, and she had fun playing with her friends, especially Bodhi. Emily brought him by, but didn't stay, claiming that she needed to meet with the gallery owner to finalize some things for her upcoming show. Another one of the kids' parents had already promised to bring Bodhi home. She apologized for not sticking around, but I think we were both eager to avoid any awkwardness with Vivian.

Earlier that morning, while Vivian was ferrying London around—she'd driven the SUV from Atlanta—I made a trip to the pet store and set up the aquarium in her room; I chose several colorful fish, and stuck a bow on the glass. When Vivian and London returned from art class, I had London close her eyes as I led her to the threshold of her room. She squealed when she opened them and catapulted across the room toward the aquarium.

"Can I feed them?"

"Of course," I said. "I'm sure they're hungry. Let me show you how much food to give them, okay?"

I tapped some food into the lid of the plastic container and handed it to her. She poured it into the fish tank, mesmerized as the fish raced to the surface and started devouring the food. When I glanced over my shoulder at Vivian, I saw that she had her arms crossed, her mouth a tight crease.

At the party, however, Vivian was all smiles with everyone, including me and my entire family. She asked my mom to pitch in when she cut the cake, and when London opened a box filled with Barbie accessories from Marge and Liz, she urged London to go over and give them a hug, which London did.

Marge leaned in afterward, muttering under her breath. "She's acting as though nothing has changed between the two of you at all," which upon reflection made me even more nervous than Vivian's earlier, chilly demeanor.

After the party, Vivian took London to the mall; with Halloween coming up, she took it upon herself to help London choose a costume. I used that time to clean up the house, filling garbage bags with paper plates and cups, and wrapping a tray of leftovers to put in the fridge. With that completed, I decided it might be best to make myself scarce for the rest of the evening, and left for my office.

I worked into the evening, focusing on the presentations for the law firms that had contacted me. As London's bedtime approached, I texted Vivian, asking if it was time to read to London, only to receive a terse response a while later that London was already asleep.

I stayed late at the office that night, but rose early on Sunday to go for a run and shower. I was having breakfast and coffee when I heard Vivian moving around in the guest room upstairs. Though I lingered in the kitchen, wondering if she might want to talk about how well the party had gone, she never made an appearance.

I returned to the office to finish the presentations—they were all fairly similar—aware that the truce between Vivian and me had ended, but unclear as to the reason. Was she was jealous that London had loved the aquarium—something I'd selected without Vivian's input? But then Vivian had been cool toward me for nearly a week, I reasoned.

I texted Vivian as soon as I got to the office, asking what time she planned to leave. She didn't respond until nearly five, informing me that she'd be leaving in half an hour and forcing me to scramble to get home in time.

When I arrived, London came running and jumped in my arms.

"I fed my fish, Daddy! And they were so hungry! And I let Mr. and Mrs. Sprinkles see them, too. I held them right next to the glass."

"Have you given them names yet?"

She nodded. "They're all so pretty, so I knew what their names should be. Let me show you."

She pulled me up the steps to her room and pointed out the various fish, reciting their names: Cinderella, Jasmine, Ariel, Belle, Mulan, and Dory "because that's who they remind me of."

Downstairs, Vivian was already waiting by the door. She hugged and kissed London goodbye. Then she half turned in my direction, uttered a perfunctory "Bye," without making eye contact, and walked out the door.

I should have simply let her go. Instead, after a beat, I followed her out. By then, she was already opening the door to the SUV.

"Vivian? Hold up."

She turned, her expression stony as I approached.

"Are you okay?"

"I'm fine, Russ," she answered, sounding anything but.

"You seem angry."

"Are you seriously asking me this?" Vivian whipped off her sunglasses. "Of course I'm angry. And disappointed."

"Why? What did I do?"

"Do you really want to get into this now?" She glared at me over the open car door.

"I just want to know what's going on…"

She closed her eyes, as though steeling herself, and when they opened again, I could see rage flaring behind them.

"Why are you dragging London along when you go out with your girlfriend?"

Her question caught me so off guard it took me a second to comprehend what she was talking about. "You mean Emily?"

"Of course I mean Emily!"

"She's not my girlfriend," I sputtered. "London and Bodhi are friends."

"So the two of you take them to the zoo? And the aquarium? Like some kind of double date?" she spat out. "Do you know how confusing that is for her? Why would you do such a thing?"

"I'm not trying to confuse her…"

"Do you know what London did yesterday? When we went to art class? She ran up and *hugged* Emily. In front of everyone!"

"London hugs everyone . . ."

"SHE HUGGED HER!" Vivian shouted. Her cheeks flushed. "I thought you were smarter than that! I thought you were better than that! You don't see me insisting that London hang out with Walter and me, do you? I haven't even told London about Walter. She doesn't even know he exists! I haven't even told her that we're getting divorced!"

"Vivian—"

"Don't!" she snapped. "I don't want to hear you try to justify why the four of you have been gallivanting around town like you're a family now. You sure didn't wait long, did you?"

"Emily's just a friend," I protested.

"Are you honestly going to stand here and try to convince me that you see Emily just because London and Bodhi are friends?" she said, sneering. "Tell me this: Are you hanging out with the parents of London's other friends, too?"

"No, but—"

"And you don't think about her? You don't call her? You're not turning to her for support?"

I couldn't deny it and my expression must have given me away.

"I've been trying my best to keep London out of this," she went on. "While you . . . You don't seem to have given any thought as to what might be best for London. Or what she might be thinking or feeling. You're just thinking about yourself and what you want—same old story. You haven't changed at all, have you, Russ?"

With that, Vivian got into the SUV and slammed the door. She backed out and roared away while I stood there, frozen and reeling inside.

I couldn't sleep that night.

Was Vivian right? Had I only been thinking about myself? I replayed all the times I'd seen Emily; I retraced the steps that had led us to the zoo and the aquarium. And I asked myself, if London had a different best friend, would I have visited those places with that friend's parents?

In my heart, I knew the answer was no, which made me wonder how much I'd been lying to myself.

I felt the repercussions of Vivian's anger a few days later, while sitting in Taglieri's office. He'd called me because he had an update on the divorce negotiations.

"I was finally able to spend time on the phone with Vivian's attorney," he said, "going through the proposed agreement section by section." He sighed. "I don't know what's going on between you and Vivian, but I was anticipating a little give-and-take, as is the norm in these kinds of negotiations. What I didn't expect was for her to escalate her demands."

"She wants *more*?" I felt a numbness spreading through me at his words.

"Yup."

"Of what?"

"Everything. More alimony. More money when it comes to dividing joint property."

"How much exactly?'

When he told me I blanched. "What if I don't have it?"

"Well, for starters... I'd put the house up for sale."

While I'd been dreading Vivian's next move, I felt as if I'd been sucker-punched.

"She also said to tell you that Vivian will be here for Halloween weekend, and that she would prefer if you didn't stay in the house this time."

"Why didn't Vivian just tell me that herself?"

"Because Vivian has decided that henceforth, she wants all communications to go through the attorneys. She doesn't want to speak with you directly."

"Anything else?" I said, in a daze.

"She also wants to bring London to Atlanta the weekend of November thirteenth."

"And if I say no?"

"She'll probably go straight to the court. And Russ..." Taglieri eyed me seriously. "This isn't something worth fighting about, because you won't win. Unless she's an unfit mother, she has the right to see her daughter."

"I wouldn't have fought it. I'm just... blown away."

"Do you want to talk about what it is that set her off?"

"Not really," I said. What was the point? "What's she saying about London?"

"For now, she wants to have her every other weekend. In the future, though, she's insisting on sole custody."

"That's not going to happen."

"Which is yet another reason to put your house up for sale. Even though I've slashed my rates for you, fighting her is going to make this an expensive proposition."

On the work front, at least, things were improving. In the weeks following London's birthday party up until the end of the month, I landed four out of the five legal firms as new clients. Though it meant I was suddenly drowning in work—as were my tech guy and the camera crew—my work with Taglieri had vastly shortened my learning curve. Meanwhile, the plastic surgeon's campaign kicked off while Marge and Liz were in Costa Rica, and he was thrilled with the results he was seeing.

As for London and me, we'd settled into a steady rhythm. The stitches in her forehead came out and when a follow-up X-ray confirmed there were no broken bones, the splint eventually came off, too. She wasn't ready for her piano lessons yet, but she managed fine in art class. On our next date night, I took her out to a fancy dinner at a place called Fahrenheit, which offered glittering Charlotte city views and elegant handwritten menus—the kind of place that Vivian would have loved.

As Halloween approached, I didn't see much of Emily.

For better or for worse, Vivian's comments had gotten to me. While I'd tried to convince myself that our relationship was platonic, I knew

389

it was more than just a friendship. I was definitely attracted to her, and in the evenings, I would find myself staring at the phone and wondering if I was somehow damaging London by wanting to reach out to Emily.

Don't get me wrong. I still called Emily almost every night, unwilling or unable to give up that comforting ritual. But in the back of my mind, I could hear Vivian's voice, and I sometimes hung up feeling confused and guilty. I knew I wasn't ready for a relationship, but was I acting as if I were, by calling so frequently? And what did I really want in the long run when it came to Emily? Could I be content to simply remain friends? Would I be happy for her if she started dating someone else? Or would I feel a twinge at the thought of what might have been, maybe even succumb to jealousy?

Deep down, I knew the answer. Aside from Marge, I considered Emily to be my closest friend...and yet I hadn't told her what Vivian had said. Why couldn't I be honest with her about the conflict roiling within me? Perhaps a part of me felt that I'd been lying to Emily all along about my intentions. I wanted more than friendship. Not now, but down the road.

And as selfish as it may seem, I didn't want to risk losing her before that, which left me even more conflicted about what exactly I should do.

The day before Halloween, I made arrangements to check into a hotel.

Marge and Liz had arrived home from Costa Rica late Wednesday night, and I didn't feel good about hitting them up for a place to stay. Nor did I want to stay with my parents; though I knew they wouldn't have minded, I didn't want them to know about my further deteriorating relationship with Vivian. At London's birthday party, Vivian's cheerful façade had led my mom to pull me aside and try to convince me that Vivian still had feelings for me. That was a conversation I didn't want to face again.

Taglieri texted that Vivian would be arriving early on Friday night, probably around seven, which meant there would be no date night with London. Instead, London and I ate at home. Afterward, she ran up the stairs to check on the hamsters and her fish while I started to clean the kitchen.

I heard Vivian push through the door twenty minutes later.

"Hello!" she sang out. "I'm here!"

My heart started to race as if I'd been caught doing something I shouldn't, simply by being in my own house. Meanwhile, Vivian breezed in like she was the one who still lived here.

Vivian poked her head into the kitchen, looking for London.

"She's in her bedroom," I said. "She ran up there to check on her critters."

"Okay," she said, nodding. "Did she eat?"

I thought you told your attorney that we weren't supposed to communicate directly. But okay, I'll play along. "Yeah, she's had dinner. No bath yet. I didn't know if you were going to take her to a movie or..."

"I haven't decided yet. I'll talk to her." She paused. "You doing okay?"

"Yeah," I said, thrown once again by her casual demeanor. "I'm fine. You looking forward to trick-or-treating?"

"It'll be fun. I picked up an amazing costume for London. It's Belle from *Beauty and the Beast*, but extra glittery."

"She'll love that," I agreed. "She named one of her fish Belle."

"Make sure you come by in time to see it."

"You want me to come by?"

She rolled her eyes, but in them I saw only disbelief, not anger—as though I were merely clueless, rather than hateful. "Of course, Russ. She's your *daughter*. It's *Halloween*. And besides, you need to be here to hand out candy for the kids who come by the house. What did you think was going on tomorrow night?"

As usual, Vivian had managed to keep me guessing.

I hadn't seen Marge and Liz since London's birthday party, so I swung by my parents' the next afternoon, before the trick-or-treating got underway. I noticed right off that Marge had slimmed down even more. She looked fantastic, but it was on the tip of my tongue to tell her not to lose much more weight, as it might make her face look too severe. Liz, too, looked like she'd shed some pounds, though not as much.

Marge and Liz enveloped me in hugs as soon as I stepped through the door.

"So this is what you look like after a vacation, huh?" I said to Marge, giving a low whistle.

"I know, pretty fab, huh? I weigh as much as I did in college now."

"You look great, too, Liz. Are you sure the two of you weren't secretly at Canyon Ranch the whole time?"

"Thank you. But no," she said. "It was all just good old-fashioned hiking and sightseeing. And like Marge, I kept my servings of rice and beans to a minimum."

"I'm jealous. I've stopped losing weight, even though I'm still running."

"How are things?" Marge asked. "When I talked to Mom last night, she said you landed some new clients? Let's go out back and talk for a while."

"All right. Let me say hi to Mom and Dad and I'll meet you outside in a few."

Visiting with my parents took fifteen minutes—Mom didn't bring up *the cancer*, thank goodness—and I found my sister and Liz on the back patio, both of them drinking tall glasses of sweet tea.

For the next hour, we talked about their trip—the zip-lines, Arenal volcano, hikes through the cloud forest and near the coast—and I caught them up on all that had been going on in my world. Just as that part of the conversation was coming to a close, my mom popped her head out and asked Liz if she'd mind giving her a hand in the kitchen.

"So ... you were told you had to communicate through attorneys, but then she showed up at the house and acted as if everything were normal?"

I nodded. "Don't ask me to explain it. I'm just thanking God for small favors."

"What I still don't understand is why Vivian got London for both her birthday and on Halloween. You should get London for some of the fun things, too."

"It's just the way the weekends are falling."

Marge didn't seem satisfied with this explanation, but apparently decided to let it drop. "How do you feel about selling the house?"

"I guess I'm torn. We don't need a place that big—to be honest, we never really did—but at the same time, there are a lot of memories there. Anyway, I don't have much of a choice. Even though my business is finally taking off, it's not like I'll have enough in the bank to pay Vivian off when we sign the papers." I paused. "It's hard for me to believe it's been almost two months since she walked out the door. In some ways, it seems like yesterday. In other ways, it feels like forever."

"I can't imagine," Marge said. She turned her head and covered her mouth, coughing from somewhere deep in her chest.

"You're still sick?"

"No," she answered. "This is just a remnant from the bronchitis. Apparently it can take the lungs months to heal, even when the inflammation is gone. I felt pretty good in Costa Rica, but right now, I need a vacation from my vacation. Liz kept us on the go the whole time—I'm still wiped out. And my knees are killing me from all the hiking."

"Hiking is good exercise, but it's rough on the joints," I conceded.

"Speaking of which, let me know if you and Emily ever want to go hiking with Liz and me. It'll be like old times."

"I will," I said. At my answer, Marge tilted her head.

"Uh-oh. I'm sensing there's trouble in paradise. Is there anything you're not telling me?"

"Not really," I hedged. "I just don't know where the relationship is going."

Marge scrutinized me. "Why can't you just be happy with what you have with her right now? Because it seems to me like she's been a rock to you these past couple of months."

"She has."

"Then just appreciate her for that, and let it be what it's going to be."

I hesitated. "Vivian thinks that hanging out Emily and the kids is confusing to London. And she's right."

Marge made a skeptical face, but in the end she folded her hands on

393

the table and leaned toward me. "So don't bring London and Bodhi," she said pointedly. "Why don't you just try going out with her?"

"Like on a date?"

"Yes," Marge said. "Like a date."

"What about London?"

"Liz and I would be more than happy to babysit. And besides, didn't you just say that London was going to be in Atlanta in a couple of weeks? Seize the day, little brother."

On Halloween night, Vivian was unusually warm, even insisting that she take a photo of me with London on her phone, which she then texted to me right away. I handed out candy to the neighborhood kids. There were so many coming by the house, I sat in the rocking chair on the front porch so I wouldn't have to keep getting up from the couch.

The next morning, I woke to a text from Vivian that said she'd be leaving around six, and could I try to be home by then?

On the way out the door that evening, she pulled me into a hug and whispered to me that I was doing a great job with London.

The first couple of weeks of November blurred together in a string of eighteen-hour days, marked by the routines that had become second nature. I exercised, worked, took care of London—who started back with piano lessons—cooked, cleaned, and made nightly calls to Emily. Thanks to my new clients, I was so busy that I didn't even have time to swing by my parents the following weekend, nor visit with Marge and Liz even once. A few things from that period do stand out in my memory, however.

The week after Halloween, I had a Realtor come by so I could put the house up for sale. She walked through and asked a lot of questions; toward the end, she suggested that I rearrange the furniture, to show the rooms to better effect. One by one, at her suggestion, the pieces ended up back where Vivian had originally placed them. Before she left, she retrieved a mallet from her car and pounded a bright red realty sign into the yard out front.

The sight of the sign made something sink inside me, and out of instinct, I called Emily. As usual, she brought me back onto solid ground, even encouraging me with the prospect of turning to a fresh page in my life, in a new home. Maybe it was the prospect of Vivian taking London to Atlanta for the weekend, but as the conversation was winding down, I found myself thinking about Marge's suggestion that I ask Emily out. Before I could gather my courage, however, Emily spoke up.

"Russ, I've been meaning to ask you—would you like to accompany me to the opening of the art show I told you about? The one that's going to include a few of my paintings?"

She sounded a bit nervous, and I could almost picture her smoothing her hair behind her ear, the way she always did when she was anxious. "I mean, it's fine if you can't, but since the opening is the weekend when London's going to be in Atlanta, I thought…"

"I'd love to," I interrupted. "I'm so glad you asked."

As the weekend of November thirteenth approached, I helped London prepare for her trip to Atlanta, which took more time than I thought it would. London was excited at the idea of visiting Vivian in her new apartment, and packed and repacked her suitcase four or five times. She fretted for days over what to bring, ultimately packing several different outfits, in addition to Barbies, coloring books, crayons, and the book *Two by Two*. Vivian had texted that she would pick London up at five, which I interpreted to mean she'd drive both ways. Of course, I'd forgotten about Spannerman's private jet, but I was reminded of that as soon as the limousine pulled to a stop in front of the house.

I carried London's bag to the car and handed it to the driver. By then, London had crawled into the limousine and was already exploring the plush interior.

It hurt to see her leaving, even if she was with her mom.

"I'll have her back here Sunday about seven," Vivian said. "And of course, you can call anytime and I'll put her on the phone."

"I'll try not to be a nuisance about it."

"You're her *father*," Vivian said. "You're not a *nuisance*." She looked away before continuing. "And just so you know, she's not going to meet Walter this weekend. It's too soon for him to meet her. I wouldn't do that to her."

I nodded, surprised—and yes, undeniably grateful.

"Do you have any big plans?" I asked, somehow eager to prolong their departure.

"There are a lot of things to do there. I think we'll play it by ear. But I should probably be going. I don't want it to be too late when we get to the apartment."

This time, there was no hug. As she turned away, however, her eyes caught the sight of the realty sign and she paused. Then, with a resolute flick of her hair over her shoulder, she moved to the open door and the driver closed it behind her.

I watched the limo pull away, feeling strangely bereft. Despite everything that had happened to this point, there always seemed to be another way to remind me that I'd lost the future I'd once imagined.

I don't know why the thought of attending Emily's gallery opening made me nervous. Emily and I had coffee together practically every weekend, we talked on the phone most nights, and I'd spent an evening drinking wine on her back patio. We'd spent whole days on expeditions with the kids. Moreover, we would be attending an event at which her work, not mine, would be on display—so if anyone should be nervous, it stood to reason it should be her.

Even so, my heart was beating faster than usual and my mouth had gone slightly dry when Emily answered the knock at her front door. One look at her framed in the doorway didn't help. I wasn't sure how artists were supposed to look at their openings, but gone was any trace of the easygoing mom with whom I was so familiar; in her place stood a ravishing woman in a strappy black cocktail dress, her hair tumbling in a glossy waterfall past her shoulders. I noticed she was wearing just enough makeup to make it seem she was wearing none at all.

"You're right on time," she said, leaning in for a quick hug. "And don't you look sharp."

I'd gone with what Vivian referred to as a *Hollywood Look*: black blazer, black slacks, and a black V-neck sweater.

"I wasn't sure what I was supposed to wear," I admitted, still feeling the imprint of her brief hug.

"Let me just make sure the babysitter has everything she needs. Then we can go, okay?"

I watched as she climbed the stairs and heard her speaking to the babysitter. At the top of the stairs, she hugged and kissed Bodhi before returning to the foyer.

"Shall we?"

"Absolutely," I said, certain that she was one of the most beautiful women I'd ever seen. "But only on one condition."

"What's that?"

"You have to give me some pointers on gallery-opening etiquette."

She laughed, the carefree sound loosening the knot of tension in my diaphragm.

"We'll talk on the way," she said, moving toward the foyer closet and grabbing a cashmere wrap. "But let's scoot out of here before Bodhi realizes he forgot something critical and it takes another twenty minutes before we can escape."

I opened the front door and watched as she led the way, noting how the dress hugged her figure just right. My eyes drifted lower until I flashed on the memory of the night she'd helped me with my bowtie, which made me flush and lift my gaze.

I backed the car onto the street and steered it in the direction of downtown, where the gallery was located.

"So, is this show a big deal for you?" I asked. "I know you've been working like crazy to get all the paintings ready."

"It's not a major exhibit at MoMA or anything like that, but the owner of the gallery does a nice job. He's been in business for a long time, so once a year, he invites his best customers to a private showing.

397

A few of them are prominent regional collectors. Usually, there are six or seven artists, but this year, I think he said he's showcasing the work of nine artists. Two sculptors, a glass artist, an artist who works in ceramics, and five painters."

"And you're one of them."

"I'm one of the painters every year."

"How many does he represent?"

"Thirty, maybe?"

"See? And you're so humble, I never would have known."

"I'm humble because my paintings don't sell for much money. It's not like anything I've done will ever see the inside of Sotheby's or Christie's. Of course, most of the artists whose work sells for a gazillion dollars are dead."

"That doesn't seem fair."

"You're preaching to the choir," she teased.

"And what role do you play at the opening?"

"Well, it's kind of like a mixer, and I'm one of several hosts. There will be wine and appetizers, and I'll hang around in the general vicinity of my work, in case any of the guests have questions or want to talk to me."

"What if they want to buy a piece?"

"Then the guest will talk to the gallery owner. It's not really my place to discuss what a painting is worth. As much as I was joking about the big bucks, I don't like to think of art in terms of money. People should buy a piece because they love it. Because it speaks to them."

"Or because it looks good hanging on the wall?"

"Or that," she said, smiling.

"I'm excited to see what you've done. I'm sorry I didn't make it to the gallery before now..."

"Russ, you're a busy single dad," she said, giving my arm a reassuring squeeze. "I'm just glad you agreed to come with me tonight. It'll give me someone to talk to when no one is looking at my work. It's a little dispiriting to stand next to your work and watch people ignore it, or avert their gaze so you won't try to talk to them."

"Has that ever happened to you?"

"Every time," she said. "Not everyone who shows up will like my work. Art is subjective."

"I like your work. What I've seen on your walls, I mean."

She laughed. "That's because you like me."

I looked over at her. "True enough."

By the time we reached the gallery, any trace of nervousness had passed. As ever, Emily made being around her easy, because she was so clearly comfortable with me. I had forgotten how liberating that feeling of acceptance was, and when we paused at the door, I found myself staring at her and wondering how different my life would have been had I married her rather than Vivian.

Emily caught me staring and tilted her head. "What are you thinking about?"

I hesitated. "I was thinking how glad I am that London and Bodhi are friends."

She squinted at me, a skeptical gleam in her eye. "I'm not sure you were thinking about the kids just then."

"No?"

"No," she said with a knowing smile, "I'm pretty sure you were thinking about me."

"It must be a wonderful thing to be able to read minds."

"It is," she said. "And for my next trick, watch this: I'm going to enter the gallery without even touching the door."

"How are you going to do that?"

She feigned disappointment. "You're not even going to open the door for me? I thought you were a gentleman."

I laughed and pulled open the door for her. The interior of the building was brightly lit, with the look of an industrial loft; a large open space, with several groups of wall partitions that rose partway to the ceiling. Paintings were mounted on the partitions, and I could see about twenty people clustered among the artwork, most holding glasses of wine or champagne flutes. Waiters and waitresses circulated, bearing silver trays of appetizers.

"Lead the way," I said. "You're the star tonight."

Emily scanned the room and we started toward a patrician-looking, gray-haired gentleman. This turned out to be Claude Barnes, the owner of the gallery. With him were two couples, both of whom had driven in from other cities to attend the show.

I snagged a couple of glasses of wine from a passing waiter and handed one to Emily while we engaged in small talk. I saw Emily point toward a set of partitions in the rear of the gallery and after the conversation came to an end, we ambled over.

I took a few minutes to examine her paintings, thinking to myself that they were not only arrestingly beautiful, but mysterious. While the paintings I'd seen in her home had been abstract, in these, I saw more realistic elements. The colors practically exploded off the canvas, and were coupled with stark brushwork. One painting in particular continued to draw my eye.

"These are spectacular," I said, meaning it. "I can't imagine how much work they required. Which is the one that was giving you fits?"

"This one," she said, pointing to the one that had caught my eye.

I studied it up close, then took a few steps back, examining it from various angles. "It's perfect," I said.

"I still don't think it's done," she said, shaking her head, "but thank you."

"I mean it," I said. "I want to buy it."

"Okaay..." she said, at once doubtful and flattered. "Are you sure? You don't even know how much it costs."

"I want to buy it," I repeated. "Really." When she saw I was sincere, she actually blushed.

"Wow. I'm honored, Russ. I'll see if I can get Claude to give you the 'friends and family' discount."

I took a sip of my wine. "Now what?"

"We wait and see if anyone comes by." She winked. "And if they do, let me do the talking, okay? I don't want be a modern-day Margaret Keane."

"Who?"

"Margaret Keane was an artist whose husband took credit for her work for years. They made her life story into a movie called *Big Eyes*. You should see it."

"Why don't we watch it together one evening?"

"Deal."

As the gallery continued to fill, I listened to Emily explain her work to interested patrons. My role, if I had one, was to take photographs using people's phones. It seemed like practically everyone who came by wanted a picture with Emily, presumably because she was the artist, but after a while I noticed that none of the other artists seemed nearly as popular.

While Emily was chatting with various guests, I wandered among the exhibits of the other artists. A few of the sculptures caught my attention, but they were so large and abstract, I couldn't imagine how they could possibly look good in someone's home. I also liked the work of some of the other painters, though in my opinion Emily's work was better.

Emily and I nibbled steadily on appetizers as the crowds ebbed and flowed. The flow of visitors reached its peak around 8:00 p.m., and then began to dwindle. While the show was supposed to be over at 9:00 p.m., Claude didn't lock the doors until the last guest left at 9:45 p.m. "I think that went well," he said, as he approached. "A number of the guests expressed interest in your work. It wouldn't surprise me if you sold out in the next few days."

Emily turned to me. "Are you sure you still want to buy that painting?"

"I do," I said, conscious that it was a luxury I could ill afford right now. But somehow, I didn't care. Claude frowned slightly, aware, no doubt, that a steep discount request would be coming. The frown vanished as quickly as it had come.

"Are there any other pieces you're interested in? From the other artists?"

"No," I said. "Just the one."

"Can we talk about this tomorrow, Claude?" Emily asked. "It's getting a little late, and I'm too tired to talk business."

"Of course," he said. "Thank you for everything you did tonight, Emily," he said. "You're always so good at these things. Your personality endears you to others."

Standing close to Emily, I knew that Claude was right.

"What would you like to do now?" I asked on the way to the car. "If you're tired, I can bring you home."

"Are you kidding?" she asked. "I've got a babysitter, and I said I wouldn't be home until midnight. I only told Claude that I was tired so we could get out of there. Once Claude starts talking, it's sometimes hard to get him to stop. I love the guy, but I only have a babysitter once in a blue moon and I'm going to take advantage of it."

"Do you feel like having dinner? We might be able to find something that's still open."

"I'm stuffed," she said, "But how about a cocktail?"

"Do you have a favorite watering hole?"

"Russ, I'm the mother of a five-year-old. I don't get out much. But I've heard that Fahrenheit has stunning views and fire pits. And since it's chilly tonight, sitting by a fire sounds perfect."

"I just took London there for date night."

"Great minds think alike."

Soon thereafter, we found ourselves at Fahrenheit's rooftop bar, warming ourselves before a glowing fire pit and taking in the carpet of city lights below. I ordered two glasses of wine from a passing cocktail waitress.

Emily sat swaddled in her cashmere wrap, eyes half closed, her expression serene. She looked extraordinarily beautiful in the rosy glow of the firelight, and when she noticed me staring, she gave a lazy smile.

"I remember that look," she said. "You used to stare at me like that way back when...a million years ago."

"Yeah?"

"Sometimes it gave me goose bumps."

"But not anymore, right?"

Her coy shrug told me otherwise.

"I know I've said that I'm glad you've come into my life..."

When I stopped, she raised her eyes to look at me. "But?"

I decided to tell the truth. "I'm not sure I'm ready for a relationship."

For a moment she said nothing. "All right," she murmured finally, with the faintest echo of regret.

"I'm sorry."

"Why are you sorry?"

"Because I've been calling too much. Maybe leading you to think that I was ready when I know I'm not. I'm still an emotional wreck at times. I still think about Vivian way too much. Not that I want her back, because I've realized that I don't. But she's still front and center, in a way that's not healthy. And you've been so generous—listening to me when I'm down, offering endless emotional support. And best of all, making me laugh..."

When I trailed off, I could feel her eyes inspecting me. "Have I ever complained that you call too much? Or that your confidences are a burden?"

I shook my head, feeling as if some epiphany were trying to surface in my chaotic brain, like an air bubble rising through water. "No," I said, "you haven't."

"You're describing a scenario in which you haven't offered me anything in return. But you have." The reddish tints in her dark hair glinted in the firelight as she pushed it away from her face. Leaning toward me, she said, "I like hearing from you, whether you're in a good mood or not. I like knowing that I can talk to you about anything, that you'll understand because we once shared a history. I like feeling that you know the real me, faults and all."

"You don't have any faults," I said. "None that I can see, anyway."

She gave a snort of disbelief. "Are you kidding? No one's perfect, Russ. I like to think I've learned some lessons over the past decade, and maybe, I'm more patient than I used to be. But I'm far from perfect."

The waitress delivered our wine, and in the silence that followed, our thoughts seemed to take a more serious turn. Emily took a sip of wine, and when she turned toward me again, I thought I saw a flash of vulnerability cross her face.

"I'm sorry," I said. "I know I'm probably putting a damper on the evening."

"Not at all," she said. "It means so much that you're honest with me, Russ. I think that's what I like most about you. You're not afraid to tell me things—that you're hurting, that you're afraid of failure,

403

that you're not ready for a relationship. You don't realize how hard it is for some people to say such things. David never could. I never knew what he was really feeling—half the time, I don't think he even did. But with you, it's different. You're so open. I always admired that about you, and it hasn't changed." She paused, as if uncertain whether to go on. "I really like you, Russ. You're good for me."

"That's the thing, Emily. I don't just like you...I think I'm in love with you."

My words seem to electrify her. "You think?"

"No," I said with growing certainty. "I *am* in love with you. It feels strange to say that when I know I'm not really ready to take further steps, but that's how I feel." For a moment I stared into the fire, trying to summon my courage. "I'm not the kind of guy you should love. You can do a lot better than me. Maybe in time..."

Saying the words hurt more than I anticipated and I broke off, feeling a knot forming in my throat.

In the silence, Emily stared at me. Then she reached over and laid her open hand on my leg, beckoning for me to take it. I did, feeling a flood of warmth and encouragement as her fingers intertwined with my own.

"Did you think that I might be in love with you, too?"

"You don't have to say that."

"I'm not just saying it, Russ. I know what love feels like. Maybe I've always loved you—God knows I loved you once with every fiber of my being. I don't think that kind of feeling just goes away—it leaves its mark on you." She held my gaze, her voice gentle. "I'm okay with waiting until you're ready. Because I like what we have now. I like that you've become one of my closest friends. And I know how much you care for me. Do you remember what I said about friendship? 'It's about someone who walks into your life, says I'm here for you, and then proves it.'"

I nodded.

"You might not believe it, but you've been doing that for me. I don't know if I'm ready for a relationship either. What I do know is that I want you in my life, and that the thought of losing you—again—would break my heart."

"Where does that leave us, then?"

"How about we just sit by the fire, you and me, and enjoy tonight. We can be friends tonight and tomorrow and for as long as you'd like. And you keep calling and we keep talking and having coffee when the kids are at art. And like everybody in the world, we'll just take things one day at a time."

I stared at her, marveling at her wisdom, and how simple she made it all seem.

"I love you, Emily."

"I love you, too, Russ." She gave my hand a squeeze. "It's going to be fine," she said earnestly. "Trust me."

Later that night, I lay awake in bed. Emily and I had lingered for another hour by the fire, letting the meaning of everything that had been said sink in. When I dropped her off at home, I felt the urge to kiss her, but was afraid of upsetting our newfound balance.

Emily sensed my hesitation and simply leaned in for a hug. We held each other for a long time beneath her porch light, and the intimacy of that moment struck me as more real and more meaningful than anything else she could have done.

"Call me tomorrow, okay?" she whispered, releasing me, but not before raising a tender hand to my face.

"I will."

And with that, she turned and went inside.

The last two weeks of November were some of the happiest in my recent memory. My anniversary passed without incident; neither Vivian nor I mentioned it when she FaceTimed with London, and it wasn't until after the call had ended that I even remembered it at all. At work, I was proving to be hugely productive on behalf of my new clients. London returned from Atlanta on Sunday night, and though she'd had a good time, she slipped back into her routine without a fuss. I spoke to Emily every day, and worked out a deal with Claude to buy her painting, which I then mounted in the family room. I saw Marge,

Liz, and my parents the following weekend, the day after Marge and Liz had met with the fertility specialist. While we were all seated in the family room together, they told my parents about their plans.

"It's about time!" my mom cried, jumping up to hug them both.

"You'll be good parents," my dad added. He sounded as gruff as always before he embraced Marge and Liz in turn. With hugs from my dad as rare as solar eclipses, I know they were touched.

Through Taglieri, I learned that Vivian wanted London in Atlanta for the Thanksgiving weekend. Actually, she wanted London beginning on Wednesday evening, through Sunday. I wasn't happy about that, but again, the every-other-weekend pattern just happened to nail every holiday. Vivian arrived on Wednesday to pick up London in the limo and whisk her off to the jet again. As I watched them pull away, I thought about how quiet the house would be without my daughter for the next four days.

The house *was* quiet that weekend. Because no one, not even me, was there at all.

Instead, that was the weekend when once more, my world began to collapse around me.

But this time, it was even worse.

How did it happen?

Like it always seems to happen: seemingly without warning.

But, of course, in retrospect there had been warnings all along.

It was Saturday morning, November twenty-eighth, two days after Thanksgiving. I'd spent the previous evening with Emily, dining out and visiting the Charlotte Comedy Zone. Once again, I was tempted to kiss her at the end of the evening, but settled instead for another long and glorious hug, one that confirmed my desire to keep her in my life for a long, long time. My feelings for her were already displacing thoughts of Vivian in a way that I hadn't anticipated, and that I hoped would continue. I felt undeniably lighter and more positive about the future than I had in months, if not years.

The call came in on early Saturday morning. It wasn't yet six a.m. when the house phone began to ring, and the sound itself was ominous. My cell phone was on airplane mode, and no one would call the house at that hour unless something terrible had happened. I knew even before I picked up the phone that it was my mother on the other end, and I knew that she was calling to tell me that my father was in the hospital. He'd had a heart attack. Or something worse. I knew she would be frantic, probably in tears.

But it wasn't my mom on the other end of the line.

It was Liz, calling about my sister.

Marge, she told me, had been admitted to the hospital.

She'd been coughing up blood for an hour.

CHAPTER 23

No

When Marge was eleven, she and my mom were involved in a car accident.

Back then, my mom was still driving one of those huge, wood-paneled station wagons. Because they were from a different generation, my parents weren't accustomed to wearing seatbelts, and as a family we rarely did.

Marge liked seatbelts even less than I did. Whereas I simply forgot to put mine on when I hopped in the car—I was still young, remember—Marge deliberately chose not to wear them, because it allowed her more freedom to punch or pinch me whenever the mood struck. Which, I might add, was way too often.

I wasn't in the car that day, and though I'm not sure how accurate my recollections are, it seems the accident was no fault of my mom's. She wasn't speeding, the road wasn't busy, and she was passing through an intersection while the light was green. Meanwhile, a teenager—probably fiddling with the radio or scarfing down McDonald's French fries—blew through the red light and broadsided the rear of the station wagon.

While my mom was a little banged up, it was Marge whom everyone was most worried about. The momentum from the crash had thrown her into the side windows, shattering the glass. While she wasn't unconscious when she arrived at the hospital, she was bleeding and bruised, and had sustained a broken collarbone.

When I entered Marge's hospital room with my dad, the sight of my sister scared me. At six years old, I didn't know much about death, or even hospitals. My dad stood over her bed, his expression flat, but I could tell

408

by his posture that he was frightened, which scared me even more. Looking down at my stricken face, he frowned.

"Come see your sister, Russ."

"I don't want to," I can remember saying.

"I don't care what you want," he said. "I told you to come here, and you're going to do what I tell you."

His tone brooked no argument and I inched toward the bed. Marge's face was grossly swollen, with deep bruises and multiple stitches, like she'd been sewn back together. She didn't look like my sister; she didn't look like anyone. She looked like a monster in a scary movie and the sight of her caused me to burst into tears.

To this day, I wish I hadn't cried. My dad thought I was crying for Marge and I felt him lay a comforting hand on my shoulder, which made me cry even harder.

But I wasn't crying for Marge. I was crying for myself, because I was afraid, and over time, I came to despise myself for my reaction.

Some people have courage.

On that day, I learned that I wasn't one of them.

The doctors didn't know what was wrong with Marge. Nurses took samples of blood and X-rayed her chest. That was followed by a CAT scan. Three different doctors came to examine her. I watched as a needle was inserted into Marge's lungs to remove tissue for further examination.

Throughout it all, Marge was the only one who didn't seem worried. Part of that had to do with the fact that since she'd arrived at the hospital, her coughing had abated. She joked with the doctors and nurses while Liz and my parents looked on with grim concern, and I thought again about how effective my sister was at hiding her fears, even from those who loved her. Meanwhile, in another part of the hospital, tests were being run. I heard the doctor whispering words like *pathology* and *radiology. Biopsy. Oncology.*

Liz was clearly worried, but not yet panicked. My parents sat like stones, barely holding it together. And I was upset, because Marge didn't look good. Her skin had a grayish pallor, which accentuated

409

her weight loss, and I found myself replaying all that I'd seen and the things she'd said over the last few months. The racking cough that never seemed to go away, the soreness in her legs. How exhausted she'd been after her vacation.

My parents and I, Liz and the doctors, were all thinking about the same thing.

The cancer.

But it couldn't be cancer. Marge couldn't be that sick. She was my sister and she was only forty years old. A little more than a week ago, she'd gone to a specialist because she wanted to have a baby. She was looking forward to being pregnant. She had her entire life ahead of her.

Marge couldn't be sick. She didn't have *the cancer.*

No.

No, no, no, no, no . . .

I was thankful that Vivian had taken London to Atlanta, because I don't know what I would have done with her all day. I spent hours drifting in and out of Marge's hospital room. When I couldn't take it anymore, I would pace the parking lot or have coffee in the cafeteria. I called Emily and shared what was going on; I asked her not to come by, but she came anyway.

Marge and Emily had a short but sweet reunion a little before noon, and in the hallway afterward, Emily held me as I shook with fear. She told me that she wanted to see me later, if I was up to it, and I promised that I'd call.

Finally, I called Vivian. When I told her what was going on, she gave a strangled gasp and immediately offered to fly back with London right away. I explained that London was probably better off with her, at least through the weekend. Vivian understood.

"Oh, Russ," she said quietly, sounding nothing like her usual brisk self. "I'm so sorry."

"Don't be sorry yet," I said, "we don't know anything for sure."

I was lying to myself, and both Vivian and I knew it. She was well aware of the history on my mother's side of the family. As I spoke again, I could hear my voice cracking.

"Do me a favor and don't say anything to London yet, okay?"

"Of course not. Is there anything I can do? What do you need?"

"Nothing for now," I said. "Thanks." Words were becoming hard to form, my thoughts beginning to scatter. "I'll let you know."

"Keep me informed, okay?"

"I will," I promised, and I knew that I would. After all, we were still married.

In the afternoon, while my parents and Liz were visiting the cafeteria, I stayed with Marge. She asked about my work, and at her insistence, I described the ad campaigns I was crafting for my clients. I think she remembered that day in the hospital so long ago, after the auto accident, and could tell how frightened I was. She knew I could speak about work on autopilot, so she kept asking questions, to distract me.

As had become her habit, she asked about Emily and I finally admitted that I'd fallen in love, but wasn't ready to tell our parents yet. At that, she cracked a grin.

"Too late. Mom and Dad already know."

"How? I haven't said anything to them."

"You didn't have to," she said. "When you called Emily on Thanksgiving, the way you felt about her was plain as day. Mom raised her eyebrows while Dad turned to me and said, 'Already? He's not even divorced yet.'"

Despite everything, I laughed. That was my dad, all right. "I didn't realize it was so obvious."

"Uh-huh," she said, nodding. "I just wish you hadn't waited until today to bring her by. I look like hell. You should have had us meet right after Costa Rica, when I was still tan."

I nodded, struck by how normal Marge sounded.

"My bad."

"I'd like to meet Bodhi, too. Since I've heard so much about him."

"I'm sure you'll have a chance."

She twisted the hospital sheet, winding it tight and letting it unfurl. "I've been thinking about baby names," she said. "I bought one of those books, you know? At work, whenever I'm bored, I look through it. I even started highlighting some of them."

Baby names? Was she really talking about baby names? I could feel pressure behind my eyes and I struggled to get the words out without my voice cracking. "Any favorites?"

"If it's a boy, I like Josiah. Elliot. Carter. If it's a girl, I like Meredith and Alexis. Of course, Liz is going to have her own ideas, but I haven't spoken to her about it yet. It's still pretty early in the process, so we have plenty of time to make a decision."

Plenty of time.

Marge must have heard herself because she looked first toward the clock, then the door of the room, which was propped open. Nurses hurried past, going about their duties as if today were no different than any other day. "I wonder when they're going to finally let me out of here," she said. "What's taking them so long? I've been here for hours already. Don't they know I have things to do?"

When I had no answer to that, Marge sighed. "You know I'm going to be okay, right? I mean, I'm not ignoring what happened this morning, but I don't feel all that bad. I feel a lot better than I did before I left for Costa Rica, in fact. I probably just picked up some parasite while I was down there. Lord only knows what the sanitary standards are like in those kitchens."

"We'll see what the doctors say," I murmured.

"If you see them, tell them to hurry up. I'd rather not waste my whole weekend here."

"I will."

Marge continued to wind and unwind the sheet. "London comes back tomorrow, right?"

"She does. I don't know what time exactly. Early evening, I'd guess."

"Why don't you bring London over for dinner with Liz and me this week? You've been so busy lately, we haven't had time for our normal sit-downs."

Watching her work the sheet, I could feel my throat tightening again. "Dinner sounds great. But none of that Costa Rican food. What with all the parasites, right?"

"Yeah," she said, looking right at me. "Trust me when I tell you that you don't want what I have."

The day crawled by.

Midafternoon. Late afternoon.

Vivian texted, asking if there was any news. I replied that we were still waiting.

Emily texted, asking how I was doing.

Scared to death, I replied.

As dusk approached, the sky began to cloud over. Marge's hospital room was bathed in flat gray light, and the TV was tuned to *Judge Judy*, though on mute. The machine monitoring her vitals beeped steadily. A doctor that we hadn't met came into the room. Though his demeanor was steady, his expression was grim and I already knew what he was going to tell us. He introduced himself as Dr. Kadam Patel, and he was an oncologist. Over his shoulder, in the hallway, I watched as a young girl in a wheelchair was rolled past the room. In her arms was a stuffed animal, a purple pig.

Just as my mother had dreamed.

I went blank, my mind tuning out almost as soon as he began to speak, but I caught various bits and pieces.

Adenocarcinoma...more common in women than men...more likely to occur in younger people...non-small cell...slower growing than other types of lung cancer, but unfortunately, it's advanced and the CT scan shows that it has metastasized to other parts of the body...both lungs, lymph nodes, bones and her brain...malignant pericardial effusion...stage IV...incurable.

Incurable...

My mom was the first to let out a cry; the plaintive wail of a mother who knows that her child is dying. Liz followed a moment later and my dad took her in his arms. He said nothing, but his lower lip trembled while he squeezed his eyes shut, as if trying to block out reality. Marge sat unmoving on the bed. Watching her, I felt as though I would topple over but somehow, I remained upright. Marge kept her gaze fixed on the doctor.

"How long do I have?" she asked, and for the first time that day, I heard fear in her voice.

"It's impossible to say," Dr. Patel answered. "Though it's incurable, it's treatable. Treatment has improved exponentially in the last ten years. It can not only prolong life, it can alleviate some of the symptoms."

"How long?" Marge demanded. "With treatment?"

"If we had caught it earlier," Dr. Patel hedged. "Before it had metastasized—"

"But we didn't," Marge said, cutting him off.

Dr. Patel stood a bit straighter. "Again, there's no way to know exactly. You're young and in good condition, both of which increase life expectancy."

"I understand that it's not a question that you want to answer. I also understand that every patient is different, which means you can't really know for sure. What I want, though, is your best guess." Marge's voice made it clear she would not be deterred. "Do you think I have a year?"

The doctor didn't answer, but his expression was pained.

"Six months?" Marge pressed, and again, the doctor didn't answer. "Three?"

"Right now," Dr. Patel said, "I think it would be best if we start discussing treatment options. It's critical that we get started right away."

"I don't want to discuss *treatment*," Marge said. I could hear anger in her voice. "If you think I only have a few months, if you're telling me it's incurable, then what's the point?"

Liz had collected herself enough to wipe her eyes. She moved toward the bed and took Marge's hand. Lifting it to her mouth, she kissed it. "Baby?" she whispered. "I want to hear what the doctor says about treatment options, okay? I know you're afraid, but I need to know. Can you listen? For me?"

For the first time, Marge turned from the doctor. The trail of her tear had left a streak on her cheek that the light caught, making it shine.

"Okay," Marge whispered, and only then, did Marge begin to cry.

Systemic chemotherapy.

Over the next forty minutes, the doctor patiently explained to us his reasoning for the course of treatment he was recommending. Because the cancer was so advanced, because it had spread throughout Marge's body and reached her brain, there were no real surgical options. Radiation was a possibility, but again, because of the spread, the benefits weren't worth the costs. Usually, patients were given more time to consider all the pros and cons of chemotherapy—including side effects, and he went over those in detail—but again, because the cancer was so advanced, the doctor strongly recommended that Marge start immediately.

To do that, Marge would need a catheter. When that part was underway, my parents and I left the room to go to the cafeteria. We didn't speak; instead, we sat in silence, each of us simply trying to process what was happening. I ordered coffee that I didn't drink, thinking that chemotherapy is essentially poison, and the hope is that the cancer cells are killed before normal cells. Too much poison and the patient dies; too little poison, and the medicine does no good at all.

My sister had already known all this. My parents and I had known all this as well. We had grown up knowing about the cancer. All of us knew about stages and survival rates and possible remission and catheters and side effects.

The cancer, after all, spread not only through human bodies. Sometimes it spread through families, like mine.

Later, I returned to the room, and I took a seat in the chair, watching as the poison began to be administered, killing as it flowed through her system.

I left the hospital when the sky had turned black, and I walked my parents to their car. To me, it seemed like they were shuffling rather than walking, and for the first time, they seemed old. Beaten down and utterly wrung out. I knew because I was feeling the same way.

Liz had asked us if she could be alone with Marge. As soon as she asked, I felt guilty. Lost in my own feelings about Marge, it didn't occur to me that the two of them needed time together, without an audience.

After watching my parents pull out of the parking lot, I walked slowly to my car. I knew I couldn't stay at the hospital but I didn't want to go home. I didn't want to go anywhere. What I wanted was to be able to rewind, to return to yesterday. Twenty-four hours earlier, I had been having dinner with Emily and looking forward to an evening of laughter.

The stand-ups at the Comedy Zone were good, and although one of the routines had been a bit too profane for my taste, the second comedian was both married and a father, and the humorous stories he related had the sweet ring of familiarity. At one point, I reached for Emily's hand and when I felt her fingers intertwine with my own, I felt as though I'd come home. This, I remember thinking, is what life is really about. Love and laughter and friendship; happy times spent with those you care about.

As I drove home, yesterday seemed impossibly distant, a different lifetime altogether. The axis of my world had shifted, and like my parents, I'd aged in the last few hours. I'd been hollowed out. And as I squinted through eyes that had gone blurry with tears, I wondered if I would ever feel whole again.

Emily texted to ask if I was still at the hospital, and when I replied that I'd gone home, she said that she was coming over.

She found me on the couch, in a house illuminated by a single lamp in the family room. I hadn't risen when she'd knocked at the door and she'd let herself in.

"Hey there," she said, her voice soft. She crossed the room and sat beside me.

"Hi," I said. "Sorry I didn't get the door."

"It's fine," she said. "How's Marge? How are you?"

I didn't know how to answer and I pinched the bridge of my nose. I didn't want to cry anymore.

She slipped her arm around me and I leaned into her. Just like earlier that day, she held me close, and we didn't have to talk at all.

Marge was released from the hospital on Sunday. Though she was weak and nauseated, she wanted to go home and there was no reason to stay at the hospital.

The first dose of poison, after all, had already been administered.

I pushed the wheelchair, my parents trailing behind me. Liz walked beside the wheelchair, clearing a path in the busy hallways. No one we passed cast a second glance in our direction.

It was cold outside. On the way to the hospital, Liz had asked me to swing by their house to get Marge a jacket. She directed me to a key hidden under a rock to the right of the front door.

I had let myself in and rummaged through the foyer closet, trying to find something soft and warm. I finally settled on a long down jacket.

Before going outside, Liz helped Marge stand so she could slip on the jacket. She winced and wobbled, but kept her balance. Liz and my parents set out for the parking lot together, then veered in opposite directions to find their cars.

"I hate hospitals," Marge said to me. "The only time I've ever been in a good mood in a hospital was when London was born."

"I'm with you," I said. "That's it in my book, as well."

She pulled at her jacket, pinching it closed around her neck. "So roll me outside, would you? Let's get out of here."

I did as she asked, feeling a brisk wind nip at my cheeks as soon as we exited the building. The few trees in the parking lot were barren of leaves and the sky was an iron gray.

When Marge spoke again, her voice was so soft I almost missed it. "I'm afraid, Russ," she whispered.

"I know," I said. "I am, too."

"It's not fair. I never smoked, I hardly ever drank, I ate right. I exercised." For a moment, she looked like a child again.

I squatted down so I could be at eye level. "You're right. It's not fair."

She met my gaze, then, and barked out a resigned laugh. "This is all Mom's fault, you know," she said. "Her and the family genes. Not that I'd ever say that to her. And not that really I blame her. Because I don't."

I'd had the identical thought, but hadn't spoken the words aloud. I knew that my mom was tormented by the same idea, and it was one of the reasons she'd barely spoken while at the hospital. I reached over and took Marge's hand.

"I feel like crap," Marge said. "I've already decided that I hate chemotherapy. I've thrown up four times this morning and now, I don't feel like I have enough strength to get to the bathroom on my own."

"I'll help you," I said. "I promise."

"No," she said, "you won't."

"What are you talking about? Of course I will."

I'd never seen Marge look so sad—Marge, who shrugged off even the biggest losses with pragmatic insouciance. "I know that's what you think you should do. And I know that you'll want to." She gripped my hand. "But I have Liz. And you have London, and your business, and Emily."

"I could care less about work right now. Emily will understand. And London is in school most of the time."

Marge didn't answer right away. When she spoke, it was as if she were returning to a conversation I didn't know we were having. "Do you know what I admire about you? Among other things?" she said.

"I have no idea."

"I admire your strength. And your courage."

"I'm not strong," I protested. "And I'm not brave."

"But you are," she said. "When I look back at the past year, and all you've gone through, I'm not sure how you made it. I watched you become the father I always knew you could be. I saw you at your very lowest after Vivian left. And I watched you pull yourself back up. All while launching a business and the struggles that entailed. Not many people could have handled the past six months the way you did. I know for a fact that I couldn't have."

"Why are you telling me this?" I asked, uncomprehending.

"Because I'm not going to let you stop doing what you need to do, just because of me. That would break my heart."

"I'm going to be here for you," I said. "You can't talk me out of it."

"I'm not asking you to abandon me. I'm asking that you continue to live your life. I'm asking you to be strong and brave again. Because London's not the only one who's going to need you. Liz is going to need you. Mom and Dad, too. One of you has to be the rock. And while you might not believe it, I know in my heart that you've always been the strongest of us all."

CHAPTER 24

———— ❧ ————

December

When I think back on Marge as a teenager, two things come to mind: roller skating, and horror films. In the late eighties and early nineties, roller skating was giving way to Rollerblading; but Marge stayed true to the old-fashioned skates that she had owned as a child—I think she had a soft spot for the disco roller rinks of her early childhood. Weekends during her teenage years were spent almost entirely on skates, usually with her Walkman and headphones on . . . even, remarkably, after she got her driver's license. There were few things she loved more than roller skating— unless it was a good horror film.

Although Marge loved romantic comedies like I did, her favorite genre was horror, and she never missed seeing the latest horror movie in its first week of release. It didn't matter to her if the film had been panned by critics and the public alike; she would happily watch it alone if she couldn't find a fellow enthusiast, as devoted to the genre as a groupie to her favorite band. From Nightmare on Elm Street to Candyman to Amityville 4: The Evil Escapes, Marge was a true aficionado of horror, highbrow and low.

When I asked her why she loved horror movies so much, she merely shrugged and said that sometimes she liked to be scared.

I didn't get it, any more than I did the allure of rolling around with wheels on your feet. Why would someone want to be scared? Weren't there more than enough scary things in real life to keep us awake at night?

Now, though, I think I understand.

Marge liked those films precisely because they weren't real. Any fright she felt in the course of the film was quantifiable; it would begin, and

420

then it would end, and she would leave the theater, emotionally spent yet relieved that all was well in the world.

At the same time, she'd been able to confront—albeit temporarily—one of the hardwired emotions of life, the root of our universal instinct toward fight or flight. By willing herself to stay put despite her fear, I think Marge felt that she would emerge stronger and better equipped to face down whatever actual terrors life had in store for her.

In retrospect, I think that Marge might have been onto something.

Vivian had returned with London on Sunday evening. Before she left, she hugged me, a longer hug than I'd expected. In it, I could sense her concern, but strangely, her body no longer felt familiar to me.

London had enjoyed her visit, but this time she mentioned that she had missed both her fish and Mr. and Mrs. Sprinkles. As soon as she got home, we went up to her room, where she told me that she'd had Thanksgiving dinner in a mansion. I guessed that Vivian had introduced our daughter to Spannerman in reaction to seeing London hug Emily at the art studio. To Vivian's mind, no doubt, I'd violated the taboo first, which gave her the right to do so as well.

I suppose I should have cared more, but in that moment, I didn't. I was worn out, and I'd known that London would meet Spannerman sooner or later anyway. What did it matter if it was this weekend, or the next time she was in Atlanta?

What did anything matter anymore?

While London was occupied with the fish, I decided to clean the hamster cage, since I'd let it slide while London was gone. By then, I was accustomed to it, and it took no time at all. I ran the mess to the outdoor garbage can, washed up, then went back upstairs, where London was holding Mr. Sprinkles.

"Are you hungry, sweetie?" I asked.

"No," she said. "Mommy and me ate on the plane."

"Just making sure," I said. I took a seat on the bed, watching her, but mainly thinking about Marge. My sister wanted me to keep living my life, to act as though nothing had changed. But everything had changed and I felt hollowed out, as empty as a junked oil drum.

I wasn't sure I was capable of doing as Marge asked, and wasn't sure I even wanted to.

"Guess what?" London said, looking up.

"What, sweetheart?"

"For Christmas, I'm going to make Auntie Marge and Auntie Liz a vase, like I did for Mommy. But this time, I want to paint fishes on it."

"I'm sure they'll love that."

For a moment, London seemed to study me, her gaze unaccountably serious. "Are you okay, Daddy?"

"Yeah," I answered. "I'm okay."

"You seem sad."

I am, I thought. *It's all I can do not to fall to pieces.*

"I just missed you," I said.

She smiled and came toward me, still holding the hamster.

"Would you like to hold Mr. Sprinkles?"

"Sure," I said, as she gently placed him in my hand. The hamster was soft and light, but I could feel his tiny claws scramble for purchase as he shifted into place. His whiskers twitched and he began to sniff my hand.

"Guess what?" London asked again. I summoned an inquisitive look. "I can read now."

"Yeah?"

"I read *Two by Two* all by myself. I read it to Mommy."

I wondered if it wasn't so much reading, as reciting from memory—after all, we had read it a hundred times together. But again, what did it matter?

"Maybe you could show me later?"

"Okay," she agreed. She put her arms around me and squeezed. "I love you, Daddy."

I caught the scent of the baby shampoo she still used and felt another ache in my heart.

"I love you, too."

She squeezed harder before letting go. "Can I have Mr. Sprinkles back?"

Marge quit work on Monday. I know because I got a text from her saying, *I've decided to retire.*

I went by her house after I dropped London off at school. Work could wait. I didn't care what she wanted; what I wanted was to see my sister. Liz answered the door, and I could tell she'd recently been crying, though only a trace of redness in her eyes remained.

I found Marge propped on the couch with her legs tucked up, wrapped in a blanket. *Pretty Woman* was playing on the television. It brought back a flood of memories, and all at once, I saw Marge as a teenager again. Back when she had an entire life in front her, a life measured in decades, not months.

"Hey there," she said, hitting the pause button. "What are you doing here? Shouldn't you be at work?"

"I know the boss," I answered. "He says it's okay if I'm a little late today."

"Smart-ass."

"I learned from the best." Marge made room, and I plopped down on the couch next to her.

"Admit it: You got my text, and you came over because you're jealous that I've finally quit the rat race." She gave a defiant grin. "I figured it was time to live a little."

I struggled in vain for a snappy comeback, and in the silence, Marge poked my ribs with her feet. "Lighten up," she said. "No doom and gloom allowed in this house." She peeked over her shoulder. "Was Liz okay?" she finally whispered.

"I guess so," I answered. "We didn't really talk."

"You should," she said. "She's actually a very nice person."

"Are you done?" I asked with a halfhearted smile. "How are you feeling, anyway?"

"A lot better than yesterday," she answered. "Which reminds me—can I take London roller skating this weekend?"

"You want to take London roller skating?" My disbelief must have shown, because Marge bristled.

"Believe it or not, I refuse to let all of you keep me cooped up in the house, and I think London will enjoy it. I know I will."

Left unsaid was that it would likely be something that London

423

would remember forever, since it would be her first time. "When was the last time you even went roller skating?"

"What do you care? It's not like I've forgotten how to do it. If you recall, I used to be pretty good."

It's not that, I thought to myself. *I'm wondering whether you'll have the strength.* I looked away toward the screen, convinced that Marge was in denial. In the freeze-frame image on the television, Julia Roberts was in a bar, confronting her roommate about money. Though I hadn't seen the movie in years, I could still recall the film practically scene by scene. "Okay," I said. "But only if you hit play so we can watch the movie."

"You want to waste your morning watching *Pretty Woman*? Instead of earning money?"

"It's my life," I said.

"Well, just don't make it a habit, okay? You're welcome to come by after work, but not before. I'll probably start needing my beauty rest."

"Just hit the play button already."

She lifted her eyebrow slightly and pointed the remote. "I just started it a few minutes ago."

"I know."

"We used to watch this together."

"I know," I said again. "Just like I also know you've always had a crush on Julia Roberts."

She laughed as the movie started up again, and for the next couple of hours, my sister and I watched the movie, calling out lines and sharing a running commentary, just like when we were kids.

After the movie, Marge went to the bedroom to take a nap while Liz and I drank coffee in the kitchen.

"I don't know what I'm going to do," Liz admitted, with the expression of someone overtaken by events she can hardly comprehend. "In Costa Rica, she seemed fine. She barely coughed and it was hard for me to keep up with her. I don't understand how she could seem so healthy a month ago, and now..." She shook her head in bewilderment. "I don't know what I'm supposed to do. I canceled my appointments today and tomorrow, but Marge basically forbade me from taking a leave of absence. She wants me to continue working at least a few days a week, insisting that your mom can fill in as needed. That we should work out a schedule, or whatever." When she raised her eyes, they were full of pain. "It's like she doesn't want me around."

"It's not that," I said, covering her hand with my own. "She loves you. You know that."

"Then why is she essentially telling me to stay away? Why can't she understand that I just want to be with her as much as possible, for as long as possible?"

She squeezed my hand in return as she stared out the window, unseeing.

"She still wants to go to New York next week," she finally added.

"You're not seriously thinking of going, are you?" Roller skating was one thing, but a sightseeing trip to one of the busiest cities in the world?

"I don't know what to do. She asked the doctor about it last night, and he said that if she was feeling up to it, there was no reason for her not to go since it's between chemo sessions. But how can I go and not think to myself, *This will be the last time Marge sees this,* or, *This will be Marge's only chance to do that that?*"

She was looking to me for an answer, but I knew there wasn't anything I could say.

Most of her questions, after all, were the same as my own, and I had no answers, either.

On Tuesday morning, the first day of December, I got a text from Marge, asking London and me to dinner that night. It was a subtle way of telling me not to swing by the house before that.

The thought depressed me, and after dropping London off at school, I arranged to meet Emily for coffee. In jeans and a thick turtleneck sweater, she looked as fresh-faced and youthful as a college student.

"You look tired," she observed. "Are you holding up okay?"

"I'm surviving," I answered, pushing a weary hand through my hair. "I'm sorry for not calling the last couple of days."

She raised her hands immediately. "Don't be. I can't imagine what you're going through. I've been worried about you."

For whatever reason, her words were a comfort. "Thanks, Em," I said. "That means a lot to me."

"Do you want to tell me what's going on?" she said, touching my arm.

For the next hour I rambled on, my cup of coffee gradually cooling to room temperature. Listening to myself, I realized that since Emily had come back into my life, I'd been careening from one emotional catastrophe to the next. Even as she held me later, I found myself marveling that she was still willing to put up with me.

For dinner that night, Liz went out of her way to cook something she knew London would enjoy—Shake'N Bake chicken, seasoned potatoes, and a fruit salad.

My mom was just leaving as we arrived, and I walked her out to her car. Before she got in, she paused.

"Marge is refusing to let me give up any of my clubs," my mom said. "In fact, she insisted that I stick to the very same schedule, but Russ…" She frowned in concern. "She doesn't how bad it's going to get. She's going to need help. It's like she's in denial."

I nodded, signaling that I'd been thinking the same thing.

"Do you know what she said to me just now? She wants Dad to come by to fix a few of the railings on the porch because they've got some dry rot. And some of the windows are sticking. And there's a leaking sink in the bathroom. She was so insistent about getting these things fixed. As if that even matters right now." She gave me a baffled look. "Why would she be making such a fuss about a few porch railings? Or the windows?"

Though I didn't respond, it finally dawned on me, what Marge was doing. I suddenly knew why she wanted me to only come by in the evenings; why she was having Liz and my mom split time with her. I knew why she wanted my dad to come over and make repairs on the house, and why she was insisting on taking London roller skating.

Marge, more than anyone, knew that each of us not only wanted private time with her, but were going to need it, before the end.

With the side effects of the initial chemotherapy treatment diminishing over the course of the week, Marge grew steadily stronger. And all of us wanted to believe her treatment was working, because we so desperately craved even a few more months with her.

I know now that only Marge understood on some intuitive level what was really going on inside her body. She bowed to treatment in the first place simply because it was what all of us wanted her to do. In hindsight, I realize that she understood, even as she'd said yes, that it wouldn't slow the progress of the disease at all.

To this day, I still wonder how she knew.

Liz and my mom organized a schedule, such that one of them would always be at the house during the day, once Marge and Liz returned from New York.

The Friday following my dinner at Marge's, my dad took a morning off work and showed up at Marge's with his tool chest and a pile of precut railings in his trunk. He began the slow process of repair and took a break at lunch; Marge and my dad had sandwiches and sweet tea on the back porch, admiring my dad's handiwork to that point and discussing the Braves' prospects for the following year's season.

On Saturday, Marge arrived at my house after art class—the very same art class where unbeknownst to my sister, London had fashioned her Christmas gift—to take London roller skating. Liz and I tagged along with them, watching from the gallery as Marge helped London inch around the rink. London, like most kids, kept trying to walk in the skates rather than glide, and it took a good half an hour before London began to master the motion. Had it not been for Marge holding both of London's hands—Marge was skating backward—my little girl would have wiped out at least twenty times.

However, by the end of the session they were able to skate side by side, albeit slowly, and London was visibly proud as she finally untied the laces with Liz's help and turned in her skates. I took a seat next to Marge while she bent over and removed her own skates.

"Your arms and back are going to be sore tomorrow," I predicted. To my eyes, she looked tired, but I couldn't tell whether it was because she was sick, or because catching London over and over before she fell was understandably exhausting.

"I'll be fine," she said. "London's not very heavy. But she *is* a chatty little thing. She talked and talked the whole time. She even grilled me on what my favorite color of fish was. I had no idea what to tell her."

I smiled. "New York will probably seem restful by comparison. You're leaving tomorrow?"

"Yeah—I can't wait," she said, perking up. "I've told Liz that our first stop is the Rockefeller Center Christmas tree. I want to get in the spirit of the holidays."

"Text me some pictures," I said.

"I will," she promised. "By the way, I know what I want for Christmas," she said pointedly. "From you."

"Do tell."

"I'll tell you when I get back. But here's a little hint: I want to go somewhere with you."

"Like a trip, you mean?"

"No," she said. "Not a trip."

"Then where?"

"If I told you, you wouldn't be surprised."

"If you don't tell me, then how can I do it?"

"How about you let me figure that part out, okay?"

With her skates off and her shoes back on, I saw her cast a last, wistful look toward the rink. It was getting crowded now, filling with children, groups of raucous teenagers, and a few nostalgic adults. By Marge's expression, I knew she was thinking to herself that she was never going to have the chance to skate again.

Today, I realized, hadn't simply been about teaching London to roller skate, or making a memory that London might hold on to forever; Marge had begun the process of saying goodbye to the things she loved, too.

Marge and Liz were gone for six days. While they were away, I worked long hours, wanting to get as much done on the new ad campaigns as possible, but mostly trying to keep myself from dwelling on my sister. As promised, she'd texted me photos of the Rockefeller Christmas tree: one of her and Liz together, and another shot of her by herself.

I had the pictures Photoshopped, printed, and then framed, with the intention of giving one set to Marge and Liz as a Christmas gift, and keeping another set for myself.

Meanwhile, I was contacted by two more law firms, including a small firm in Atlanta that had stumbled across my recent work on YouTube. As I started to put together the requisite presentations, I found myself reviewing the past six months.

When I'd started my agency, it seemed as though all my worries were business- or money-related, and at the time, I'd found the stress overwhelming. Things, I'd thought, couldn't get much worse, yet I could distinctly remember Marge reassuring me that everything would turn out fine in the end.

She was right, of course.

On the other hand, she couldn't have been more wrong.

The holidays continued to approach.

"What are your plans for Christmas? With London?" Marge asked me. It was Sunday afternoon and she'd just woken from a nap, but still looked tired. We were on her couch, where she'd wrapped herself in a blanket, even though the house felt warm to me. She and Liz had returned from New York the day before, and I wanted to see her before London returned from Atlanta. "Have you and Vivian discussed that yet? Christmas is only two weeks away, you know."

As I stared at my sister, it seemed to me that she'd lost even more weight since I'd seen her at the skating rink. Her eyes had a sunken look about them, and her voice sounded slightly higher and thinner, somehow.

"Not yet," I said. "But again, it's falling on one of her weekends."

"Russ, I know I've said it before, but it's not fair for you not to have any holidays with London."

No, it wasn't. But there wasn't much I could do about it, so I attempted to change the subject.

"How was New York?"

"It was amazing," Marge sighed. "But the crowds...wow. There were lines down the block just to get into some of the stores. The shows were fantastic, and we had some truly unforgettable meals." She mentioned some of the musicals they'd seen and restaurants where they'd eaten.

"It was worth it, then?"

"For sure," she said. "I had the hotel arrange a couple of romantic evenings while we were there, too. Champagne, chocolate-covered strawberries, rose petals trailing to the bed. I'd also brought along some new lingerie to show off my newly svelte figure." She waggled her eyebrows. "I think I blew Liz's socks off."

"Why didn't you want her wearing socks?"

"Really? That's your thought process?"

"When my sister starts talking about her love life, I choose to retreat into naïveté," I explained. "It's not like I share details about my love life."

"You don't have a love life with Emily yet. And if you ask me, it's about time you did something about that."

"We're in a good place right now," I insisted. "We talk every night on the phone, see each other for coffee. And we went out on Friday night."

"What did you do?"

"Dinner. And karaoke."

"You did karaoke?" That caught Marge by surprise.

"She did. Then again, it was her idea. She's pretty good, too."

Marge smiled as she burrowed deeper into the couch. "That sounds like fun," she said. "Not really sexy or romantic, but fun. Any bites on your house yet?"

"There have been a few nibbles here and there, but nothing official yet. My Realtor says that December is always slow. She wants to do an open house in January."

"Let me know when. Liz and I will come by as ringers, and talk up the place in front of potential buyers."

"You have better things to do than go to an open house."

"Probably," she conceded. "Then again, you always seem to end up needing my help in one way or another. I've had to take care of you my whole life." She glanced in the direction of the kitchen, where Liz was preparing lunch. "I'm supposed to have more chemo this week. Next Friday, I think. I'm not looking forward to that at all." She sighed, a flicker of apprehension crossing her face. She turned to me. "With that in mind, we should probably do our thing on Thursday."

"What thing?"

"Our trip, remember?" she said. "My Christmas present?"

"You do realize that I still have no idea what you're talking about."

"That's okay. I'll pick you up at seven. Liz can get London ready for bed, if that's all right with you."

"Of course," I said. She stifled a yawn and I knew it was time for me to go. "I guess I should take off. I've got a ton of work I want to get done before London gets home."

"Okay," she said. "I'm looking forward to Thursday night. Make sure you dress warmly."

"I will," I promised. I rose from the couch, hesitated, then leaned back over to kiss my sister on the cheek. Her eyes were closed. "See you later."

She nodded without answering, and by the sound of her breathing, I knew she had fallen asleep again, even before I'd reached the front door.

Vivian delivered London around 7:00 p.m. that evening. While the limousine idled out front and London was in the bath, we spoke briefly in the kitchen.

"About Christmas," she said, cutting to the chase. "I think it would be best if we spend it here. For London, I mean. It'll be her last Christmas in this house. I can just stay in the guest room, if that's all right with you." She reached for her purse and pulled out a slip of paper. "I've already bought some things, but it might be easier if you picked up some of this other stuff, so I don't have to haul everything back here. I made a list. Just save the receipts and we can split it all up at the end."

"Whatever's easiest," I agreed, thinking back to what Marge had said about the holidays, knowing she'd be pleased. "I saw Marge today," I said, leaning against the counter.

"How's she doing?"

"She's already beginning to sleep a lot."

Vivian nodded, lowering her gaze. "It's just awful," she said. "I know you think Marge and I didn't get along that well, but I always liked her. And I know she doesn't deserve this. I want you to know that. She's always been a great sister."

"She still is," I said, but even as the words came out, I wondered how much longer I'd be able to say them.

After school on Wednesday, Emily and I planned to take the kids out to a Christmas tree farm, where you could choose and have your own tree cut down. Much of the place was decorated like Santa's village, and kids could meet Santa before visiting his workshop, where hot chocolate and cookies were served. Even better, the farm would deliver and set up the tree in its stand, something I needed since I suspected that my Prius would otherwise be crushed beneath the weight of the tree.

When I mentioned the plan to Marge, she insisted that she and Liz meet us there.

It was nine days until Christmas.

In the gravel parking lot, Marge emerged from the car. When I hugged her, I could feel the sharp ridges of her ribcage, the cancer slowly eating away at her from within. She seemed to have more energy, however, than she had just after she returned from New York.

"And this, I take it, is Bodhi," Marge said, shaking his hand with touching formality. "You're so tall for your age," she remarked, before proceeding to ask about his favorite activities and what he wanted for Christmas. When the kids became visibly antsy, we let them run off toward the farm, where they were quickly lost between evergreen triangles.

Emily and I trailed after them, strolling with Marge and Liz.

"How is your holiday season shaping up, Em?" Marge asked. "Are you going anywhere?"

"No," she said. "We'll just do the family thing like we usually do. See my sister and my parents. Ever since London learned to ride a bike, Bodhi's been begging for one, so I guess I have to get him one—even if I'm not so confident about my ability to teach him to ride."

"You'll help her out, won't you, Russ?" Marge said, elbowing me.

I grimaced. "Marge has always been good at volunteering me for things."

"I seem to recall that," she laughed. "Russ said you had a good time in New York?"

The two of them fell behind a bit, engrossed in their conversation. I looped my arm through Liz's, and followed the path the kids had taken.

"How's the schedule working out with Mom?" I asked.

"It's working, I guess. I cut back to three days a week at work, so your mom is going to come on the other two weekdays."

"Marge seems to be doing well today."

"She was a little fatigued this morning, but she perked up on the ride over. I think doing things like this makes her feel like there's nothing wrong with her, if only for a little while. She was the same way when we were in New York."

"I'm glad she wanted to come. I just don't want her to get run down."

"I've said the same thing to her," Liz said. "And do you know what her response was?"

"I can't imagine."

"She told me not to worry so much, because she 'still has something important to do.'"

"What does that mean?"

Liz shook her head. "Your guess is as good as mine."

As we stopped and waited for Emily and Marge to catch up, I pondered my sister's cryptic words. She had always been one for surprises, and I wondered what last mysteries she had up her sleeve.

The next evening, Marge and Liz arrived at my house at seven on the dot. As soon as Liz walked through the door, London took her hand and led her up to the bedroom to show her the aquarium.

Marge was bundled in a scarf and hat, despite the relatively mild temperatures. She also wore gloves and the oversize down jacket I'd brought to the hospital.

It seemed impossible that less than three weeks had passed since she'd been rushed to the hospital.

"Are you ready?" she said impatiently, clearly ready to leave.

I grabbed my jacket and dug out a pair of gloves and a hat, even though I couldn't imagine needing them. "Where are we going?"

"You'll see," she said. "Come on. Before I chicken out."

I was still mystified, but as we began to turn down roads I recognized, I suddenly understood what she had in mind.

"You're not serious," I said as she pulled up to the gates and shut off the engine.

"I am," she said firmly. "And this is your Christmas gift to me."

As I looked up, the water tower loomed—impossibly, immeasurably tall.

"It's illegal to climb the water tower," I said.

"It's always been illegal. That never stopped us before."

"We were kids," I countered.

"And now we're not," she said. "You ready? Get your hat and gloves. It'll probably be windy up top."

"Marge..."

She stared at me. "I can make the climb," she said in a voice that left no room for dissent. "After another round of chemo, maybe I won't be able to. But right now, I still can, and I want you to come with me."

She didn't wait for me to answer. Getting out of the car, she strode toward the steel maintenance ladder, leaving me paralyzed with indecision. By the time I scrambled after her, she was already six feet in the air. Which meant, of course, that I had no choice but to start climbing. If she got tired, if she became weak or dizzy, I had to be there to catch her. In the end, it was fear for her that spurred me to follow.

Marge hadn't been lying. Though she had to take a break every twenty feet or so, she would inevitably start up again, moving relentlessly higher. Below me, I could see rooftops, and I caught the scent of chimney smoke. I was grateful for my gloves, as the metal rungs were cold enough to make my hands stiffen up.

When we finally reached the top, Marge inched her way over to the spot where I'd found her on that terrible night back when she'd been in college. Just like then, she let her feet dangle over the narrow walkway, and I quickly moved to her side. I put my arm around her again, in case she got dizzy.

"You must be feeling the cold," I said.

"Speak for yourself," she retorted. "I put on long johns before I came."

"Fine," I said. "Then slide your butt closer to me so I can get warm, too."

She did, and for a while we took in a bird's-eye view of the neighborhood. It was too cold for the nighttime sound of crickets or frogs; instead, I caught the faintest murmuring of wind chimes and the sound of the breeze as it rustled the branches of trees. That, and the sound of Marge wheezing, low and wet. I wondered how much pain she was in. The cancer, after all, always brings pain.

"I remember when you found me up here, drunk as a skunk," she said. "Well, not all of it—I actually don't remember much at all about that night, other than that moment, when you suddenly appeared."

"It was a rough night," I said.

"I sometimes wonder what would have happened had you not shown up. I wonder if I really would have jumped, or maybe fallen. I was so heartbroken about Tracey at the time, but I look back now, and can't help but think it was a good thing. Because in the end, I found Liz. And what Liz and I have is nothing like what I had with Tracey. Ever. She and I just work, you know?"

"Yeah, I know. You guys have something that everyone wants."

"I'm worried about her," Marge admitted. "She's so good at helping other people get through their problems, but I think she gives so much at work, she doesn't have much left for herself. And it scares me. Because I want her to be okay. I want her to be happy." She stared out into the distance, almost as if trying to see into the future. "I want her to one day find somebody new, someone who loves her as much I do. Someone she can grow old with."

I swallowed, forcing the tightness from my throat. "I know."

"When we were in New York, she swore she has no interest in ever finding someone else. And I actually got really mad at her. We had an argument, and afterward I felt so bad about it. We both did, but..."

"There's a lot going on, Marge," I said, my voice soft. "She understands. And she'll be okay." If Marge heard me, she gave no sign.

"Do you know what else scares me?"

"What's that?"

"That she's going to lose contact with London. She loves that little girl so much...London is a big part of the reason we wanted to have kids of our own. And now—"

"Liz is always going to be part of the family," I cut in. "I'll make sure that Liz plays a big part in London's life."

"What if London moves to Atlanta?" Marge pressed.

"She'll still see Liz regularly," I assured her.

"But you're only going to have her on the occasional holiday and every other weekend, right? Maybe a couple of weeks in the summer?"

I hesitated. "I honestly don't know what's going to happen with London," I said. Vivian had been more generous, and less volatile, since learning about Marge. But then, she was the least predictable person I knew, and I was leery of making specific promises I couldn't keep.

She turned toward me. "You have to fight for her," Marge urged. "London should live with you."

"Vivian won't let that happen. And I doubt that the courts will, either."

"Then you have to figure something out. Because let me tell you something—girls need their fathers. Look at me and Dad. He might not have been the most expressive guy in the world, but I always knew at some really deep level that he was there for me. And look at what he did for me when I came out. We stopped going to church, for God's sake! He chose *me*—over God, over our community, over everyone. And if you're not around for London when she comes to her own crossroads in life, she's going to feel abandoned by you. You have to be there for her—every day, not just now and then." She fell silent for a moment, as if winded by her efforts. "Anyway, she's used to you being the primary parent now," she added. "And you're great at it."

"I'm trying, Marge," I said.

She grabbed my arm, her voice fierce. "You have to do more than that. You need to do whatever you can in order to remain in London's life. Not as a weekend or vacation dad, but as the parent who's always there to hold her when she cries, pick her up when she falls, help her with her homework. To support her when she can't see a way forward. She needs that from you."

I stared down at the empty streets below, washed by the halogen glow of streetlights.

"I know she does," I said quietly. "I just hope I don't fail."

On Sunday morning, the Christmas tree was delivered and London and I spent the first part of the day decorating it, stringing lights among the branches and conferring over the placement of every single ornament. When I called Marge and Liz later that afternoon to see if they wanted to come by for some eggnog, Liz answered the phone and said they wouldn't be able to make it.

"It's been a pretty bad day," Liz said. Marge had undergone her second round of chemo on Friday, the day after the trip to the water tower, and I hadn't seen her since. According to Liz, the nausea and pain were worse than the first time, and Marge had barely been able to leave her bed.

"Is there anything I can do to help?"

"No," she answered. "Your mom and dad have been here pretty much all day. They're still here." She lowered her voice. "Your dad— I think it really kills him to see Marge like this. He keeps finding new things to repair. It's hard for your mom, too, of course, but she's been through it so many times that at least she knows what to expect. He's trying so hard to be strong for Marge, but it's destroying him inside. He just loves her so much, his girl. They both do."

I found myself thinking about what Marge had said that night on the water tower, about being the kind of dad who is there for everything, always. Even, it seems, at the end.

"He's a great father, Liz," I said. "I hope I can be half the dad he is."

On Monday, London's last day of school before winter break, I finally got around to the Christmas list that Vivian had left me. Work had kept me busy most days, and in my binary focus on "clients" and "Marge," Vivian's list had slipped off my radar. Luckily, Emily still had some last-minute shopping to do, so the two of us drove from store to store late that morning. With Christmas only four days away, I was worried that some items would be sold out, but I was able to find everything on Vivian's list.

Halfway through our shopping, Emily and I took a break for lunch. There was a café at the mall and though the food smelled good, I had little appetite. On the scale that morning, I saw that I'd begun to lose weight again. I wasn't alone; Liz was losing weight as well, and I noted that she sometimes looked disheveled, as if she no longer cared about her appearance. Her hair, often tied back in a careless ponytail, was losing its luster. My mom and dad, too, were suffering. My dad seemed to have acquired a defeated hunch in the past few weeks, and my mom's face was more deeply lined with worry with every passing day.

But our suffering was nothing compared to Marge's. Walking was becoming painful for her, and often, she struggled to stay awake for more than an hour. When I visited, I sometimes sat with Marge in her darkened bedroom, listening as she seemed to struggle to draw breath, even as she slept. Occasionally she whimpered in her sleep, and I wondered if she were dreaming. If only, I thought, she could dream the kind of dreams that would make her smile.

Thoughts like these preoccupied me, even in Emily's company, no matter what the surroundings. When my lunch arrived, I stared at it blankly, picturing Marge's emaciated face. I took only a single bite before pushing the plate aside.

If Marge couldn't eat, I guess there was a part of me that felt like I didn't deserve to, either.

"You need to come by the house," Marge said without preamble, right after I answered her call. I'd just dropped Emily off a few minutes earlier.

"Why? Are you okay?"

"Do you really want me to answer that question?" she said, with a trace of her old sardonic humor. "But yes, I'm feeling better than I was, and I'd like you to come by."

"I have to pick up London from school in a little while. And drop off the gifts beforehand."

"Swing by here on the way and leave the gifts with us," she said. "London won't find them that way."

When I reached her house a few minutes later, I started unloading the bags from the trunk. When I looked up, my mom appeared in the front doorway. Even with her help, it took two trips to unload everything.

"I'm not sure where to put all this," I said, staring at the mountain of bags on the kitchen floor. Did London really need all this? I wondered.

"I'll put it all in one of the closets," my mom said. "Go on in. Marge is waiting for you."

I found Marge on the couch, wrapped in a blanket as usual, with the living room shades drawn. The lights from the Christmas tree cast a cheerful glow, but in the days since I'd seen her last, she seemed to have aged years. Her cheekbones stood out in sharp relief below the sunken pits of her eyes, and her arms looked ropy and flaccid. I tried to mask my dismay at her appearance as I took a seat beside her.

"I heard it was a rough few days," I said, clearing my throat.

"I've felt better, that's for sure. I'm on the mend now, but..." She cracked a smile, a ghost of her irrepressible self. "I'm glad you came by. I wanted to talk to you." Getting the words out seemed to be an effort. "Emily called a little while ago."

"Emily?"

"Yeah," she said. "You remember her, right? Gorgeous hair, has a five-year-old son, the woman you love? Anyway, she called me because she's worried about you. She says you're not eating."

"She *called* you?" I said, feeling my irritation rise. Now Marge was going to worry about *my* health?

"I *asked* her to keep an eye on you and let me know how you're doing," Marge said in a bossy voice I remembered from childhood. "Which is why I then asked you to come over." She scanned me with a critical eye. "You better eat a decent dinner tonight, or I'm going to get seriously angry with you."

"When did you discuss 'keeping an eye' on me with Emily?" I demanded.

"When we went to Santa's village for the trees."

"You have better things to worry about than me, Marge," I said, conscious of how sulky I sounded.

"That's where you're wrong," she said. "That's something that I won't let you take away from me."

Tuesday, December twenty-second, was London's last day of school before the winter break, and that was when I planned to wrap all the gifts. Before I'd left her house the previous day, Marge asked if she could help with the wrapping, since the gifts were over there anyhow.

When I arrived at the house with wrapping paper after dropping London off at school, my first thought was that Marge looked better than she had the day before. Simultaneously, I hated that I had begun to make those kinds of evaluations every time I saw her, only to see my hopes elevated or dashed depending on how she seemed to be doing.

Liz was home with her that day, and she exuded a forced good cheer as we brought the gifts to the kitchen and began to wrap. At Marge's request, she made us all cups of hot chocolate, thick and foamy, although I noticed that my sister drank little of hers.

Marge wrapped a couple of the smaller gifts before settling back in her chair, leaving the rest to Liz and me.

"I'm still not happy that you're calling Emily to check up on me," I groused.

Despite her condition, Marge was clearly enjoying my discomfort, as evidenced by the gleam in her eye. "That's why I didn't ask your permission. And if you're interested, we didn't just talk about that, by the way. We talked about a lot of things."

I wasn't sure I liked the sound of that. "What things?"

"That's between me and her," she said. "But for now, what I want to know is whether you ate last night. Full report, please."

"I made steaks for London and me," I sighed. "And mashed potatoes."

"Good," she said with satisfaction. "Now, have you spoken with Vivian about the plans for Christmas this year? Other than that she'll be coming to Charlotte?"

The tradition in my family had been to gather at my parents' on Christmas Eve. My mom would make an elaborate dinner and afterward, we'd allow London to open gifts from the relatives while *It's a Wonderful Life* played on television. On Christmas morning, at our house, Vivian and I would have London to ourselves.

"We haven't gotten into the specifics yet," I said. "She doesn't come in until tomorrow. We'll figure it out then."

"You probably need to get her something," Marge pointed out. "For London's sake, so she can see her mom opening some gifts. It doesn't have to be anything big."

"You're right," I said. "I didn't think of that."

"What did you get Emily for Christmas?"

"Nothing yet," I admitted.

"Any thoughts yet? You're cutting it a little close..."

"I don't know," I said, looking to Marge and Liz for inspiration. "A sweater, maybe? Or a nice jacket?"

"Those could be part of it, but she told me what she's getting you, so you'll have to do better than that."

"Like jewelry or something?"

"If you want, I'm sure she'd appreciate that, too. But I was thinking that you need to do something from the heart."

"Like what?"

"I think," she said, drawing the words out, "that you should write her a letter."

"What kind of letter?"

Marge shrugged. "You write for a living, Russ. Tell her how much she's meant to you these past months. How much you want her to remain in your life. Tell her..." Marge said, lighting up, "that you want her to take a chance on you again."

I squirmed. "She already knows how I feel about her. I tell her that all the time."

"Write her a letter anyway," Marge urged. "Trust me. You'll be glad you did."

I did as Marge suggested. With London in tow—piano lessons weren't until the New Year—I drove directly from school pickup to the mall, where I found some gifts for Vivian: her favorite perfume, a scarf, a new novel by a writer she liked. I also picked out an embroidered silk jacket for Emily, one that I was sure would complement her rich coloring and slightly Bohemian style, and a gold chain with an emerald pendant that would accent the color of her eyes. Later, after London had gone to sleep, I sat at the kitchen table and wrote Emily a letter. It took more than one draft to get it right; despite the wordsmithing I did for my job, writing from the heart was entirely different, and I found it difficult to strike that delicate balance between raw emotion and maudlin sentimentality.

In the end, I was happy with the letter, and grateful that Marge had made the suggestion. I sealed it in an envelope and was about to put the pad and pen back in the drawer when I suddenly realized that I wasn't yet done.

Working until long past midnight, I wrote Marge a letter as well.

Vivian got in a little past noon the following day, not long after I'd returned from dropping off the gifts at Emily's. With the tree already trimmed, London and I had spent the morning decorating the mantel and hanging the stockings. It was a little late in the season, but London didn't mind at all. She was proud to be old enough to help.

I let Vivian visit with London for a while before signaling my desire to speak with her. Retreating to the kitchen while London watched TV in the living room, I asked her what she wanted to do for Christmas Eve. At my question, she stared at me as though it were obvious.

"Well, aren't we going to your parents' place, like we always do? I know that it might feel a little strange considering what's going on, but it's Marge's last Christmas and I want London to spend time with her and the family, like she always has. That's why I came home in the first place."

Even though we weren't in love anymore, I thought to myself, there were still moments when I was reminded of some of the reasons I'd married Vivian in the first place.

Christmas Eve and Christmas Day unfolded much like they always had.

The atmosphere was a bit stilted on Christmas Eve at first, for obvious reasons. Everyone was polite to each other and there were kisses and hugs all around when Vivian, London, and I showed up at my parents'. But by the time I finished my first glass of wine, it was clear that everyone's sole aim that evening was to make the gathering enjoyable for London's sake—and Marge's.

Vivian appreciated the gifts I'd gotten her; for me, she'd bought some running gear and a Fitbit. Marge and Liz oohed and aahed over the vase that London made for them, especially marveling at the colors of the fish that London had painted. Tears shone in their eyes when they opened the framed photos that had been taken in New York, and my sister took the envelope containing the letter I'd written with a tender smile. London received a bunch of Barbie stuff from pretty much everyone, and after the gifts were opened, we put on the movie *It's a Wonderful Life* while London played with her new toys.

The only truly notable event of the evening took place after we'd finished opening the gifts. From the corners of my eyes, I watched as Marge and Vivian slipped from the living room, sequestering themselves in the den. The low hum of their voices was barely audible behind the partially closed door.

It was odd to see the two of them speaking so intimately, let alone in private, but I knew exactly what was happening.

Vivian, like all of us, had wanted the chance to say goodbye.

On Christmas Day, once London had opened the rest of her gifts, I left the house so Vivian could have some time alone with London. To that point, we'd been together almost continuously during the previous forty-eight hours, and if I needed a break from her, I was certain that Vivian felt the same way. Cordiality, let alone forced gaiety, in the midst of a divorce and custody dispute, wasn't easy for anyone to maintain.

I texted Emily, asking if I could drop by and received a quick response, urging me to do so. She had a gift for me, she said, and she wanted me to see it.

Even before I got out of my car, she was skipping off the porch toward me. Up close, she threw her arms around me, and we held each other in the pale sunlight of a cool December day.

"Thank you for the letter," she whispered, "it was absolutely beautiful."

I followed Emily inside, picking my way through a maelstrom of new toys and torn wrapping paper, at the center of which stood Bodhi's shiny new bicycle. She led the way toward the Christmas tree, and reaching behind it, pulled out a flat, rectangular package.

"I thought about giving this to you before Christmas, but with Vivian staying at the house, I thought it would be best to give it to you here."

I tugged at the wrapping paper and it came off easily. As soon as I saw what Emily had done, all I could do was stare, the memory coming back to me in a rush. Overwhelmed, I couldn't speak.

"I had it framed, but you can change it to something else," Emily said in a shy voice. "I wasn't sure where you might want to hang it."

"This is incredible," I finally said unable to tear my eyes from the image. Emily had painted the photo of London and me dancing outside the aquarium, but it seemed even more real, more alive than the photo somehow. It was by far the most meaningful gift I'd ever received, and I wrapped my arms around Emily, suddenly understanding why Marge had been so insistent that I write Emily a letter.

She'd known that Emily was giving me a gift from the heart, and Marge wanted to make sure I matched it with one of my own. Once again, Marge had been looking out for me.

The year rolled toward its inevitable conclusion. Vivian went back to Atlanta. I'd closed the office for the week, and spent most of my time with London. I visited with Marge and Liz every day—Marge continued to rebound, rallying our hopes—and saw Emily three times, though twice in the company of the kids. The lone exception was New Year's Eve, when I took her out for a night of dinner and dancing.

At the stroke of midnight, I almost kissed her. She almost kissed me too, and we both laughed about it.

"Soon," I said.

"Yes, soon," she answered.

And yet, as romantic as that moment was, I felt reality beginning to take hold.

In 2015, I thought I'd lost everything.

In 2016, I suspected I'd lose even more.

CHAPTER 25

For Auld Lang Syne

Marge's romantic plans for Liz in New York weren't without precedent. Around the five-year mark of their relationship, Marge had surprised Liz with an elaborate scavenger hunt on Valentine's Day.

When Marge initially revealed her plans to me, I'll admit I was shocked because it seemed so unlike the sister I knew. After all, she was an accountant, and while generalizations might be unfair, she always struck me as more of a smart-alecky pragmatist than a mushy paramour.

While Marge rarely showcased her romantic side, she could clearly hit it out of the ballpark when she chose to do so. Indeed, the scavenger hunt proved to be the work of a master planner. New York was child's play by comparison.

The centerpiece of the Valentine's Day scavenger hunt—which involved locations all over Charlotte—was a series of ten riddles. The riddles were set to verse and led to specific reveals. A sample:

Today, dear Liz, we'll have some fun,
To remind you that you're my only one,
So visit the spot where it's all about you,
On early mornings and late at night, too,
Then look to your left, my darling dear,
And your very first clue will there appear.

Marge had taped the first clue—a small key—next to the bathroom mirror, which led Liz to a post office box that she had to open with the *key. Inside the box was another riddle . . . and so it went. Some of the clues were tougher than others; one required Liz to finish a glass of champagne to find the next clue, which was glued to the bottom of the champagne flute. At the time, I was stunned by the breadth and inventiveness of Marge's scheme.*

Looking back, I'm no longer surprised by Marge's elaborate Valentine's Day plans, or her meticulous footwork. I no longer think of it as out of character. Because drawing up blueprints for other people's happiness was what she did best.

My sister, the accountant, always had a plan—especially for those she loved.

My memories of early 2016 are distilled into a series of vivid moments, set against the muted backdrop of my day-by-day existence.

The backdrop consisted of work, where I wrote, filmed, edited, and designed ad campaigns; London's care, before and after school; my daily run; and Emily, whose nightly phone conversations and occasional dates nourished and sustained me. Those routines made up the regular fabric of my days, and also served as temporary distractions from the peaks and abysses that marked that period of my life. With the passage of time, I'm sure I've forgotten more than I remember. Some things I willed myself to forget.

But other memories will remain with me forever.

About a week into the new year, Marge went in for further tests. While I didn't accompany her to the hospital, my parents and I joined Liz and Marge when it came time to hear the results.

We met the doctor in his office, across the street from the hospital. He faced us across a heavy wooden desk, a handful of family photos arranged next to a large stack of files. On the walls were shelves filled with books, and the usual assortment of framed diplomas, plaques, and citations. The only incongruous element was a large framed poster from the film *Patch Adams*. I only vaguely remembered the film—it starred Robin Williams as a caring, kind, and funny doctor—and I found myself wondering if Dr. Patel aspired to be a doctor with similar attributes.

Had there ever been anything humorous said in this room? Did any patients ever laugh when talking to their oncologist? Could any joke minimize the horror of what was happening?

To us, Marge appeared to be improving slightly—she'd had more energy since the holidays, and her pain didn't seem quite as acute. Even her breathing seemed less labored. All of that should have pointed to good news. I could see the hopefulness in my parents' expressions; I noted the confident way Liz was holding Marge's hand. We'd shared our secret hopes amongst ourselves during the previous week, trying to draw strength from each other.

Marge, however, didn't look hopeful. There was an air of resignation about her from the moment she took her seat, and I knew right then, with certainty, that Marge would be the only one who wouldn't shed a tear that afternoon. While the rest of us had remained stuck in various stages of grief—denial, anger, bargaining, depression—Marge alone had already moved on to acceptance.

Marge knew—even before the doctor said a single word—that the cancer hadn't slowed its progression. In truth, she'd known all along that it had spread even farther.

"Please don't ask me how I'm doing," Marge said. "Mom and Dad just left, and Mom kept asking me that over and over. And Dad keeps asking what else needs to be fixed. I wanted to say *me*, but didn't think they could handle the joke." We were sitting on Marge's sofa, as had become our custom, staring at the empty space where the Christmas tree had once stood. My dad had removed it a few days earlier, but the furniture hadn't been rearranged yet, leaving a barren space in the corner of the room.

"It's a hard day for them," I said. "They're doing their best."

"I know," Marge said. "And I love that Dad keeps coming around. We've talked more than we have in years, and not just about baseball." She let out a breath before suddenly wincing. A wave of pain—somewhere, everywhere—made her entire body tighten before it finally passed.

"Can I get you something?" I asked, feeling more helpless than ever.

"I just took a pill," she said. "I don't mind the painkillers, other than that they make me sleepy. They don't work as well as I want them to, of course. They blunt the pain a bit, but that's about it. Anyway..." She looked toward the kitchen, where Liz was at the table, coloring with London. Lowering her voice, she said, "I told Liz I'm not doing another round of chemo." Her expression was grim, but resolute. "She was pretty upset about it."

"She's just scared," I said. "But do you really think that's the right decision?"

"You heard the doctor," she countered. "It's not working. And on the downside, it makes me feel even worse. All I do is vomit and sleep, and my hair is starting to fall out. I'm losing whole days after the treatment, and I don't have that many days left."

"Don't say that," I pleaded.

"I'm sorry. I know you don't want to hear it. Nobody does." Marge squeezed her eyes shut, wincing again at another wave of pain that, to me, took far too long to pass. "I'm guessing London doesn't know I'm sick, am I right?"

I shook my head. "She doesn't even know that Vivian and I are getting divorced yet."

Marge opened one eye to peer at me. "It's probably time that you tell her, don't you think?"

I didn't answer, because I didn't even know where to start. There was too much to lay on a six-year-old: divorce and Marge dying and moving—maybe even as far away as Atlanta—leaving her father and her friends behind.

I didn't want London to deal with any of it. *I* didn't even want to deal with it. As I felt the tears building behind my eyes, Marge reached over and placed her hand on mine. "It's okay," she soothed.

"No, it's not okay. None of this is okay." I could hear my voice begin to crack. "What am I going to do about London? What am I going to do about you?"

She squeezed my hand. "I'll talk to London about me, okay? So don't worry about that. It's something I've been wanting to do. As for everything else, I've already told you what I think."

"What if I can't? What if I let you down?"

"You won't," she said.

"You can't know that."

"Yes, I can. I believe in you."

"Why?"

"Because," she said, "I know you better than anyone. Just like you know me."

The following Friday, in mid-January, Vivian flew into town to pick up London for the weekend. When I broached the idea that it was probably time to tell London about our impending divorce, she suggested that we do it when they got back. After all, she said, she didn't want to ruin London's weekend.

The next morning, my Realtor staged our first open house, and as promised, Marge and Liz were there, loudly talking up the house to each other in front of potential buyers. Afterward, my Realtor called to tell me that she'd detected some genuine interest in the property from one couple in particular, who were relocating with their children from Louisville.

"By the way, your sister missed her calling as an actress," the Realtor remarked.

On Sunday evening, shortly after their return from Atlanta, Vivian and I sat our daughter down at the kitchen table and gently broke the news.

We kept the discussion at a level appropriate for a six-year-old, emphasizing that both of us still loved her and that we would always be her parents. We told her that she had nothing to do with the fact that we could no longer stay married.

As she'd done the first time, Vivian led the discussion. Her demeanor was loving and I felt that she struck the right tone, but London burst into tears nonetheless. Vivian held her and kissed her as she cried.

"I don't want you to get divorced," London pleaded.

"I know it's hard, sweetheart, and we're so sorry."

"Why can't you just be happy with each other?" London said, still sobbing. Her naïve incomprehension triggered such a profound wave of guilt that I despised myself.

"Sometimes it just doesn't work," I tried to explain. The words sounded meaningless, even to me.

"Is that why the house is for sale?"

"I'm afraid so, baby girl."

"Where am I going to live?"

At her question, my eyes flashed toward Vivian, silently warning her not to say *Atlanta*. Her expression was defiant, but she held her tongue.

I put a hand on London's back. "We're still working on that. And I promise that no matter what happens, your mom and I will both be around to take care of you."

Eventually, London calmed down, though she was clearly still confused and shaken. Vivian went upstairs with her and started getting her ready for bed. When she came back down, I intercepted her at the door.

"How is she?" I asked.

"She's upset," Vivian answered, "but according to my counselor, that's normal. In the long run, she'll be fine as long as you don't make the divorce more acrimonious than it has to be. That's when kids suffer the most in these situations, and you don't want to do that to her."

I bit back a retort—I wasn't the one making this acrimonious, after all—knowing it was pointless.

Vivian gathered her things—the limo and the jet were waiting, after all—but she paused in the doorway. "I know it's a bad time, with Marge and everything," she said, "but we need to get our agreement squared away sooner rather than later. You just need to sign it, so we can be done with all this." And then she was gone.

Swallowing my rage, I started up the steps so I could finish tucking London in.

In bed, her eyes were red and swollen, and she barely looked at me.

Later that night, for the first time in years, she wet the bed.

In the days following our discussion with London, she was noticeably subdued and spent even more time in her bedroom than usual. The bed-wetting continued; not every night, but two more times, and she no longer wanted to read *Two by Two* before going to sleep. While she let me kiss her goodnight, she no longer reached up to put her arms around my neck for a hug.

On Marge's recommendation, I spoke to her teacher at school about what was going on between Vivian and me. The teacher assured me she hadn't noticed anything amiss, other than a recent incident at the drinking fountain. London had somehow spilled water on her blouse one morning, and immediately burst into tears. She was inconsolable, and resisted both the teacher's and her classmates' attempts to comfort her.

My daughter, in other words, was struggling. After her piano lesson on Thursday, I spontaneously suggested we go out for ice cream, but her reaction was tepid. I finally persuaded her to go, but she barely touched her ice cream on the drive home, oblivious to the mess the melting cone made in the car. Later that evening, as she was playing with her Barbies, I overheard her talking to herself as she leaned young Barbie toward Ken.

"I don't want to live with Mommy in Atlanta," Barbie said to Ken. *"I want to live here with Daddy. Daddy is fun and we go on date nights and he lets me cook, too. And I want to play with Bodhi every day and see Nana and Papa and Auntie Marge and Auntie Liz."*

That night, I couldn't sleep, replaying the scene that London had enacted over and over in my head. Marge was right, I thought. Emboldened, I called Taglieri the following morning, making it clear to him that I was willing to do whatever it took to ensure that London lived with me.

That same day, my Realtor called to let me know that I'd received an offer on the house.

"Well, you've certainly stirred up a hornet's nest," Taglieri said. It was Wednesday, five days since I'd conveyed my instructions to Taglieri,

452

and he had called me into his office to discuss the response. I fidgeted in my seat as he went on. "I got a letter from Vivian's attorney yesterday."

"And?"

"If you choose to fight her on the custody issue, it's going to get very ugly. Basically, the attorney warned me that they're going to aggressively pursue a claim that you're an unfit father."

I blanched. "What does that mean?"

"For starters, they want to bring in a psychologist to evaluate London, and do an assessment of her needs and preferences. I mentioned that as a possibility to you early on, if you remember. London's so young, I'm generally of the opinion that it's of limited use, but depending on the psychologist they use, they're hoping to submit a report that bolsters their claims. Some of the allegations are frivolous. They're claiming that you don't feed London a healthy diet—that you sometimes feed her sugary junk food for dinner, for instance, or that your failure to get her to dance class resulted in her getting kicked out. But there are other claims that the psychologist might explore on a deeper level."

"Like what?" I felt slightly nauseous as Taglieri went through the possibilities.

"That you're forcing London into a relationship with your new girlfriend, Emily, before she's ready."

"Emily's son Bodhi is London's best friend!"

"I hear you. And hopefully, the psychologist will confirm that. But you never know until they file their report with the court." He paused. "There are also more serious allegations in the letter—that you purposely endangered London by pressuring her to ride her bike down a hill, knowing she was still inexperienced and couldn't handle the challenge. Also that you failed to contact Vivian right away and that you purposely minimized London's injuries when talking to Vivian to cover up for your ineptitude."

"That's...that's not the way it happened!" I stammered, feeling myself flush. "Vivian knows it was an accident. She knows I'd never purposely endanger my daughter!"

Taglieri held up his hand. "I'm just letting you know the substance of the letter. But there's one more thing, and you're going to have to stay calm, all right?"

I squeezed my hands into fists, feeling the veins at my temples throb.

"In the letter," Taglieri went on, "the lawyer mentions that you have 'date nights' with your daughter. That she gets dressed up in an adult-like fashion and that the two of you go out to romantic destinations."

"So?"

"Russ…" Taglieri gave me a pained look. "It's disgusting, but the lawyer is suggesting that your relationship with London might be unhealthy, if not outright inappropriate…"

It took me a second to grasp the implication. When it hit, it took my breath away.

Oh, God… Vivian wouldn't do this… not in a million years would she do something like this…

I actually felt light-headed, black spots swimming at the edge of my vision. I was mortified, repulsed, and furious—but even those terms weren't strong enough to describe the way I was feeling.

"It was only innuendo," Taglieri cautioned, "but the fact that it was mentioned in the letter at all troubles me. At the very least, it signals that they're prepared to paint a very negative, if not downright sickening, picture of you."

I barely processed Taglieri's words. Vivian wouldn't do this… How could she even *hint* at something like this…?

"I'm going to get on the phone with the attorney later, because we can't just ignore these kinds of implied threats. It's an attempt to intimidate you, and it's also incredibly unprofessional. At the same time, it gives us a sense of just how far Vivian might go to get custody. And if it goes to court, I want to emphasize that you never know what a judge is going to decide."

"What do I do? I know London wants to live with me…"

"Like I said, let me talk to the attorney. But what would be best, as I told you early on, is for you and Vivian to work it out. Because, as your attorney, I can't say I feel optimistic about your chances when it comes to winning this thing."

For the rest of the day, I staggered around as if I'd received a massive body blow.

I didn't go to work. I didn't go home. I didn't visit Marge or Liz, or drop by my parents' place.

In my speechless fury, in my horror, I didn't want to talk to anyone. Instead, I texted Emily and asked if she could pick London up from school and watch her until I got back into town. She asked me where I was and what was wrong, but I couldn't answer. *I need a few hours alone,* I texted back. *Thank you.*

Then, getting into my car, I started to drive.

Three and a half hours later, I was in Wrightsville Beach, where I parked my car.

The sky was overcast and the wind was bitter. I walked the beach longer than it took me to make the drive, and as I walked, my mind circled from London to Marge to Vivian before starting anew. With it came uncertainty and fear and relentless waves of emotion. I alternated between rage and confusion, heartbreak and terror, and by the time I returned to the car, my cheeks were wind-burned and my soul was numb. I hadn't eaten all day, yet I wasn't hungry in the slightest.

I made the drive back to Charlotte and picked up London long after the sky had turned black. It was past London's bedtime, but thankfully, Emily had fed her. I couldn't summon the energy to speak to Emily about what had happened just yet; there was so much I still didn't know how to put into words.

It was Marge to whom I eventually turned, mainly because she left me no other choice.

It was the last Friday in January, and I had agreed to stay with Marge while my mom ran to the pharmacy to refill one of Marge's prescriptions. By this time, the cancer had progressed to the point where no one was comfortable leaving Marge alone, even for a little while. The living room was illuminated by a single table lamp, and the shades had been drawn at Marge's request. She said bright light made her eyes ache, but I knew the truth: She didn't want us to see her clearly, for even a single glance was enough to reveal how sick she really was. So much of Marge's hair had fallen out that she'd taken to wearing an Atlanta Braves baseball cap whenever she was awake. Even though she was wrapped in a blanket, her continued weight loss was evident in her bony hands and painfully skinny neck, in which her Adam's apple protruded, knoblike. Her breathing sounded wet and thick, and she had long bouts of coughing and gagging that sent my mom and Liz into a panic. They would pound her back in an effort to dislodge mucus and phlegm, which often came out bloody. She slept more than sixteen hours a day, and her appearance at the open house two weeks earlier was the last time she'd left the house.

She could no longer walk more than a few steps on her own. The cancer in her brain had affected the right side of her body, as if she'd had a stroke. Her right arm and leg were weak, and her eye had begun to droop. She could only offer half smiles.

And yet, as I sat beside her, I found her as beautiful as ever.

"Emily came by yesterday," she said, the words emerging slowly, and with effort. "I like her so much, Russ. And she truly cares about you. You need to call her," she said with a pointed look. "You have to talk to her, let her know what's going on with you. She's worried about you."

"Why did she come by?"

"Because I asked to see her. I wanted to spend some time with the woman my brother loves. The new-and-improved model, I mean." She forced a weak smile. "That's what I called her. I think she was pleased."

I smiled. Despite her decline, Marge was still Marge.

She gathered her strength for a moment, and went on. "I think it's time that I talk to London, too."

"When?"

"Can you bring her by this weekend?"

"She won't be here. She'll be in Atlanta with Vivian."

"Then how about after school today?"

My sister, in her own way, was telling me that time was running out.

I was suddenly unable to swallow. "All right," I whispered.

"I want to see Vivian, too. Can you set that up?"

My stomach tightened at the name and I looked away. Still furious and mortified, I could barely tolerate the thought of Vivian, let alone the idea of asking her to visit my dying sister. Marge saw my expression but pressed on.

"I need you to do this for me," she said. "Please."

"I'll text her," I said, "but I don't know whether she'll come. She's usually on a tight schedule."

"See what she says," Marge pressed. She blinked, and I noticed that even her lids were slowing down. "Tell her it's important to me."

I reached for my phone and texted Vivian; she responded almost instantly. *Of course*, the text said. *Tell Marge I'll be there around five.*

I let Marge know and watched as she closed her eyes. I thought she was about to fall asleep before she opened them again.

"Have you accepted the offer on your house yet?"

I shook my head. "We're still going back and forth on the price a bit."

"That's taking a long time."

"The potential buyers have been traveling. According to my Realtor, we're close, though. She's thinking we'll sign next week."

"That's good, right? So you'll be able to pay off Vivian?"

Again, the sound of her name made me recoil. "I guess."

Marge stared at me. "Do you want to tell me what happened? Emily said that you were gone all day Wednesday but wouldn't talk to her about it."

Rising from the couch, I peeked out the window, to make sure my mom wasn't pulling into the drive. I didn't want her to hear what was going on; the last thing she needed was even more stress in her life. Taking a seat again, I brought my hands together and told her about the meeting with Taglieri and the letter that Vivian's attorney had sent.

"Well," Marge said when I finished. "This isn't completely unexpected. She's been very clear all along that she intends to bring London to Atlanta."

"But . . . the *threat*. She's playing so . . . *dirty*."

"What does your attorney say?"

"That he doesn't like my chances. And that he still thinks Vivian and I should work something out between us."

Marge was silent for a moment, but her gaze was almost feverish in its intensity. "First, you have to know what you really want."

I frowned. "Why do you keep saying that? We've talked about this already. I've told you what I want."

"Then do what you have to do."

"You mean go to court? Play dirty, like she is?"

She shook her head. "I don't think that would be good for London. And London is your priority."

"Then what are you suggesting?"

"I think you know," she said, closing her eyes again.

And as I studied her weary face, it finally dawned on me that I actually did.

On the way back from Marge's, I called Emily, asking if we could meet for lunch. She agreed, and we arranged to meet at a bistro not far from her home.

"First, I want to apologize for not telling you what was going on," I said as soon as we sat down. "To be honest, I didn't even know how to begin."

"It's okay, Russ," she said. "Sometimes we all need to process things on our own first. Don't ever feel pressured by me—I'm here whenever you feel ready to talk. Or even if you don't."

"No, I'm ready now," I said, touching her hand. Taking a deep breath, I told her everything—about London's distress, my instructions to Taglieri, and Vivian's response. As I spoke, she brought her hands to her mouth.

"I can't imagine how you must have been feeling," she said when I finished. "I would have been . . . shell-shocked. And completely, utterly furious."

"I was. I still am," I admitted. "For the first time, I feel like I actually hate her."

"With good reason," she said. "Maybe it's not such a bad idea to let

458

the psychologist talk to London. You'll probably be able to put these crazy allegations to rest right off the bat."

"There's still the issue of the bicycle accident."

"Kids have accidents, Russ. That's why the law requires them to wear bicycle helmets. Judges know that."

"I don't want this custody battle to play out in court. I don't even want London to have to meet with a psychologist about this. If she needs counseling to help her deal with the divorce, that's different. But I'm not going to put London in the position of having to choose between her mom and dad." I shook my head. "I'm trying to stay focused on what's best for London. And I know she needs me in her life as a consistent, everyday presence—not in an occasional, ad hoc way. So I'm going to do what I have to do."

I knew I was being vague, but there were some things I just couldn't tell Emily.

She nodded before sliding her water glass toward her. Rather than raising it to her lips, however, she rotated it on the table. "I saw Marge yesterday," she said.

"I know. She told me. How do you like being labeled the 'new-and-improved model'?" I cracked a grin.

"I'm honored." Then, with a sad smile: "She's such a good person."

"The best." There was nothing else really to say.

After school, I brought London to Marge's. Because she'd been to the house numerous times in the past month, she'd known that Marge was sick, even if she didn't realize the seriousness of her illness. When Marge opened her arms, she went to her as usual and gave her a tender hug.

When I mouthed the question, *Do you want me to stay?* Marge shook her head.

"I'm going to visit with Nana for a little while, okay, London? Will you keep an eye on Auntie Marge for us?"

"Okay," she said, and I left them alone in the living room. My mom and I sat on the back porch off the kitchen, not saying much of anything.

A short while later, when I saw London enter the kitchen, I went back inside and held her as she cried.

"Why doesn't God make Auntie Marge better?" she choked out.

I swallowed through the lump in my throat, squeezing her small body to mine. "I don't know, sweetie," I said. "I really don't know."

Vivian texted that she planned to go straight to Marge's after her flight landed, and as a result, she didn't arrive at the house until half past six.

As soon as I saw the limo out front, I thought of the letter from her attorney. I left the front door open but retreated to the kitchen, feeling a wave of disgust toward her wash over me. Even though she'd just spent more than an hour with my sister, I still had no desire to speak to her.

I heard Vivian enter the house, and then London's tremulous voice, asking Vivian if she really had to go to Atlanta. Despite Vivian's promise that they were going to have a terrific time, London began to cry. Footsteps pounded as she ran to the kitchen and threw herself into my arms.

"I don't want to go, Daddy," she sobbed. "I want to stay here. I want to see Auntie Marge."

I scooped her up and held her as Vivian entered the kitchen. Her expression was unreadable.

"You need to spend time with your mom," I said. "She misses you all the time. And she loves you very much."

London continued to whimper.

"Will you take care of Auntie Marge while I'm gone?"

"Of course I will," I said. "We all will."

With London in Atlanta, I passed most of the weekend at Marge's, just as I'd promised my daughter. My parents were there too, alongside Liz.

We spent long hours at the kitchen table telling stories about Marge, as if our vivid memories and outrageous accounts of Marge's exploits would help keep her alive longer. I finally told my parents and Liz about the night I rescued Marge from the water tower; Liz re-created the romantic scavenger hunt. We laughed about Marge's roller skating and horror movie obsessions, and reminisced about the idyllic day that Marge and Liz had spent with Emily and me at the Biltmore Estate. We marveled at Marge's wit, and the fact that she still viewed me as a little brother desperately in need of her superior guidance.

I wished Marge had been there to hear all the stories, but she was with us for only a few of them. The rest of the time, she was sleeping.

On Sunday evening, London returned from Atlanta. Vivian said goodbye to our daughter near the limo and didn't come inside.

It was the last day of January. Marge and I were both born in the month of March; she on the fourth, and I on the twelfth. We were both Pisces, and in the world of the Zodiac, people born under that sign are said to be compassionate and devoted. I'd always believed that to be truer of Marge than me.

Her birthday, I realized, was less than five weeks away, and I knew she wouldn't be around to celebrate it.

Like Marge, I just knew.

CHAPTER 26

Saying Goodbye

My parents didn't have the most active social lives when Marge and I were young. While my dad might grab a beer every now and then with friends, it was relatively rare, and my mom hardly went out at all. Between work, cooking, cleaning, visiting her family, and raising kids, she didn't have a lot of extra free time. Nor did my parents dine out as a couple very often; dining out was considered an extravagance, something I can remember them doing perhaps half a dozen times. When you consider birthdays, anniversaries, Valentine's Day, Mother's Day, and Father's Day, six dinner dates in eighteen years isn't much.

That meant that when they did go out, Marge and I would be giddy at the thought of having the house to ourselves. As soon as their car pulled out of the driveway, we'd make popcorn or S'mores—or both—and start watching movies with the volume turned up way too loud, until, inevitably, one of Marge's friends would call. Once she got on the phone, I would suddenly be forgotten . . . but I was usually okay with that, since it meant even more S'mores for me.

Once when she was thirteen or so, she convinced me that we should build a fort in the living room. We found a coil of clothesline in the storage shed and ran it from the curtain rod to the grandfather clock to an air vent and back again to the curtain rod. We pulled towels and sheets from the linen closet, fastening them to the line with clothespins. Another sheet went over the top, and we furnished the fort with pillows pulled from the couch. Marge hauled in a propane-fueled camping lantern from the garage. We somehow got that lit without burning down the house—my dad would have been furious had he known—and Marge turned out all the lights before we crawled inside.

Setting the whole thing up had taken more than an hour, and it would take almost as long to take it all down and clean up, which meant we were only able to spend fifteen or twenty minutes in the fort before my parents got home. Even when they did go out, they never stayed out late.

I still recall that night as a near-magical experience. At eight years old, it was adventurous and new, and the fact that it was also against the rules made me feel older than I was, more like Marge's peer than a little kid, for the very first time. And as I looked at my sister in the eerie glow of the lantern in our makeshift fort, I can distinctly remember thinking that Marge was not only my sister, but my best friend as well. I knew even then that nothing would ever change that.

On February 1, the high temperature hit seventy-one degrees; five days later, the high was only fifty degrees and the low dipped to twenty-four. The wild temperature swings that first week of February seemed to weaken Marge even further. With every passing day, Marge grew worse.

Her sixteen hours of sleep a day lengthened to nineteen hours, and every breath was a struggle. The paralysis on her right side grew even more pronounced, and we rented a wheelchair to move her around the house more easily. Her words started to slur and she had hardly any appetite, but those things were nothing compared to the pain she was experiencing. My sister was taking so many painkillers that I suspected that her liver was turning to mush, but the only time she seemed to feel any real relief was when she slept.

Not that Marge ever mentioned the pain. Not to my parents or Liz, and not to me. As always, she was more worried about others than herself, but her suffering was evident in the way she winced, and the way her eyes would unexpectedly blur with tears. Witnessing her agony was torture for us all.

Often, I would sit with her in the living room as she slept on the couch; other times, I sat in the rocking chair in the bedroom. As I stared at her sleeping form, memories would roll back through the years, like a movie playing in reverse—a movie in which Marge was the star with the most memorable lines of all. She was forever vivid, forever alive, and I wondered whether my memories would remain that way, or whether they would slowly fade with the passage of time. I struggled mightily to see past her illness, telling myself that I owed it to her to remember everything about the way she was before she got sick.

On the day that the temperature plunged to twenty-four degrees, I remembered something that my father had told me about wood frogs, which can be found in North Carolina to as far north as the Arctic circle. As cold-blooded creatures, wood frogs were susceptible to frigid temperatures and could freeze completely solid, to the point that their hearts stopped completely. And yet, the frog has evolved in such a way that glycogen continues to break down into glucose, which acts a bit like nature's antifreeze. They can remain frozen and immobilized for weeks, but when the weather finally begins to warm, the wood frog blinks and its heart starts back up; there's a quick breath, and the frog hops away in search of its mate, as if God had merely hit the pause button.

Watching my sister sleep, I found myself wishing for a miracle of nature just like that.

Strangely, the rest of my life continued to move forward apace.

Work remained a sometimes welcome distraction, and my clients' enthusiasm for my work product was a rare bright spot during that time. I met with my Realtor and signed on the dotted line; the couple from Louisville asked for a long escrow, because they wanted their kids to finish out the school year there, so the closing was set for May. And over lunch one day, Emily casually asked me for the name of my Realtor, revealing that she was thinking of selling her house, too.

"I think I need a fresh start," she said, "in a place where I didn't live with David."

At the time, I suspected she was just trying to show moral support for my own decision to sell, a decision she knew I still harbored

464

ambivalence about. But a few days later, she texted me a photo of the new FOR SALE sign in her front yard.

Nothing remains the same for long; her life, like mine, was moving forward. I just wished I knew where mine was heading.

My dad continued to show up at Marge's house with his toolbox nearly every afternoon. What began as "necessary repairs" on the house gradually turned into extensive remodeling. He had torn out the entirety of the guest bathroom on the day Liz and Marge attended my open house, intent on upgrading it to the kind of bathroom he thought his only daughter deserved.

My dad was a dinosaur when it came to technology. To that point in his life, he'd seen no reason to purchase a cell phone. His boss always knew the location of the job site and everyone else on the crew had one, so he could always be contacted. Who else would call him anyway, he wondered? Why be bothered?

Yet my dad came to me right after the new year, and asked me to help him buy a phone. Since he didn't know anything about "those cellular gadgets," he asked me to select one for him. "Just make sure it does all that fancy stuff," he said, "but isn't too expensive."

Though my Dad hadn't mentioned it, I chose a phone that I felt would be simple for him to use as well. I set him up on my plan, and then spent some time with him showing him how to make and receive calls, as well as text. To his contacts, I added the information for Marge, Liz, my mom, and me. I couldn't think of anyone else to add.

"Can it take pictures?" he asked. "I've seen phones that can do that now."

Pretty much all phones have done that for years, I thought to myself, but I said only, "Yes, it does."

I showed him that function and watched as he practiced taking pictures and then examining them. I also showed him how to delete the ones he didn't want. Though I had the sense that much of the information was overwhelming, I watched him carefully tuck the phone into his pocket and head out to his car.

I saw him again at Marge's house the following day. She'd risen from her nap and our mom had chicken soup waiting. Marge ate half the bowl—less than we'd hoped—and when the tray was taken away, our dad took a seat beside her. He looked almost shy as he began to show her photos of various faucets, sinks and towel rods as well as options for floor and wall tile. Obviously, he'd been at the home improvement store, and this was the only way he could make sure that Marge was part of the design process.

Marge knew that our dad had never been a man of words, nor had he ever been openly affectionate. But through his labors, she could see that in his own way he was shouting his love for her at the top of his lungs, hoping that she could somehow hear what he'd always found so difficult to say.

Dad took notes as she made her selections, and when they were finished, Marge leaned closer to him, giving him no choice but to hug her. "Love you, Daddy," she whispered. Then, rising from the couch, he lumbered out of the house. Everyone knew he was off to purchase her selections, but after a few minutes, I realized that I hadn't heard him start his car.

When I got up to peek through the curtains at the driveway, I saw my dad, the strongest man I'd ever known, sitting in the front seat of his car with his head bowed and shoulders heaving.

Wonderful aromas always floated from Marge's kitchen these days, as my mom tried desperately to make food that would tempt Marge into eating more. There were soups and stews and sauces and pasta; banana cream and lemon meringue pies and homemade vanilla ice cream. The refrigerator and freezer were stuffed, and every time I came by, she handed me food for my refrigerator, which had gradually filled as well.

Whenever Marge was awake, my mom would set a tray in front of her; by the second week of February, my mom had begun to feed her because her left side was growing weaker as well. She would carefully raise the spoon to her lips, wiping her mouth between bites, and then offer my sister a sip of something to drink through a straw.

While Marge ate, my mom would talk. She would talk about Dad and the way the young new owner of the plumbing business was giving Dad a hard time for missing so much work. By that time, my dad had probably accrued years of vacation time, but the owner was the kind of guy who was never happy, a man who demanded more from the employees while demanding less of himself.

She described the tulips she'd planted for my dad and the lecture she'd attended with her Red Hat Society friends; she also regaled Marge with things that London had told her, no matter how inconsequential. More than once, I heard my mom pretend to be upset that no one had notified her in advance about Marge's and London's roller-skating adventure.

"I picked you up and dropped you off so many times at that rink that my tires made tire grooves in the parking lot asphalt—and you forgot to mention when my *granddaughter* was trying it for the very first time?"

I knew that she was only half-teasing, that she would have loved to have been there, and I silently berated myself for it. My mom, after all, not only wanted to see London on skates that day; she'd wanted to see her own daughter, skating with abandon and joy on her face—one last time.

As the second week of February rolled around, I had the sensation that time was simultaneously speeding up and slowing down There was a slow-motion quality to the hours I spent at Marge's every day, marked by long stretches of silence and sleep; on the other hand, each time I showed up, it seemed that Marge's deterioration was accelerating. One afternoon before pickup, I stopped by and found her awake in the living room. She and Liz were speaking in low voices, so I offered to leave, but Liz shook her head.

"Stay," Liz said. "I was about to touch base with one of my clients anyway. It's an emergency. You two talk for a bit. I'm hoping this won't take long."

I took a seat by my sister. I didn't ask her how she was feeling, because I knew it was a question she hated. Instead, as always, she asked about Emily and work, London and Vivian, her voice slurred

467

and tinny. Because she tired so easily, I did most of the talking. Toward the end, though, I asked if I could ask her a question.

"Of course," she said, her syllables running together.

"I wrote you a letter for Christmas, but I never heard what you thought about it."

She smiled her half smile, the one I'd grown used to. "I haven't read it yet."

"Why not?"

"Because," she said, "I'm not ready to say goodbye to you just yet."

I confess that I sometimes wondered if she'd ever have a chance to read it. Over the next three days, whenever I went to the house, Marge was always asleep, usually in her bedroom.

I would stay for an hour or two, visiting with Liz or my mom, whoever happened to be around. I would admire the latest repairs or renovations that my dad had undertaken, and more often than not eat a large plate of food that my mom would put down in front of me.

We almost always stayed in the kitchen. I thought at first it was because no one wanted to disturb Marge while she was sleeping, but I discounted that when I realized if that my dad's hammering wasn't enough to wake her, our low voices wouldn't either.

I finally figured it out one afternoon, when Liz stepped outside to sweep the porch. At loose ends, I wandered to the living room and took a seat in the spot where Marge and I usually sat.

My dad was working away quietly in the bathroom, but I realized I could hear a strange, rhythmic sound, like a malfunctioning fan or vent. Unable to pinpoint its origin, I moved first to the kitchen and then to the bathroom, where I spotted my dad lying on his back with his head beneath the new sink, in the final stages of hooking it up. But the sound was fainter in both those places; it grew in volume only as I began to make my way down the hallway, and it was then that I knew what was making that horrible noise.

It was my sister.

Despite the closed door, across the far reaches of the house, what I'd been hearing was the sound of my sister breathing.

Valentine's Day fell on a Sunday that year. Marge had planned a special gathering at her house, even inviting Emily and Bodhi, and I brought London over as soon as she got back from Atlanta.

For the first time in two weeks, London and I arrived to find Marge sitting upright on the couch. Someone—maybe my mom, maybe Liz—had helped her apply a little makeup. Instead of the baseball cap, Marge wore a gorgeous silk scarf, and a thick turtleneck sweater helped disguise the weight she'd lost. Despite the tumor ravaging her brain, she was able to follow the conversation, and I even heard her laugh once or twice. There were moments when it almost felt like one of our usual Saturday or Sunday afternoons at our parents'.

Almost.

The house itself had never looked better. My dad had finished the guest bathroom and the new tiles and sink gleamed, reflecting state-of-the-art fixtures. He'd also spent the last week repainting all of the interior trim in the house. My mom had laid out a veritable banquet on every surface of the kitchen, and as soon as Emily arrived, my mom made her promise to take a mountain of leftovers home with her, including whatever was left of the pies.

We rehashed a lot of family stories, but the highlight of the evening was when Liz presented her Valentine's Day gift to Marge. She'd made a photo album of the two of them that opened with photos of each of them as infants, and progressed through their entire lives. On the left-hand pages were photos of Liz; on the right, Marge. I knew that my mom must have helped Liz compile the photos and as Marge slowly turned the pages, I watched my sister and Liz grow up in tandem before my eyes.

Eventually the album began to feature photos of the two of them together, some taken on exotic trips while others were merely candid shots taken around the house. No matter how formal or casual, however, each photo seemed chosen to tell a story about a particularly meaningful moment in their lives together. The entire album was a testament to their love, and I found myself close to tears.

It was the final two pages of the album that broke me.

On the left was the photo of Marge and Liz beneath the Rockefeller

Center Christmas tree in New York, the last trip they would ever take together; on the right was a photo that looked to have been taken only a couple of hours earlier, with Marge looking exactly as she did right then.

Liz explained that my dad had taken it, and that unbeknownst to her had left to get it developed at a nearby drugstore. Upon his return, he asked Liz to add it to the last page of the album.

All eyes turned toward him.

"I've always been so proud of you," my dad choked out as he looked at Marge, "and I want you to know that I love you, too."

The day after Valentine's Day, the waiting began.

I now believe that on Valentine's Day, Marge used much of her last remaining reserves of energy. She slept almost the entire day Monday and ate no solid food from that point on, sipping only tepid chicken broth through a straw.

While my mom and dad were a constant presence at Marge's house, I drifted in and out, mainly because of London. She had been unusually volatile since learning the truth about Marge, occasionally throwing a tantrum or bursting into tears over trivial things. She would get particularly emotional when I refused her requests to visit Marge, but it was difficult to explain to London that her aunt was almost always sleeping now.

However, a few days following the Valentine's Day celebration, Liz called me at home in the evening.

"Can you bring London by?" she said urgently. "Marge wants to see her."

I called up to London, who was already upstairs in her pajamas, her hair still wet from her bath. She raced down the stairs and would have rushed straight to the car, but I managed to block the door in order to get her to put on a jacket. When I pointed out that she wasn't wearing shoes, she randomly grabbed a pair of rubber boots from the closet and slipped those on, despite the fact that it wasn't raining.

I saw she was holding a Barbie, refusing to put it down even while donning her coat.

When we arrived at Marge's house, Liz gave London a hug and kiss and immediately pointed her in the direction of the master bedroom.

Despite her fevered rush to the car, London hesitated for a moment before starting slowly down the hall. I trailed a few steps behind. Again, I could hear my sister, the sound of life leaving her with every breath she took. Inside her room, the bed-stand lamp spilled a warm pool of light onto the hardwood floor.

London paused just inside the doorway.

"Hi...honey," Marge said to her, the words slurred, but understandable.

London cautiously approached the bed, moving quietly so as not to disturb her sick aunt. I leaned against the doorjamb, watching as London reached Marge's side.

"What...do you...have there?" Marge asked.

"I brought you a present," London responded, handing over the doll she'd been clutching all along. "It's my favorite Barbie because I've had her since I was little. She's my first Barbie, and I want you to have it."

When London realized that Marge didn't have the strength to take it, she set it beside Marge, propping it against my sister as she lay beneath the covers.

"Thank you. She's pretty...but you're...prettier."

London bowed her head and raised it again. "I love you, Auntie Marge. I love you so much. I don't want you to die."

"I know...and...I love you...too. But I...have something... for you. Auntie Liz put it...on the dresser. One day...when you're old enough...maybe you can...watch it with your dad...okay? And maybe...when you do...you'll think about me. Can you...promise me...you'll do that?"

"I promise."

My eyes flashed to the dresser. I saw the DVD that Marge had given my daughter and I blinked back sudden tears as I saw the title.

Pretty Woman.

"Marge thinks I should still have a baby," Liz told me over coffee in the kitchen, a few days later. Her expression was a mixture of fatigue and bewilderment.

"When did she tell you this?"

"Well, she first brought it up when we went to New York," she said. "She keeps pointing out that I'm healthy enough to do it, but..." She trailed off.

I waited for her to go on, but she seemed lost. "Do you want to do that?" I asked in a tentative voice.

"I don't know, Russ—it's all just so hard to contemplate right now. I can't imagine doing it on my own, but she brought it up again yesterday." For a moment she picked at the grain of the kitchen table, making a small groove in the wood. "She told me that she'd already made financial arrangements, in case I felt differently down the road. That I'd be able to afford IVF, a nanny if I wanted, schooling, even."

When I tilted my head, trying to figure how and when Marge had made these arrangements, Liz ran a hand over her hair, trying to corral loose strands into her messy ponytail.

"Apparently right after she'd passed the CPA and became an accountant, she bought a bunch of life insurance. Two different policies, in fact. She added to them over the years, and it's quite a lot of money. The larger policy lists me as the beneficiary, and it's more than I'll ever need, even if I did decide to have a child on my own. She recently changed the beneficiary on the other policy, to your parents. So your dad can retire. I asked about you..."

I raised my hand, interrupting. "I'm glad it's going to you and my parents," I said. She looked confused, as if none of the information she'd recited really made sense to her.

"What I kept wondering when she told me about all this," Liz continued, "is *how did she know?* I asked her, and she said that because of her family history, and even though she wasn't sure who the beneficiaries would eventually be—early on, I think she listed you and your parents—she wanted to make sure she had it just in case she ever needed it."

"She never told me."

"She never told me, either," Liz admitted. "When we were discussing having a baby before she got sick, I guess I never really focused on the cost. We do okay and we've saved a bit, but mostly I guess I always trusted that if Marge thought we could afford it, we could..." For a

472

moment, her expression verged on desperation. "I can barely hold myself together. I told her that I didn't think I was capable of raising a child without her. She was always the more maternal one. And do you know what she said to that?"

I looked at her, waiting.

"She said that I was her inspiration and that any child that I raised would make the world a better place. And that if there's a heaven, she promised that she would watch over our child forever."

The following day, it was my turn to say goodbye.

When I arrived at the house, Marge was sleeping as usual. I stayed for a while, keeping an eye on the clock so as not to be late to pick up London from school, but before long the baby monitor in the kitchen crackled and both my mom and Liz hustled back to the bedroom. A few minutes later, my mom returned to the kitchen.

"Marge wants to see you," she said.

"How is she?"

"She seems pretty coherent, but you should probably head back now. Sometimes she starts to get confused, and doesn't stay awake long."

Observing my mom's steady demeanor, I could see that she was every bit as strong as my father, for she was bearing the unbearable, each and every day.

I held my mom for a moment, then walked down the hall to the bedroom. As on Valentine's Day, Marge was wearing a pretty scarf, and I guessed that she had asked Liz to put it on her before I came in.

I pulled a chair from the corner of the room and scooted it toward the bed. Liz backed out of the room as I reached for my sister's hand. It felt warm but lifeless in mine. Unmoving. I didn't know whether she could even feel it, but I squeezed it anyway.

"Hi, Sis," I said to her softly.

At my voice, she blinked, then struggled to clear her throat.

"Read," she said, the word coming out garbled.

It took a moment for me to understand what she meant, but then

I spotted the envelope that Liz had placed on the bed stand, and I reached for it. Opening it, I pulled out the single sheet of paper, took a deep breath and began to read.

Marge,

It's late at night, and I am struggling to find the words that I wish would come more easily. In truth, I'm not sure it's even possible to convey in words how much you've always meant to me. I could tell you that I love you, and that you're the greatest sister a guy could ever have; I could admit that I've always looked up to you. And yet, because I've said those things to you before, it feels painfully inadequate. How can I say goodbye to the best person I've ever known, in a way she truly deserves?

And then it occurred to me that all of what I need to say can be summed up in just two words.

Thank you.

Thank you for looking out for me all my life, for trying to protect me from my own mistakes, for being a living example of the courage I so desperately wish I owned. But most of all, thank you for showing me what it means to truly love, and be loved, in return.

You know me: the maestro of grand romantic gestures, of candlelit dinners and flowers on date night. But what I didn't understand until recently was that those tender, orchestrated moments mean nothing unless they occur with someone who loves you just the way you are.

For too long, I was in a relationship in which love always felt conditional—I was forever trying, and failing, to become someone worthy of true love. But in thinking about you and Liz and the way you are with each other, it eventually dawned on me that acceptance is the heart of true love, not judgment. To be fully accepted by another, even in your weakest moment, is to finally feel at rest.

You and Liz are my heroes and my muses, because your love for each other has always made room for your differences and celebrated everything you had in common. And in these darkest hours, your example has been a light that helped me find my way back to the things that matter most. I only pray that someday I, too, will know the kind of love that you two share.

I love you, my sweet sister—

Russ

My hands shook as I refolded the letter and placed it back in the envelope. I didn't trust myself to speak, but Marge's wise gaze told me I didn't need to.

"Emily," she wheezed. "You...have...that...with...her."

"I love her," I agreed.

"Don't...let...her...go..."

"I won't."

"And...don't...cheat on...her...again..." and here she managed the ghost of a wicked smile, "or...at least...don't tell...her..."

I couldn't help but laugh. My sister, even at death's doorstep, hadn't changed a bit. "I won't."

It took her a little bit to catch her breath. "Mom and...Dad... need to...see London....Be part...of her life."

"They always will be. Just like Liz."

"Worried...for...them."

I thought of my mom and all the loved ones she'd lost; I thought of my dad, weeping in the car.

"Do...it."

"I will. I promise."

"Love...you."

I squeezed my sister's hand then leaned down and kissed her on the cheek.

"I love you more than you will ever know," I said. After offering a tender smile, she closed her eyes.

It was the last time I ever spoke to her.

My dad packed up his tool chest that night, and all of us kissed Liz goodbye. Now it was time for the two of them to be alone.

I don't know what, if anything, they said to each other over the next couple of days—Liz never told us, other than to say that Marge enjoyed a day of surprising lucidity before she finally slipped into a coma. I am glad that Liz was there for that, and I pray that they both had a chance to say most of what was left to be said.

A day later, my sister died.

The funeral, at the gravesite, was a short affair. Marge had apparently given strict instructions to that effect, but the brief ceremony attracted dozens of mourners, all of them bundled up under the cold and gloomy sky.

I gave an abbreviated eulogy, of which I have little memory, other than that I spotted Vivian standing at the edge of the crowd, far from my family, Liz and Emily.

Prior to the funeral, London had asked if she could dance for her Auntie one last time. So after the mourners had dispersed, streaming away to their cars, I helped London attach her gauzy wings. With no music, and only me as an audience, London fluttered gracefully around the freshly turned earth, like a butterfly flitting in and out of the shadows.

This much I know: Marge would have loved it.

EPILOGUE

At the park, I sit in the shade while London runs and climbs and plays on the swing. It's been hot the last couple of weeks and the air is so thick with humidity that I keep spare T-shirts in the trunk of my car to change into at times like this. They don't stay dry for long, but I suppose that's typical for late July.

In the past four months, the Phoenix Agency has signed three more legal firms as clients, and now represents firms in three different states. I've had to find a new office, and two months ago, I hired my first employees. Mark had two years' experience with an Internet marketing firm in Atlanta, and Tamara is a recent graduate from Clemson, with a degree in film. Both of them are "digital natives," and text using both their thumbs, as opposed to the hunt-and-peck method preferred by their boss. They're intelligent and eager to learn, and they've made it possible for me to spend time with London this summer.

Like last summer, my daughter is constantly on the go. Tennis, piano, and art, along with dance at a different studio, one run by an instructor who inspires hugs from the kids. I drive her to and from her activities, and work while she's busy; in the afternoons, we can often be found at the neighborhood pool or at the park, depending on her mood. It amazes me to see how much she's changed since our first summer together. She's taller and more confident, and when I'm driving her here and there, I can often hear her sounding out the words she sees on billboards.

My house isn't as large as my former home, but it's comfortable and both of Emily's paintings—the one I'd bought at the show, and the one she'd painted of London and me—grace the walls of the living room. Even though I've been living there since late May, there are still boxes I haven't yet unpacked, and I had to rent a storage unit for the furniture from my previous home that I no longer needed. I'll probably sell most of it eventually, but with all the recent changes in my life, I just haven't had the time. I'm still getting used to living in Atlanta, after all.

Vivian and I met the day after the funeral, and in less than an hour, we had worked everything out. Though I offered, she declined my offer of alimony, and as for the property settlement, she asked for only half of the equity in the house, savings, and investment accounts. She let me keep the funds in our joint retirement account, but then again, money for her was no longer the concern it once was. At that same meeting, she revealed that she was secretly engaged to Spannerman—others would learn of it after our divorce was finalized—and while I could have been hurt by that, I found to my surprise that it didn't bother me at all. I was in love with Emily, and like Vivian, I'd reached the point where I was ready for a new chapter in my life.

However, money had never been the real bone of contention between us—custody was. So I was both relieved and a bit skeptical when she leaned over and said in an earnest voice, "I want to apologize for the letter my attorney sent." She placed a hand over her heart. "I was venting in her office, and didn't realize how my words would get twisted. I know you would never do anything inappropriate with London, and when I finally saw the letter my attorney had sent, I felt sick to my stomach." She sighed. "I can't imagine what you must have been thinking about me."

She closed her eyes, and in the moment, I chose to believe her. Part of me longed for that; I didn't want to think she had ever been capable of such things—but the truth is, I'll never know how things actually transpired.

"When Marge asked to see me that night, she told me flat-out that London needed both of us, that I would be hurting London by pursuing sole custody. Needless to say, I was angry. At the time, I felt it was none of her business. But her words affected me more than I wanted to admit... and over time I began to realize that she might be right." On her wrist, she twisted a thin gold bracelet around and around.

"Whenever London came to Atlanta, all she did was talk about you. How much fun she had with you, the games you played together, the places you went." Her voice trembled. "I never wanted to take London from you. I just wanted her with me. So when Marge said you would move to Atlanta...I was floored. I never imagined that you'd leave Charlotte, or your parents. I always felt that you started your own business because you weren't serious about finding work in another city." At my protest, she held up a hand. "That's why I wanted sole custody in the first place. Because I love London, too, and only seeing her every other weekend was killing me. I guess I never believed that you would go to such lengths to remain in her life."

She looked directly at me. "You're a great father, Russ. I know that now. If you're willing to move to Atlanta like Marge said, and you want to split time with London, I think we can probably figure something out."

Which is exactly what we did. For starters, London was allowed to stay with me in Charlotte to finish out the school year; two days later, the moving van filled with our stuff rolled toward Atlanta. When Vivian travels—which still keeps her out of town three or four nights a week—London stays with me. I also have my daughter every other weekend, and London and I have a standing date night on those Fridays she's with me. To avoid a repeat of the past year, Vivian and I have decided to alternate holidays in the future. So I can still read bedtime stories to my daughter when she stays with her mom, I bought a mini iPad, and London props it against a pillow to see me via FaceTime. Even better, once school starts, I'll still be able to pick her up at school every day, and she'll stay with me until Vivian finishes at work. I'm assuming that means that London and I will have dinner sometimes; other times, London will have dinner with her mom; but I'm confident that Vivian and I will figure it out.

I find myself being thankful to Vivian for all those things, cognizant that in all the years I've known her, my ex-wife has never once failed to surprise me.

Even, sometimes, in good ways.

I dreaded telling Emily that I was moving.

Most people would applaud my decision to choose my daughter over a new romantic relationship, but I also knew that a woman like Emily comes along once in a lifetime. Charlotte and Atlanta were close enough for a short-term relationship, but could it really work in the long run? Like me, Emily had been born and raised in Charlotte and her parents and sister lived nearby. We hadn't been seeing each other for very long; to that point in our relationship, we hadn't so much as even kissed.

"You could do better than me," is how I began the conversation. There were smarter and kinder men, wealthier and better-looking suitors, I went on. When Emily interrupted me to ask what this was about, I spilled everything: my conversations with Marge; my meeting with Vivian the day after the funeral; the realization that I needed to move to Atlanta. For London. Could she forgive me?

Standing, she put her arms around me. We were in her kitchen at the time, and in that moment, my eyes flashed to her studio, where she was working on yet another painting. It was one she intended to give to Liz. As she'd done with the image of London and me, Emily was painting a version of the photo taken of Marge and Liz beneath the Rockefeller Center Christmas tree.

"I've known for a while that you were going to move to Atlanta," she whispered into my ear. "Marge told me when I went to see her. Why do you think I put my house up for sale?"

Emily and I now live less than a mile from each other. We're each renting for the time being, because we both know that it's only a matter of time before we start shopping for rings. There are those who might think it's too fast—my divorce was finalized only three months ago—but to this I would respond, *How many people have the chance to marry their closest friend?*

For London, knowing that Bodhi not only lives here but will go to the same school—there's an excellent one nearby—has made her transition that much easier. Right after I watched London zip down the slide, I glanced toward the parking lot and saw Emily pulling in. Bodhi jumped out and made a beeline toward London, and when Emily smiled and waved, I knew with certainty that my day had gotten a whole lot better.

And by the way, if anyone's interested: On Emily's first night in Atlanta—she moved here a week after London and I did—we celebrated with champagne and ended up in bed. Ever since, I've felt as if I've finally come home.

It hasn't been easy for my parents, or for Liz. On the weekends that Vivian has London, I make the drive to Charlotte, and I visit my parents. Liz is often there, and our conversations drift to Marge as a matter of course. These days, we no longer weep at the mention of Marge's name, but the aching emptiness remains. I'm not certain that any of us will ever completely fill the void.

Yet there are glimmers of hope.

When Liz and I were chatting last weekend, she asked me in an offhanded way whether I thought she was too old to become a single mother. When I assured her to the contrary she merely nodded. I didn't press her, but I could see that Marge's gift to Liz was already bearing the fruit of possibility.

Later that same afternoon, my dad mentioned that the owner of the plumbing company was running it into the ground and he wasn't sure whether he wanted to stick around to watch that happen. When my parents came to visit London and me in Atlanta earlier this week, I caught my mom looking through the real estate section of the newspaper.

As I mentioned before, my sister always had a plan.

As for me, Marge had known all along what I needed to do, and in the weeks following her funeral I often wondered why she hadn't simply told me to move to Atlanta instead of letting me fumble my way to the answer on my own.

Only recently did I figure out why she'd held back: After a lifetime of looking to her for guidance, she knew I needed to learn to trust my own judgment. She knew that her little brother needed just one more push to become the man she always knew I could be—the man who finally had the confidence to act when it mattered most.

It was a year to remember and a year to forget, and I am not the man I was twelve months ago. In the end, I lost too much; the grief I feel about Marge is still too fresh. I will miss her always, and know that I couldn't have weathered the past year without her. Nor can I imagine who I'd be today without London, and whenever I look at Emily, I clearly envision a future with her at my side. Marge, Emily and London supported me when I needed it most, in ways that now seem almost preordained.

But here's the thing: With each of them, I was a different person. I was a brother and a father and a suitor, and I think to myself that these distinctions reflect one of life's universal truths. At any given time, I am not the whole me; I am but a partial version of myself and each version is slightly different from the others. But each of these versions of me, I now believe, has always had someone by his side. I'd survived the year because I'd been able to march two by two with those I loved the most, and though I've never admitted it to anyone, there are moments, even now, when I feel Marge walking beside me. I'll hear her whisper the answer when I'm confronted with a decision; I'll hear her urging me to lighten up when the world is weighing heavily on me. This is my secret. Or rather, it is *our* secret, and I think to myself that I've been lucky, for no one should ever be forced to march through life alone.

ACKNOWLEDGEMENTS

There are always so many to thank in the aftermath of completing any novel.

My children, Miles, Ryan, Landon, Lexie and Savannah, who continue to inspire me.

Theresa Park, my agent, and Jamie Raab, my editor, have been by my side for twenty years, and I'm always grateful for their insights and efforts when it comes to making my novels as good as they can be.

At Park Literary + Media, the brilliant, resourceful and supremely capable team of Emily Sweet, Abby Koons, Alex Greene, Andrea Mai, Vanessa Martinez and Blair Wilson. They do for authors what no one else in the industry can, and I owe much of my success to their far-reaching efforts.

At United Talent Agency, Howie Sanders and Keya Khayatian have been my essential advisers, tireless advocates and creative brain trust for almost twenty years. They've seen me through many dramatic ups and downs, and their strategic brilliance and unflagging loyalty are unparalleled. I'll never be able to repay Larry Salz for all of his strenuous efforts on behalf of NSP TV, but I'm deeply grateful nonetheless. David Herrin will always be my guru and oracle when it comes to the business of data and social sentiment, a genius in his own right. Danny Hertz was indispensable to my team, and I wish him all best in his exciting new career.

Scott Schwimer, my indefatigable entertainment lawyer and friend, has been my sword and my shield for twenty years now. His personal loyalty and keen business sense go far beyond what anyone could expect from his lawyer; he's also been a patient, reassuring sounding board for me through all kinds of challenging situations.

My publicists Catherine Olim, Jill Fritzo and Michael Geiser have gone above and beyond the call of duty these past few years. No one could ask for more vigilant and talented representation in the world of PR—their personal commitment and professional effectiveness have always amazed me.

LaQuishe "Q" Wright is the undisputed leader in her field of entertainment-related social media, and she never fails to wow me with her savvy and professionalism. Mollie Smith has also been a hugely valued member of my social media team, whose reliability, responsiveness and design sense continue to enhance everything I do.

At Hachette USA and UK, the team of people I have to thank is too numerous for me to cite in full, but I hope they know how much I appreciate the specific efforts of each of them. To name just a few:

Arnaud Nourry
Michael Pietsch
Amanda Pritzker
Beth DeGuzman
Brian McLendon
Anne Twomey
Flamur "Flag" Tonuzi
Claire Brown
Chris Murphy
Dave Epstein
Tracy Dowd
Caitlin Mulrooney-Lyski
Matthew Ballast
Maddie Caldwell
Bob Castillo
Kallie Shimek
Ursula Mackenzie
David Shelley
Catherine Burke

At Warner Bros. TV, I'd like to thank Peter Roth, Susan Rovner and Clancy Collins-White for their support and gracious professionalism. Likewise Stacey Levin, Erika McGrath and Corey Hanley for their efforts at NSP TV.

My appreciation also extends to Denise DiNovi and Marty Bowen, fabulous producers who've brought many of my novels to life on screen.

To Peter Safran, his lovely wife Natalia, Dan Clifton and the talented Ross Katz, I want to express my heartfelt appreciation for their work on *The Choice*.

Others who also deserve my gratitude include Jeannie Armentrout and Tia Scott, who keep things my life running smoothly for me on the homefront.

Andy Sommers, Mike McAden, Jim Hicks, Andy Bayliss, Theresa Sprain, Dr. Eric Collins are all consistently helpful in various areas of my life, and I can't thank them enough.

My gratitude also extends to Pam Pope and Oscara Stevick, who do great things with numbers.

There are also some special friends who deserve my appreciation, including Michael Smith, Victoria Vodar, David Geffen, Dr. Todd Lanman, Jeff Van Wie, Jim Tyler, Chris Matteo, Paul DuVair, Rick Muench, Robert Jacob, Tracey Lorentzen, Missy Blackerby, Ken Gray, Dr. Dwight Carlbloom, David Wang and Catherine Sparks.

Given space constraints, I am necessarily omitting countless other people deserving of gratitude, but I hope they know how much their efforts have meant to me. The creative business is a group enterprise, and I've had the privilege of working with an extraordinary team almost every step of the way.

With over 105 million copies of his books sold, Nicholas Sparks is one of the world's most beloved storytellers. His novels include thirteen number one *New York Times* bestsellers. All Nicholas Sparks' books have been international bestsellers and have been translated into more than fifty languages. Eleven of his novels have been adapted into major films – *The Longest Ride*, *The Best of Me*, *Safe Haven*, *The Lucky One*, *The Last Song*, *Dear John*, *Nights in Rodanthe*, *Message in a Bottle*, *A Walk to Remember*, *The Notebook* and *The Choice*.

For all the latest news from Nicholas Sparks, sign up for his e-Newsletter at www.nicholassparks.com, and follow him on Facebook and Twitter: @NicholasSparks.

Join us at

For competitions galore,
exclusive interviews with our lovely
Sphere authors, chat about
all the latest books
and much, much more.

Follow us on Twitter at
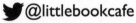 @littlebookcafe

Subscribe to our newsletter and
Like us at **f** /thelittlebookcafe

Read. Love. Share.